Also by Christoph Hein

The Tango Player

The Distant Lover

Willenbrock

Settlement

Settlement

A Novel

Christoph Hein

Translated by Philip Boehm

Metropolitan Books
Henry Holt and Company New York

Metropolitan Books
Henry Holt and Company, LLC
Publishers since 1866
175 Fifth Avenue
New York, New York 10010
www.henryholt.com

Distributed in Canada by H. B. Fenn and Company Ltd.

Originally published in Germany in 2004 under the title *Landnahme*
by Suhrkamp Verlag, Frankfurt am Main.

The translation of this book was made possible, in part, by a grant from the PEN Translation Fund.

The translation of this work was supported by a grant from the Goethe-Institut that is funded by the German Ministry of Foreign Affairs.

The translator also wishes to thank the National Endowment of the Arts for its support of this translation.

Library of Congress Cataloging-in-Publication Data

Hein, Christoph, 1944–
[Landnahme. English]
Settlement : a novel / Christoph Hein ; translated by Philip Boehm.—1st U.S. ed.
p. cm.
ISBN-13: 978-0-8050-7768-1
ISBN-10: 0-8050-7768-5
1. Men—Germany (East)—Fiction. 2. Germany (East)—Fiction. I. Boehm, Philip. II. Title.
PT2668.E3747L3613 2008
833'.914—dc22

2008009021

Henry Holt books are available for special promotions and premiums.
For details contact: Director, Special Markets.

First U.S. Edition 2008
Designed by Linda Kosarin
Printed in the United States of America
1 3 5 7 9 10 8 6 4 2

Settlement

Procession

The four men standing on the rostrum at the top of the stairs smiled unwaveringly at the crowd gathered in the market square. One of the men checked his watch several times before signaling to the musicians, who then struck up the Duke of York March. When they spoke among themselves the men did not smile; their faces looked worried; they were nervous.

"We can't wait any longer," said the oldest. "Who do they think they are? Their royal highnesses? They're only the prince and princess of the carnival."

"Don't get so worked up, Sigurd," said a short, stocky man. "I'll go and fetch them." He nodded to the others, then turned and opened the heavy door to the Rathaus and went inside.

The prince was standing in the middle of the hall. Without saying a word, he nodded when the stocky man came in and explained that everyone was waiting for them. The prince looked over at the princess, who was sitting on a bench, holding a tissue to her face.

"It's time. We have to go out there now, we can't put it off any longer," the stocky man repeated. Then he, too, looked at the princess, who dabbed some powder on her cheeks, took a quick look at a hand mirror, and stood up. She was visibly pale; despite her forced smile it was clear she had just been crying. The man walked toward her.

"Half the town is out there waiting on the square," he said, looking at her imploringly.

He offered his hand and led her to her place beside the prince. Then he went to the door, opened it, and gestured toward the square with a grand sweep of his arm. The couple walked the few steps outside and onto the rostrum without looking at each other or touching.

The princess was dressed completely in white. She had her hair pinned up and was wearing a crown. The prince had on a white silk suit and, like his consort, he was smiling—even if his lips were pressed into more of a grimace. The four men stood beside the prince and princess, and joined them in waving to the crowd below. The brass band had taken its place at the foot of the stairs and now played the Presentation March.

Over two hundred people had assembled on the square in front of the Rathaus. Many came with small children they held by the hand or hoisted onto their shoulders to give them a better view of the prince and princess. The children had silver and red stars painted on their cheeks, foreheads, and noses; a few wore paper hats or beanies with devil's horns or lined caps embroidered with the faces of animals and scary monsters, which the parents pulled down over the children's ears, since it was icy cold. All eyes were fixed on the royal couple and the four men on the rostrum, who never stopped smiling as they waved down to the crowd, first with one hand, then the other. The men wore shiny red and gold paper hats that contrasted oddly with their dark suits. Behind them gathered the princely guard—five sturdy girls costumed in short skirts and knee-high red boots, led by a majorette in a red coat. The girls moved to the music and stamped their feet to keep warm. Their eyes beamed with pride as they peered between the shoulders of the men, searching the crowd for friends and acquaintances.

The man on the rostrum addressed as Sigurd turned toward the band. When the conductor glanced up, he gave a sign, and after a few measures the music stopped. The stocky one who had escorted the prince and princess out of the Rathaus produced an oversized gold key made of papier-mâché and presented it to the prince. The band played a fanfare, after which Sigurd stepped up to a microphone and announced that the key to the city had been presented and so the procession could begin. He glanced once more at the bandleader, who struck up another fanfare, and then stepped away from the microphone and waved to the crowd, beaming away as he conversed in hushed tones with the men next to him.

All four were in their late fifties and somewhat stout. They appeared confident, almost smug, and were evidently important, influential people in town—"imposing figures," they might be called. In their pointed, heavily decorated carnival hats they looked more worn-out, tired, and fat than comical.

After the fanfare, the musicians launched into the next carnival song, raising the volume to cover the occasional false note. The prince and princess and the four men stepped back from the balustrade at the edge of the rostrum and one of the men urged the princely guard forward, letting his hands brush up against the girls' waists and backsides as if by accident. For a moment the five girls stood frozen in place, then, at the majorette's command, they started to dance, kicking their legs up as high as they could while constantly blowing kisses to the crowd. Occasionally one of them lost her balance and fell out of step; then she began all over, her face crimson as she rejoined the line, blowing kisses more energetically and enthusiastically than ever. Some of the people in the square clapped to the music, others waved at the girls, shouting their names to get their attention. Because the balustrade blocked the view of the rostrum, the people below could see little of the girls' legs; they could only guess what the princely guard was doing by the movement of their upper bodies.

The prince of the carnival never stopped waving, and never turned to look at his princess. For her part she went on smiling bravely; yet even in her magnificent white dress she appeared helpless and lost. Sigurd again made his way to the microphone and shouted something no one could understand over the music. He took the prince and princess by the arm and hustled both to the stairs. As they descended the steps, the young man declined to offer his arm to the princess; the couple walked side by side, still refusing to touch or look at each other. The girls of the princely guard followed, tossing their legs up at each step, anxious lest they hit someone or lose their footing. The majorette kept glancing right and left as she directed the movements of her comrades. Before she reached the bottom of the stairs, her left foot caught on a cable that had been taped to the stone landing, pulling the microphone off the rostrum; it fell to the ground with a loud bang that reverberated over the amplifiers until one of the men picked it up and brought it to safety.

A gentleman approached the stairs carrying a little girl who was in tears. He climbed up a couple of steps toward the stocky man, who shook his head to show he was too busy and had no time at the moment. The gentleman with the little girl refused to be brushed aside; he climbed two steps higher and explained that the girl had lost her grandfather and they should use the microphone to page him. The stocky man then held the microphone to his mouth and called out for the missing grandfather to come and pick up his grandchild. The man scanned the crowd, and when no one responded he asked the child for her grandfather's name. The girl stuttered a reply and the man spoke into the microphone that the grandfather was named Grandpa and he should please report to the rostrum right away. Then he again turned to the girl and asked for her name. But his manner came across as too forceful, too brusque, and the frightened girl made a face as if she would again start sobbing.

An older man leading a child by the hand approached the Rathaus steps. He waved at the girl, trying to catch her gaze, and moved toward her as fast as the short steps of the child at his hand allowed. It took a few moments for the girl on the rostrum to discover her grandfather; she gave a great sigh of relief and then burst into tears. As the grandfather reached the stairs, the howling child ran down the steps and into his arms.

The gentleman who had first found the child looked at the short, stocky man now coiling the microphone cable.

"Hello, Woodworm," he finally said in a low voice.

The man interrupted his work and looked up, squinting.

"Are you speaking to me? Is there something else?" he asked with a note of suspicion.

The man replied with a friendly smile. He climbed a step and asked, "Don't you recognize me, Woodworm old boy?"

The stocky man sized him up, then turned away without saying a word. Carefully he tied off the cable and nestled the microphone inside the bundled cord. Then he looked at the gentleman and shook his head slightly. "No. I don't think I do. You're not from Guldenberg, are you?"

"No, I'm not. But I used to live here. A long time ago. Years—no, by now it's already decades."

"I don't remember you. Were we in school together?"

"All through grade school," said the stranger. "I take that back—just from third grade on. We even shared a bench for a couple of years."

The man holding the microphone reached up and started to run his fingers through his hair till he felt his carnival cap, which he hastily took off, folded up, and stashed under his arm. His hair had thinned and grayed; the deeply receding hairline exposed his whitish scalp.

"No, I don't remember you."

"Pill-peddler. That's what they used to call me."

"Doesn't ring a bell. Sorry."

"Thomas Nicolas. We used to sit at the same desk."

"And what brings you here, Herr Nicolas?" asked the one addressed as Woodworm. Then he corrected himself: "I mean Thomas."

"Sheer chance. I was passing through and thought I'd see what had become of my old town."

"And do you like what you see? There's been of lot of building and restoration in the past few years."

"I noticed. Everything's gotten smaller. The church, the Rathaus, this square. Back then it was all bigger. A lot bigger."

The other man looked puzzled, and the stranger smiled and continued: "Or else I've just grown bigger myself, maybe that's it."

"I'm sorry, I have a lot to do. What with the carnival and all. I have to take care of the parade, the festivities. Perhaps we'll see each other some other time."

He left for a moment through the open Rathaus door. When he came back he was again wearing his paper hat. He spoke to the three men who had been standing next to him on the rostrum and now were waiting for him. They hurried down the stairs and took their places behind the prince and princess. The conductor quickly signaled to the musicians, the music started up, and the procession slowly lurched into motion.

Before the procession—led by the band, the prince and princess, and the local VIPs—disappeared down the street, the man who had been addressed as Woodworm glanced back. Thomas Nicolas, the stranger paying a short visit to his old hometown, was standing on the Rathaus steps, smiling at his former schoolmate.

Thomas Nicolas

It was the middle of September—the school year had just begun—when Fräulein Nitzschke brought a new boy to our third-period class. Fräulein Nitzschke was our class advisor; she also taught us grammar and spelling and German history. She was in her late forties and unmarried and insisted on being addressed as Fräulein. Whenever parents called her Frau Nitzschke, she would correct them with a gentle but insistent smile, as if she attached particular significance to the fact she wasn't married. She was a gaunt woman—flat as a board front and back was what the older boys said on the playground—and her cheeks were always heavily powdered, which was very unusual and got the grown-ups in town to talking. People suspected she had bad skin or some kind of disease, but no one knew for certain. When she walked among the school benches and leaned over one of the pupils, we could smell her sweet-scented makeup.

Fräulein Nitzschke led the newcomer up to her desk, took her seat, and then waited until the class had quieted down and everyone was looking at her, or rather at the boy standing next to her, staring grimly ahead.

"We have a new boy joining us," she said at last. "And I'm sure he'd like to introduce himself."

She looked encouragingly at the boy, who kept eyeing the class, sizing us up.

"Please tell us your name."

He shot her a brief glance and mumbled something without looking anyone in the eye.

At that point the class began to fidget. The boy had said his name so quietly, so halfheartedly, that hardly anyone could understand him. Somebody shouted out "Louder!" and everyone laughed. But we'd realized as soon as he opened his mouth that his German was different, that he spoke one of the raw eastern dialects. That he was another refugee who'd been sent to our school because his family had been driven out of Pomerania or Silesia.

Just after the war our town had been flooded with them. They'd been housed with people who had to be pressed by the local authorities and sometimes even the police into clearing out one or two rooms and taking in the strangers. Everyone hoped they would either soon move on or that the authorities would assign them apartments of their own. Even if Bad Guldenberg had suffered less damage from the bombers and the fighting than the district seat and the neighboring villages, there was still much to be rebuilt, and neither the town nor its inhabitants had money to construct new housing. Moreover, since materials were scarce, even the most pressing repairs took a long time to complete.

Now, five years after the war, when Bernhard showed up in our class, it was clear that a number of these DPs had decided to settle in Guldenberg for good. The new eastern border had been recognized as permanent, so that the once-German provinces on the other side of the Oder River were now Polish, and there was no chance of the expellees ever being able to return to their former homes. As a result, our school had more than its share of their children. By third grade most of them had learned to speak our dialect, although every now and then some odd word or usage would give them away, or the fact that their pronunciation was a little throatier. But no matter how they spoke, you could easily spot them because they were poorly dressed, with darned stockings and mended sweaters and round leather patches stitched to the elbows of their jackets. Their shoes were always old and cracked.

The commotion in the classroom did not faze Fräulein Nitzschke. "That's right—Bernhard Haber," she said, carefully enunciating the name. Then she turned to the newcomer. "Come see me during recess, Bernhard, and I'll put you down in the class register. But now go and take your seat."

Bernhard Haber searched the rows of double desks for a place to sit. The others also looked around, just to confirm what they knew already—that every one of the flip-up seats was taken. When the teacher realized this, she stood up and slid her own chair alongside her desk.

"You can use mine for the moment, Bernhard. We'll straighten things out during recess. The custodian will bring a chair in for you."

She turned to the class. "Bernhard is a year older than you. He comes from Poland and wasn't able to attend school regularly in the past few years. So he's missed a thing or two, and I think it's better for him to join the third grade, at least for the time being. We'll see how much he knows, and I expect all of you to do whatever you can to help him."

"A Pollack," said a boy from one of the back rows in a low voice.

The new boy had stepped over to the chair the teacher had provided; he now turned to face the class. Without raising his arm, he clenched his hand into a fist and held it for a moment in front of him, searching the class for the boy who had made the remark.

"That was a very, very ugly thing to say," said Fräulein Nitzschke. "I don't want to hear that word ever again. Never! Do you understand? And Bernhard isn't Polish; he's German, just like you."

After recess we found an extra chair had been brought to the classroom, but the new pupil had to share a desk with two girls, who squeezed together to make room.

When Herr Voigt came in to teach arithmetic, everyone stood up while he made his way to the blackboard, where he greeted the class and took his place at the teacher's desk. Then we sat back down, flipping our seats with a loud bang. As always, Herr Voigt scanned the classroom like a raptor in search of prey. When he caught sight of the new boy, he looked him over from head to toe, amused.

"So . . . I see we have a new boy with us," he said with obvious scorn. "And what's your name?" Without waiting for an answer, he opened the class register and read aloud what Fräulein Nitzschke had written about Bernhard Haber.

"Hmmm, it says here you're ten years old. Well, if they've stuck you in the third grade, I'm guessing you're not exactly a whiz at numbers, am I right?"

The whole class laughed. The new pupil had placed both hands on his desk. He kept his eyes fixed straight ahead and said nothing.

"Stand up when I talk to you. And look at me. Did you come here with your parents?"

"Yes."

"Well, at least you're not an orphan. They cause nothing but trouble. Does your family have an apartment? Or a room somewhere?"

"Yes."

"Good. And does your father have work?"

"No. Not yet."

"So he's living at the town's expense. What's his profession?"

"He's a carpenter."

"Good. Carpenter is good. If he knows what it means to work and doesn't have two left hands, he'll find something soon enough. There's plenty of need for carpenters."

He paused for a second and then went on, with a malicious smile. "Or maybe your father doesn't really like to work? We've seen that kind before, too."

The new boy stood by his seat with his head downcast, his hands gripping the slanted desktop. His face was bright red as he replied, "No. My father doesn't have two left hands. He has one left hand."

"And where are you from? Where were you born, boy?"

"In Breslau."

"What did you say?"

"We come from Breslau."

Herr Voigt shook his head and looked at the class with open-mouthed indignation. He raised his arm and pointed at one girl: "Kathrin, what's the name of the city this new boy comes from?"

"Wrocław," said the girl, standing so quickly that her seat flipped back up.

Herr Voigt nodded, satisfied. Then he turned again to face the new pupil: "Or do you think Italy is still inhabited by the Romans? From here on you better remember that it's the Italians. And what about Istanbul—I bet you people from Outer Pomerania still call it Constantinople or Byzantium, am I right? So, you come from Wrocław, in the Polish People's Republic. Understand?"

Bernhard Haber stood completely still and looked Herr Voigt straight in the eye.

"One more time, then. Where are you from?"

"I come from Wrocław."

"Right. Now sit down. We want to start our lesson."

Bernhard Haber stood defiantly next to his desk a moment longer. Before he sat down, he blurted out, "But I was born in Breslau."

Herr Voigt had turned to write something on the blackboard. Now his arm holding the chalk slowly dropped. As if in slow motion, he spun his upper body around and fixed his eyes on the new boy, who had evidently caught him off guard. For a moment we thought he would start yelling. But all he did was stare at Bernhard with contempt and give him a menacing smile.

"So," he said at last, his words sounding practically like an acknowledgment, "you're one of those. Well, don't you worry, I'll soon have you singing a different tune."

He turned back and went on copying some problems from the open book in his left hand onto the dark, gray board full of scratches. Bernhard Haber carefully looked over his new classmates, most likely trying to gauge their reaction to his showdown with the math teacher. He seemed intent on memorizing the exact details of every one of our faces. And we stared back, so that for a moment our eyes locked while Herr Voigt went on quietly explaining the problems he was copying out on the board.

The next morning a new desk had been brought in, as well as two flip-up seats. The custodian had set it up in the back of the room, right by the coatrack, and the new boy sat down. When Fräulein Nitzschke came to teach during third period, she made him trade places with a girl in the first row.

Bernhard Haber didn't own a real satchel; all he had was a cloth bag that had been stitched from an old gray military coat, which he carried like a rucksack. The bag was too big to fit in the space under the desktop, so he had to keep it by his desk during the lesson. The other pupils whose satchels were too big for their desks kept them on hooks mounted on the chair frames, but Bernhard's bag didn't fit that, either. So it just lay in a grubby heap on the oiled wooden floor.

Soon enough, on the third day, when Willy was called to the front of the class, he made a point of walking right next to Bernhard and kicking the bag so that it flew a full six feet and collided with Fräulein Nitzschke's desk. The whole class perked up. Willy was not only the strongest boy in our grade, he was also our best soccer player, and he'd clearly scored a goal with that shot. If it had been during recess and not class time, someone would have been bound to kick the bag back to him. But Fräulein Nitzschke didn't kick it back; she asked Willy what he thought he was doing. He claimed that it was an accident, that he had tripped over the bag and almost broken his leg. No one believed him and we started to giggle. But there was nothing Fräulein Nitzschke could do except tell Willy to return the bag to Bernhard and apologize. Willy picked up the bag with two fingers, as if it were too filthy to touch, took it to Bernhard, and mumbled some form of apology. Bernhard didn't say a word and acted as if it didn't concern him at all. He didn't even check to see whether anything inside had been broken.

At recess, as soon as Fräulein Nitzschke had left the room, Bernhard stood up, went over to Willy, and in one move grabbed his hair, jerked his head down, and put him in a headlock. He pressed until Willy cried out, then made a couple of rapid movements with his arm. When he let go, both of Willy's ears were fire-red and he was moaning, loud enough for all to hear. No one ever tripped over Bernhard's bag again, not even by accident.

Bernhard lived with his parents at Herr Griesel's farm, over on Gustav-Adolf-Strasse, across from the old cemetery, which hadn't seen any new funerals in years; after the war they buried people in the forest cemetery behind the TB hospital. Old Man Haber couldn't find any carpentry work in town, despite the fact that there was plenty of need for carpenters. And it was true that he didn't have two left hands—but he didn't have any right hand at all; his right arm had been amputated just below the shoulder joint. As a Soviet prisoner of war, he had been sent to a labor camp near Perm in the Urals and forced to work in a mine. One day he and four other prisoners were carrying sacks of flour and pickled fodder-beets into the storeroom when a drunken guard accidentally shifted his truck into reverse, causing it to lurch backwards, so that Haber's arm got caught between the tailgate and a support pillar. He was immediately taken to the doctor in the hospital barracks, but she couldn't save the arm. If the accident had happened underground, Haber would have bled to death before they managed to bring him up. After the accident he was of no use as a miner, and following four months on a kolkhoz, where he was of no help either, he was released.

Because his hometown had been ceded to Poland after the war, Haber was sent to the eastern part of Germany, under Soviet occupation. He managed to obtain permission to travel to Breslau, or Wrocław as it was now known, to look for his family. After four weeks he found them in a village twenty-five miles north of the city. His wife was with her mother and their only surviving son: one year after the war ended Bernhard's brother had been so malnourished he was sent to a Polish hospital, where he died. When Haber found them, all three were living with a Polish farmer who himself had been resettled in the wake of the war. As an invalid, Haber then applied for an exit permit for his entire family, which he received six months later, four years after the war.

Upon his arrival in Germany he was unable to provide the address of anyone who could house his family; all his relatives had lived in Silesia until the end of the war, and he had no idea as to their current whereabouts. In the end, the Habers wound up in Guldenberg because our town was listed as needing carpenters when the officials filled out the resettlement forms, using a list that had probably been drawn up according to someone's whim. Although Haber pointed out that he was crippled and wouldn't be able to work in his trade, the border guard merely nodded and refused to reconsider his decision, promising the carpenter that he would be helped further upon his arrival. The local authorities were informed, he assured Haber, and had plenty of experience helping war cripples get back on their feet.

But the Guldenberg authorities were neither informed nor especially willing to help. All they did was issue ration cards and assign the Habers to farmer Griesel, who gave them two tiny attic rooms, one of which could be heated with a cylindrical stove—the other was icy cold in winter.

Bernhard's mother helped Griesel's wife with the farmwork in return for food. His father, on the other hand, spent four months looking for work but couldn't find a thing, not as a carpenter or in any other trade. Laborers were in demand, but the one-armed man was regretfully turned away everywhere he looked. He lacked the skills and expertise for office work; he was practically illiterate, having never had any use for reading or writing, neither in his trade nor during the war nor as a Soviet prisoner. Haber was the only war cripple in Guldenberg, and his injury only reminded townspeople of the defeat and the humiliation of having to surrender to the Allies. His missing arm was the obelisk that Guldenberg never erected for the lost war and the town's seven fallen soldiers.

The new year came, and in January farmer Griesel began servicing his equipment, replacing any broken or damaged parts and sharpening the blades. He asked the refugee he'd been forced to house whether he might help with the woodwork, and so Haber set up a small shop inside the barn, next to the parked handcarts and the two carriages and beneath a loft stacked with bales of straw. Using the few tools at his disposal, Haber sawed, planed, drilled, and sanded the needed pieces. After school his son helped with whatever he couldn't handle alone: together they were able to perform rough carpentry jobs and produce wagon shafts, staves, and spokes. The farmer was satisfied with the work, and though he only paid in kind, he did send other clients, so that Herr Haber was soon able to buy some tools that he urgently required to make a new start.

That summer the carpenter helped with the harvest. Because he knew how to handle horses, Griesel lent him a carriage, and Haber transported grain and straw from the fields to the mill, the state-run collection points, and the barns. He also helped pack the sacks and took pains to accomplish no less than any other harvest hand. He was indifferent to pity or mockery; he seemed not to notice remarks about his missing arm, and curtly brushed aside any praise of his adroitness.

Once the harvest was in, he converted Griesel's old tobacco shed into a workshop: he could no longer use the barn because some of the electrical tools and machines he had acquired ran on diesel fuel, and the farmer was afraid the sparks might ignite the straw. Meanwhile the shed that had been used for curing tobacco stood empty; after the war, the farmer had been forced to give up growing tobacco, since the state quota system stipulated what to plant, and he could no longer dedicate even the tiniest plot for the more profitable crop.

Eighteen months after resettling in our town, carpenter Haber went to the Rathaus to apply for a trade license. He presented whatever documents he had managed to save, along with two affidavits in lieu of papers he could not provide from Lower Silesia. Over the next two summers he continued to help with the harvest and worked in Griesel's fields, as he and his family couldn't live off the little he earned doing woodwork. The locals preferred to patronize one of the three carpenters who had been working in town for years—two of them for generations—instead of going to Haber's paltry workshop, either because he was a refugee who had settled unbidden in their town or because they didn't care to order a table or a cabinet from a one-armed craftsman attempting to ply his trade in a makeshift shop with a ridiculously small number of tools.

The local housing authority was unable to assign Haber a dwelling of his own, and constructing a new house was out of the question: Haber had no illusions as to what he could build by himself or how much help he might expect from his neighbors. And so for three years, until the fire, Haber went on living with his family in the two attic rooms of the farmhouse, and working in his shop inside the old tobacco shed.

Although Bernhard Haber had been prevented from entering the fourth grade, where he actually belonged, and placed instead in my class, he still had to work hard to keep up and avoid being sent to an even lower grade. He was not without talent and once he understood something he never forgot it, but he was a little slow on the uptake, as we said; he would sit for several minutes poring over an assignment as if in a daze. You can see him thinking, Fräulein Nitzschke once said. She didn't intend it in a mean way, but the class was amused by her remark and frequently made use of it to describe our classmate, even if none of us dared repeat it within his hearing.

After school he had to help his father in the carpentry shop, which meant that he frequently failed to finish or even start his homework. He was completely incapable of learning anything by heart, such as a song or a poem. When a teacher called on him he would stand beside his school bench as though petrified, his eyes fixed on a corner of the room, while he searched desperately for the right words. If we tried to prompt him he would mumble our cue out loud without understanding the meaning, and then, unable to add another word, would go on repeating the line we had provided as if he were using it to fish the remaining words out of his memory, until finally the teacher would take pity and ask him to sit down, recording his unsatisfactory performance in the class register.

He was utterly hopeless at Russian. He was unable to master the vocabulary, because he didn't have time to study at home. Because the different linguistic structure and the unfamiliar characters confused and confounded him so much that even with the simplest exercise he would stare at the teacher in mute desperation, as if hoping for some supernatural inspiration—he had clearly stopped trying to figure it out on his own.

Every year he seemed the most likely pupil to be held back, but then with amazing regularity his grades would improve during the last decisive weeks, just enough so that he would squeak through and pass to the next grade. We knew the teachers helped him, since repeating a grade was not only a scary threat for us children, but the teachers, too, had an interest in seeing their pupils pass. If too many were held back, it was seen as a failure on the part of the faculty and a sign of substandard pedagogical skills. So the teachers took care to send home the dread letter only when it was absolutely unavoidable; otherwise they turned a blind eye. Because Bernhard was a quiet student who never disturbed the class or caused trouble during recess, the teachers decided to drag him up into the next class each year, holding back a different student whose grades were not necessarily worse but who was a true troublemaker. Moreover, his teachers realized that Bernhard was unlikely to ever need more than a third-grade education, as he was clearly not a budding scientist but rather someone destined for a life of manual labor, building roads or working in the fields. In this way, Bernhard, who spent barely any time with his classmates and, apart from his impressive obtuseness, caused no problems in class, was moved from one grade to the next. As a consequence, the amount of material he didn't understand grew with every passing year, especially because each new curriculum relied on some mastery of previous subjects, which Bernhard had failed to grasp. He sat in his place without saying a word, always ready to defend himself; only his blank look revealed his desperate attempt at comprehension.

Even though Bernhard was a full year older than the others in our class, he was one of the smallest. In sports, where we had to line up according to height, he would stand with the puny kids on the left, yet whenever we chose teams, he was one of the first to be picked. When we played field handball, once he took possession of the ball no one got in his way; he would run circles around everyone, then make straight for the penalty area and hurl the ball into the goal. He was just as much in demand for soccer; he never let anyone steal the ball from him, and any boy who tried to foul or trip Bernhard would spend the rest of the game on the sidelines, rubbing his shins, unable to play. Whenever the game called for stamina and strength, he had no match; but if a sport required adroitness as well, that was another story. On the parallel bars, Bernhard tried to make up for his lack of elegance and control with a wild burst of strength; when the bending bars threatened to break, the coach, afraid the boy might hurt himself in a moment of frenzied exertion, and ignoring Bernhard's protests, sent him back to the bench. His indefatigable enthusiasm and his fearless, unsparing efforts always earned him an "A" in sports and physical fitness despite his pronounced clumsiness, and this "A" looked strangely out of place on his report card, which was otherwise filled with very different letters.

Bernhard didn't have a single friend in our class. In the schoolyard he often talked with an older boy who was also a refugee—his father had fallen in the war and he lived with his mother and two sisters. This boy and his family had been resettled at the edge of town in one of the old barracks that had belonged to a large estate, an enormous property that was first run as a state farm and later given to the cooperative. Before the war the three one-story buildings had housed harvest hands and seasonal workers from Pomerania, and during the war Russian and Polish laborers. Each barrack had a long, blank façade broken only by a row of closely spaced doors and two tiny windows placed at even intervals. The townspeople still referred to the barracks as the Polish Settlement, and for that reason we thought it right that the refugees were housed there, since they had been expelled from Poland and spoke a Polish-sounding German. The older boy from the Polish Settlement seemed to be friends with Bernhard; at least I never saw him spending that much time with any other boy from school.

In any event, no one in our class mixed with him during the breaks. Now and then a teacher would ask one of the better students to help the weaker ones, and one girl became Bernhard's tutor and undertook to help him with his homework. Because Bernhard never invited the girl to his house—he seemed determined that none of his schoolmates should see where he lived—and because he either forgot their meetings or purposely ignored them, the girl soon began to lose heart and then gave up trying altogether. Occasionally she would go over to him during the short breaks—when we weren't allowed outside—look over his notebook, point out a mistake, or else provide a missing answer, which he quickly jotted down. But even then he would thank the girl with just a nod of his head, as if it were all the same to him. He showed as little interest in us, his classmates, as he did in the teachers or the work. In the face of his indifference, we quickly lost interest in him as well and began to avoid him, especially because he would rabidly defend himself whenever he felt attacked, offended, or annoyed.

His one true friend was his dog, a young mixed-breed terrier farmer Griesel had given him as payment for a week's field work, which he gave the unusual name of Tinz. He even tried to bring the dog to school. When the bell rang he tied the terrier to the school's low picket fence and told the dog to sit down and wait. The dog sat and looked at Bernhard attentively.

"Sit and no barking," Bernhard said. Then he went inside, turning around several times to make sure that Tinz was doing as he'd been told and keeping quiet.

During our first lesson the custodian came to our classroom and, after consulting with the teacher, asked Bernhard whether the dog in the yard belonged to him. When Bernhard gave a silent nod, the custodian said that bringing animals to school was against regulations, that it was cruel and a public nuisance and he didn't want to lay eyes on the beast in his schoolyard ever again.

The next morning, Bernhard again brought the dog to school. Again he tied Tinz to the fence and ordered him to sit and wait, which he did. For three days the terrier set the mood for the entire school. Especially at recess, the girls from every grade crouched in front of the dog, talking to him, kissing him, and trying to play with him. Although Bernhard had told everyone not to feed him, they gave Tinz bits of their homemade sandwiches, let him lick their hands, and competed for the dog's affection. During class, too, the animal offered a distraction, as the children attempted to look out the window from their seats or on their way to the blackboard. Tinz so disrupted the normal routine that on the dog's second day Bernhard was summoned to the principal's office. But the discussion did not produce the desired effect, since Bernhard tied the terrier to the fence for a third day as well. Then the principal came to our classroom and threatened Bernhard with the most severe punishment if he brought his dog to school again. He would expel Bernhard, even though ours was the only school in Guldenberg, which meant he would have to take the bus every day to the next town, or possibly to the district seat. Then he ordered Bernhard to take the dog home at once: whatever lessons he missed would have to be made up after school, as punishment.

After that, Tinz stayed in Griesel's farmyard. For weeks and months the girls asked Bernhard about his dog, and he was pleased to see that everyone, apart from the teachers, missed having Tinz at school.

At the beginning of sixth grade, the teacher once again changed our seating arrangement, just as she did every year—always in the very first hour of the first day of school. Planting herself in front of the class, Fräulein Nitzschke would open her small notebook and tell us who had to pack up his things and move. This always sparked protest among us boys, and sometimes tears among the girls, who were particularly outraged at being torn apart from each other, as they put it. But within a week the girls were already best friends with their new bench mates, and whispered together exactly as they had with their predecessors. These regroupings were very important to Fräulein Nitzschke—that much we understood—and presumably she spent days brooding over the new arrangements before making her decision. Children who disturbed the class were set off to the side, and the better students were mixed with the weaker ones; but she would also put students together for no apparent reason, at least none that we could discern. If we felt the move was unfair and asked for her reason, all she would say was that there were pedagogical considerations she didn't have to explain to us.

The worst thing that could happen to a boy was to be placed next to a girl. Then all the other boys would howl with malicious delight, and the jubilation was all the greater if you had escaped being seated next to a girl yourself. Still, perhaps in deference to our childish embarrassment, Fräulein Nitzschke only did that when there was no other seat available, or when a pupil was especially loud and incorrigible. Meanwhile, until our name was called we would stand by the windows or lean against the walls of the classroom with our satchels tucked under one arm, anxiously awaiting our fate.

At the beginning of sixth grade, Fräulein Nitzschke assigned me to the bench in the second row closest to the door: I lost my nice seat by the window from the previous year. As I took the two steps to my new place I listened carefully for the next boy or girl to be called—we would be sharing a desk for at least a year.

"Bernhard Haber," said Fräulein Nitzschke.

I slammed my satchel on the desk so loudly that I turned in

shock to the teacher and hinted at an apology. Then Bernhard sat down on our bench without deigning to look at me. He unpacked his things, laid them out on the desk in front of him, and seemed completely uninterested in the rearrangement taking place. When I could no longer stand the silence, I muttered something about the teacher and her yearly rearrangement of the seats. Bernhard merely glanced in my direction and returned to unpacking his things from the shapeless cloth bag he still used instead of a satchel. Having Haber as a bench mate was better than having a girl, but after the girls he was lowest on the list.

We spent two years on the same bench, until he was finally kept from moving to the next grade. In the middle of the seventh grade we wound up with a new teacher for physics and mathematics who gave Bernhard an F in both subjects, so that when I advanced to eighth grade he no longer sat next to me.

During those two years we didn't speak much, and in the first six months hardly at all. At the beginning I kept trying to engage him in conversation. When he did respond with more than a nod or a shake of the head, his replies were always terse and mostly monosyllabic. Perhaps he didn't want anything to do with us because he was a year older. Many of the older children refused to speak with the younger ones. They teased and picked on them in the schoolyard, but they never actually talked to them. Or maybe Bernhard didn't feel at ease in our class, or in our school; maybe he missed his hometown and the village in Poland where he had spent the last years.

Most of the expellees were strange; they had a strange way of talking, pronouncing the words very differently than we did, and using expressions that didn't sound German and that no one in town understood. So it was natural that the refugees and their children stuck together. They spoke differently and lived differently, had experienced different things. They came from a Germany that wasn't our Germany.

They had been expelled from their country and were not

at home in ours. They had settled among us, were living in our town, but in reality they continued to inhabit their vanished homeland. They never stopped talking about all they had lost, and no one in town wanted to hear about it, because even though the townspeople hadn't been forced to leave their homeland, things hadn't been so rosy after the war for them, either. Even those who hadn't seen their homes hit by bombs or suffered other losses in the war had to struggle to make ends meet. And the local authorities forced anyone who was relatively well off and owned an apartment or a freestanding house to take in strangers, either people from a neighboring town who had been bombed out of their homes or refugee families. And not everyone could put them up in a feed loft or a makeshift attic or, like farmer Griesel, in some unused rooms. Most people had to clear one or even two rooms to accommodate the uninvited guests, and share their kitchen and toilet, and if they owned a bath they couldn't exactly bar the strangers from using it.

Everyone envied the people who didn't have to take in refugees or who only had to house them for a few months (even though some, like my parents, owned large apartments or houses), and stories circulated about how they had managed this. My father never spoke with me about it, not even later on, but I sensed that it had something to do with the Skittles Club he visited twice a month, whose members consisted of local businessmen. Locals claimed there was more than skittles going on there but no one knew exactly what. When I asked Father about it he laughed and said that surely I wouldn't begrudge him the pleasure of drinking beer with his friends twice a month. He told me that the Skittles Club was very old and used to be called the Green & Gold Skittles Club, and later the German Skittles Club. After the war it was dissolved, but members still met every other Friday in the Eagle Tavern. Much later, long after I had left Guldenberg, I heard that the

Skittles Club had been revived and registered under a new name: the Guldenberg Green & Gold Carnival Association. In any case, neither my father nor the other members were assigned refugees for more than a short period before they were accommodated elsewhere, so that we were able to keep our rooms, which was fine with me, as I heard nothing but bad stories about the refugees from the other families. They used electricity without paying and stole food from the ice box and the cellar and were no better than Gypsies. Even the people with no firsthand experience of the refugees had little good to say about them. Since most homes hadn't been designed to house so many, tensions flared practically every day between the owners and the refugees, and if there was a fight in a pub or on the fairgrounds you could bet that it was between refugees and locals. The Guldenbergers didn't consider the expellees proper Germans and cursed them behind their back as Pollacks, or else called them "the other Russians," to distinguish them from the real Russians—that is, the occupying soldiers.

And so Bernhard was a Pollack. That's what we called him at school, although only when he wasn't around, because none of us had any desire to get into a scrap with him.

One Saturday, a year after Bernhard's father had set up shop in the tobacco shed, it burned down. Just after the church bells had rung six o'clock, the sirens on the water tower at the fire house started wailing. For minutes the whole city was filled with the rising and falling howl, until all the volunteers from the fire brigade had assembled in front of the building. They hauled the old red engine out of the garage in front of the tower and hastily donned helmets with leather neck guards and black jackets with silver insignia. The helmets had been provided when the fire brigade was established and had never seen any real action: there hadn't been a single fire since the end of the war. It was as if everything that could possibly burn had been consumed during the hour-long bombardment of the city in the very last year of the fighting. For the practice drills, which were staged a few weekends in the summer, the volunteer firemen would wear their black caps or the old helmets from before the war.

All the children ran after the firefighters as they drove out of the hangar. Some had come with their bicycles and tried to keep up with the engine. Two older boys were leaning far over their handlebars and were holding on to the coiled hose affixed to the vehicle. They let the red engine pull them through the town, although the firemen sitting on the side benches of the open vehicle threatened them and even swatted at their hands with wooden ax handles.

The word spread fast that Griesel's old tobacco shed was on fire, and I raced with two classmates down the road to Niedermühle, where the building stood just behind the city limits sign. When we got there the fire engine was parked away from the fire, the hoses had been unrolled, and the portable motor pump stood between the blazing shed and the river. Four firemen were positioned at each of the two nozzles, at a respectful distance from the blaze, and pointed the jets of water at apparently random places in the flames. Two others kept shooing the children back and shouting loudly. Herr Keller, captain of the fire brigade, who worked in the town hall as doorman and custodian, forbade his men from going closer to the flames.

"It's wood," he told everyone who approached him. "Dry wood. You have to let it burn itself out."

Keller said the same thing to a policeman who showed up on his bicycle and stood beside the fire captain while holding his bike. The men's pristine helmets glowed red in the light of the flames. Keller and two of his men walked around the shed, followed by the policeman, pushing his bicycle. They gruffly sent away the children who wanted to join them.

The full width of the roof was aflame, and thick, dark smoke was billowing out of the ventilation slits that ran above the shed's large double doors. Here and there a single flame came shooting out through the smoke, which rose, almost perpendicularly, for several yards before slowly wafting toward town. Occasionally a joist would come crashing down inside, sending a torrent of smoke and sparks through the vents and into the sky, where it came back down as glowing rain. When Keller finished making his rounds, he ordered the men to break off trying to put out the fire in the shed and direct their energies instead to dousing the meadow between the burning building and the barley field, to prevent the fire from spreading.

When the one-armed Haber showed up with his son and saw the firemen steadily hosing the meadow with river water, he started screaming at them, asking why they weren't trying to save his shop instead of dumping water in the meadow to no purpose. Before the men could answer, the main roof truss collapsed with a crash and a gigantic storm of sparks. A few seconds later the burning side-planks toppled into the shed's interior and out onto the rutted muddy driveway. Glowing bits of wood flew through the air and landed at the feet of the watching firemen, who shrank back and again shooed away the children.

Haber refused to be pushed aside; in a dazed silence he stared at the fire that was destroying what little he had, while Keller went on explaining why the men were directing the water at the meadow, to keep the flames from spreading to the winter barley. Then he added, "Looks like someone wanted to knock off early and forgot to switch a machine off. Or maybe you had a parabolic heater? Those things cause half the fires in our district. It's horrible, they ought to be banned."

The carpenter shook his head without saying a word or taking his eyes off the fire. Meanwhile about a hundred spectators—mostly children—had gathered behind the firemen. They were standing in groups, watching the burning shed with interest and discussing the work of the firemen, who went on steadfastly watering the meadow and attending to the pump motor, which was tired with age.

An hour later the last wall collapsed in a spray of sparks, and all that was left of the shed was a tall, glowing mountain of ember and ash, with a few pieces of blackened iron jutting out. At Keller's command the men now turned the nozzles there. The embers let off a loud hiss when the water hit, and turned into a dirty gray muck. The policeman, who had left soon after he appeared, returned in a car with a colleague. They climbed out, waved Haber over, and interrogated him as they bent over the hood, where they had set down their fake-leather shoulder bags. One of them opened a notebook and slowly took down every word the carpenter spoke. My two friends and I moved over near the policemen, but not so close as to be chased away; as we watched the burning shed, we took pains not to miss a word between Haber and his interrogators.

The unknown policeman, who had come by car from the district seat, asked Haber to list every machine he had kept in the shed, specifying which were electric and which were diesel-powered. When the carpenter again got worked up about the firemen who, in his opinion, had simply stood there and let his shop burn down, the policeman from the district capital said, "We all do what we can, citizen."

"Or not."

"I don't understand, Herr Haber. I don't see what you're getting at."

"If you lived here you'd understand."

"Very well, citizen. I need to take down some information. And later, once we've investigated the site, I'm sure we'll have some more questions for you."

"Firefighters, they call themselves," said Haber. "All they do is stand around and let everything burn."

"There wasn't much they could do. Nobody can do much when it's all wood that's burning."

"Especially if they don't want to."

"They're all doing what they can. We have to put people's

lives first. And in this case nobody could do anything. Was it your shed?"

"No. I was leasing it. I just owned the shop inside."

"You're a carpenter?"

"Yes."

"These days everything is electric. That's why there's so much trouble."

"I did not set fire to my own shop." The carpenter was indignant.

"I didn't say you did. We'll see what we see. We'll find out whatever there is to find out, Herr Haber," the policeman responded, his voice loaded with meaning. "I tell you, people are constantly amazed by how much we can establish after a fire. They think everything's been completely destroyed, and then we find some piece of evidence that clinches the case. These days we use the latest methods and techniques and we get to the bottom of everything. Murder, homicide, arson—we solve it all, citizen."

"Well, it wasn't me. I can swear that by God Almighty."

"This has nothing to do with God Almighty. You can leave him out of it. We solve things scientifically."

"Why should I want to set fire to my own shop?"

"There doesn't have to be intent, citizen. Negligent arson is also a punishable offense."

"Negligent arson? What are you suggesting?"

"For the moment I'm not saying anything. First we have to investigate the site of the fire, and if we determine, and for your sake I hope we don't, that some electrical appliance wasn't switched off, then, my good man, then you can be happy there were no human casualties. And if it is indeed private property, as you say, then you should be doubly happy. If the site belonged to the people, then all I can tell you is: prison is not a nice place."

"Everything in the shop was switched off. Like every day

when I finish work. You don't need to teach an experienced carpenter that—it's in his blood."

"So you say. I'd prefer to rely on my investigation."

"You don't have to."

"Oh? And why not?"

"All the machines were turned off."

"I'm sure you *think* you turned everything off. Maybe you turned everything off every day but one. Today."

"I can prove it to you."

Haber fished something out of his jacket pocket and held it up, right under the policeman's nose.

"What's that?"

"A fuse."

"So? What's that supposed to prove?"

"That's the main electrical fuse. I unscrew it every evening and every morning I screw it back in. I promised the farmer I would do that. And that's what I did back home, too, when I had my own shop, back then. Every evening I unscrewed the fuse and every morning I screwed it back in."

"We'll see. Everything will be sorted out. If you unscrewed the fuse, that's fine. Maybe the wiring wasn't sound."

"It's only a year old. I had to put in everything new. The shed never had electricity before; the farmer didn't need it. I paid for it all myself. I had to have the cable laid out here, the service mast erected, and pay for three hundred yards' worth of wire. All myself. The whole thing cost as much as a new rototiller."

"Well," said the policeman, and then went silent. He scrutinized the carpenter, then stuck his notebook in his bag and stared at the glowing pile of embers without saying a word.

"It was arson," said Haber finally.

The policeman whistled through his teeth and made a face. Then, without taking his eyes off the smoldering remains of the shed, he said, "That remains to be seen. The investigation will determine if that's the case. Let's not have any hasty accusations, citizen."

The policeman pointed a finger at Haber and sighed, then once again took the notebook out of his shoulder bag, opened it to an empty page, licked the pen, and then held it over the paper.

"Is there someone you suspect?" he asked. "Can you give me a name? Have you noticed anything?"

"Have I noticed anything? I certainly have. Ever since I've had to live here. Since I was resettled here as a refugee."

"I'm talking about the fire, about the fire and nothing else. I want you to tell me if you've noticed anything that might shed light on the cause of the fire."

"Write down the entire town. If you want to know the perpetrator, just write down Guldenberg."

"Enough," the policemen said, threateningly. He was annoyed because he had thought the carpenter really was going to name someone, and had already started writing in his notebook.

"I'll pretend I didn't hear that," he went on. "Otherwise it might cost you dearly, citizen."

"It's true. This is the second time I've lost everything. The second time I've been ruined. In Breslau I lost my fully equipped shop to the Poles. I had to give everything up and didn't get a penny. And now this. Now I'm bankrupt for the second time in my life."

The policeman shook his head. "You have Hitler to thank for the first time, and this here is fate. Fire is a force of nature. We're powerless against it. You can see for yourself. We'll find out if it was arson, Herr Haber, nothing escapes us. And if there's some bandit out there, we'll nab him, and you'll get every penny back. Of course, if it was fate, or even negligence, then it's a different matter."

"For me it's the end. I might as well end it all right now."

"You shouldn't say things like that, Herr Haber. Everybody makes do, one way or another."

"Right. One way or another. And one time or another it's all over."

The policeman snapped his notebook shut, then placed it, along with the pen, inside the black bag he had slung over his arm. He laid his hand on the other man's shoulder. "Don't go throwing in the towel just yet, Herr Haber. Come morning, everything will look a lot better. This doesn't mean you're finished."

He walked over to his colleague and together the two men strode importantly in the direction of Captain Keller. Haber stood, a broken man, before the remains of his workshop, from which occasional flames were still flaring, his mouth half open. Bernhard went over and for a moment reached his hand to his father's shoulder; Haber looked at his son, then stroked the back of his son's neck with his left hand, his remaining hand. Both stared at the embers and the gray-black machine parts. Eventually the only sounds to be heard were the noise of the pump and the stream of water and the hissing as it hit the embers. Many of the children had left. About thirty people were standing around, watching the glowing remains of the shed, observing the firemen as they extinguished the embers, and casting stolen glances at Herr Haber, the carpenter, standing there with sunken shoulders, and his son, Bernhard.

After nine o'clock my father showed up. By then it was pitch dark and he was looking for me. Since none of my classmates had wanted to go home, I had stayed near the shed and the firemen.

"There you are," said Father, after placing his hand on my shoulder and crossly turning me around. "I thought I might find you here. No supper for you tonight, boy—and now home."

But then he stopped and looked at the burned-down shed as I told him what the police and Herr Haber had said. When I reported that the carpenter had told the policeman to write down the whole town of Guldenberg as the arsonist, Father gave a quick snort and laughed.

Then he mumbled to himself, "He's not so wrong about

that," and took me by the hand. "Now come along." We went over to Herr Haber, who together with Bernhard was still staring at the glowing remains of the shed.

"Good evening, neighbor," my father said to the carpenter, though we didn't live anywhere near them.

I was certain that my father had never spoken to Herr Haber before in his life. The carpenter may have come into our pharmacy once or twice; being a cripple, he likely needed various medications and bandages, but my father didn't work at the counter. For that he had hired Frau Brendel, an older woman whose husband had died in the war and who after being widowed had trained as a pharmacist's clerk. My father kept to the large room behind the salesroom—his laboratory, as he called it, where he concocted his mixtures, processed the orders, looked over the incoming consignments, and occasionally took inventory. An old brown door adorned with a beveled rosette mirror connected the salesroom to the laboratory; as a rule, Father left it open so he could keep an eye on what was going on in the pharmacy. He also had a narrow glass pane built into the wall in back of the pharmaceutical cabinet, so that he could see into the outer room without having to get up from his chair in the laboratory. That meant that whenever the bell rang, Father could see who had come in the pharmacy, and he only went into the front room for acquaintances or important people he wanted to greet personally. Then he would stand beside the cash register and talk while Frau Brendel went up and down the row of cabinets carrying a small silver tray, opening the heavy old drawers with the porcelain markers, taking out the packets, and placing them on the tray with whatever prescriptions she had already filled. While Father had probably seen Herr Haber through this spyglass, and while he may have recognized the name from his prescriptions, I was sure he'd never gotten up from his chair on the carpenter's account. After all, Herr Haber was one of those unfortunates who'd been expelled from the East. We had taken two of them in ourselves for six months, right after the war—Frau Happe, who worked in the church office, and her daughter, who had trouble walking and who back home had mended other people's laundry. They had been assigned two rooms in our house, one of which had a hotplate and running water, so they were only allowed to use our kitchen when there was no other choice. My father would never have gone into the front room on account of a refugee like Herr Haber; he had too much work to do in the pharmacy for that, so I was puzzled why he was speaking to the man now and even calling him "neighbor."

Haber turned to him, and I could see he had tears in his eyes.

"This is bad for you, very bad," my father said. "I'm sorry."

The carpenter stared at my father without understanding, as if he were trying to interpret the meaning of the words. Then he nodded helplessly, without hope, but grateful for the sympathetic remark.

"Let's go," Father said to me, "there's nothing we can do here. We can't help and we're only in the way. And it's already your bedtime."

He had placed his arm over my shoulder, and we walked that way back home. I talked the whole time about the fire and the firemen, Herr Haber, and the policeman from the district seat, just to escape the reprimand I knew was coming, but Father didn't say a word. When we reached home, Mother gave me a careful looking-over; she presumed I'd been given a hiding.

"Where were you? Go in the kitchen, your supper's in there."

Father let me go with a little smack on the head.

"There was a fire," he told Mother. "Griesel's tobacco shed burned down—that old wooden barn right by the mill, where Haber with the one arm has his woodworking shop. Or rather had, since there's nothing left of it. Now he's lost everything a second time, this Haber."

"The poor family," said Mother. "Maybe we can help them somehow."

"How do you intend to help them, Katharina? The man simply landed in the wrong town. In his shoes I'd pack my bags and move on. The town doesn't want him, there's nothing to be done."

"What are you getting at? Was it arson? Did someone set fire to the barn?"

"That's certainly what Herr Haber thinks. And he's probably right."

"But who would do such a thing?"

"I'm sure I could come up with a couple names if I thought long enough. My dear, if I were in his place I wouldn't stick around for the next warm welcome."

"My God." Mother gaped wide-eyed at Father, as if he himself had set the carpenter's shed on fire. "What a wicked thing to say! Do you really think anyone in our town is capable of doing such a hideous thing?"

Father smiled. He looked at me and asked, "Is the carpenter's son still in your class?"

I nodded and Mother said, "He's even sharing a bench with Thomas."

"Good," said Father. "Then I hope you know what you have to do."

I nodded without hesitating. Then I turned red and asked, "What do you mean? I mean, what exactly should I do?"

"You should stand up for him, Thomas, and make sure no one in your class is mean to him, you understand? His family has it hard enough. We don't have to make the rest of their life hell in the bargain."

I nodded again, although I didn't have a clue how I was supposed to stand up for Bernhard. He didn't need anybody to stand up for him, not from our class or the whole rest of the school; he could stand up for himself, and he did, too. On that very first day he'd made sure that no one ever dared pick a fight with him. The boys stayed out of his way, and I was more likely to need his protection than vice versa, the way Father meant. But I didn't want to explain all that, so I just nodded.

Bernhard didn't come to school on Monday, which allowed us all to speak freely about the fire—by far the biggest thing to happen in town in a long time. Many of us had seen the shed in flames Saturday evening, and the others had gone on Sunday to see the ashes. The fire brigade had hosed down the meadow until midnight to keep the dry grass and stubble from catching fire. Then the captain ordered the hoses rolled back up, had four men lift the pump and remount it on the back of the fire engine, and posted two men to keep watch overnight. Before the vehicle drove away, they all made one more pass around the barn.

Everyone in class was convinced it was arson. A few people knew or at least claimed to know that the police had found three separate sources for the fire, that the barn had been doused with gasoline in several places, and that the police had roped off the site to search for clues in the barn and surrounding area. One boy from the other sixth-grade class claimed to know who had started the fire. The older children pushed him to give a name but he refused to say anything else except that he knew who had done it. Naturally we also discussed the possibility that Bernhard's father himself might have burned down the shed for the insurance, so that he might be given a proper workshop in the middle of town. The authorities now had to find some other space for him, an empty room somewhere suitable for a shop, and we figured he had a good chance of getting something in a more central location. Certainly it couldn't be farther away than Griesel's old tobacco shed. As we saw it, there was something to the argument that the fire hadn't been such a bad thing for him, even if he hadn't set it himself, although he had lost a few things in the process. But no one felt much sympathy: the whole event was far too exciting.

When Bernhard returned to school the next morning, some of us watched him out of the corner of our eye. No one talked with him about the fire, and Bernhard remained as closed off as ever. One of the girls wanted to express her sympathy. No sooner did she open her mouth than he cut her off to ask about the homework he had missed, and had her loan him her notes from the previous day's lessons—without paying the girl herself any more attention.

That day for second period we had Fräulein Nitzschke. After she greeted the class and we were allowed to sit down, she spoke about the misfortune that had befallen Bernhard's family and exhorted us to do everything we could to help our classmate. I wondered what she meant by that, and I was sure all the others were asking themselves the same thing, if they'd even listened to Fräulein Nitzschke's drippy speech in the first place. How were we supposed to help this refugee boy when he was so pigheaded and tight-lipped? I watched him in secret: Bernhard was staring at the teacher as blankly as if she were talking about the North Pole. When Fräulein Nitzschke stepped over to our desk and stroked his hair, he gave me a look to let me know that if I even thought of laughing, at recess he'd give me a couple of warm ears, as we used to say. So I bit my lip and tried to look uninterested while Fräulein Nitzschke bestowed her endearments—which we all hated—on Bernhard. She asked him if he wanted to say something about what his father intended to do. Bernhard shook his head, and Fräulein Nitzschke went back to her desk and began the day's mind-numbing lesson.

Bernhard never said a single word about the fire to us. The authorities did indeed determine it was arson. The police spoke with a few people who lived on the outskirts of town near the old mill, asking whether they had noticed anything unusual, whether they had seen any strangers around, which is how we learned they were looking for an arsonist. Father commented that you can spend a long time looking for something you don't want to find. When I told him that many of my classmates thought the one-armed carpenter had set the old tobacco shed on fire himself, he smiled and touched my chin so that I would look him in the eye, and asked, "And you? Do you share their opinion?"

"I don't know," I said. "I don't have an opinion."

"No," he said, "old man Haber didn't start that fire. I don't know who did, but I'm sure it wasn't him. What's more, any one of us, not just the refugees, could find himself in a similar position, just like that. A town is capable of doing many things, my boy. One tiny slip-up in a cozy little nest like ours and you can suddenly find there isn't enough air to breathe. I'll tell you something about these quaint little houses with their nice gardens in front: all these charming little flowerbeds are fertilized with depression and reek of raw nerves and mental illness. I should know, because everybody gets their pills from me. And if I could sell that kind of thing, they'd buy a couple of 'ultimate pills' to get out of here. So my boy, and now go eat your supper and then to bed."

Two months after the fire, the city administration assigned Haber space in an old mattress factory on Molkengasse that had partly burned down on one of the very last days of the war, and let him set up a new shop in several empty rooms on the ground floor. The owner, an old widower, had died of smoke inhalation trying to contain the fire as it spread through the building. He had no children and was evidently without heirs, as no one had put in a claim for the ruined factory after his death. The windows on both of the upper stories had been knocked out, and the roof had been patched with heavy cardboard to keep out the rain and prevent further deterioration. The only usable rooms were on the ground floor: one of them was fully tiled, like a butcher's slaughtering room. The authorities had given old man Haber a contract for the ground floor, along with the assurance that he would receive special consideration once the building was repaired and the upstairs rooms, which would one day become apartments, were allocated. But they warned Haber that that was a long way off—probably a very long way off—because the city owned a number of damaged buildings that were only partially usable, and the old mattress factory wasn't a priority for repair, since there was too much that needed fixing, and in fact they were considering tearing it down and putting up a new building, which might actually prove cheaper. Along with the lease agreement and all the necessary permits from the various departments in the Rathaus that dealt with the allocation of space for commercial purposes, Haber received a certificate entitling him to a special apportionment of supplies, in the event he wanted to repair the building himself. In that case, he was told, he might acquire the entire structure for life and free of charge, after the work had been completed and had passed inspection. Frau Steinmar, the case officer who handed him the forms, said, "Those are the rules, Herr Haber, I'm sorry. I can see you won't be able to fix up the building." And then she shrugged and added, "There's nothing better available. You've seen for yourself how things are in Guldenberg."

"Thank you. I'm satisfied. The old factory rooms are just the right size for me. And sandwiched between the other buildings like that, no one will dare set them on fire."

"Do you really think that someone from our town—"

"Thanks very much for your trouble."

"And you're sure you want to set up shop there? The only reason it's empty is because the roof might collapse."

"I know. I've seen it. I'm satisfied."

"I'm sorry. We honestly don't have anything else. There are just too many refugees, too many people to resettle."

"I know."

"I mean . . . I don't want to offend you, Herr Haber. It's just that we're a small city. We've also had to make sacrifices, and we weren't spared the bombings, either."

"Right."

"I realize that you've lost everything, but none of us are living a life of plenty. Look at it this way: if the rooms were in order, then they would have been given away a long time ago. The building would have been assigned to someone else, someone from here."

"I know."

"So in that regard it's lucky for you that the house is so run-down."

"Yes."

The city gave Haber a loan, which enabled him to open a bank account and purchase a circular saw and the tools he needed most, since all of his equipment was destroyed in the fire. Even though he had taken out insurance, the policy didn't pay anything, since he had set up shop in a wooden structure, which, according to the terms of the policy, was not allowed in his line of work.

Haber took a board, fashioned a sign, and turned to Herr Satern, who owned the stationery shop, which also sold a few books and homemade postcards with scenes of the town and the two nearby tourist attractions—the Luther Stone and the Bismarck Tower. He had Satern inscribe *G. Haber—Architectural Woodwork and Cabinetry* in a thick, curvy script. Then he hung the sign over the entrance to the former mattress factory. The board served as a makeshift cover over the factory logo embedded in the stucco, but the old Fraktur lettering could be seen both above and below the new sign.

"He's not exactly going to get rich here in Guldenberg," was Father's commentary, "but these days it'd be a lot if he manages to earn enough to feed himself and his family."

Old man Haber had next to no work. The refugees who had flooded our town were in no position to hire a tradesman. They sawed and nailed their boards themselves and built whatever they needed in a rough-and-ready way. The locals, too, had little money to spare, and if they were willing to splurge on a craftsman, the last thing they would do was hire one of the refugees, who were only adding to the town's general misery. Before the war, Guldenberg had housed five carpenters, and each had plenty of work. When the Habers arrived, only three of these remained, but the townspeople always turned to them.

Apart from that, it was a riddle to us how old man Haber with his one arm could pick up a large board and cut a curve or run a bench plane. Now and then I heard the grown-ups talking about him; some felt sorry for him, but no one wanted to hire him, at least none of our friends and relatives. Everyone in my family shared my father's opinion: "Ordering something from a one-armed carpenter might be the decent, Christian thing to do, but you'd have to be dumb as a bag of rocks." He had nothing against the man but thought that sympathy for the refugees shouldn't cloud good common sense.

A year after the fire the Haber family was able to leave Farmer Griesel's attic and move into an apartment on Mühlenstrasse. The previous tenant had taken off in the night for West Germany. He had been party secretary at the machine works, and the townspeople now reported with a sneer that he had fled to the West, along with the party funds, the list of members, and many of the more important documents from the factory. His flight created a stir in Guldenberg that lasted a week. Even at school the teachers commanded us to exercise greater vigilance. The history teacher spoke repeatedly of the class enemy attacking, and warned of sabotage, diversionary actions, infiltration, and agents, while we listened in disinterested silence. These catchphrases meant nothing to us, and among ourselves we lumped them all into one category we called "sabotrators."

The former party secretary's three-room apartment was sealed off for a week, after which the furniture was hauled away. Several weeks later the dwelling was transferred to the carpenter, and so Haber and his family moved in.

To help his parents with the move, Bernhard was allowed to skip two days of school, despite his being a poor student.

Farmer Griesel hitched up his horses and carted the larger pieces of furniture over to Mühlenstrasse, while Bernhard transported the boxes and smaller pieces using his dog cart. His father had mounted a shaft onto an old wooden handcart with metal-rimmed wheels, and Bernhard had taken some old straps off the wagon that the farmer no longer needed because they were torn in several places and fashioned a makeshift harness. After fitting the harness to his dog, Bernhard hung the traces on the cross-yoke, creating a passable dog cart. This cart was piled high for the move, and Bernhard pulled together with Tinz while also steering the cart. After the successful operation, Bernhard could frequently be seen driving his dog cart well beyond the farmyard, with Tinz hauling him through the parks and around the town. When the going was difficult, Bernhard would walk alongside and help push; when they came to level, asphalted stretches or well-worn park trails, Bernhard would jump into the cart and let Tinz pull him, while he steered with outstretched legs, occasionally dragging one foot as a brake.

He didn't have his dog for long—just two years. Tinz died a few months after the move, during the summer vacation. His body was found one day, by the river, a hundred yards from where we used to swim, hidden in some bushes. Some small children found the dog's body because it was attracting insects and had begun to stink. The excited children ran home and told everyone they saw about their find. A man from the Polish Settlement, whose own children were spending the day at the swimming hole, finally stopped them and had them lead him to where the dog had been found. Using a pole, he pulled the carcass out from under the bushes, looped some string around the dog's neck, pulled it up the bank, and buried the decomposing animal alongside the road with the help of a sand shovel that he borrowed from some children playing on the beach. When he came back to the river, he cleaned off the shovel in the water, returned it to the children, and said, "Somebody killed that dog. With a wire snare. That's horrible, who'd do a thing like that?"

The man asked if anyone knew who the animal's owner was. Several girls said they did, and the man told them to go to the owner and let him know. They should explain that the animal had been buried immediately because it had been dead for several days, and they should say where it was and show him the place; it was marked with an ash branch. They should also warn the owner not to dig up his dog unless he wanted to catch scabies, because the animal was already quite decomposed.

Two of the girls ran off right away to look for Bernhard Haber and report the dog's death to him. I never learned how Bernhard reacted to the news. I didn't see him that summer. I never saw him during any school vacation. Maybe he left town or visited relatives and friends in Poland, though I doubt that his family would have had the money for such a long trip. More likely he had to spend his vacations in the shop helping his father, which is why we never saw him in town or at our swimming hole.

On the first day of seventh grade, Fräulein Nitzschke rearranged our seating once again. I stayed with Bernhard but we were moved to the second bench in the middle row. During the first recess, Bernhard turned to me and said quietly, "Listen. I'm saying this to you and to everybody else."

Then he went silent and looked at me angrily. I tried to withstand his gaze and said, as casually as I could, "Why are you whispering? If you have something to say to everybody you should say it so they can hear."

He took a deep breath and then went on, just as quietly. "Listen. Whoever it was that killed Tinz, I'm going to kill him. Let everybody know."

I nodded, scared, and turned bright red, as if I myself had been the one who killed his dog. Bernhard screwed up his eyes and squinted at me. I pulled my satchel out from under the bench and acted as if I were searching for something. I could feel that he was still staring at me, and I didn't dare raise my head.

"What do you know about it, Thomas?"

"Nothing. I don't know anything. What should I know?"

He waited without saying a word.

"I didn't even know your dog was dead," I lied. "Did someone really kill him? Maybe he just died somehow."

Bernhard looked at me.

"It must have been a crazy person, Bernhard. It had to be a crazy person—no one from our class would do that."

I spat the words out hastily. The idea that Bernhard would kill one of my classmates, maybe stab him, sent shivers down my spine. He had said it so quietly and coldly I was convinced this was no idle threat.

We never found out who killed Tinz; at least I never heard anything about it, neither back then in Guldenberg nor later on. As Bernhard had commanded, I delivered his message to my classmates during the next recess. The boys laughed, but I could tell they were convinced he was serious. The girls, on the other hand, were openly scared and spent the day chattering about Bernhard and his dead dog. At some point the class started saying that a man from the Polish Settlement or a field hand from the barracks had killed Tinz, but that was just a rumor: I never heard a name spoken, and no one provided any precise information. Nor did I learn who started the rumor. The truth was that everyone in the class was worked up over the dog's death, and even more over Bernhard's warning. Everyone, that is, except for Bernhard Haber himself. He never mentioned his dog again. When one girl told him how sorry she was to hear about Tinz, and how despicable it was to kill a little innocent dog, he looked at her uncomprehendingly and turned away without saying a word.

Three weeks later Herr Engelmann, the principal, came into our room. He stood in front of the desk where Fräulein Nitzschke was sitting and asked Bernhard to stand. Then he talked about how someone had killed our classmate's dog, and he hoped that this person, whoever he was, whether from our school or somewhere else, would have the courage to confess and apologize.

"It has come to my attention," he went on, "that Bernhard Haber has issued severe threats toward this unknown person. By so doing, Bernhard, you have intimidated and frightened your fellow pupils." He looked directly at Bernhard. "That is something I cannot and will not tolerate. I am not only responsible for your education and schooling, I am also responsible for the safety and protection of each and every one of you."

Then he spoke for a long time about how he was accountable for the pupils in his school and had to ensure that they were free from harm, and that he had authority to take whatever steps were necessary. Like the captain of a passenger ship, he had to shoulder this responsibility, but he also had the right to exercise his duty. In case of danger he was authorized as a representative of the state and would not hesitate to use his power to keep the children entrusted to him out of harm's way.

The whole class understood exactly what the principal was talking about, especially as he had made Bernhard stand up, yet none of us quite grasped what powers he could use against us or Bernhard. We were amused by the reference to a ship's captain, and later spent a long time talking about the comparison, which struck us as odd, because we had never pictured the small, pale man as a suntanned sea wolf sporting a white uniform. As for authority, we knew that a captain could marry people aboard his ship, as well as conduct emergency christenings and commit to the deep the bodies of those who died at sea. But none of these events was likely to happen at our school, so for the next several days in the schoolyard we debated without result about what powers our principal was entitled to. Finally we accepted one boy's theory that Herr Engelmann had originally wanted to go to sea but had been turned down because of his size and was now leading his able-bodied crew inside the teachers' lounge, which was off limits for us. In any case, from that day on, whenever we spoke of him we always referred to the principal as Captain.

After he had finished his speech, Herr Engelmann looked at Bernhard Haber expectantly but the boy just went on staring at him, unmoved and evidently unimpressed. Finally, the principal asked him to make a statement. Bernhard shrugged his shoulders as if bored and asked, "May I sit down?"

Fräulein Nitzschke's face appeared behind the shoulder of the principal, who was a head shorter than she. Highly agitated, her cheeks intensely red, she demanded that Bernhard apologize, twice—once for his impertinence toward the principal and once for the threat that had terrified his classmates and for which there really was no excuse. The principal laid his hand on Fräulein Nitzschke's arm to signal that she should leave the matter to him.

"You threatened your classmates," he said to Bernhard, as we listened with bated breath. "What a monstrous thing to do."

"No," said Bernhard, looking down at me.

"And you're a coward as well."

Bernhard slowly shook his head and looked down at the floor.

"I said," he began. He faltered before finally saying, "Somebody killed Tinz, my dog."

"That is bad, and very regrettable," said the principal. "But it's no reason to terrify your classmates."

Bernhard stared at his shoes without saying another word.

"Look at me! Did you understand me, boy?"

Bernhard nodded without looking up.

"Then tell everyone here that you regret saying such a stupid thing. That you were careless and rash and are sorry for what you said."

Bernhard clenched his teeth and went on staring at his shoes.

"Well, come on! We're waiting. And we'll wait for as long as it takes for you to apologize."

The class was completely still. We all had our eyes on Bernhard, who was standing motionless beside his seat, his head bowed. He didn't seem the least bit embarrassed to be the center of attention, nor did he appear at all on edge but, rather, disinterested.

"Well? I'm not hearing anything." The principal cupped his hand behind his ear. He was beginning to sweat.

"Say something, Bernhard. Say what you have to say," Fräulein Nitzschke again broke in. She looked at Bernhard, practically pleading, while casting worried glances at the principal.

Bernhard gave an audible moan, then looked at Fräulein Nitzschke, pressed his lips together, and seemed to be patiently waiting for whatever was coming.

"If you don't apologize, boy . . . If you don't take back those bad things you said, I'll have to expel you from school. I won't have any choice—it's my duty. Your parents will have to enroll you in another school, in Eilenburg, or somewhere else, and you'll have to take the bus or the train every day. Maybe the other school won't even take you; there are plenty of reasons not to. You might wind up having a pretty long commute, maybe so long you'll have to sleep there, in a dormitory, and then you'll only be able to see your parents during vacation. You'd better think about that, my boy, and on the double."

The principal scrutinized Bernhard with a worried face, then glanced at our teacher, who was nervously crumpling her handkerchief. Now he looked helpless, as if he and not Bernhard had been called on the carpet for some disgraceful deed.

"I'm not going to put a black mark down in your record, boy. I won't even give you a written reprimand, but only because that's not severe enough for something like this. That was a threat of murder. And if I took it seriously, if I thought for a second that you really meant it, then I would have no choice but to inform the police and the district attorney. Do you understand?"

Surprisingly, Bernhard nodded, but he did not look up. The

principal was relieved that the wrongdoer had finally shown some kind of reaction, and once again demanded an apology. Bernhard stood next to me, unyielding, and made no move to comply with the principal's request. The class was gradually getting restless; everyone was beginning to whisper. Some were annoyed by Bernhard's obstinacy and stubbornness, while others approved of his stance and hoped he wouldn't give in anytime soon. Fräulein Nitzschke and the principal seemed not to notice the quiet commotion; both stared fixedly at Bernhard Haber, tilting their heads forward a little, as if that might help the boy open his mouth and finally utter the apology they demanded.

I looked up at Bernhard, who stood next to our bench unruffled. I admired him. I wasn't as strong as he; I wouldn't be able to stand there that long, refusing to deliver what the teacher, the principal, and the entire class were waiting an eternity for him to say. I knew I would have given in a long time before and said what was expected, whether I meant it or not.

Tiny beads of sweat broke out on the principal's forehead. He bit his lower lip, and we could literally see him thinking things through, struggling to deal with Bernhard, straining to bring the matter to some conclusion without sacrificing his authority.

"Bernhard," he finally said, "you are sorry, aren't you? You apologize for making such a rash and foolish statement? You regret saying it and would like to tell your classmates that you're sorry? Agreed?"

Bernhard gave a curt nod, so quick you could barely see it—you might have mistaken it for an involuntary twitch of his head. But the principal seemed satisfied.

"Well, I'm happy to see it, my boy," he said, breathing a sigh of relief. "I'm happy to see it. And now that's the end of that and I never want to hear anything like it again, neither from you nor from anyone else."

As he spoke these words he scanned the classroom, as if

any one of us might have come close to saying something similar. Then he turned to Fräulein Nitzschke and, pleased with himself, said, "Well that's that. You may now proceed with your lesson, Fräulein Nitzschke."

He gave the class another stern looking-over, told Bernhard to sit down, and walked to the door. Bernhard looked at me as he slowly slid onto the chair. His face revealed nothing—no trace of shame or regret. Nor was there any hint of triumph, although he had stood his ground: the little head-nod didn't count; the principal couldn't seriously consider that an apology. Bernhard had bested the principal in front of the entire class, he had won the battle, and we had all seen him do it. Still, despite his sensational victory, Bernhard seemed completely indifferent. He acted as if he'd had nothing to do with any of it. When the principal reached the door, he turned around and said, in a quiet voice, as if he were speaking to himself, "That boy needs a good whipping. And by someone who has two good arms to do it."

Then he left our classroom. Everyone in the class had heard him. Bernhard's faced suddenly turned white.

"Eye for an eye," he hissed. "Wire snare for wire snare."

Fräulein Nitzschke froze and shuddered briefly as if suddenly frightened.

"So . . . shall we get on with it, then?" she said, forcing a smile, and clapped her hands.

I don't know for certain if she heard Bernhard's remark or if she simply preferred to ignore it. Ten minutes later the bell rang for recess, and we ran into the schoolyard to talk about the whole incident and Bernhard and his victory over pale little Herr Engelmann, who thought he was a captain on the high seas. Bernhard stood with the refugee children from the seventh grade; they were leaning against the shut door of the church that bordered the other side of the schoolyard, eating their sandwiches and talking. I was sure he said nothing about his successful encounter; at least he didn't appear to be boasting about his triumph. As always he spoke little and remained composed. Perhaps it meant nothing to him to have defeated the principal so magnificently; perhaps he was simply better than all of us.

Even now that his family had a new apartment, where he possibly had his own room, he never invited his classmates over. If it was absolutely necessary for one of us to seek him out because an urgent message from school had to be delivered, or because he'd been sick and needed his homework, he would crack open the door, tell the classmate he'd be right there, then shut the door and reappear a few minutes later with his jacket and accompany his visitor downstairs while listening to whatever information needed to be conveyed. If he had to make note of something, he would sit down on a step and scribble it in his ungainly handwriting on a piece of paper he fished out of his jacket pocket. We couldn't help notice how intent he was not to let anyone into his apartment. We wondered whether he actually had his own bed. In the years after the war our town had no rich people, but even amid the general destitution there was a kind of poverty for which one could only have contempt.

In any case, the carpenter stayed in the city, and Bernhard stayed in my class. When I started eighth grade our paths separated, as he had to repeat the seventh grade, and after that I had just one year left before I switched to the comprehensive preparatory high school in Eilenburg. That meant I had to take the hour-long train ride twice every day and didn't get home until late afternoon or sometimes in the evening. I didn't have time to see any of my old friends, not to mention people like Bernhard, with whom I had no real connection.

For four years I took the train to Eilenburg, and during the summers I went on bicycle tours with two new friends from high school. Once we were away for seven weeks straight, biking all the way across Bavaria. We stayed in the saddle the entire time except for four days, when we were able to store our bikes at a farmstead in the Bavarian Forest belonging to a classmate's uncle. Our aching bottoms didn't improve, though; quite the contrary, since we spent these days seated in two collapsible boats this uncle had borrowed from a neighbor, trying with all our might to navigate the Menach, upstream and downstream. But we never managed either way without capsizing, with the result that we had to spend our nights in tents that were soaked through. For me there was no reason to look Bernhard up once we stopped going to the same school, and after high school and passing my exams I went to the university in Berlin and seldom came back to Guldenberg. Now and then during brief visits home I would hear something about him, from Father or some old school friends. I never spoke to Bernhard myself. Actually, in the two years I shared a desk with him we never really spoke, either; Bernhard didn't want to. Whenever I said something to him, he would nod or shake his head, and only if it was unavoidable would he grumble a short answer.

Only once in the years I knew him did we have a longer conversation. It was his fourth winter in our town, and I ran into him late one afternoon near the railroad sidings. I was returning from my piano lesson with Frau Lorentz, the widow of an inspector, who lived in a little house by the pond. After the war ended, Frau Lorentz stopped receiving her widow's pension. Her husband had served the old regime, as people now said, and had he not died of a heart attack in the third year of the war, he would have had to face charges and undoubtedly been sent to prison. I never found out much more about it. Father brushed aside my questions and said that a lot of things happened back then, now times were different and people were suddenly seeing things in a different light. Some people were lucky and others not, and some had to pay for things they were not responsible for. In any event, Frau Lorentz could no longer pick up her money each month at the Rathaus as she used to; instead she now received a tiny pension, and had to teach piano, English, and stenography just to survive. Once a week I would go to her place, where I had to sit on the stool in front of her grand piano and play what I had practiced at home. She would sit on a chair close beside me, so close I could smell her perfume. If I played too slowly or hit the wrong note she would place her hands on top of mine and press my fingers on the keys. She was never satisfied with me, and if she'd had her way I would have spent several hours a day at home practicing. Once a month, always on the first Thursday, I brought her an envelope Mother had sealed using the blank margins from a sheet of stamps—it contained payment for the lessons Frau Lorentz gave my brother and me. Every month she received twenty marks, which I always checked, as long as the seal could be opened easily and without leaving a trace.

On this one winter afternoon I was ambling home past the railroad sidings. Freight trains seldom passed here. Now and then one of the sealed, rusty red cars was left there for a few days. When that happened you could always find a few of the older children around the sidings, playing with coins or knives. Some children had money in their pockets, but we all had knives—folding pocketknives from our fathers or grandfathers, or else a hunting knife in a leather sheath you could wear on your belt. And a few were proud possessors of army knives they had found in the woods. One boy even had an honor dagger, a sheath knife with a swastika embossed on the hilt. He said he had found it on a dead body and enjoyed telling in great detail what the dead soldier had looked like. We were always playing with the knives—during class, at recess, on the way to school, at home. At all hours of the day we were whittling or notching some piece of wood, throwing the knives, or playing the dangerous finger-fillet game in which you jab your knife as fast as you can between your spread fingers without hurting them. As long as it was light out and the switchmen had work to do, or were sitting in their mobile quarters with the cylindrical stove heater, everyone kept a respectful distance from the uncoupled cars. When the men finished work and went home, we fell on the abandoned cars and tried to open the heavy sliding doors, which were made of iron and thick wooden planks and were latched shut in many places. Even the unlocked bolts and hooks could hardly be budged, rusted as they were and bent from being hit so often. Indeed, we never managed to open any of the properly locked cars. When we banged our iron bars against the large metal latch bolts and their enclosures, the noise was so great that we stopped trying, out of fear we might get caught. The only cars we managed to get into were the empty ones that had been left open, but these were completely empty, as if they'd been swept clean, and we seldom discovered anything in them apart from a leftover broom, a few heavy cast-iron parts, or a cleaning rag—nothing of any use to us. Still, we would take the broom and cast-iron parts and drag them for a ways until we got bored and tired of carrying them, then toss them somewhere in a ditch.

On this particular day in January there was not a single car on any of the three rails. The bumpers placed at the end of two stretches of rail were completely overgrown with weeds; the small wooden abutment and the iron buffer could hardly be seen amid the leafless branches, which were covered with old, crusted snow. I had taken the path through the allotment gardens, to check what was going on at the sidings before heading home at sunset. Even from the garden plots I could see that there were no cars, but I noticed someone walking on the tracks, so I went closer. It was Bernhard; he had his little cart with the metal-rimmed wheels that Tinz used to pull. He was gathering things and putting them in a sack on his cart.

When I came within a few steps of him I said hello. He glanced up, nodded, and went on picking up pieces of coal and collecting them in the old potato sack. The pieces were small, very small—even tiny. In fact, what Bernhard was collecting was waste; he was sifting little bits out of the sparkling pile of slack that had slipped between the tines of the coal-sifter. To recover these pieces, Bernhard would dig into the slack with both hands, then carefully shake his fingers so the coal dust trickled through, leaving the bits he considered worth collecting in his sack. I almost asked him what he was going to do with all that trash, because you couldn't put it in an oven: pieces that small would only stifle the flames, not burn. After our last coal delivery, once Father's apprentice and I had brought the coal into the cellar, there was a whole mountain of this slack outside our cellar window; at least two hundredweights' worth, according to my father, and he had to talk to the dealer twice before the man hauled the waste away and had two sacks of usable coal delivered in its place.

The pile of slack ran for fifty yards alongside the tracks. I watched Bernhard, stamping my feet to keep warm, and didn't know what to do. It seemed somehow wrong just to leave, since I had seen him digging around in the waste and he was bound to think I'd tell about it at school. So I stood there undecided and watched him sifting through the black dust with his bare fingers. Bernhard paid no attention to me. Having quickly taken note of my presence, he didn't take his eyes off his hands, which kept moving back and forth while the black dust ran through his fingers.

"A shovel would be good," I said.

Bernhard grumbled something.

"Or some kind of sieve. Like the construction workers have."

"I don't have one."

"That's pretty shitty work. You'll get all filthy."

"Everything's got a price. And I can always wash my hands."

I wiped the encrusted snow off a signal lamp, put my bag down, stuffed my woolen gloves in my coat pockets, and pulled up my sleeves. I poked around the coal dust hesitantly with my shoe, picked up a few individual pieces with my fingers and set them aside. When Bernhard looked at me, I squatted down and began sifting through the mess with both hands, just like Bernhard. At the same time I tried to start up a conversation, but he returned to monosyllables.

"Why do you suppose they dumped the coal here?"

"Don't know."

"No need to do that if they're transferring it."

"Hmm."

"When did the coal get here?"

"Don't know."

"It must have been here at least a few days. It's frozen solid."

"Day before yesterday it wasn't here."

"Well, I'm sure they didn't keep the coal here very long. Certainly not overnight or it would have grown legs and run off."

"Probably."

"So you think this crap will burn? If you put it in the oven the fire will go out. No air can get in."

"Shovel in a little bit at a time. Then it works."

"I guess it could if you did it that way. It really is garbage, though. I mean, you can't actually call it coal. They should pay us something for clearing it off the tracks. Nobody else would do it."

"Um-hm."

"Have you already taken a sack home or is that your first one?"

"There's not that much here."

"No, there's not. It could be hours before we're finished."

By then my hands were covered with a thick black paste from the cold, wet coal dust, and I wondered why I had ever gotten involved, but I couldn't just stop now and take off. I had to keep at it for at least an hour, or half an hour, so as not to look ridiculous. Why the devil had I gotten mixed up in this? They were waiting for me at home, and if I showed up hours late looking like a pig I'd better be prepared for what was coming.

"Don't you have a sack with you?" asked Bernhard.

"No. I didn't know. I just happened to come by this way."

"How will you get the pieces home? Don't you have anything you could use?"

"Like what?"

I was about to say that I just wanted to help him pick through the coal bits, so that he could fill his sack more quickly. But then I realized that Bernhard would have no idea what I meant; after all, we weren't friends. He wouldn't have understood; he would have just looked at me and tapped his forehead as if I had a screw loose. So I simply kept quiet.

"I have another old sack. You can have it. It's got a hole in the bottom. You'll have to tie it off, then it'll work."

He got up, walked over to his cart, and tossed me a folded sack. It had more than one hole, so I had to tie four knots in it. That made it pretty small, which was all right with me.

"You don't mind?" I asked.

"Mind what?"

"That I pick up coal here."

"There's plenty."

"I meant because you were here first."

"Doesn't belong to me. Doesn't belong to anybody."

"Not that it's worth a lot, right?"

"Um-hm."

"Garbage like this isn't coal, at all. It's just garbage."

"Um-hm."

Half an hour later Bernhard tied up his sack and started packing up his cart without even opening his mouth to say good-bye. My own sack was barely half full, even though it was tiny because of the knots.

"You going?"

"Yeah."

"I think it's time for me to get home, too. It'll be dark as pitch before long. We can walk a ways together, at least up to the parade grounds."

He didn't answer. He stopped for a moment and the metallic clang of the wheels ceased temporarily. Then he went on, without saying a word. I held my bag in front of me with both hands—if I'd thrown it over my shoulder I'd have gotten myself completely filthy—and went running after him.

"Toss it on," said Bernhard without stopping, pointing his thumb at the cart.

I tossed the sack onto the cart and grabbed the cross-yoke where he used to harness his dog and helped him pull. On our way home the lamplighter passed us three times. He was riding his bike; the long pole he used to light the gas lamps was affixed to the bicycle frame. When he came to one of the cast-iron lampposts, he would stop and awkwardly remove the pole from its mount, thread the hooked tip into the small metal ring that hung next to the lamp glass, and pull it down a bit, whereupon the small glowing mantle would flare up brightly.

I wondered what to do with my sack. The best would be if Bernhard took it with him, because I didn't know what Father would say if I showed up at home with it. Besides, I had to think up some excuse since I was late and completely filthy.

"Do you have any animals at home?"

Bernhard had stopped abruptly and surprised me with his question.

"Animals? What do you mean? What kind of animals?"

"Just animals."

"Like a dog or something?"

"Yeah."

"No, we don't have a dog. We don't have any animals. Well, just a little kitten. My father isn't a farmer. He's a pharmacist. He owns the drugstore at the market square, the Lion Pharmacy."

"I know. But you could still have animals. A cow's good, or a goat, for the milk. A pig is best, they don't cost anything. They can live off scraps. My father says that anybody can raise a pig."

"We don't have anything like that. Just a cat."

"Why would you have a cat? If it were at least a dog, a fierce watchdog. What good is a cat?"

"My mother wanted one. It just lies around on the sofa all day."

"And what do you do with your scraps? Do you just throw them away?"

"No. Tine takes them. She's our household help."

"Oh. Otherwise I could have picked them up. I mean, before you threw them away."

"If you want I can talk to my parents—then you could pick them up."

"No, that's okay."

"Do you have a pig?"

"Of course."

"Like I said, Bernhard, if you want I can mention it at home, then you can get the scraps for your pig."

"If your woman gets them, then it's all right. I just meant instead of throwing them away."

As abruptly as he had stopped he now grabbed the shaft and went on, almost knocking me over. I tried to keep the conversation going, but he answered in single syllables or not at all. At the parade grounds he halted and waited for me to take my sack off the cart. I asked if I should bring him back the sack. He let the shaft drop on the ground, poked his finger in one of the holes, and then said I should just throw it away, it was no longer of any use. He picked up the shaft and went on with his cart.

When I reached the little plant nursery I dumped the sack in a ditch; I couldn't show up with it at home. Father would question my sanity. When I tossed it over the withered, leafless bushes I felt relieved. After a few steps I turned back, opened the sack, and scattered the contents in portions around the tree roots. Then I took the empty sack and stuck it in an oil drum that was rusting away in front of the nursery.

The next morning I nodded to Bernhard and greeted him cordially, but he said nothing about our operation and was as terse as always. In class they called him Woodworm because of his father's trade, just as I was known as Pill-peddler. But I'm not sure he knew that, because we only called him Woodworm behind his back. I don't think anyone would have ever dared say it to his face.

Marion Demutz

Spring is on its way. Today I sat with my face in the sun, which is already warming things up. The roads are lined with dirty piles of leftover snow that was swept onto the shoulder—now crusted over and so well trodden that your foot leaves no print. The trees at the parade grounds have already sprouted buds half an inch thick, and the front gardens are blooming white and blue with late snowbells and wild sweet violets. This weekend I'm going to take a long walk in the woods to look for some branches I can stick in a vase so that they'll bloom for Easter.

This year I've been waiting for spring like never before. Last October I discovered three little lumps on my right upper arm. My doctor sent me straight to the hospital, where they performed a biopsy. In the end they told me it was all treatable, but during the weeks I spent waiting for the results, I made peace with the world in my very own way. I completely cleared out my apartment. I went through all my drawers and both armoires; I looked over all my clothes and threw a lot of them away. I also gave the kitchen a thorough scrubbing, along with the pantry and refrigerator, and got rid of whatever I no longer needed or didn't think I'd miss in the next weeks. Some of the things that wound up in the trash I had never really needed at all; I have no idea why I bought them in the first place. I bustled about the apartment as if before a move; let's face it, it could have been a very big move indeed.

When you look at things in the light of day, I said to Susanne, you don't really need much at all—at least if that light has revealed three cherry-size lumps. At some point, I thought to myself, you'll no longer be in the position to go through everything in your apartment. Then Katja or some complete strangers will come and close down and clean out the place. I wouldn't want them to speak ill of me or make fun of all the things they might discover in my small apartment, even if I were lying helpless and maybe even unconscious in a hospital, even if I were already dead and buried. At least my apartment should be in order, I told Susanne, so nobody would have any cause to talk.

And now I've cleaned up the whole place and suddenly I have a lot of room again. I thought I'd be leaving my apartment forever, that I'd have to give it up to someone else, but now I'm back after all. Just for a little while, of course—and that's something I have to come to terms with. All my life I've had an eternity ahead of me, a multitude of years, what seemed like an infinite reserve of time. Not anymore. Ever since last fall I realize all I have is a remainder, a few years, maybe ten, maybe a lot less than that. I'll live to see this spring and possibly one more, but probably not many others. My time has shrunk—a little strip of snow in the sun, vanishing slowly and relentlessly. Perhaps I ought to be counting the days I have left, but I feel calm and happy. Now all the unrest has finally disappeared from my life, and I am enjoying every single day. I've never sensed and tasted the coming spring so intensely. Each single day is a joy; I even find delight in breathing. All the things I hardly ever noticed now give me great pleasure, and I can only shake my head thinking I had to grow so old to understand what it means to be alive. I used to consider all sorts of things important, and I was always fretting about what the future would bring. Now I no longer have any future, at least none worth mentioning, and yet I'm more contented than ever. Now I'm a foolish, happy, old woman. I wasted my time on all sorts of routines and defenses, and was so concerned about so many stupid things that I practically forgot about living. Ever since I cleaned out my apartment, though, the silly fears that used to keep me awake all night are gone. I feel like a young girl: light-hearted, happy, carefree, and I could sing the whole day long. I do, too, because today I'm a lot happier than back then when I was a naïve girl surrounded by admirers.

In three years I'll be sixty; I don't think I look it, now that I have my figure back and weigh the same as I did when I was eighteen or nineteen. That's the nice thing about this disease: it carries the odor of death, but it does make you slim. My nose is kind of shapeless, but I never liked my nose much anyway. When I was little I used to think it was horribly ugly, a real snout. I always dreamed of having a thin nose, preferably with a little bump to make it interesting. The most important thing was that it be narrow and that you couldn't see the nostrils. Back then I thought I had the ugliest nose in the world. I couldn't do anything about it; mother had a cucumber stuck in her face as well; she probably never heard anyone compliment her sweet little nose, either. But I really liked my figure. My bottom wasn't fat and I had a fine waist; I had a decent bust and even better legs. Just cut off the nose and I'd be fine. I spent hours in front of the mirror, but no matter what clothes I wore or what makeup I used, it didn't help. Nothing I did to my nose made it any smaller or narrower; it just turned bright red, as if my friend Caroline or Father had given it a tug.

When I say I never liked my nose, I don't mean that it was any uglier than the noses of the other girls. No, compared to those geese I had a nose like Queen Cleopatra's. The hair salon where I did my apprenticeship had a plaster bust of her in the display window, though nobody knew exactly why.

In eighth grade all the girls called me Simone, because I had the same hairdo as Simone Signoret in *The Adulteress.* I saw the film three times, and would have seen it even more, just on account of Simone Signoret, but they never showed the same film more than three days in our town. Since you were supposed to be sixteen I had to secretly borrow my mother's high heels so I'd look more grown up and they'd let me in. Anyway, the hairdo wasn't the only reason they called me Simone—it simply accentuated the general resemblance.

Later I saw *The Crucible,* where Signoret wore a completely different hairstyle. I didn't like it, though, and refused to try it, but my friends and acquaintances still talked about my resemblance to the actress.

I think that the only one in the class who didn't realize how much I looked like Simone Signoret was Bernhard, since he never went to the movies and had never seen her—his family didn't have any money for movies. And Bernhard, out of all people, happened to be my boyfriend.

We went out for three years, but it wasn't the real thing. Just a little kissing and petting, nothing more. Shortly before I left for vocational school he showed up in my class. He had failed a grade and was a good deal older because he came from Poland, where he hadn't had any schooling, or at least not any proper schooling, and he'd had to repeat a grade when he was younger. Most of the girls talked badly about him; not only because he had failed a grade, but mostly because he was uncommunicative and unsociable. The boys respected him because he was very strong and wouldn't hesitate to use his strength when someone crossed him.

For a while we sat together in the first row. Our teacher placed all the pupils according to their performance; the best sat in the back because they knew everything anyway, while the dunces, as he called us, had to sit right in front so he could keep an eye on us. Based on the report cards we could figure out who we'd be sitting next to in the upcoming year, unless a new person joined our class, or someone who'd been kept behind.

I can't say I was madly in love with Bernhard; he wasn't good-looking enough for that. He was strong and muscular, and I liked the fact that no one would ever pick a fight with him. Although he was two years older than everyone else, he was the shortest boy in the class. I was a good three and a half inches taller than him, and when we went out the other girls talked about us behind our backs, making nasty comments about the difference in height. That didn't bother me, at least not very much. What did make me mad were the dumb remarks and mean jokes about the two dunces who were meant for each other. I couldn't think of a retort, at least not right away—only always hours later. Still, somehow that brought us closer.

At first Bernhard didn't talk to anyone in the class. In the schoolyard he'd stand around with some other boys who weren't in our class and smoke cigarettes on the sly. He didn't talk much with them either, but they treated him with respect. When he did say something, they all listened and nodded in agreement. In our class, though, he didn't have any friends. Also he never copied anyone's homework right before school; he'd just let the teacher yell at him if he didn't have anything to show. He'd stand next to the desk, look down at his shoes, and refuse to answer the question. If a teacher made a joke at his expense, he would turn around and quickly look the class over.

We understood and never laughed at any of these jokes, even if they were funny and right on target. We knew that come recess Bernhard would track down anyone who even grinned and in one punch give him a bruise that would last for days.

I don't know what Bernhard liked about me. Maybe the girls were right and it was just that I was in the same boat as he was. Not that I was a refugee child, but I couldn't follow the teacher any better than Bernhard, and when they handed back our assignments, the two of us always had the same grades, which weren't exactly impressive. Then we'd look at each other, just for a split second, without saying anything or making a face, while the teacher trotted out the usual warnings and lectures and the others crowed about their good grades. Maybe it was those seconds that brought us close enough that one day after class—we'd both been promoted to the eighth grade—Bernhard said to me, "Let's go down to the river. Or do you have to go straight home?"

I was completely baffled. Bernhard hadn't said a word to me the entire year, and somehow I had come to terms with having a desk mate I could never whisper to during class or slip a note to or ask for an answer. And then, after we'd spent a whole school year sitting on the same bench, he suddenly invited me to go for a walk. I was so taken aback all I could do was nod, and I probably turned bright red. Finally, after I'd recovered my composure, I hastily added: "No, I don't have to go straight home. I was planning to go down to the Mulde myself."

We walked together in silence. When we reached Molkengasse, Bernhard suggested we drop our books off at his father's shop. I gave him my satchel, and he took it and his funny, homemade schoolbag through the factory yard gate. Several minutes passed before he came back out. He said his father needed him to help out in the shop, and he had to promise he'd be back soon.

"You have to help him a lot?"

Bernhard nodded.

"It's dumb, isn't it, without an arm, especially when you're a carpenter and need two hands," I said, as we walked across the green.

"In Guldenberg it's dumb even if you have two arms," Bernhard said blackly. I laughed and said he was right and that after I finished school and my apprenticeship I wanted to move to a big city like Leipzig or Berlin.

"I'm going to the sea," he said. After a moment he added, "When I get out of school I'm going to disappear somewhere near the sea. Maybe an island."

"As a sailor? Or a fisherman?"

"I don't know. What I do there doesn't matter so much. The main thing is that I'm near the sea."

"Have you ever been?"

"No. We don't have money for that."

"Neither do we. In my family it's all save save save. We even save on water. We're only allowed to bathe once a week, and then two people have to share the same water. Katja—that's my little sister—and I take turns going first. If I go after her it's like old dishwater—dirty and soapy and cold as hell."

"We don't have a real bathtub. Just an old wooden thing you can barely stand up in, much less sit down."

"No bathtub? I wouldn't like that. There's nothing like lounging in the tub. When it's my turn to go first, I sit in the warm water and dream away, no matter how long they knock on the door. They can't get me out until my teeth are chattering from the cold. Katja stays there for hours, too, when she goes first."

"That must be great. In my house by the sea I'll have a bathtub. And a real bathroom, with everything it's supposed to have."

"And when you're finished bathing in the tub you can jump in the sea and start all over."

"Exactly. That's what I'm going to do."

"Are you going by yourself? I mean, are you going to live there alone by the sea?"

"I don't know. By myself or with . . ." He stopped, looked at me, and added, "We'll see."

"I'm going to have a big bathroom later on, too. That means more to me than kitchens or bedrooms, let me tell you. A bathtub, and tiles, and a big mirror. And it has to be warm. No skimping on coal in my house. Or water, either, that's for sure."

Bernhard nodded. We climbed down the bank by the bridge and sat down on the fallen trunk of one of the willow trees that grew along the river, reaching their branches out over the water.

"In any case, I'll be glad as anything to be done with school," I said as we stared at the Mulde and the bits of wood and trash floating by.

"Yeah, I'm not much for school, either. I prefer things that are real. And I know how to work, too. I can leave them all in the dust, teachers as well as students. I'd like to challenge one of the teachers to a match. Let me tell you, when it comes to hauling sacks or cutting trees or training dogs or whatever you want, none of the teachers could keep up with me. I'd like to see one of them even come close.

"I believe you. You're strong. Like a bull," I said, and laughed out loud: "Bernhard the Bull."

Bernhard felt flattered and grinned. Then we went on sitting next to each other in silence. Bernhard was dreaming about his sea, perhaps, and I was wondering why he had asked me out on a walk. I didn't know if it was just a whim that meant no more to him than anything else in our class. Would he forget all about it tomorrow, and go on ignoring me? Or had he asked me here because I meant something to him? I wasn't about to say anything about being in love, or even think it. But why else would he be sitting here with me, staring at the water without saying anything?

I had noticed that he occasionally looked at me in class in secret; almost all the boys did that, because I was the only girl with a real bust. Whenever I wore my yellow blouse with the lace insert I could bet all the boys were staring at my breasts. And of course during calisthenics, which we took together with the parallel class. Herr Stieglitz had the boys from both classes and Fräulein Gertz had the girls. If I had to do gymnastics on a beam or a vault and there were boys nearby, their eyes would practically fall out of their sockets. Bernhard would stare at me as well, but he never said anything, whereas the other boys would make noises and lewd remarks I just laughed at. Bernhard would watch me in silence, and when I caught him looking, he turned his head away as if he weren't interested in me at all. "So why did he ask me down to the river?" I asked Susanne, back then.

"I think I better go," he finally said. "My father is waiting for me."

He stopped and looked me in the eye for at least a minute. I thought he was going to kiss me, and I was afraid he might hurt me. He stood up, waited for me to clean off my dress, and then we walked back to Molkengasse, side by side. I waited in front for him to come out and give me my satchel.

"It was nice at the river. I mean, with you."

And then he shook my hand and said, "So, see you tomorrow."

I was completely mystified. I didn't know whether I was his girlfriend now or not. He hadn't kissed me, and he hadn't grabbed me or petted me either. Really he hadn't done anything except sit next to me without saying much. Maybe, I thought back then, that's what love is like, and people just have the wrong idea. Maybe, I thought, life really is different than in the movies, just like Mother always says—and the way she said it you had no choice but to believe her.

I slept badly that night. I was afraid I'd do something stupid the next day and would look ridiculous. I made up my mind not to say anything and wait for him to speak to me. And if he didn't say anything, the way he hadn't said anything the whole year he'd been sitting next to me, then he wouldn't get a peep out of me, either. I'd forget the walk and he could get lost as far as I was concerned.

When I stepped inside the classroom—I must have looked terrible, what with the little sleep I got and being so nervous—Bernhard was already in his seat.

"Well," he said, which coming from him sounded like a very warm and friendly greeting. He even stood up to take my satchel and stash it under the bench. Karla noticed that and immediately told her friend, and so from that moment on, the entire class considered me Bernhard's girlfriend.

We went together for three years—our last year of school and the first two years of our vocational training. I trained as a hairstylist, and Bernhard became a carpenter. He did his apprenticeship in Spora with a carpenter named Mostler, since his father didn't have a license and wasn't allowed to train anyone. Bernhard's father had been unable to obtain a new license in Guldenberg because the other carpenters didn't want him to have one, as he explained to me. Not having a license was just as bad as not having an arm, and he knew a thing or two about that.

Bernhard and I got along well; I think he really did love me. As far as I was concerned he was the first boy who was actually interested in me and didn't just stare at my breasts and try to fondle them. That was all, though; I can't say I was in love with him. I felt flattered by his attentions, but he didn't exactly cause my heart to pound the way it did when I was twenty and saw Butzer, who played piano with the Kettlers. I met him after a concert in Halle and went out with him for three months. Just looking at him made my knees shake, and when he touched me I felt hot all over.

Bernhard was really just a friend. A very reliable friend who could be taken at his word. He never talked much, but once he said something, he stuck to it, regardless of what happened later, and even if it hurt him. We went out so long everybody thought we would get married someday. Even my mother eventually got used to the idea, although she had dreamed of me finding a better match. Bernhard and I never talked about it. He probably thought it was already settled. And I avoided thinking about it, since I liked him and was happy to be with him, but I had dreams of a completely different sort of marriage, with a man who would take me away from all of this and with whom I'd have a wonderful life. I considered marriage something final and fairy-tale-like. Of course I wasn't expecting a prince—after all, I was no longer a child—but I hoped my husband would have something different, something extraordinary about him, like a hero from some magical country who would make me happier than I had ever been, and make me the envy of all my girlfriends. My wedding would be a dream come true, and my unknown future groom belonged to the world of my dreams—which did not include Bernhard. He was the son of a one-armed carpenter and was going to be a carpenter himself; and as the child of refugees, no, he wouldn't be the envy of anyone in Guldenberg. The longer we were together, the more it seemed understood that we would eventually get married—everything was pointing in that direction. Caroline, my best friend, wouldn't stop teasing me about it until one day I burst into tears and she was stunned. She didn't understand me; I didn't even understand myself. Somehow things we don't want just happen, I told Susanne, because there isn't any other way, and that's probably what we call fate.

At least he would be a carpenter and not a mechanic like my father, who came home every week with a pile of clothes smeared with oil. You had to scrub them for hours and still the dirt and stink wouldn't come out. No, I definitely didn't want a mechanic, and since that's what nearly all the boys I knew were planning to be, none of them made the first cut. A carpenter doesn't get that dirty; you can just shake out the shavings and sawdust and then wash his work clothes along with the other clothes, without worrying whether some greasy rag you'd overlooked would ruin the good sheets. Mother always got into a state when she was fishing the clothes out of the boiling suds with her wooden tongs and discovered a shop rag that Father had simply tossed into the hamper. A carpenter was a cut above that, and somehow I had resigned myself to being with Bernhard, even if I had dreamed about a different life. Who else was I going to find in our dump of a town? The visitors who came to Bad Guldenberg for the resort were all old and mostly sick; many of them smelled bad, too. That I later met Butzer was an unexpected stroke of luck, even if it only lasted a few months and Butzer wasn't exactly nice to me. He was a pig, just as everyone who'd ever had anything to do with him said. They warned me against getting involved with him. He really was a pig, too, but that didn't bother me at the time. I loved him like I never loved any other man, before or after, and I always knew it wouldn't last. Even when I was living in his apartment he had other women, and didn't bother to hide it. Still, I'm glad that I was with him. That was something in my life I wouldn't want to have missed. Never, not then when we were together, and not after it was over, and not now, even if nobody but Susanne understands me and everyone feels sorry for me.

With Bernhard it was different. And if this whole thing hadn't happened and Mother hadn't gone berserk, and Father, who otherwise let me get away with anything, hadn't forbidden me to see Bernhard anymore—in other words, if this whole brouhaha the entire city was talking about hadn't happened, even though most people only knew about it secondhand, then I might have become his wife, and might still be married to him, and today I'd have a house with a garden in front and one in back and my own car and help with the cleaning. And instead of the two children I have who turned out badly and don't want anything to do with me, I'd have two who were well brought up, like in better homes, where they get a good education and a decent job, or even go to the university, and who might inherit something when I'm gone because in the meantime Bernhard Haber has built up quite a fortune. But then I wouldn't have met Butzer, because with Bernhard I would never have gone to hear the Kettlers. If I know Bernhard he wouldn't have wasted money on a concert like that, because back then he never had any money; he never picked up the tab, we each paid for ourselves. That's how it always was with him.

After our walk along the Mulde, and above all after Karla saw him pick up my satchel, I was considered his girlfriend. Three weeks later our teacher noticed it and moved us apart, which was fine with me, because I ended up next to Katharina, and even though she was pretty much a Goody Two-Shoes, at least she wasn't as stiff and uncommunicative as Bernhard and I could talk with her during class.

When I recall my time with Bernhard, I see us walking together around town, down by the Mulde, or through the gardens of the health resort. He's walking next to me, bending his head down a little as if he had to watch where he was going, ponderously, like he was carrying a heavy burden, glancing at me only now and then and saying nothing. And I talk and talk, blabbing about whatever pops into my head, and I'm happy to have someone who'll listen.

Listening is something he did well, and he never forgot anything. I had to be fiendishly careful not to contradict myself, because then he'd pick up on it and tell me what I'd said days or weeks before. There was no point in talking about school; we had no need to, since it had no value for either of us. And what was there to say about the teachers' arrogant comments and the gibes of some of our classmates—that's just the way it was, and we learned to live with it. I felt that he really liked hearing me talk about our future. I drew a picture of my future life and sketched out his, and he was mostly surprised by what I told him about his prospects. Then he would nod in agreement.

Neither of us was interested in politics or current events. Now and then in class we'd discuss some issue about world peace and our progressive allies, but most of our classmates had little interest in that; the only ones who raised their hands to speak were Karla and Fred, whose parents were especially progressive. We all suspected that they would become big politicos—the head of some state firm or the mayor of a city—and so we let them talk. The rest of us listened patiently to all the political business and blurted out something if they were asked to state their position, some of the usual nonsense we used to laugh at. Bernhard and I were never asked; we never had to state our positions. Once I said something really stupid that caused everyone in the class to laugh out loud, and after that the teacher never called on me if we were talking about politics. And as a rule Bernhard only answered when there was something he wanted to say, and he never wanted to say anything about things like that. If they called on him anyway he would stand beside his desk, head down, and just stay silent no matter how long the teacher tried to cajole him into saying something—the whole period if necessary. Bernhard wouldn't say a word. Punishments were of no use. If he was sent to detention, he would just accept the punishment, and either do the extra work after class or not—you could never tell with him. The teachers ultimately gave up wanting to educate him. They simply let him advance with the class and stopped arguing with him. So as not to waste an entire period with a single, stubbornly silent pupil, they avoided every conflict with Bernhard. His thick skull had defeated them. Both of us could rest assured they wouldn't call on us when the subject was politics. We might say something that might make the whole class laugh, and the teacher would have to spend hours explaining why what we had said was completely in error, and that the world was a lot more complicated than we imagined, that we had to learn to think politically, that appearances aren't enough, and neither is what people call common sense, because some people couldn't be expected—and here he always looked at Bernhard and me—to show much sense of any kind.

When I think back on our time at school, I have no idea

how it all happened—it must have been May, because I remember I had spent the Whitsun holidays with Caroline at Lake Müritz. Bernhard had never been political; at least he'd never said a thing about politics, either at school or on our walks. Perhaps it was just some crazy idea of his—that's possible, because now and then he would do something that made everyone shake their heads and when I asked him about it he would say, "I just wanted to."

My parents suspected that somebody was behind it, that someone had put him up to it, and that he was a fool who'd let himself be used, but I don't believe that. Bernhard always did what he wanted, and when he felt that someone expected him to do one thing, then he was sure to do or say the exact opposite, even if he hadn't intended to originally, and even if it hurt him. After all, that was his real problem with school: he knew exactly what people wanted from him, and that's exactly what he refused to do. I was different in that respect: I always wanted to say what they wanted to hear, but I just never came up with the right answer, so if I said or did something dumb, it was certainly not because that was my intention. I wasn't as brave as Bernhard, who didn't care if he set everyone in the class against him and even annoyed the teachers. For him it was very important to get his way; I learned that the hard way, and that's why I don't believe that Bernhard let anybody talk him into doing anything—that just wasn't his style.

He didn't talk to me before and he didn't talk to me after. The only reason he ever gave for what he did was: I just wanted to. And then there was no point in asking any more questions.

We met regularly after our walk to the river. Mostly we went outside of town, to the alum works, to the old mill, and very often to the forest cemetery, or else we took a walk in the woods or along the Mulde. We seldom went to the resort gardens, since all the old people there stared so rudely. And we only went to the market square or the parade grounds, where most of the young people hung around, if there was a fair or some kind of show everyone wanted to see. Otherwise we preferred to be alone; that's how Bernhard wanted it. He said that the others in class were dumb immature brats he didn't want to have anything to do with.

"All of them?" I asked. "Surely not all of them."

He gave a disdainful snort and told me I'd better watch out with my girlfriends and the ones I thought were my friends because soon enough I'd be in for a nasty surprise, because he knew people. Later I often had cause to think about that remark, because I wound up getting nasty surprises from everybody—all the ones I trusted and loved. Everybody but Bernhard. He never disappointed me: I broke things off with him before I could be disappointed, under pressure from my parents and all sorts of friends. But back then I was really upset by what he was saying and asked him, "Isn't there anybody you love?"

"Yes," he said. He was silent for a very long time and then said, in a hoarse voice, "You."

I was scared, because I realized then how much he loved me and I knew I didn't really love him.

"I don't mean that. I want to know who you like apart from me."

He thought for a long time, and then said, "My parents."

"And apart from your parents? Don't you have any friends? Isn't there anybody who understands you?"

"Yes," he said. "Tinz. I loved him."

I didn't have to ask who Tinz was; I already knew. I think the whole town knew about Tinz. They said he had threatened to kill whoever killed his dog.

"That doesn't count," I said. "Tinz was a dog, it doesn't apply to him."

"Well, in any case, I named somebody," Bernhard countered, "and Tinz counts for me."

"That's just terrible if apart from your parents all you love is a dog."

"Maybe," he said. "Maybe for you."

"You're a little crazy," I said quietly, to myself. Bernhard could get very mad if he heard you say things like that. If you somehow implied that he didn't have a whole lot of sense, then he'd throw a real fit, even with me. But it was true nevertheless. I mean, I wasn't exactly a brain myself. But in practical things I did fine. At any rate, a lot better than Bernhard, who judged everything by how he wanted it to be. I, on the other hand, felt that if anyone, and that included our teachers, wanted a specific answer, then I would try to give it, and I didn't feel I had to bite my tongue off in the process. I tell people what they want to hear, especially when I'm looking for peace and quiet. Banging your head against the wall is just plain stupid, and people who keep on doing that shouldn't be surprised when it starts to hurt. Bernhard was like that. Banging his head against the wall was his whole life plan; you could see that even back in school, or during his apprenticeship. Still, he didn't end up worse off than me; after all, I'm not exactly the happiest person in the world, and I certainly haven't had it easy. It would have been a big help to me if I hadn't had to count every penny. I always wanted a few marks in the bank, back when I was young, and of course now that I'm older, too, but it wasn't meant to be, though somehow I've managed to make do, at least so far.

There was no talking with Bernhard. If he was convinced of something, no one could get him to change his mind, not the smartest or the strongest person in the world. He took his punishment on the chin, whether it was a bad grade or some other penalty, and he never showed whether it made him angry or not. You couldn't even tell if it made any difference to him at all. At any rate he never let anyone change his mind. The only exception was me. Now and then I could persuade him one way or the other, because I knew how you had to start with him.

At first everything seemed normal. We went out together, and in class they talked about us. Some of the girls wanted to know how well he could kiss and how far he got with me, how far I'd let him go. I told them something to shut them up, and maybe to impress the stupid hens a little. In reality we went a whole half a year without his ever even trying to kiss me. I had thought out exactly what I would do in case he did. I had an exact plan, since I didn't want to let him do it just like that. But when he didn't even try, I quietly packed that plan away. At one point I started getting uneasy. All the girls in my class, even the ones without a steady boyfriend, had kissed—all except for me. If I'd been smarter I might have suspected that he was from the opposite shore—meaning that he was homosexual—but I didn't have any idea about that back then. I wondered whether I was just a kind of friend to him, a buddy, and didn't mean anything to him as a girl—though I felt I was too good for that. In any case, all the plans I'd thought up in such detail were useless, because I was the one who wound up kissing him, I mean, properly. It was on a Monday, in the forest cemetery. We were sitting on an iron chain that wasn't a chain at all: it was stiff and didn't move. I was talking and Bernhard was listening. And when he looked at me and was again about to ask his usual "Really?" I bent over quickly and kissed him on the lips.

It happened very quickly and I didn't feel a thing. I still remember the way he beamed. I'd never seen his face light up like that. With that tiny kiss I must have made him infinitely happy. He was suddenly all sunbeams, I never saw anything like it ever again, not with Bernhard, not with the boys after him, and certainly not with Butzer, who never seemed to care, whether we were kissing or even making love. With Butzer I was probably the one who was beaming.

Bernhard just smiled blissfully away, without saying or doing anything. I remember thinking that all that was missing was for him to close his eyes and keel over, and then we'd really be in a mess. But he didn't; he just smiled. I thought that after that it was his turn to kiss me, since he was the boy after all, and I didn't want to make a fool of myself. He should kiss me to even things up, so he couldn't spread it around that it was only me who kissed him, though I knew Bernhard would never do that. But he didn't kiss me, he just reached for my hand on the way home and held it until we could see people's houses. That was all there was, and at home I wondered for a long time why I had kissed him and not the other way around. As far as my kissing him went, I came up with plenty of reasons that were crystal clear, at least to me, but I couldn't explain his behavior, because it was definitely peculiar. Other boys would have hardly let an opportunity like that escape them, and if possible would have even reached for my breasts, which they were always staring at anyway.

Much later I asked him why. At first he acted like he didn't know what I was talking about, and then he stroked my ear the way I like and said, "It was beautiful. So beautiful I didn't want anything more."

That was his entire explanation. It didn't tell me much, but that's the way he was. Later on he did kiss me, and he proved a real marathon kisser. He wanted to do it all the time. Just like he had always listened to me talk, now he wanted to kiss me all the time, which kind of got on my nerves, because with him it was just one big mouth attack, and I didn't feel a thing, just his wet lips and his tongue, which I didn't like. I always told him to leave that out, but all my appeals were in vain. To this day I remember constantly saying to him, "Enough of that." I remember it exactly because Butzer used the exact same words to put me off when I wanted to kiss him. That's the way it goes.

My mother urged me to invite Bernhard over, because she wanted to meet him, but he always found some excuse not to come. Mother chalked it up to his being shy, or ashamed because he came from a poor family and wasn't as well dressed as we were. That may be, I said, but on the inside I had to laugh. Bernhard was by no means shy, and he didn't care how he was dressed. If someone in class said something about his old pants or his ridiculous knitted cap, he just smiled, cold and scornful, and didn't even get mad. The truth was that Bernhard despised the Guldenbergers who had always lived here. He was a refugee, and they weren't very popular, and so he despised everyone else. That's why he didn't want to sit down to coffee with my parents, though he would have been served cake, which he certainly didn't get at home, made with good butter and real whipped cream. In the three years we went together he was in my house a total of five or six times when my parents were there; otherwise he came over only when my mother and father were away.

During his visits nothing happened I didn't want to or that I couldn't square with my conscience. I showed him my room; he looked at it a long time, as was his custom, then we sat down in the living room or cooked something in the kitchen, mostly spaghetti, which he loved to eat, with some drippings or a sauce I whipped up. He never tried to force himself on me. Not even the time when a pot slipped out of my hands and spilled water all over me. After I mopped up the mess in the kitchen I had to change into something dry. I had left the door to my room ajar to keep talking with him, and I undressed down to my underwear. He didn't try to come into the room, and he didn't even try to peek through the door crack, which amazed me.

On his first visit I showed him the entire apartment. He stopped for a long time in the bathroom, and I had to call him twice before he came to the kitchen. He hemmed and hawed and when I finally asked him to say what was on his mind he said, embarrassed, "I'd like to take a bath in the tub. If that's all right."

Now I was the one who was embarrassed. I knew that they didn't have any bathtub at his house; he had told me himself, and I understood that he'd like to have a chance to lie down in the warm water. On the other hand, that meant that he'd have to undress. He'd be completely naked in our apartment while my parents were out. That thought made me a little uneasy, not to mention the fact that my parents could of course come back early, or Grandmother might stop by to fix me a meal. I imagined Bernhard sitting stark naked in the tub and hearing me answer the door.

Bernhard noticed my hesitation and said, "It was only a thought, Marion."

I shook my head. "No, you just have to be patient. It'll take half an hour for the water to warm up."

I fetched a bucket of wood and three pieces of coal from the shed outside and got the fire started. Then I sat down with Bernhard in the living room and we waited until the water in the narrow bath-stove got warm. By then we were both embarrassed; I barely said a word. Every five minutes I kept running to the bathroom to check on the fire and see how hot the water was, and in the meantime I looked for a towel I could give Bernhard that Mother wouldn't notice later in the basket with the dirty laundry. When the water began to boil, I told him I was filling the tub and he could get ready.

"What do you mean get ready?" he asked, surprised.

"You're not going to take a bath with your clothes on, are you? Or were you planning to undress there?"

"Yes, in the bathroom. It's simpler that way."

I nodded, even though the bathroom was tiny and none of us changed our clothes in there.

"You can lock the door if you want. From the inside."

"I saw that."

He stood up, took the towel, nodded, and left. I sat in the living room all by myself and kept hoping no one would show up—not my parents or my grandmother or any of my friends. Because if someone were to come right then—and the smoke from the chimney made it obvious that somebody was home—I'd be the one in hot water. After ten minutes I snuck into the hall and listened. I heard him whistling, very quietly. I went to the bathroom door and knocked.

"Bernhard?"

"Yes. What is it?"

"You can take some shampoo if you'd like. I mean, if you want to wash your hair. The yellow glass bottle that says 'shampoo.' Just don't take too much. Father always gets mad when I take too much."

"All right, thanks. I see the bottle. What's shampoo?"

"For washing your hair. Some kind of soap with egg yolk so it foams up."

"With egg yolk? Yes, of course. We do that, too. We make it ourselves."

"So, everything's fine?"

"Yes."

He was clearly not in a rush to leave the bathtub, and I stood outside the door and didn't know what to do, whether I should wait for him in the living room or go outside to ward off any potential visitors and keep them from coming into our apartment. I also hoped that Bernhard wasn't doing anything silly that might make it obvious that someone had just taken a bath. I'd have to give the bath-stove a thorough cleaning, I couldn't forget to do that, because it was only lit once a week, on Saturday, and in the winter when there was a hard freeze, Father put some coal in it to keep the water inside from freezing. But if he noticed that I had actually heated it up, he would yell at me, not just because of the waste; he and Mother were also bound to grow suspicious and pepper me with questions.

Bernhard had started whistling again, and I stood in front of the door, trying to make up my mind.

"Do you want me to soap your back?"

The question just slipped out; I really startled myself. I listened and waited anxiously for his reaction. The bathroom had grown still. I wanted to tell him it was a joke, but it was too late for that, because what's said is said, and I asked myself what he thought of me now. I think a whole minute must have passed before he answered.

"No, no need. I can do it myself."

I breathed a sigh of relief.

"Good. I said it because I like having my back soaped up. When I'm sitting in the tub and my mother washes my back. It's real nice."

"Right. I can do it myself."

"Okay, then, I'll wait for you in the living room."

He didn't answer. When he finally showed up in the living room half an hour later I turned red as a beet. He was dressed and his hair was tousled.

"That was good. I let out the water. Is that all right?"

"Yes. I'll clean up."

"It's already clean. And I wiped everything down as well."

"I should clean out the tub in any case. I bet you left a ring."

"Do you have a comb I could use?"

"I can give you mine. Or I'll cut your hair if you'd like."

"No. Thanks. Thanks a lot for the bath. It's all right."

"If you want I can talk to my parents. I'm sure they'd let you take a bath here every now and then."

"No. Don't do that. I just wanted to see what it's like."

I ran my fingers through his wet hair, and then we kissed. I told him that he tasted much better freshly washed, and he laughed.

Bernhard never took another bath at our house, although whenever my parents were away I told him he could.

We were both relieved when we finally finished school. There wasn't much to say about our grades; we'd both passed, or maybe "survived" is a better word, and we laughed at our report cards. We had already arranged our apprenticeships: the only requirement in the contracts was that we successfully complete school and had a diploma to show for it. The following September I was to start my apprenticeship at the Heidepriem Hair Salon, and Bernhard would be going to Spora every day to start his training as a carpenter. Once a week we'd take the train to the vocational school in Eilenburg. The classes for hair stylists and carpenters were in the same building; we had them on Tuesday and the carpenters had theirs on Friday. I was looking forward to my apprenticeship, I'd always wanted to be a hair stylist, ever since I was little, and I never regretted it, even though I got this awful skin allergy ten years ago because I was always getting those chemicals on my fingers. I was very proud when Frau Heidepriem picked me, although three other girls had applied for the apprenticeship—and all three had better grades.

"You know," she told me, "my girls don't have to be whizzes at math, I have a cash register for that. And I don't care if they can write long letters without mistakes. What I do insist on is that they get along well with the customers. You can't be sassy, but you don't want to overdo the politeness, either. The only thing that counts is that your clients come back. And it's not enough that their perm is done right. There are other things in life, and in a hair salon, those may be more important. And that's *veda,* my child. Please don't ask me now what that is. I can't explain it to you; I only know that some people have it and others don't. A very smart man once explained it to me, and I certainly don't mean my own husband. This man told me that I had *veda* and that's why I was so successful with my clients. And unless I'm very mistaken I think you have it, too, girl. You have *veda,* so don't disappoint me."

Frau Heidepriem was pleased with me and I stayed on with her after my apprenticeship, so I must have had something of this *veda,* but outside of my professional life it didn't help me much. Or maybe you need a different kind of *veda* for men and love, and that's something I certainly didn't have. I had no idea that I had some kind of *veda,* and to this day I've never found out what that might be. But my boss was pleased with me, and so were my clients.

At the graduation ceremony, in the school auditorium, Bernhard and I were the last to receive our diplomas, since they handed them out according to class rank. The class teacher made a few remarks about every student—which for us were pretty brief and consisted of the usual admonitions. That same day we rode our bikes to Spora. Bernhard had promised Herr Mostler, the carpenter where he was supposed to begin his training in September, that he would take him his diploma the moment he got it, and he talked me into biking there with him. Because my parents wouldn't be back before evening, I ran home, tossed my schoolbag in the middle of the living room, set my diploma on top, and got my bike out of the shed.

Bernhard had said we were going for a bike ride. He didn't tell me we were headed for Spora and the carpenter who would be his master until we were on our way, but I didn't care. And I didn't realize until after the fact why in the world I had to be there when he showed Herr Mostler his diploma. When we got to Spora, I wanted to wait for him outside the shop, but he took my hand and said I should come along. Before he took his diploma out of his bag, he introduced me to Herr Mostler and his two journeymen. Bernhard wanted to show his master and future colleagues that he had a girlfriend. Like his diploma, I was a trophy, a proof of his manliness. At the time I was proud of that, proud of him and proud that he wanted to claim me like that. The men said something naughty I only half understood, but I sensed what they meant and laughed out loud along with them. Herr Mostler led us to the shed next to the shop, where the boards and beams were stacked for drying, and asked Bernhard to identify the different types of wood. He answered nearly everything correctly, even though all you could see were a few cut boards and in some cases just a narrow edge.

"That's good, my boy. You have a carpenter's eye. If you work hard, you'll become somebody—then you can forget your report card. We'll see you on the first of September, at seven o'clock. And don't oversleep, boy, or you'll be in trouble."

When we left, the boss gave me a small turned table leg

that was lying in the trash, because it was cracked and unusable. I had lifted it out of the box with the sawdust and scraps of wood.

"This is so nice. Why are you throwing it away?"

"What do you mean, nice? That's trash. The work was for nothing. I was almost finished and then it split—see here, diagonally through the grain."

"It's still pretty. It shouldn't be thrown away."

"Who would want that? I can't use it in a table. Would you like to take it, love?"

"For free?"

"Of course. I'll give it to you. Since you're Bernhard's girl."

"Thank you."

"And what do you intend to do with it?"

"I don't know. Maybe use it as a candlestick."

"Sounds good. But you can't hold me responsible for anything you two do together by candlelight, understood?"

Bernhard turned red, and the journeymen laughed, this time at him. I looked Herr Mostler in the eye and said, "I bet you'd like to be there to supervise, wouldn't you?"

"Pretty sassy girl you got there," he told Bernhard, looking at me. "Watch out she doesn't wind up wearing the pants."

Bernhard stuck the turned piece of wood in his bike rack and we set off. For a long time he didn't say a thing, although we were riding alongside each other.

"What are you so happy about?"

"I just am."

"Tell me."

"I've done it," he said. He took hold of my bike seat and shoved me ahead.

"What have you done? Any chance I might find out?" I asked, since he didn't volunteer any more.

"I've passed school, I have a good job, and now I'll show everybody."

I glanced at him briefly. As always, he had his head down,

but I could tell he was happy. He was beaming like he had when I kissed him.

That first year of our apprenticeship we seldom saw each other. During the week, Bernhard didn't come back from Spora until late, and on the weekends he needed to help his father, who had something for him to do every week. Since he only had one arm, Bernhard's father always put off some tasks for the weekend. Bernhard was supposed to take over his father's carpentry shop after he finished his apprenticeship and had earned his master's diploma, and so he had to work at his father's place even in his free time. A few times I went into their shop and watched them; afterwards I would undress completely in the bathroom at home and shake out each article of clothing. The tiny bits of wood had stuck everywhere, and even if I had just washed my hair I had to rinse it again. Bernhard hardly had any time for me. All that was missing was that I fix a hot lunch and take the pot to him and then we would have been just like an old married couple. I told him our relationship wasn't very exciting and that I'd like to have a little more fun, since, after all, I wasn't forty, or eighty. He nodded as if he understood and then said he had to go help his father.

In the summer after our first year in training we went camping for two weeks. Naturally not just the two of us; my parents would never have allowed that, and I'm sure his wouldn't have, either. I went with Sylvie, who had been in the class parallel to ours at school and was now completing her apprenticeship as a secretary in the city administration. She'd never really been my friend, at least not a real friend, more an acquaintance; and the fact that we went on vacation together was sheer happenstance, because my best friend Caroline and her parents had managed to get a vacation room on the Baltic.

I ran ino Sylvie at a birthday party, we started talking, and since she was in the same position as I was we agreed to go camping as a foursome. Each of us could tell our parents that we were camping with another girl, and the boys—Bernhard and Sylvie's friend, Norbert—could serve up the same story at their homes. We had planned to go to the Süsser See, since someone had told us that the campground there was excellent but didn't cost more than elsewhere, and that the water was good and you could have all sorts of fun. The trip was only supposed to take five hours by bike, and so I agreed. Bernhard did whatever I asked him to, anyway, at least so I thought.

Just getting there was a disaster and should have made me suspicious. Instead of five hours it took us nine. Somebody's bike was always breaking down, and once one of the tent bags fell right in front of Norbert so that he crashed into it and we had to scrape him off the pavement. The boys kept quiet during the trip, while Sylvie and I were cursing like sailors; and when we finally reached the campground at twilight and paid the fees, we had the boys set up our tent and went to bed without so much as a thank-you. Instead of supper we ate a kind of chocolate, some disgustingly sweet bar that Sylvie had in her bag that made you feel full after a few bites. Once we were finally in our sleeping bags, listening to the boys setting up the second tent in the dark and cursing to themselves, Sylvie whispered, "One thing I can assure you: I'll be glad when all this is over and I'm back at home in my own bed."

"You can write that down in your prayer book. And in mine," I said.

Suddenly we jumped and sat up in our sleeping bags. A motorcycle had pulled up right next to our tent; then someone shouted, a dog barked, and finally the whole campground was awake and cursing.

Sylvie groaned, and I said, "Well it was your brilliant idea to come here."

"What? You mean you'd rather spend these two weeks at home? That's not what I'd call a vacation."

"But pedaling yourself to death just to land at some godforsaken place where a bunch of jokers spend the whole night trying to see who can make the most noise—does that sound like a vacation to you? It doesn't to me."

"Oh, come on. Maybe it won't be so bad. I mean, it's just the first day. So . . . what's your Bernhard like? Not very talkative, is he?"

"Let's say I don't have to struggle to get a word in."

"That's not so bad. And otherwise?"

"And otherwise what?"

"You know, how is he in other ways? Real passionate, or do you have to get him going first?"

"He's pretty subdued."

"Watch out, those still waters can run pretty deep, and you can fall in. Really deep, too, if you know what I mean."

"Don't worry, I'm keeping an eye out. I wasn't born yesterday. And yours? How's Norbert?"

"Mostly he likes to grope at me. His hands are always after something. With him I have to be very careful what I put on. If there's any skin showing, his fingers will find it. Is yours the same way?"

"Um-hmm."

"Always excited like that? My mother says it comes from the boys eating too much meat. At that age they should eat nothing but vegetables. But that wouldn't help with Norbert."

"Hmm . . . I think Bernhard eats too many vegetables as it is."

"Really? What do you mean?"

And then she started giggling, and I couldn't stop myself either. We were laughing and snorting so loudly that we had to crawl inside our sleeping bags. When we sat back up, I had tears of laughter in my eyes, and I'm sure Sylvie did as well.

"Too many vegetables! Hey, that doesn't sound so good."

"I mean, because his parents don't have much money. They're refugees, you know."

"I know. No meat at all, that can't be good, at any age."

She started laughing again; her head disappeared inside her sleeping bag. Through the canvas we could see shadows in front of our tent.

"What's going on with you two? Are you asleep or do you want to take a little walk? Just to look around."

A hand started tugging at the zipper, then pulled it down, and Norbert's head appeared in the door of our tent. Sylvie yelled at him and told him to get lost, she was completely exhausted. Norbert was startled and looked at us with his mouth half open; baffled, he slowly pulled his head back and rezipped our tent.

After he was gone, Sylvie asked, "That was okay, wasn't it? They should leave us in peace."

I was tired and muttered my agreement. People were running past the tent; you could hear the grass swishing; you could hear them talking; somewhere someone was playing music. I had so looked forward to spending two weeks away from my mother's nagging voice and my father's constant lectures, which really grated on my nerves. I'd figured it couldn't help but be wonderful to finally get out of the house for a few days. Now I felt so helpless, so alone, that I'm sure I would have started bawling if I had been by myself in the tent.

Mother worried about me all the time, and whatever I put on, she always had to voice her opinion, which led to our constant quarrelling. And Father knew everything, he always knew what needed to be done, and when, and he was always right, which drove me crazy—I mean, how do you deal with a father who knows everything, and reminds you of it, day in and day out? I'm sure I've made a few mistakes in my life, back then as well as today, and there are some decisions I wish I hadn't made, or else that I'd made completely differently, but at least they belong to me—I don't believe that being perfect always is the only right way to live. The messes I made are still my own, and my mistakes are also a part of my life. But at that moment I missed my parents, and I no longer cared for the idea of camping out. I could feel the ground through the sleeping bag and the air mattress and was sure I'd wake up the next morning with a sore back. And I couldn't even bear to think about my clothes packed in those bike bags. After fourteen days wadded up like that they were bound to look like someone pulled them out of a trash bin.

"Are you asleep?"

"Yes," I grunted. I stared at the canvas tent wall, which I could barely make out; more than anything else I wanted to yell at Sylvie and ask how on earth she thought anyone who wasn't used to living in the middle of a train yard could possibly fall asleep in this stupid tent with all this noise and racket.

"What's the matter with you all of a sudden? Did you want to go on a walk with the boys? Now, in the dark?"

"No."

"My mother would say anyone who does that is man-crazy."

"Well, I'm not."

"Do you even know what it means?"

"Just leave me alone."

"I have an aunt. Everyone in the family says she's man-crazy. She's actually very nice. We really get along. She has this cute little dog, a cocker spaniel I can romp around with all over her apartment for hours. Do you know what man-crazy means?"

"They chase after men. A woman who wants a man."

"Wrong. Every woman wants a man, doesn't she? No, man-crazy is something else."

"And how do you know?"

"I just do."

"And what do you know?"

"They're women who don't wear any panties."

For seconds it was completely quiet in the tent.

"Never? They never wear panties?"

"Nope."

"Even during their period?"

"I don't know. Once I asked Aunt Bärbel. Not so direct, of course. I didn't want to tell her she was man-crazy. She laughed and told me never to let anyone look under your skirt, especially another woman."

"That's disgusting. Just thinking about it—no, I couldn't last a minute."

"I feel the same way. And besides, if the material rubs me a bit I don't mind. That's why I prefer wearing another pair of panties on top of that."

"And if you were climbing the stairs, or walking on a wall—I think I'd die."

"And you can get all sorts of diseases, too. I mean it's all pretty sensitive. We women are pretty delicate down there, not like with the guys. We have to constantly watch out and keep ourselves warm. The boys can just pull out their ding-dong and pee away, even outside in winter, while we could catch our death doing that."

"No panties! That's so vulgar!"

"Of course. Man-crazy is a kind of disease. Either you have it or you don't."

"And how do you catch it?"

Sylvie didn't know how to answer that.

"Have you ever . . . I mean, with a boy . . . ?"

"What?"

"You know."

"Kissed?"

"No! Come on, not just kissed."

"You mean, held it?"

"Yes, held it, and even more. Ines, who was in my class, says she's gone a lot further. She's not a virgin anymore."

"My God! Is that true?"

"I don't know, that's what she said. She doesn't care what the boys in class say, either. They say very mean things about her, but she just laughs and acts proud of it."

"Maybe she's lying."

"Maybe. Could be, because she always has to be the center of attention."

"Does she have a boyfriend?"

"Always. And more than one. Anybody can kiss her—I've seen that myself."

"Is she sick?"

"Sick? What do you mean?"

"I mean, is she man-crazy?"

"No question about it."

"So, she doesn't wear panties?"

"Of course she wears panties."

"But, then . . ."

I didn't say any more because I really didn't want to know. I couldn't fathom the idea that women or girls our age would go around without any panties. Least of all that they would do so by choice. I wasn't entirely clear what man-crazy really meant, and I noticed that Sylvie didn't know a whit more than I did, so I figured I might as well keep my mouth shut and my eyes closed and pretend I'd fallen asleep since I couldn't get any reliable information out of her. I really didn't like her all that much anyway, and I didn't want to chatter the night away with just anybody.

We only had one cooker to fix our food and make tea, or rather to warm up the water, since we could never get it very hot, so we could forget about cooking. The cooker had a bright aluminum part where you placed your pot, and a tiny pan below where you put some whitish tablets and lit them with a match. Maybe our pot was too big, or else we took too much water, or else the thing was meant less for camping and more for dollhouses, where everything worked but only if you pretended. In any case, we had to pour lukewarm water over the tea leaves, and our dehydrated soups lumped up in the pot. No matter how long we stirred it, the powder wouldn't dissolve, and we ended up eating a thickish paste that tasted like Maggi seasoning and a ladle or two of murky water. After three days I refused to eat any more, and instead I bought some rolls and stuffed myself with them until I was full to bursting. On top of that I ate some August apples that Bernhard and Norbert rounded up. After sunset they would roam through the gardens and orchards and steal what they could carry. Otherwise we passed the day at the lake, swimming or reading. Or else we lay in our tents and slept or dozed away. I couldn't go for a walk. The boys and Sylvie didn't want to. I would have gone by myself, but apart from the highway and the road to the lake, the campground was surrounded with fields of grain and potatoes. A narrow strip of furrowed sand ran around the lake: once, when I tried to walk around it, after ten minutes my legs were bright red and swollen from all the thistle prickles.

On the third day, the boys came to our tent and wanted to talk. They sat around on our air mattresses, hemming and hawing. Bernhard didn't say a thing, and it wasn't until Sylvie got mad and was about to throw them out that Norbert started talking.

"How would it be, I mean, what do you two think, maybe we could switch."

"What do you want to switch, Stork Legs? What are you getting at?"

"I thought, well, Bernhard and I were thinking . . . we don't have to spend the whole vacation, you know, in the same tent. That's boring."

"Is that what you thought?"

"Yes."

"Oh, that's a great idea. So, Marion and I should move into your tent, right, and you two can stretch out here?"

"Huh? What do you mean?"

"I thought you wanted to switch, right? Marion, didn't he

just say that it would be less boring if he and Bernhard slept in our tent and we moved into theirs?"

"That's not what I meant."

"What was our deal? What did we talk about before vacation? Did you forget?"

"If you don't want to, we'll just leave it."

"We had a deal, right? Is our deal off?"

"All right. Forget it."

"There you go again, always pushing. I don't want to, understand?"

"Calm down, Sylvie. It was just an idea. If you don't want to, okay. We'll just stay the way we are."

"You never stop, do you? You promise not to annoy me, and then it's just a matter of time before you do."

"Let's go," Norbert said to Bernhard. "We're obviously getting on their nerves."

"Yeah, get lost, both of you. And I don't want to hear or see you for the next few hours, understand?"

I was relieved. I knew the boys would make the suggestion; I had been expecting it since the first day, and I hadn't had any idea how I was supposed to react. I wanted to, and I didn't want to, and above all I didn't want to be a dumb prude, which the boys would have thought I was had I said no. But Sylvie had read them the riot act, and I was relieved that she had taken the decision away from me.

"Well, I think the two of them got the message, Sylvie. They won't dare bring that up again."

"I'm not so sure. I know Norbert, and he has a one-track mind. All he thinks about is groping and grabbing."

After a week the weather turned bad. Each day it rained for hours; everything in the tent was damp, and my feet were constantly cold. I lay awake long into the night until I got warm enough to sleep. At one point I lost my patience. I had noticed after a couple of days that Sylvie always had something to discuss with Bernhard. She worked for the municipality and acted really important, as if she was the mayor, or his right hand. She kept talking about this meeting or that conference and about decisions that didn't interest any of us, but Bernhard, the little fool, listened to her, the same way he always listened to me. Sylvie was a real activist, involved with everything political, exactly the way she had been at school. If we were supposed to elect a board or a committee or a delegation, she would always put herself up as a candidate, and if she didn't get elected she was terribly upset. Most of the time, though, she did get elected, because there were never enough candidates to fill all the offices. Every day she ran around with her Young Pioneers kerchief, which nobody else did except for the little ones. She believed in it; she really believed in the politics and the speeches, and she knew all the political songs by heart and sang them loudly, too, so everybody noticed, especially the teachers. I couldn't give a fig for politics; I kept myself out of it and only said what I had to. I said what they expected me to say, and that was easy enough to guess. In any event, there at the Süsser See, Sylvie started up again about all that, and my Bernhard listened. I couldn't imagine it would interest him. We had never discussed politics, never—not me, and certainly not him.

At first I thought nothing of it. I read my paperback novels or dozed away in the sun and didn't worry about them. When I asked Bernhard to go swimming or ride into town with me, and he said he didn't want to because he was talking with Sylvie, I laughed and didn't think twice about it. I laughed at both of them, since a conversation with Bernhard was always very one-sided, but after two or three days I'd had all I could take, and in the evening I told Sylvie that she better keep her hands off Bernhard and stop talking nonsense to him all the time. She flew into a huff and told me that I didn't understand, it's not what I imagined, and that Bernhard, unlike me, had social interests and didn't want just to drift into tomorrow but rather to help shape it. I told her I was very impressed but would she kindly shape her own tomorrow, and not mine or

Bernhard's; otherwise I'd shape something of hers, for instance her face. During the night I said some more things to her, though I usually never think of the best things to say until the next day. She acted as if she was asleep, but I knew she had heard every word.

The next day I straightened Bernhard out. I asked him if he had gone camping with Sylvie or with me, and told him to make up his mind, because there was no way I was going to be the odd one out, I'd rather leave. He was startled; my outburst had caught him off guard, and he insisted they'd just talked about professional and political things, and that of course we had come here together and nothing had changed.

"It seems to me it has," I said.

"But, Marion . . ." he answered, at a loss.

"Then prove it," I said, and left him standing there.

I would have preferred to start home that second, but I was a little scared of riding the bike all that way by myself, and besides, it was constantly raining, and I'd be soaked through in minutes.

The rest of the vacation passed somehow. The whole thing was boring, and I looked forward as never before to sitting down to a proper meal at home. I knew that Mother would spend an entire day beating around the bush, trying to find out if anything had happened that she ought to know about. And that's exactly what she did. She probed and probed, but the most direct question she could manage was whether we had gotten any closer to each other.

I acted as if I didn't know what she meant. But when her prying finally got to be too much, I told her that she wasn't going to become a grandmother, because I hadn't slept with Bernhard, if that's what she wanted to know, and besides, there was such a thing as coitus interruptus, if a girl didn't want to get knocked up. Mother turned red and claimed she hadn't been thinking of anything of the kind and that I had no right to talk to her like that and she was amazed at the kind of words that came out of my mouth and that I certainly didn't learn them from her. When I refused to take back anything and didn't apologize, and just gave her an angry look, she finally left the room.

I hadn't lied to her. I didn't sleep with Bernhard, not at the Süsser See and not later, either. I wasn't afraid of losing my virginity; after all, I was old enough, and at sixteen none of my girlfriends was still a virgin, if I could believe them. But Bernhard didn't make me go tingly all over. He was nice to me and very kind, but when I was next to him I never felt the kind of heady rush or crazy trembling the other girls talked about. At times I felt sorry for him, and I cursed myself for not being nicer to him; but that's the way it was, and I wasn't about to force myself to go further.

At the Süsser See, Bernhard and Sylvie avoided talking alone after I raised a stink. They were both a little afraid of me, and that was fine as far as I was concerned. Sylvie spent the remaining days sitting with Norbert and gabbing away at him, and when the sun finally reappeared, Bernhard lay down next to me in the sand and listened to me. When it rained we all sat in our tent, which was a little bigger than the boys', and played cards. I never played so much skat in my life.

The trip back home wasn't so terrible, perhaps because I knew what to expect, or because I was so happy to have survived our vacation and the tent. One thing was for sure: that was the last time I ever went camping—I'm more the hotel type.

After our trip I seldom saw Bernhard; sometimes two whole weeks would pass without our meeting. I had my work and my girlfriends, and during the week he stayed in Spora until late, and otherwise he had to help his father. I only saw Sylvie and Norbert from a distance; we avoided one another. Sylvie stopped coming to the salon; after our trip she switched to a different stylist, or else she had a friend do her hair—a lot of people did that.

In the second year of his apprenticeship Bernhard made his big scene. It came without warning, even for me, and I have no idea what had gotten into him. My guess is that he kept meeting with Sylvie after our miserable vacation and she talked him into it. I knew that whenever I'd worked on him long enough, eventually he reached a point when he couldn't reply and then I had him, he would do as I asked. Maybe Sylvie had a similar hold on him. I'm not suggesting that he was afraid of women; he just wasn't very clever, and any girl could make him feel embarrassed. That was my experience with him, and my guess is that if a woman had a different experience, she just hadn't made enough of an effort. Bernhard spoke very little, and he was very stubborn, but he was also easily influenced, if you knew how. There was something mule-like about him—a stubborn beast that wouldn't respond to words or whips, but then, after you'd given up, would suddenly take off in the desired direction, because it had finally dawned on him what was wanted. When I told him something, he first had to chew on it and digest it thoroughly before it sank into his head. He was a little slow on the uptake, and mistrustful, just like his father and the rest of the family, and they all did these strange things with their eyes when you spoke to them. They didn't completely squint, they just narrowed their eyes as if they were anxiously waiting for what might come next. Maybe that was normal where they were from. Maybe everyone there was mistrustful, or maybe they had lived through terrible things and were afraid they might happen to them again in our town. Mother once said that Bernhard was a true peasant. At the time I thought she was trying to insult him, and me in the bargain, but later I understood that she meant something else. Bernhard *was* a peasant. Perhaps they acted as they did because of what happened in their homeland or when they were expelled, since the other refugees were also a little odd, or else they had suspicion in their blood, inherited from their ancestors, and they carried it farther and farther, to the end of the world. I don't know. I know his family didn't exactly receive me with open arms—more like an intruder, whom you keep a wary eye on at all times.

Of course things were different between Bernhard and me, but he never really opened up, though I didn't realize that until the end, when my parents and all kinds of people were asking me about him and I had nothing to tell them. I went out with him for three years and still I didn't know any more about him than anyone else and couldn't say what had gotten into him.

For two or three years Guldenberg had had an agricultural cooperative that consisted mostly of new farmers with small landholdings who had assigned everything they had to a collective farm where they worked the fields and raised their livestock together. At first none of the locals joined the collective, and the old farmers, whose families had been working the same land for generations, resolutely refused to give up their property, despite the collective's successes being reported every day in the paper. The Guldenberg collective was named "New Way": my father said it was nothing but a club for lazybones and starving paupers who'd thrown in their lot together and took turns wearing the one pair of pants they owned. That's how people in town talked, too, and in my salon I never heard a single good word about the collective, especially since many of the new farmers were refugees, and they weren't exactly beloved by the locals. One customer once said that the collective really ought to be called "No Way." Everyone laughed, even Frau Heidepriem, but then she said that she didn't understand the first thing about politics and didn't like people in her salon talking about it either. Everyone immediately understood, and so we went back to chatting with our clients about men and children, hairstyles and actors.

Farmers in the collective had to work less than the other farmers. They had a regular workday and even an annual vacation, something the old farming families shook their heads at, because that couldn't bode well. In truth, the collective harvested far too little grain, as everyone knew, even if the papers printed something different, and their cows didn't produce any better than those of the private farmers—actually, they produced far less. Still, the collective farmers were given preference when it came to supplies and could borrow any kind of machine or tractor they needed, while the private farmers had to wait weeks, and bring in their harvests with horses, old mechanical combines, and open-frame wagons.

In the spring they renamed the collective, changing it from New Way to Dawn. Father said they did it to avoid the No Way slur, and that it was just a naïve trick they might be able to fob off on the journalists but not on anyone who'd ever seen the inside of a stall. I couldn't have cared less about the whole business; after all, I was a hair stylist, and in the salon we had other problems. What I needed was a decent pair of scissors, from Solingen, because what we had worked all right if you wanted to pluck the clients' scalps, or perhaps do a little pruning in the garden, but not for the elegant cuts you could see in the West German magazines our clients showed us when we asked how they wanted their hair done. Frau Heidepriem was never at a loss for words. When one of her clients brought her the stylish photo of an actress and explained that she needed the same hairstyle as Sophia Loren, the boss said "Fine, now go and bring me Sophia Loren's hair as well." I couldn't be that sassy with the clients, particularly not as an apprentice. I had my own problems, and believe me they had nothing to do with all the hoopla over the collective, and Frau Heidepriem made sure that the subject never came up again in her salon.

The papers were full of reports about the collective, publishing photos of the members when they won yet another bonus, while those who refused to join were listed by name and classified as enemies of the peace who had learned nothing from the last war. But that was always on the first or second page, which no one in the salon read anyway. We flipped right past to the fashion and film pages or the news about Guldenberg. We also paid special attention to the birth announcements and obituaries, since we could talk about that with the clients, and we actually cut out the monthly and weekly movie programs. Frau Heidepriem and the two stylists who had stayed on after their apprenticeship would spend hours studying the lottery results, because they had formed a ticket club and every week pooled their tips to buy several tickets. They could afford to do that; they earned well enough and received hefty tips from some of their regular customers. They also got the tips that were intended for me when I took care of a lady nearly all by myself; the rule in the salon was that the trainer always had the right to the trainee's tips. In any event, we were always talking at work, day in and day out, but we never wasted a word about New Way or Dawn, and I didn't talk about it with Bernhard, either.

A few weeks after the name change, we heard a rumor that all the collectives were to be disbanded, because they weren't paying their way and didn't produce enough. A campaign was started to dismantle them nationwide. From then on, private farmers would receive stronger support and no longer be disadvantaged when it came to the distribution of seed and fertilizer. Their contributions to feeding the people had been insufficiently recognized: from now on, the depots would loan equipment strictly and fairly according to regulations. Certain newspapers supposedly reported this openly, and some articles evidently went so far as to say that our country should follow a German path and not the Russian one. Our paper didn't report on this at all, and the omission was glaring. For months the front page had had nothing but news about the collectives and agriculture, and now they were hardly mentioned.

I heard about these things from Father. Ever since the beginning of the war he had been friends with Herr Ebert and Herr Griesel, two local farmers whom he had helped after hours because their field hands had been drafted and they couldn't manage the work on their own. In turn, after the war was over and there was hardly anything to buy, both farmers helped our family: once a week we went to one of their farms and brought back eggs and flour, and occasionally even a piece of meat. Father would meet regularly with the two farmers in the old Preussischer Hof, a tavern, now renamed the Deutscher Hof. Neither Herr Ebert nor Herr Griesel had joined the collective, although they had been heavily pressured to do so. They took care of their farms entirely on their own, with help from their wives and children and occasionally a few people looking to earn some extra pennies. Both farmers had told Father about the many injustices and how the deadbeats in the collective were being mollycoddled at every turn. When the news from Berlin finally made the rounds, they were relieved to have stayed independent and hoped that things would at last look up for them. They refused to speak with the farmers from the collective. They wouldn't even say hello, because those weren't true farmers, at least not like they were, and they doubted a single one would survive the dismantling of the collective, since they'd never learned to work. The farmers were convinced that after Dawn was dismantled, these individuals would sooner or later give up their farms and look for jobs in the machine works.

A few weeks later Father told me that our local secretary of agriculture had been transferred for disciplinary reasons and was going to be put on trial. Together with some other functionaries who, like himself, had been taken in by foreign propaganda, he had tried to weaken socialism in the countryside, and in so doing had actually abetted the return of capitalism. Our paper didn't mention any of this, but the rumor went around town and various people assured Father that there had been noisy assemblies in the Rathaus, and that the party cells in the residential part of town and in the machine works had been put on high alert. Now, once again, the paper went back to trumpeting the collective's successes on the front page; every day there was something else about the "battle of the harvest" the collectives were fighting, and once again prizes and bonuses were handed out to the collective farmers and their photos were printed in the paper.

One evening Herr Griesel paid us a visit. He had never done that before, and he spent three hours in the living room with Father. Mother and I stayed in the kitchen so as not to disturb the men. After Griesel had left, Father told us that Dawn was not going to be dismantled. A new decision had been made in Berlin, and now the collectives were to be enlarged and strengthened. There was going to be a campaign to persuade private farmers, the ones who had always delivered their targets, to join. According to the new policy, all the country's farmers would soon be working in agricultural cooperatives and private farming would become a thing of the past.

Most of the farms in Guldenberg lay just outside the old town's fortifications or else were completely isolated. There were five farmsteads within the city limits, and they had been in the same families for generations; their owners possessed the most land and were well off, as they had the benefit of experience. The new farmers, those in the collective, had only been raising crops and livestock since the land reform after the war; before that they had been workers who'd never seen a cow before and didn't know how to handle horses. Or else they were refugees who had owned land in the east and had then lost everything and were left completely high and dry. The state had given them a parcel of land and an apartment or maybe a house, and that was all—barely enough to keep body and soul together. They had a couple of chickens and a goat, and very few of them had two or three heads of sheep and a cow, but none of them had a real pasture or a team of horses like the old established farmers. Herr Griesel and Herr Ebert each had more cows and horses than the whole Dawn collective put together. And now the most successful farmers, the "kulaks," as they were called, were to be forced into the collective. Herr Griesel had said that the new district secretary had been to his farm three times and each time with people Griesel didn't know. They had tried to persuade him, and threatened him in the bargain. Two days earlier they had announced an audit and promised they would uncover more than enough to put him on trial for crimes against the people's agriculture and be dispossessed. They had given him exactly three weeks to apply for membership in the collective; after that they couldn't guarantee what would happen, since his case would then be in the hands of the district attorney.

Herr Griesel hadn't dared refuse them or order them off his property. He had shaken his head and kept repeating that he was a good and honest farmer who hadn't incurred any debts and had always delivered his full quotas on time. In the meantime, his wife had completely fallen apart, moaning and groaning because she could already see him in prison. Now Griesel was considering joining the collective or escaping to the West. But because he couldn't take his farm with him, and because he was incapable of abandoning it, he would sign.

"And what did you say to that?" my mother asked my father.

"Nothing. I didn't say anything. What could I say?"

"It's good you didn't. It's better that way, Richard. Who knows where it will all lead? Best not to say anything."

"I'm glad I'm not a farmer."

"And why did he come to you? What did he want from you?"

"I have no idea."

"Didn't he say anything? Does he want you to help him?"

"No. How can I help? Maybe later on, with the harvest again."

"Or maybe not," said Mother.

"What's wrong with you? Why shouldn't I help him with the harvest anymore? I've been doing it for years. And you like his potatoes better than the ones in the store."

"Better stay out of it. We don't want to get caught up in something."

"You're imagining things again, Trude."

"Maybe. Maybe not."

"Have you heard some kind of rumor?"

"You know yourself that they're launching a campaign. And if you say something against it, well, people have disappeared for far less. And the same applies to you, girl. You just keep out of it in that salon of yours. If one of your ladies starts in on the subject, you just say you don't understand a thing about it, and keep your mouth shut. Do you understand, Marion?"

"You don't have to tell me that. I'm not stupid. And Frau Heidepriem takes care of those kinds of things. She doesn't want politics in her salon."

"Good for her. And you do the same."

"What's gotten into you, Trude?"

"It's just none of our business, that's all I'm saying."

Once again the paper was printing daily reports about the collective: Father read the passages aloud over supper. The district secretary was pictured several times in conversations with the farmers from the collective; he had told the paper that Eilenburg could become the first completely collectivized district in the country and an example for the entire republic. There were only a few farmers left who were still stuck in their backward ways and now had to be patiently persuaded to support progress. Guldenberg in particular should make an effort if it didn't want to miss the boat. At 7:00 p.m. Father always turned on the German-language broadcast of the BBC. Because the station was jammed and the announcer was almost impossible to understand, Father kept turning the dial and moving the radio to get better reception. Whenever there was any commentary about the situation in East Germany, Mother and I had to be as quiet as mice so that Father could catch everything.

Once the BBC broadcasted a report about a village near Guldenberg, and Mother and I listened every bit as attentively as Father. We wanted to see if we recognized any of the names and whether they said anything about our town. They mentioned our river, and for a moment I was so proud I was almost sick in my stomach. The man on the radio said that the unprofitable collectives were supposed to have been dissolved weeks earlier, but that some hard-liners had now gotten the upper hand and immediately launched a counterinitiative that was to be implemented with force. Party functionaries in Berlin had been removed from office and arrested, and efforts were heightened throughout the country, particularly to bring the experienced, successful, and well-to-do farmers into the cooperatives, and that they would be the next victims of forced collectivization.

"Forced collectivization," Father repeated after the broadcast, and added, "So it is coming."

"Did you hear? The man from London mentioned the Mulde!" I interjected.

"Um-hmm. They're well informed. They have their people everywhere."

"And Herr Griesel and Herr Ebert will join the collective?"

"They won't have any choice in the long run. You're sitting in the hot seat, I told Griesel. If they stop delivering what he needs, if he can't buy what he has to have to run the farm, then he has no prospects. But he doesn't want to join. His family has been there for ninety-eight years, and he doesn't want to give up before they make one hundred."

"But he wouldn't have to work so much. They have an eight-hour day in the collective. They even have vacation."

"That's what they say in the paper, girl. They say a lot of things in the paper."

"You mean, you don't think it's true? You think they're lying?"

"I don't know. It's all propaganda. You shouldn't believe a word. Don't talk about it. If that's the way they want it, then there's no use banging your head against a wall. And that's exactly what I said to Griesel."

Everyone in the city knew that the agitators would soon show up at the five farms in Guldenberg. They were already in the villages and farmsteads surrounding the town. Then, one Sunday in June, at ten in the morning, they descended on Herr

Griesel and the four other farmers. A week later, Herr Griesel told Father the whole story. According to him, they showed up simultaneously at all five farms. Seven men came to Griesel's, the head of the Dawn co-op, the local secretary of agriculture, a man from the district office, and four youths. For a while the group stood in front of the locked gate. Then one of the young men climbed over the wall and opened the gate. Because Griesel's dog was back in his kennel that Sunday morning, the group went straight across the farmyard up to the house. The dog ran around at night free, unchained, and Griesel had thought of letting him out of his kennel when the agitators showed up. But then he thought that if his dog attacked one of the functionaries—and given how ferocious he was, that was bound to happen—then he would have even more trouble to contend with.

The men knocked once, then walked right into the house and made their way to the kitchen, where Griesel and his wife were waiting. They sat down on the chairs, without waiting to be asked, and started hammering away at Griesel and his terrified wife. The man from the district was the main speaker; the others listened to him in silence and nodded in agreement when he said something they found particularly significant. Once he was done with his speech, the head of the co-op said, repeatedly, "We need you, Hannes."

Griesel said that he had never been on a first-name basis with this man and was surprised that he called him Hannes.

When the two men had finished speaking, they looked at Griesel and his sobbing wife and waited for the farmer to say something. Griesel looked back at them in silence, then spat right on the tiles in the middle of his kitchen, and said to his wife, "Be quiet. Stop blubbering. I'm signing."

And that's what he did. When the agitators began congratulating him he roared at them: "Out!"

That Sunday, four of the five farmers in Guldenberg signed. The fifth, Herr Hausmann, had a telephone; he had been warned that the agitators were on their way. He locked the gate to the yard and the door to his house and unchained his dog. When the group appeared in front of his farmstead, he kept them standing there at the locked gate, then put a bathrobe on over his Sunday suit, went to the stable, which had a window that opened onto the street, opened the window, and told the agitators that he was sick and couldn't receive any visitors. Then he waited with his wife in the kitchen until the Wild Hunt, as he called it, had moved on. If the others had been as clever they would still be independent—at least that's what Herr Hausmann said Sunday evening in the tavern, but in the end it didn't help him. Two days later another group showed up and pushed their way into his cowshed, and Herr Hausmann finally signed, because he was the last farmer in the whole district who hadn't applied to join the co-op, and the party would not tolerate it.

The same Sunday the agitators showed up at Griesel's and the other farmers' in Guldenberg, I was wearing my patent-leather shoes for the first time—black with buckles from the Gerhartz Shoe Shop. I had wanted to buy them for a week, but I had to wait until I had enough money. On Thursday I ran to Gerhartz's right after work and put my money down on the table in front of old Frau Gerhartz, who was still traipsing about the store. Then I grabbed the fabulous shoes and without even trying them on ran all the way home. There I immediately slipped into them and showed them to Mother. She liked them, too, except she thought they were much too expensive, even though I told her the price was less than what I actually paid. But since I had bought them with my own money she couldn't say anything. After that I wrapped them in the tissue paper and put them back in their box.

I wore them on Sunday for the very first time. Father didn't notice; he didn't even see them, though I put them on right under his nose, and Mother kept looking at them. After breakfast Mother went to church and Father put on his work clothes and marched off to his beloved garden plot at the Hüfnermarkt, while I cleared the table and washed the dishes. At ten o'clock I met a few girlfriends from my old school at the parade grounds. We hadn't planned to get together, but those of us who had been in the school choir kept meeting there the way we always had. There were three or four girls, at most; some had moved away and some didn't come as regularly as before. A few had work at home or were meeting their boyfriends: of course we all had boyfriends. When I got there, Traudel was sitting on the bench, and Kathrin was standing in front of her. They looked me up and down in silence before they said hello. I was happy I hadn't put on my windbreaker, because the way those girls were staring at me I'm sure they would have found something nasty to say about that old rag. They noticed the shoes right away. Traudel even knew how much they cost, since she had tried them on at Gerhartz's herself. She said they didn't fit her because her instep was too high, which was why she couldn't wear shoes with buckles. She didn't say they were too expensive, and I didn't bring up the price. I sat down next to Traudel and crossed my legs to keep my shoes in view.

"Can I tell her?" asked Kathrin, and before Traudel could answer she went on: "She's getting engaged!"

"Who? You, Traudel?"

"Can you believe it?" Kathrin went on. "A real engagement, with rings, and a family party. If I showed up at home with a ring I think my parents would go crazy. Just on account of the money. As it is, every time the subject comes up they start yammering on about how much a wedding will cost."

"Really, Traudel? Is it true?"

Traudel nodded proudly.

"Do you really want to marry Paul?"

"I don't know. I mean, getting engaged doesn't mean getting married."

"Find a safe mooring and then go on looking, right?"

"Something like that. After all, I've been with him for two years."

"That's how long I've been with Bernhard. Even longer. But I wouldn't even think about getting engaged."

"I wouldn't either in your shoes."

"What's that supposed to mean? What are you trying to say? You don't like him, right? Well, you don't have to—the main thing is that I like him."

"You don't have to get snippy. I just mean that Bernhard's a little strange."

"Strange? Watch your tongue or you'll wind up looking strange yourself."

"What I mean is that he goes for years without so much as opening his mouth. I can't remember ever hearing him say two sentences together . . ."

"So what if he doesn't say much? It's better than if he spent the whole day babbling about the different kinds of motorcycles he says he's going to buy."

"You'll see that machine sooner than you think. Paul's going to buy that new model for us. Maybe even with a sidecar."

"Sure. And a house too, with a garden, right? Then you can nail your bridal wreath right over the front door."

"Stop it, you two. Did you come here to quarrel?"

"At least Paul doesn't pick on people he doesn't know," Traudel said.

"Do you mean me? Or Bernhard? Who are we picking on?"

"Oh, come on. You call that normal? My father says we haven't seen anything like it in a thousand years."

"What are you getting at? Spit it out before you choke on it."

"Well, what would you call it? Going to people you don't know and putting a gun to their head?"

"I have no idea what you're talking about. Do you, Kathrin?"

"She means Bernhard. He's with that group that's going around trying to force the farmers to join the collective."

"Bernhard? What are you talking about?"

"Your Bernhard, that's what. He's always there. That's a genuine activist you've got there. If you want to you can see the gang in action. Today they're running around Guldenberg. Supposedly they won't stop until everybody's signed up."

"Bernhard's with them?"

"He's one of the most fanatical. He's with the group working on Griesel."

"Griesel? Are you serious?"

"Can you imagine? Of all people, Griesel. The man who took him in back then, Bernhard and his whole crooked family. He took in one-armed Haber, who God knows couldn't have been good for much. He fed and looked after those refugees, and this is how Bernhard thanks him."

"Why don't we go over there? Then you can see for yourself, Marion?"

"Who else is in the group? Sylvie?"

"Of course. She was always like that. Her whole family is red. Red as a bloody beet."

"Sylvie, hmm. Well well well, now I'm beginning to see. The whole picture."

"What does Sylvie have to do with it?"

"She was always after him. Last summer I let her have it, too, and then she stopped. But if it's true that Bernhard is running around with her, then we're finished. And there's no coming back, either."

"See for yourself. Come on, let's go."

We passed by the plant nursery and up Gartenstrasse until we reached the old cemetery and Gustav-Adolf-Strasse, where Griesel had his farm. I was one step ahead of the others, they could hardly keep up with me. I didn't want to walk next to Traudel and Kathrin, I didn't want to talk to them. I had to get my thoughts straight and clear my head.

I had seen that Sylvie and Bernhard got on well together. But why was he taking part in this political stuff? It had never interested him, no more than it had me, and I knew that his parents didn't have anything to do with it; they were still mourning the old days when they were well off. Sylvie must have talked him into it somehow. She had wrapped him around her little finger in a way I'd never managed to. She must have had something I didn't, something that appealed to Bernhard, and it couldn't have been her looks. Sylvie had the face of a mouse, she was a pale timid little shrew who couldn't stand the cold, with tiny eyes always looking around suspiciously, always on guard, and at the same time always eager never to miss a thing. Her eyes really were like a little rodent's, close together and fidgety. When you looked at her you started to get twitchy yourself, because the eyes kept darting this way and that as if they were checking the air around you. Her nose jumped right out of her face; it was like a weapon, that nose, sharp enough to draw blood. And she had thick legs, regular potato mashers: no calves or ankles, it was all one line, without any shape, like blank pieces of pine that had been set aside to be made into a pair of legs sometime later. You'd never see her picture in the papers, and it would never cross your mind to compare her with a film star.

But there was something about her the boys found intriguing. It had been that way in school, too. Back then, there were two or three really good-looking girls everyone wanted to imitate, their hairstyles and clothes, and there were the sassy girls who set the tone. I belonged to both groups, even if the other girls in my class didn't think so highly of me. I was good-looking and always perfectly dressed. And I was never at a loss for words: after the last thing had been said, and the subject had been closed, everybody knew I'd still come up with some comment I had to say out loud, even if it earned me a black mark in the class register. I couldn't help myself; whatever popped into my head I had to get out, no matter what it cost.

And then there were the girls who didn't stand out in any way: they weren't pretty, and they didn't dress well enough to be noticed. They were constantly whispering with their friends—girls who were just as unremarkable as they were—but as soon as someone else appeared they went quiet. Like little gray mice. If one of them came to school with a big bright ribbon in her hair, no one said hey, fantastic, that looks great, because with these girls it only looked ridiculous, and if you wanted to be nice to them you simply overlooked it.

Sylvie was one of these little gray mice, but she always had two or three boys around her, and she was probably the first one in our grade to have a steady boyfriend. When it came to breaking up, she was always the one who ended things, and there was always a new boy eager to claw his way into her good graces. It wasn't her looks, that was clear; maybe she had a certain smell that attracted the boys, a smell that only they could smell, a smell that ugly flowers use to attract bumblebees and honeybees. She had something I didn't understand and the other girls didn't, either. None of them could figure out why boys would cluster around her and burst out laughing whenever she tried to be funny.

Griesel's farmstead was right across from the cemetery. It had a long, high wall that faced the street, unbroken except for two small stable windows, a large gate, and an ancient door to the farmyard. This door was never used; the gate, on the other hand, was wide open all day long, offering an unobstructed view of the stable and cowshed and the manure pile. The living quarters lay to the right, behind the wall, and could be seen upon entering the yard. There was no work done at Griesel's farm on the Sabbath, so the gate was shut on Sundays. When we got there, seven people were standing outside the gate—the agitators. A narrow footpath ran along the other side of the road, and beyond that the ground sloped up to the cemetery wall. Children were sitting on the grassy slope, watching the goings-on in front of Griesel's.

"Well, what did I tell you?" asked Traudel and nodded her head at the group gathered outside the gate. I had stopped and was looking at the people. I knew some of them, in particular Bernhard and Sylvie, who were standing together.

"And you really knew nothing about all this?"

I didn't answer, but just kept moving forward, very slowly. Herr Trebel from the town hall was kicking against the gate with his boots and calling out for Griesel to open up, open up at once. He looked at the others in resignation, then turned back to the gate and shouted that they had plenty of time and would stand there until someone came out and opened up. Bernhard had seen me coming, I was sure of that. He had glanced in my direction, then quickly turned the other way and was now avoiding me. I kept on going, slowly but surely, until I reached the group and was standing next to Bernhard and Sylvie.

"Hello, Bernhard," I said.

He turned around and acted surprised to see me. Sylvie said something to me, but I kept my eyes fixed on Bernhard and didn't react to her. Bernhard was embarrassed and could scarcely look at me.

"It's a nice Sunday," I said. "I was expecting you to come and get me."

"I'm busy now. I'll come by in the afternoon."

"Can I talk to you?"

"It's a bad time now, Marion. We'll see each other in the afternoon."

"I have to speak to you now."

"All right. What is it?"

"I have to speak to you alone."

"That's impossible. I'm busy here."

"Oh? Doing what?"

"You can see for yourself."

"Yes, I see. Just come here for a second. When Herr Griesel opens the gate, you can go. You can go and march on in with the others. Well?"

"I'll be right back, Sylvie."

"Do you have to ask Sylvie's permission?"

"What's the matter with you?"

"I want to talk to you alone. And what I have to say to you isn't meant for your friend Sylvie."

"So what is it?"

"Tell me what's going on here."

"We have an assignment."

"Aha. An assignment. And who gave you this assignment? Sylvie?"

"It comes from the state."

"I'm impressed, Bernie. Really. Bernhard Haber has been given a state assignment. That's great. And Sylvie? What's she doing here?"

"Sylvie's part of it."

"Part of what? Part of you? Since when?"

"We're both in the group supporting the cooperative. We want to convince the farmers to join. It's better for them and better for us."

"What does any of this have to do with you? I always thought you wanted to be a carpenter. And now all of a sudden you're becoming a farmer?"

"Of course not, we're on a common mission with the farmers."

"Who is we? You and Sylvie?"

"The city council, the district, the parties, the youth organization."

"I see, and you belong to all of that? I had no idea you were so involved."

"Sooner or later you have to decide something in life, Marion."

"Right. And you've decided on Sylvie."

"This doesn't have anything to do with Sylvie. It's completely my own decision."

"So how come I knew nothing about it? When did you

become so progressive? When did that happen? In a tent at the Süsser See?"

"That didn't have anything to do with it."

"I see it differently, Bernhard, very differently."

"I have to go now. I'll see you this afternoon. I'll pick you up around three, all right?"

"Are you sure you wouldn't rather pick up Sylvie?"

"See you at three, then."

"I don't know if I'll have time at three. I don't think I'll have time today."

"I'll come anyway."

"Do what you see fit. Especially since you're doing it anyway. And tell Sylvie hello for me. Don't forget that, Bernhard."

He slinked back to the group with his tail between his legs. I saw Sylvie say something to him and then look in my direction. What she must have seen in my eyes—I don't know how she didn't burst into flames right there on the spot and drop dead, and the earth open up and swallow her. I went back to Kathrin and Traudel, who peppered me with a thousand questions. I told them I'd seen enough and wanted to go back to the parade grounds.

"I don't know if he's going with her or not," I said to the girls on the way back. "I only know that I'm not going with him. Not anymore. As far as I'm concerned, we're through."

When Traudel congratulated me, I told her very rudely that in the future she should have the sense to keep her mouth shut and her nose out of other people's business.

That afternoon Bernhard actually did come trotting over and rang our bell. After the fifth time, Mother sent me out. She told me not to avoid him but tell Bernhard flat out that from now on he should call on someone else, on his new friends, for instance. I went to the hall, opened the door a crack, and told Bernhard that I didn't have any time for him. When he asked when we could see each other, I said, "I don't know, Bernhard. I don't trust you anymore. You go for months without saying a thing, and then you pull something like this. I think it's better that we split up."

He was shocked; he hadn't expected that, which surprised me, since he must have known we weren't a great match. He asked me to take a walk with him so we could talk about it; I said that I had already decided and I didn't care to waste another word on the subject.

"It's over, Bernhard, over and done with. Besides, you have Sylvie."

When I held out my hand to say good-bye, his eyes were swimming in tears, which I hadn't expected at all.

"It's better this way," I said, friendly. When I closed the door and went back inside, I almost felt sorry for him. I hadn't said, "See you later," since that didn't seem right to me, and I didn't really want to see him later anyway.

Late that afternoon Father came back from the playing field, where he'd been watching a soccer match. I was standing in the bathroom, teasing my hair, when he knocked briefly. He came inside, sat down on the edge of the tub, and watched me in silence. A few of his friends and colleagues from work had told him about the agitators and about the fact that Bernhard had gone with them to pressure the farmers into joining. The way Father told it, the agitators forced their way into Griesel's farmstead—it must have been shortly after my talk with Bernhard—and finally got him to sign the application.

"And your Bernhard was there."

"He's not 'my Bernhard.' "

"He's a strange one. After all, it was Griesel who took him in back then."

I shrugged my shoulders and focused intensely on my hair.

"I'm worried about you, Marion. That boy's not for you."

"You don't need to worry about me. I've finished with Bernhard. Once and for all. Didn't Mother tell you?"

I looked at him in the mirror; he seemed pleased. Then he got up, blew on the back of my neck and gave me a kiss, and went out. During supper my parents kept sneaking glances at me, but I kept my feelings to myself. That evening Mother came into my room and wanted to talk about Bernhard and console me, but I told her that it wouldn't have lasted much longer anyway.

"Now I'm waiting for my dream prince," I said, and we both laughed. She said she was relieved that I wasn't taking it too hard.

Then next morning, when I showed up at work, Frau Heidepriem took me aside to tell me about Bernhard and his performance on Sunday.

"Everyone has to find his own path to salvation," she said, "but I won't have politics in my salon. So don't you go starting up with anything. Don't misunderstand me, girl, I'm not at all against politics, but everything has a time and a place, and my salon is never the time or place for that."

I told her that I never discuss politics, in or out of the salon, and that none of it interested me in the least, not the politics and not the farmers. I finished by saying, "And I have nothing more to do with Bernhard Haber. It lasted far too long and now it's over."

"Very good," said Frau Heidepriem, beaming at me. "I knew I could rely on you. You have *veda,* girl. And now go and open the door. It's already nine o'clock."

I never spoke with Bernhard again. We occasionally saw each other, and twice I visited his big new workshop to place an order, but there was no personal talk. He's been married a long time now, though not to Sylvie, as I would have predicted. A few years after the incident, he married a girl from Spora, but it didn't affect me in the slightest, since by then I had other friends and other interests.

Today I sometimes wonder what would have become of me if we had stayed together and maybe gotten married. And then I'm happy and relieved, since he's not one of my better memories. With the little love I had for Bernhard it couldn't have lasted long, and we would have ended up hating or despising each other—like so many married couples in town, as I knew from clients who told me everything while they were sitting in the chair or under the dryer, at least after they'd been coming to me for some time. As I stood behind them and our eyes met in the mirror, they'd tell me everything, young or old. It just came bubbling out of them. They told me about their happiest days, and their children, about their husbands and their marriages, and a few said quite openly that they would kill their men if an opportunity presented itself. In the salon I learned things I never thought possible, things that were far more disgusting and unbelievable than anything I'd seen at the movies. When I was finished with a client and had done my best with her hair, she would quickly wipe her tears, and by the time she was paying at the cash register she was herself again, strong and proud and ready to face the world. I think the churchgoing women told me even more than they told their priests.

As for me, I told everything to Susanne. When there was anything important, I went to her. And that's why back then I wanted to have my first kiss at the forest cemetery, right next to her. I often went there with Bernhard to see my older sister, whom I had never known. Susanne was born two years before me and lived only fifteen months. She came down with tuberculosis, and the doctors at the forest hospital couldn't do anything. I've gone to visit Susanne my whole life, ever since first grade. I planted flowers on her grave and watered them, and I told her everything. Whenever I came home after visiting her, I always felt a lot better.

Bernhard didn't say anything when I first suggested we go to the cemetery; unlike the others in our class, he didn't find the idea of walking in a graveyard strange. At some point I told him about my sister, and he nodded, as if it were completely understandable. He said he'd like to visit his grandfather, who was buried a couple hundred miles away, where no one in the family could travel.

"Were you close to your grandfather?" I asked him.

He nodded, jutting out his lower lip, and said, "My grandfather was the only one who . . ."

Then he stopped and wouldn't finish his sentence. Now and then I asked him, but he never said any more about his grandfather. Perhaps he loved him the way I loved my sister. Or even more, since he had actually known him, while I had never even seen Susanne. In any case, I kissed Bernhard at Susanne's grave because I thought I'd waited long enough, and that seemed to me exactly the right place. If anyone was to know I had a boyfriend it should be my older sister; maybe she would enjoy watching me kiss him, in case she was looking. We sat on the tiny rusted chain around Frau Grambow, who lay next door, and who'd been lying there for thirty-two years and eighteen days before Susanne died. I talked, and Bernhard listened, and then I kissed him. It was beautiful, very beautiful. And it was good that nothing more happened between us, and that I didn't marry him. No, Bernhard was the last man I needed.

I thought about Frau Heidepriem, my old boss, who died later on, and told Susanne that even though I never married, and even though I have two children who want nothing to do with me, I really did have *veda,* whatever that is.

Peter Koller

After the flood had subsided for good, they hauled the rest of the wooden bridge away and that May began constructing the new stone bridge. Giant low-loader trailers were parked on both sides of the Mulde, and sand piles and stacks of stone blocks surrounded the crew cars where the workers lived and which looked like old discarded circus wagons.

In those days we frequently went to the river after the men had finished work, to watch them cook their meals in the crew cars, or wash up and shave, or sit on the riverbank in their work clothes and toss a fishing line into the water and drink their beer. It wasn't warm enough to swim in the river, but we went down to the Mulde as often as we had six months earlier, when a section of the Autobahn had been closed for repairs and all the traffic was rerouted to the next entrance along a detour that led over our wooden bridge. I was still in school, and spent almost every afternoon with my friends on the landing next to the bridge. We studied the passing cars and had fun feeling the old wooden structure tremble and creak under each vehicle that crossed. That traffic must have been the final straw, because the following winter the bridge could not withstand the ice floes.

The traffic from the Autobahn was rerouted over our bridge for about half a year, and we never got enough of watching the automobiles, guessing all the makes and models, and placing bets as to who was right. In those days there weren't many cars in Guldenberg—perhaps eighty people owned their own, and most of those were prewar models that they maintained as well as possible with makeshift repairs: Greschel the butcher even had one with a special wood-gas carburetor he used to take out on drives. The detour gave us a chance to see the cars speeding on their way from Berlin to Munich—cars we knew only from pictures in the papers or the hobby cards we all collected. We dreamed about these automobiles: when we sat on the bridge, when we stood around the schoolyard, talking among ourselves—even in bed that's all we thought about. Now and then a few boys talked about girls, but we were more interested in the machines clattering over our bridge than in thin hips that still didn't have much to show, front or back. You could see cars from all over Europe, the latest models; for us it was a perpetual auto show in motion, a daily presentation of every car in the world that money could buy. Because they had to drive very slowly over the bridge, that was the best place to look them over, size them up, and make our expert pronouncements.

That's when Bernhard and I first started talking, back then on the bridge. Before that I'd seen him in the schoolyard but never spoken with him. It was already suppertime, and most of the boys had left. Because it was getting dark, we made no bones about taking out our cigarettes and smoking one, or half of one: we used to cut them in two with a razor blade to make them last longer. What we really cared about was lighting the cigarette, then taking the first two or three drags, and, finally, flicking the butt so it arced as high as possible and landed precisely on the targeted spot. That was fun for us and earned respect; in those days I found the actual smoking boring, and I couldn't stand the smell that stuck to my fingers. The little kids showed up and stared at our cigarettes, ready to race one another to pick up a discarded butt, just in time to salvage one or two last puffs. We shooed them away and told them to go home, since staying on the bridge was too dangerous, and besides, we had declared it off limits.

On one of those evenings, four of us were sitting on the landing when this white Opel came to a full stop in the middle of the bridge and died, right before our eyes. We had spotted it earlier, since it had approached the bridge very slowly, jerking all the time, its motor sputtering as if gasping for air. Then there was a loud backfire and it gave up the ghost. An older man in a suit with a scarf around his neck climbed out of the car, unlatched the hood, and opened it without turning off the headlights. He then went to the trunk, took out a pair of gloves and put them on, banged on the motor a few times with a wrench, then stared at the engine compartment for a long time as if he were looking for something, and finally closed the hood. He stood by the car for a moment, undecided, and looked around, at a loss as to what to do. He waved to us, and all four of us immediately went over. He slowly took off his gloves and tossed them on the hood. In the twilight I had the impression that his skin was very tan, and I was eager for him to open his mouth and say something to us. I wanted to hear his voice, which was bound to have something of the same splendid shimmer of his skin. Perhaps he would address us in a foreign language, or speak with an accent that hinted at far-off lands full of promise. But once I was standing in front of him I realized his skin was really just yellow—an unhealthy, dirty yellow like the fingertips of a smoker. He asked us where he could find a shop that could fix his car, and we told him how to get there. He opened the driver's door and switched off the headlights. Then he went to the rear door, took out a soft brown overcoat and put it on. Finally, he reached for a wide-brimmed felt hat the same color as his coat and put it on before locking the car. When he started off toward town, I told him he shouldn't leave his car on the bridge, or else he should leave his lights on, because there was a lot of traffic here and the bridge was very narrow. He stopped, nodded, looked at his car, and asked us to help him push it. He sat at the wheel and we pushed his car back off the bridge onto the shoulder of the road. He had let down his window and was sticking his head out. I was standing right behind him, pushing against the car frame, and as I did this I pulled out the little button that locked the left-rear door. The man didn't notice, and when he locked up his car again, this door was open. We accompanied him to the bridge. Then we sat down on the landing while he went on into town by himself.

After the man had disappeared in the darkness, I jumped down from the landing. Before I could say anything, Bernhard asked me if we wanted to take a closer look at the car. He grinned, and I realized he had noticed my little maneuver. All four of us went to the parked car, opened both of the back doors, and quickly searched the entire vehicle. We found maps, dirty cleaning rags, a box of candy, and an empty thermos. Since the trunk was locked we thought we'd make do with the candy and the thermos and disappear, when suddenly Bernhard dismantled the back of one of the rear seats and stuck his head into the trunk. A few seconds later he opened it from within and crawled out. Inside we found a spare tire, a plastic box with a red cross on top, and a small black suitcase made of artificial leather. We took out the suitcase and the plastic box and opened each. The suitcase contained two folders with papers, crumpled clothes, and a toiletries kit. The plastic box had bandages and tablets and other first-aid necessaries. Each of us snatched something. We all grabbed quickly so that no one quarreled. I got my hands on the toiletries kit. I liked it because it was made of leather, or faux leather, and was small enough to fit comfortably in my jacket pocket. Then we closed the trunk and the plastic box, placed them both back inside, straightened the backseat, closed all the doors we had opened, and headed home.

When we reached the entrance to our local museum we passed Schrader's old diesel delivery truck going in the opposite direction—he owned the smithy and the repair shop. Someone was sitting next to him, perhaps the old man whose car we had plundered, but between the darkness and the miserable light of the gas lanterns we couldn't tell, especially since the truck's headlights blinded us. When they drove past we turned around and howled and waved after them. I had reason to be pleased with my loot, even if I didn't know what I could use it for. The others had stolen things that were even more useless. Bernhard was lugging the car jack; when I asked him what he intended to do with it, he answered that something like that always came in handy and he would give it to his father, who was bound to have some use for it in the shop.

"And where will you tell him it came from?"

He shrugged his shoulders. "Found it," he said.

After that I saw Bernhard more often. Occasionally during recess he would come over to me and my friends and listen without taking part in the conversation. He would stand there like a lost little boy, and since he wasn't in our grade, we'd barely speak to him. At some point he mentioned our joint thievery and asked about my travel kit: I told him I didn't know what he was talking about, and that he better keep his mouth shut, which he did.

Six months later, when the cars were no longer being rerouted through our town, ice destroyed the bridge. In the middle of February we had a flood that nearly reached the old high-water mark. The bridge had tapered wooden deflectors set in front of the pilings designed to break the ice, but these floes proved too big, and instead of breaking up they simply accumulated in great stacks on the upstream side of the bridge. As a result, watches were posted day and night; the men used long iron poles with hooks on one end to break the floes into pieces they could then maneuver under the bridge and past it. Now and then an especially large floe smashed into the pilings so that its peak sloped up above the bridge, which then made a loud grinding sound, and anyone standing on it could feel the vibration running through his entire body. Positioned on both banks, the men tried to pull the ice off the wooden breakers with their hooks and then strike the ice so that it split or cracked into fragments the water could carry away. Just as we had watched the cars six months earlier, we again sat on the wooden landing and watched the men—and made bets on their attempts to loosen the floes from the pilings and pull the stacked icebergs apart and lead them safely under the bridge.

After two days we were shooed off the bridge. It was Barthel, one of our policemen, who constantly marched through town with his German shepherd, which he held on a short leash with his right hand. He would sling his black service bag over his shoulder and would open it importantly when he had something to take down, ordering the dog to sit when he needed both hands for writing. The dog always looked ready to spring whenever anyone approached his master—so it seemed to us—and never took his eyes off the newcomer for even a second. Barthel talked a lot about his dog: apparently it was a certified police dog, extremely well trained, and a match for any criminal. When Barthel came toward us, we sensed what he was going to say. A little earlier he had spoken with the men on the town side of the river; the men had pointed at us, and then Barthel had climbed up the bank and come straight to us.

"Get lost," he said coarsely.

When we protested, the dog took a step in our direction. I didn't know whether he did it on his own, if he sensed our resistance and was trained to react aggressively, or whether his master had given him an imperceptible signal using the leash. In any event the dog's muzzle was just inches away from my legs, the animal snarled, and the blood froze in my veins when I saw the dog's sharp teeth in front of me and smelled his breath. I didn't move and tried to grin nonchalantly while slowly putting my hands in my jacket pocket. I tried to take my eyes off the dog's bared teeth and avoid his stare and pretend to be unaffected, but I couldn't, I was literally glued to the dog's sharp muzzle, his hanging tongue frothing with saliva, and his dirty-yellow eyes that were just a handsbreadth away. Suddenly Bernhard spoke to the dog. He said "come" or "come here," stuck out his hand, and the dog turned away from me, laid its ears back, and looked at Bernhard.

"Here, boy, come here," he said again, and motioned with his fingers as if he wanted to stroke the dog's neck. The dog gave a quiet growl that no longer sounded threatening. Bernhard bent over and actually patted the dog's long muzzle and the fur between his ears. He ran his fingers over the dog's eyes, which closed appreciatively, while the hind legs yielded as if preparing to sit down. Barthel, the policeman, jerked on the leash and called his dog; the animal stood up again but kept his head stretched out so that Bernhard could continue scratching. Barthel then took the end of the leash and landed a whack on the dog's rump; the dog gave a brief yowl before snapping at Bernhard's hand. Bernhard managed to pull back just in time, but the dog snapped again and bit Bernhard in the calf. Bernhard screamed and jumped off the landing. His pants were torn. He lifted the trouser leg and saw he wasn't bleeding, but the dog's teeth had left a clear mark on his skin. The policeman was startled as well. He had pulled the dog back and was now holding him by the collar. He scolded him while patting him on the head. We had all seen how he had sicced the animal on Bernhard. Bernhard rubbed his calf and then inspected the tear in his trousers. He rolled down the pant leg, straightened himself up, and glared at Herr Barthel, dark with rage.

"You'll have to pay for the pants."

"The pants and some additional compensation for pain and suffering," I said, taking a place beside Bernhard.

"I told you to get off the bridge. I warned you that it's dangerous. And if you annoy my dog, he'll snap at you. You and no one else are to blame. You can't treat a trained police canine like a little lapdog—they're always dangerous. You stuck your hand out; he considers that an attack and will defend himself."

"You sicced him on me. The dog was completely calm. I was even able to pet him."

"You don't pet strange dogs, at least not if you have a brain in your head. My dog is aggressive; when he's attacked he defends himself."

"You sicced him on me."

"Nonsense. If I had let him loose on you there wouldn't be much left of you, boy. He just nibbled at you, he's playful. You saw for yourself; you're not even bleeding."

"My pants are ruined. You have to replace them."

"Your pants were already gone. They're worn through, and that tiny rip was there already, I'm sure. I'm not paying you anything, not a penny. You get enough from the city as it is. Always holding out your hand, always getting coddled, as if we'd been waiting just for you. Who the devil asked you here? And now get lost, all of you. Off the bridge. You have to learn not to provoke strange dogs, at least not ones that are well trained. We don't do that in these parts. That's not done here."

"Everyone saw it. You sicced the dog on me to bite me. And you'll have to pay for my pants."

"And what else?"

"The pants and compensation," I repeated.

The dog kept staring at Bernhard, who didn't appear to be the least bit afraid of the animal, even though he'd just been bitten. In fact he seemed to get along very well with the beasts.

"That's it. I've had enough," said the policeman. "End of discussion. And get off that bridge like I told you."

Then he turned around and walked toward town. The dog walked alongside and kept looking back at us until his master smacked him one with the leather leash.

"He'll have to pay for that," I told Bernhard. "We saw it, we'll all testify. The man is a public danger, siccing a dog like that."

"The idiot," Bernhard growled as he carefully examined the hole in his pants. "My mother will be furious. What if he doesn't pay?"

"Then you take him to court. You have enough witnesses. We'll all back you up."

All the boys that were standing or sitting around nodded.

"Take him to court? A policeman? That costs a lot of money, and they won't believe us."

We stayed a few minutes on the bridge, out of pride and because the policeman had a bad conscience and surely wouldn't come back. On our way home I told Bernhard that he really had a way with dogs and asked him if he hadn't been afraid, because I had nearly soiled my pants. I put my hand on his shoulder, and I think he understood that it was a sign of thanks. He said he knew how to handle dogs—any dog there is. No, he wasn't afraid of any animal. He said that no one should be afraid of dogs because dogs acknowledge and fear our physical size and will therefore never attack a human unless they're pushed to do it. If you are afraid of them they become aggressive and dangerous, because then they want to be leader of the pack, since they're descended from wolves and are used to living in packs, where there's always one animal who decides everything, who manages to assert himself againstall the others and they have to submit to him. I told him I could care less about dogs, but I might get a big watchdog that everybody would respect and who would have to obey my every word.

"That dog would never have snapped at me if Barthel hadn't told him to."

"I know. We saw that. You had that beast practically eating out of your hand."

"Yeah, I know how to handle dogs."

"That's for sure," I said.

We reached a point where our paths went separate ways. I was very glad the dog hadn't torn my pants.

Two days later the bridge was closed to all traffic, including bicyclists and pedestrians. Whoever wanted to get to the other side had to drive to Grehna and take the ferry that had been set up after the village had been bombed and its own bridge destroyed.

The water level subsided at the end of March, and specialists came from out of town to inspect the bridge. They stayed in Guldenberg for four days, climbing up and down the bridge and donning rubber suits that came up to their chins so they could enter the water and examine the condition of the pilings. After they left, the bridge remained closed, and three weeks later our local paper reported that, according to an engineers' report submitted to the commission, the bridge in Guldenberg was beyond repair and had to be torn down. As it was, it had only been erected after the war as a provisional emergency bridge.

The Wehrmacht had detonated the old stone bridge during the last days of the war, in order to slow the advance of the Americans, but just one day later, after the German detachment had left, the inhabitants surrendered to the Americans, who were already on the other side of the Mulde. The story went that a policeman climbed over the remains of the pilings, carrying a white flag to surrender the town to the American army: all the German soldiers had left, and the town leaders, the mayor, and two full-time city employees had fled. That same day, with the help of a pontoon bridge they were carrying, the Americans entered the city, which was overflowing with refugees. The American officers created a new municipal administration with people who spoke a little English. They didn't care at all what profession the new town fathers had practiced or what they had done during the Nazi period. The new administration held office for two weeks—really just nine days—since the Americans left at the end of April, and the Russians moved in five days later, on May 4. They commandeered the best buildings: the old post office became the new Red Army headquarters, and the three highest-ranking officers along with their adjutants took over Tefler's large estate. The same day they occupied the town they chased the administrators appointed by the Americans out of the Rathaus. All positions were filled with Communists and people named by the Communist Party, so that all the offices previously held by businessmen and civil servants were taken over exclusively by blue- and white-collar workers. A narrow wooden footbridge was erected across the Mulde, as the Americans had dismantled their collapsible bridge and taken it with them, and the Russians had no such technology—they were using horses to haul their gun-carriages. Russian soldiers built the footbridge; the Germans had to deliver the wood and do the dirty work.

The footbridge served the men going back and forth across the river—women considered it too dangerous, and children were expressly forbidden to set foot on it, according to a posted decree. One month later a ferry was added, built by the three local carpenters and workers in the sawmill; it could even transport horse carriages across the river. Construction of the wooden bridge began that same June, and was completed shortly before winter. Not three months later it was damaged by river ice and had to be closed for repairs for two weeks in the spring. One of the ice deflectors had shifted a few inches, and the inspectors discovered some splintered beams and bent iron blades where the deflector joined the bridge piling. The deflectors were then bolted to the base of the bridge, and concrete and iron stakes were sunk in the river to support the icebreakers and pilings.

This construction lasted a few years, as there was little flood water and the ice usually broke up by the time it got to us. But eight years after the wooden bridge was constructed, just months after we had watched the detoured traffic rumbling across it, the water rose to a record high, and the river carried enormous ice floes downstream, destroying three of the five pilings, so that the bridge had to be closed once again. In May they began the demolition, and workers from the sawmill dismantled the wooden construction. Huge stacks of boards and piles of blackened, tar-soaked planks appeared along the riverbank, and every week a few friends and I would steal wood from the unguarded storage site and cart it home in a wheelbarrow. There was an immense amount of wood, but since half the town was fetching firewood for the winter, they finally put up a fence, and when that proved insufficient for stopping the thefts, employed a night watchman with a dog. Even so, by the end of May all that was left were the man-sized planks that were too heavy and unwieldy to haul without a wagon or a hoist.

That same May they began building the new stone bridge, a few yards away from the earlier provisional bridge, on the site of the original bridge—the one that had been blown up. The remnants of the first stone bridge, which had jutted out of the water during all these years, defying flood and floe, were either cleared away or used in the new bridge. The bridge builders came from Leipzig. Most of them arrived by bus every morning and left in the evening; two men slept over during the week in a construction trailer that had been set up directly along the river, where they could heat water and spend the night.

So instead of meeting up in the market square as usual, once again we ran down to the river late in the afternoon, since the new bridge brought some variety to our lives. We watched the men work on the foundations until twilight, then climb on the bus that took them home, unwashed and in their dirty clothes. After that we would watch the two men who lived on site eat their supper, play cards, and drink beer in front of the trailer where they slept, while tending a small wood fire in an iron grating. Now and then they'd call out to us to get lost or send our sisters, and then we'd answer them, but mostly we just sat on the stack of lumber or the hewn blocks of stone near the construction truck, talking among ourselves as we did at the market square, while lazily taking in the scene.

In June we were invaded by potato beetles. The half-inch-long yellow-orange bugs buzzed into town and covered the streets, sidewalks, and roofs. Carpets of their black-striped wing cases descended from the buildings, and all the sandy paths and asphalt streets were covered with a thin, yellowish mush of squashed beetles. The town had never seen these disgusting bugs and larvae until after the war; since then they came every year in May and June, covering the crops in the fields surrounding the city. The plants had huge holes in the leaves where the beetles had eaten, and the schoolchildren were given several days off to pick the pests off the leaves and put them in jars to take to a collection point, where they were paid a penny for every ten bugs or larvae. Despite this the bugs destroyed whole fields early every summer, leaving the potatoes to rot in the ground, and all that could be done was till them back into the soil. Since no one could remember seeing them before the end of the war, people in town decided that they had come with the Allied warplanes, and had been deliberately released all over our country. They said the Americans had used them as a weapon against the German Reich to spark a famine that would force the Wehrmacht to surrender sooner. Wherever they came from, they hadn't missed a single year since the war, and nothing could stop the defoliation and inevitable damage to the harvest—not the gigantic tank trucks equipped with spray arms twenty yards long that soaked the sprouts with pesticides, nor the hordes of schoolchildren who happily traipsed up and down the fields as if on a school outing, surely causing more harm than good, and who welcomed the potato beetles as they would an excessively hot summer day, when we were all allowed to go home after third period, or those special cold days when the coal cellar was picked clean and the principal could do nothing but wait for a new delivery. Up to now, however, the bugs had never ventured into town: they had always camped in the fields outside the old town wall, encircling the city like a besieging army.

But around the end of June, after the beetles had already fallen on the fields, new legions came and began attacking the town. They sat jammed together on the trees, they crawled across the streets and along the walls, and you could no longer tell the colors of the flowers in the beds, so completely were they covered by the black-and-yellow-striped bugs. Housewives picked the bugs off their garden plants day after day, then trampled them or burned them, only to look out their windows the following morning and resign themselves to the fact that their carefully and lovingly tended flowers and shrubs were again covered with the yellow-and-black swarms. The beetles stuck to the leaves in dense ranks, seemingly motionless. After they had eaten and nothing was left of the leaf except a few large holes, they dropped to the ground, where they lay still for hours before flying off to their next feeding place—the ones that didn't get trampled, at least. It was like an invasion. Time and again we would hear a woman or a small child cry out when a beetle landed in their hair or on their face, or if they accidentally squashed one with their bare hands and the disgusting slime got on their skin. The municipal administration posted notices on the town's four kiosks and on telephone poles, informing citizens of the proper course of action. But within three days the notices were no longer legible. Beetles had landed on the announcements and had been squashed there, so that we could no longer read the pointless suggestions of the mayor, who held forth on hygiene and vigilance but in fact had no idea what to do about the plague.

The bridge builders cursed all day long. They threatened to stop work and go home. They were scared of the beetles, afraid they might carry some disease. We laughed at them and told them the bugs were harmless, dumb, and sluggish and did nothing but eat leaves, so there was no reason to be afraid of them. The beetles would destroy half the harvest—not that the bridge builders cared about that—but otherwise they weren't the least bit dangerous. One of the workers listened to me skeptically, then jumped to his feet and started stomping on the sandy ground in front of him, crushing the dead beetles with his heavy work shoes. We doubled over laughing.

I put two beetles on my palm and poked them with a fir needle to get them to fight each other, but they were so frightened they wouldn't budge, so I flipped them into the air.

"They're actually very nutritious," Bernhard suddenly chimed in, "lots of vitamins and proteins."

"What are you talking about, boy?" said one of the workers.

"You can eat those beetles. They're not bad fried. A little like chicken. You dust them in flour, fry them in oil, and add a little salt and pepper. Make a nice meal."

I looked at Bernhard but he kept a straight face, and I wasn't sure whether he was serious or if he was trying to make fun of the workers.

"That's the most disgusting thing I've ever heard," said another one, shaking his head. "I just can't believe it."

"He's just trying to pull your leg, Karl."

"It's the honest-to-God truth. Try it some time. You'll be thankful for the tip."

"Get the hell out of here, you little toad. Trying to pull something on an old man. Beat it."

"It's true. Believe me. Fry them up a bit with a little salt and pepper, and that's it. They're best if they're still alive when they go in the pan. Then they're especially crispy."

"Get out of here, you little bastard, before I give you a taste of something else. What a jackass. That boy deserves a good hiding."

We moved on, because even though most of the men were laughing, one was so worked up we weren't sure he wouldn't start using his fists. A boy in our group asked Bernhard if he really would eat the beetles and I told him to shut his mouth. We walked up to the road and watched the workers from there. I stood next to Bernhard and nodded to him.

"Nice job."

All he said was: "What a bunch of idiots. Scared of a little bug. Like girls, or babies."

"They're from the city, that's all. They don't know about things like that."

"Still. How can you be so dumb?"

"Maybe they'll try your recipe."

"They're probably dumb enough. Maybe we should make them a little surprise."

"What do you mean, Bernhard?"

"I don't know. Something with the pretty little beetles."

He grinned and squinted.

"What, for example?"

"Let's think about it. We're bound to come up with a nice surprise for them." He gestured loosely toward the construction site.

Then he said quietly, "Whatever we come up with we should do just the two of us. In case there's trouble—know what I mean?"

I nodded. We looked over at the site one more time and thought about what we might do while the others kept talking about the fried potato-beetle.

The next day we still didn't know what we wanted to do, but there were fewer beetles. The town was full of the sticky yellow goo, but there were only a few bugs on the chewed-up leaves in the gardens. Maybe they had overeaten, or else run out of food. Or maybe the army of beetles had moved on to lay siege to other towns and villages.

Meanwhile we were excited about something else. The whole town was glued to their radios, trying to make out what they could through the hissing and bleeping used to jam the forbidden stations. Stalin's organs—as we called the jamming—

were again in full force. In Berlin there was some commotion in the streets, but only the western stations reported that. They talked about a strike spreading through the entire country. Our newspapers said nothing about it, and in town everything was quiet; in any case, there were no more people on the streets than usual, and they weren't striking but shopping or walking. At school we discussed the rumors, and at home my parents spent every minute in front of the radio, their ears pressed against the material stretched over the round speaker hole, listening to the rasping and whistling. Each time they made out a few words, they repeated them, and then went back to listening. None of it interested me; I found it amusing the way they sat there in front of the console, listening with their eyes wide open. Naturally, playing records was out; everyone had to be absolutely quiet so they wouldn't miss a word.

I had arranged to meet Bernhard in the afternoon. Since the bugs were getting scarce we had to act quickly. That morning we had visited the construction site and taken an empty round carton that had been filled with the coarse-grained soap powder the workers used to clean the heavy grease from their hands in the river. We didn't know how we might use it; we had just found it and tucked it away, like we did with everything we thought might come in handy. When I met Bernhard after school, we collected enough potato beetles in the gardens of the health resort to fill the stinky old carton. Bernhard stuck it under his jacket, and we went to the river. We still didn't know what we were going to do with the carton and the bugs. The only things we could think of were the sort of dumb pranks little children do, but we wanted to do something that would get the workers really steamed up.

When we reached the green we suddenly saw a dozen workers heading toward the market. They were dressed in their work clothes, a few were wearing caps or broad-rimmed hats, and they all had their tool belts buckled on and were carrying hammers. They were talking excitedly among themselves and didn't even notice us, although they nearly ran us over. I don't even think they saw us. Something important was going on that they were very preoccupied with. Bernhard looked at me; we realized right away that for the next hour no one would be bothering us at the construction site.

We were right: none of the workers was there, and no children, either. We had free range of the place and could rummage through what we wanted. The crane had been shut down; the door to its cab rattled when we shook it but wouldn't open. Nor could we get inside the crew car where the two workers spent the night. I had Bernhard hand me the carton with the beetles and went to the wooden bench at the riverbank, where I found some old rags, a dirty towel, and a can of soap. Suddenly Bernhard called me over. He was standing by a truck with a large wooden structure mounted on the bed where the workers kept their tools. When I looked up at Bernhard he laughed, reached for the handle to the makeshift shed, and opened it. I looked around: no one was in sight, and I raced over.

"How did you get it unlocked?"

"They left it open. These idiots."

We looked all around before going in. Instead of lowering the wooden stepladder, we jumped onto the truck and climbed into the shed. Inside was dark; the only window had been blocked with a board, so we had to leave the door cracked in order to see. To the right was a shelf with large drawers containing nuts and bolts. Over that, hanging from leather loops, were the tools: wrenches, nippers, trowels, screwdrivers, pipe wrenches, mallets, crimping tools, metal shears, and saws and planes of various sizes. In one corner we found a whole mountain of cast-iron couplings. To the left, in front of the blocked window, was a workbench with some smaller parts scattered on top and a blowtorch that was practically new.

Bernhard and I looked at each other, then each went about inspecting the treasure in front of us. It was Bernhard who began making a pile of the tools. When I saw what he was doing, I snatched a few for myself.

"Don't take so much," I told him, as his pile grew bigger and bigger. "You won't be able to carry all that. And we can't come back a second time."

"I know," he replied, laying a miter square on his pile.

Suddenly he whistled through his teeth. I glanced up; he went to the door and looked around. Then he reached under the workbench and pulled out a rope hoist with an electric winch.

"That's it," is all he said.

"You can't get that out. It's too heavy. And how do you intend to take it through town without anyone seeing?"

"This is what I need. The rest doesn't interest me at all."

"When they see it's gone they'll turn the whole town upside down. Let's only take a few small things they won't miss right away. They'll just look around and order some new ones. But an electric motor isn't something they're going to give up that easily."

"And they shouldn't, either. I want to teach them a lesson they won't forget. I'll hide the thing and won't get it until they're finished with the bridge and the workers have left. After a few months nobody will be looking for the motor."

"No. Forget it. Take the other things and let's get out of here."

I stuffed my pockets full and tucked the blowtorch under my arm, beneath my jacket. I jumped out of the truck and tried walking a few steps. The unwieldy device pressed against my ribs, but I could walk with it, and nothing rattled in my pockets. When I turned around, Bernhard was standing outside the truck, struggling with the winch. He called over for me to help; I shook my head and stayed where I was. Without saying another word, he hoisted the motor on his back and held the suspension in his hands. He left the cable inside the shed. Shaking my head, I started off. I could hear Bernhard panting behind me. When I reached the embankment, I waited until he caught up to me with the motor.

"And what now? Where do you plan to put the thing? Best if you'd toss it down the embankment and we disappear."

Bernhard again heaved the motor onto his back and set off toward the floodplain. My guess was he wanted to hide it in Korsitzke's stretch of forest. I followed because I wanted to find out what he was planning. Besides, I didn't want to go straight back into town; I didn't want to run into the workers, who would be returning to the site sooner or later. After we'd gone a couple hundred yards, Bernhard lay the motor in the grass. I thought he was taking a break. When I approached him he said that one of us had to go back to fetch the box with the potato beetles. Otherwise the workers would know who had looted the shed in their absence. I had no desire to return to the construction site, though I really didn't want to stay there next to the rope hoist, waiting for Bernhard, either.

"All right, why don't you do it," I finally said. "I'll keep an eye on things here."

Half an hour later he came back and said everything was taken care of and I didn't have to worry about a thing.

"I'm not worried," I answered. "It's just that you're a little crazy."

Bernhard looked at me, enraged. For a moment I thought he was going to hit me, but then he took the motor and went on. He hid it in the roots of a toppled tree, then strewed leaves and broken branches on top. Of course anyone who did come this way was bound to see the motor. Bernhard intended to come back at night and fetch it home. After that we took a long detour back into town through the allotment plots, then by way of the train station. Two policemen we'd never seen before were standing in front of the post office. Just to be safe we crossed the street, but they called us over anyway. The policemen wanted to know what I was carrying under my jacket. I took out the blowtorch and showed it to them. One of them asked what it was and why I was hauling it around. I explained that I was building a rabbit cage. Then he wanted to see what I had in my pockets, and I had to unpack everything and lay it on the sidewalk. As I took one tool after the other out of my pocket and put it on the sidewalk, I looked at Bernhard. He appeared completely calm and looked with seeming indifference at the policemen. When they asked him to empty his pockets, he acted bored as he showed them that he didn't have anything.

"And where did you steal all this?" the policeman right in front of me asked as he poked around the tools with the toe of his shoe.

"It all belongs to my father. I need it for the rabbit cage."

The policeman glanced at his colleague, who waved his hand in disdain.

"Fine, get lost. But let me give you a good piece of advice: don't let us see you on the streets again today. If I catch you two again I'm taking you in. Is that clear?"

I nodded, pocketed the tools, and stuck the blowtorch back under my arm. The policemen didn't pay us any more attention, and we hurried on our way.

"If one of the workers had come by and seen that . . ." was all Bernhard said.

"Yes," I said. "Then it would all be over. And if you had dragged that winch of yours along—my God."

"There's another policeman. What's going on today?"

"Let's go back along the moat and past the old gas plant."

"I don't have anything on me. Nobody can do anything to me."

"Okay, come on."

Something was going on in town; there were policemen I'd never seen before, and everybody seemed restless—in a hurry, nobody paid any attention to us, which was fine with me. I was extremely glad the police didn't stop us again, because I now regretted our having taken the tools. I really couldn't use them, and if Father discovered them he'd ask some questions that I wouldn't know how to answer, at least not to his satisfaction. At Brunnenstrasse, Bernhard and I went our separate ways.

When I got home nobody was there. I took the tools to my room and hid them in my wardrobe. Then I went back into town. On my way I again sensed the strange mood. As if something deep inside the city machinery was slowly vibrating with motion. Something was different: people walked differently, they talked differently, and I had the feeling I'd missed something. But everyone was heading toward the market square, so I just followed the crowd. On Kirchstrasse I met three boys from my class. I asked them what was going on and they told me there was a strike, that nobody was working, and everyone was gathered at the market square.

"And the police?" I asked.

"There's no sign of them at the market. And the Rathaus is closed. A few people tried to get in, but the large door is blocked up good and proper. Either the administration has taken off or else they've barricaded themselves inside."

"A strike? That's illegal."

"Right. Anyway, the only ones striking are the men from the machine works and the bridge builders from out of town. The others are just standing around, gawking."

"And why are you leaving?"

"I was there for three whole hours. Nothing's going to happen, and I have better things to do than stand around all day, so I'm taking off."

"That's incredible—a strike. I never thought I'd see anything like that in a dung heap like ours."

"I was surprised, too. But it's pretty boring. Anyway, I'm going. So see you tomorrow."

"Are we having school tomorrow?"

"I'm not sure. Why? Are you planning to go on strike yourself, Koller?"

"If everybody strikes, then there's no school."

"My father says that they'll arrest a few people this evening and during the night and then by tomorrow the whole thing will have blown over."

"Anybody want to come along to the market square?"

"Not really."

"I have to get home. I don't want any trouble from my parents."

We said good-bye with a casual wave.

Several men were assembled at the market square next to the large whitewashed wooden stand, where an enormous plywood peace dove lorded over the square, surrounded by three flags that were kept up all year long. The men were talking among themselves. A number of people had gathered on the sidewalks around the square to watch—and that was all that could be seen of the strike. I took a slow turn around the square. Three people I knew spoke to me, telling me to get home as fast as I could, that it was no place for children. I nodded and kept an eye out for either of my parents or a teacher, but I didn't see any of them. I was disappointed. I knew strikes from the movies, or from newsreels, and there were always thousands of people marching wildly through the streets, singing songs and shouting slogans, waving banners or posters. Here there were no more than thirty people, almost all men, and no one was shouting anything or singing songs—it really was boring. After half an hour, three of the men from the bridge boosted one another onto the stand and pulled down the flags and threw them into the street. That happened with hardly a word, and nobody shouted or cheered the way they had in the movies. Now and then you could see somebody peering through a window: the curtains were pulled back a bit and you could make out a nose and a pair of eyes that watched the goings-on for a few minutes. I also saw a few heads appear in the windows on the upper story of the town hall and then disappear before they were discovered by the crowd below. Once the flags were tossed on the street and covered with dirt, things quieted down again; everybody simply stood around and waited, the way they did every other day.

Half an hour later nothing had happened, so I strolled very slowly and calmly straight across the square, right past the bridge builders, who formed the largest group around the peace dove. They cast a brief glance in my direction but didn't pay any more attention to me, so that I was able to stand there a few minutes, listening. They weren't talking very loudly; they were agitated, and clearly at a loss as to what to do next or how long they should stay. One of them suggested going back to work at the bridge, but the majority halfheartedly rejected that proposal. The men didn't have a leader; they needed someone who knew what to do, someone they could follow, like I had seen in the movies. One of them shoved me and told me to get lost and run on home, this wasn't child's play. I grinned at him. If you only knew, I thought, wouldn't you ever be surprised, you asshole. When you get back to your stupid truck you'll be in for a sight, you'll never forget this dumb strike, it'll cost you, my friend, and I bet they'll make you pay for everything we took, Bernhard was right to take as much as possible, I'd like to be there when you get back, I'd like to see your stupid face then, this isn't child's play, you don't know how right you are.

I walked on slowly to the pharmacy, pushing my way through the people who were standing on the sidewalk watching the men on the square and talking. Four boys from my class were hanging around the old gas station, of which the only thing left was a rusty old pump—the hose had been removed, and the small booth where the leaseholder sat had been carried off piece by piece so the stones could be used for other construction. We greeted one another with a nod of the head.

"Hi."

"You just getting here? Where were you?"

"At home."

"There's something going on here. A strike. Neat, huh?"

"It's actually pretty boring."

"Still, it's illegal. And they say all hell's broke loose in Berlin."

"Maybe something will happen here."

"I don't think so. The police haven't even shown up."

"I'll bet they're afraid. They're scared to death they might get hammered."

"No, I've seen them."

"Where?"

"And there are more of them than you think. They've brought in reinforcements from all around the area."

"So where are they? Where'd you see them?"

"Around the train station and outside the post office. My guess is they're stationed all around the market square."

"They can't do anything."

"Just wait. You want to bet? What are you willing to put up?"

"I don't know, I think I better be going now."

Then Bernhard appeared. He had come down the Old Leipzig Road, glanced around the square, and then steered straight for us.

"What are you doing here?"

My school friends gave Bernhard an annoyed look, but he didn't respond. He turned to me with a pathetic look—as if I should answer the question, as if I could tell them why he was here, why he was hanging out with us, why no one else wanted to spend time with him, and why he had been born into this world in the first place.

"Leave him alone," I said as the silence grew hostile. "He's all right."

Two of the boys took off, and we waited with Karl and Freddie and the others for something to happen. At one point Freddie said that the only people standing around the memorial were locals and the bridge builders, that there wasn't a single refugee, even though enough of them had made themselves at home here. I grabbed him by his lapels and asked what he meant by that.

"Nothing," he said. "I was just making an observation."

"I see," I said. "An observation. You better keep your observations to yourself. Or else I might get angry, understand?"

"If the shoe fits, put it on," he answered, freeing himself.

"That's exactly right," I said, and stared him down until he couldn't stand it anymore and turned his head away.

"This is boring. Let's go," he said to Karl, and together they went off.

We didn't say anything, just looked at each other a moment and then watched them leave. The square was very quiet, despite the workers who had assembled there.

"I have an idea, Koller," said Bernhard.

"An idea. What is it?"

"Come on. Let's walk over to the bridge builders."

"Why?"

"I just want to tip them off that the town is full of police. That they better get back to the bridge."

"That's not a good idea. I mean, if we're standing here and watching, nobody can get on our case. But if we go over there, that's a different story. If someone from school sees us, and they will, then you better be ready for what happens."

"We're not striking, Koller. We're just watching. All we're doing is crossing the square, that's not illegal. Come on."

He ambled slowly across the square, over to where the workers were standing next to the wooden memorial with the flags, and I followed. The workers from town were bunched together in smaller groups. I knew a few of them and said hello. They told us to leave and go home. The bridge builders were standing in front of the town hall: twelve men in work jackets and dirty, heavy corduroys, with tool belts made of leather or cloth and carrying hammers. Two men who looked bored turned in our direction but didn't say anything. Bernhard spoke to one of them.

"Excuse me."

"What do you want, boy?"

"I wanted to tell you that there are masses of police in town. At least fifty."

"Did you see them?"

"Yes. At the train station. And the post office. The road out to the field hands' barracks. They're everywhere."

"We don't give a shit about the bulls."

"I heard they were planning to go to the river. To the bridge."

"So?"

"Well, that's what one of them said. Two or three of you should go there and check on them."

"They won't find many of us there, boy. It's good you told us, now take off. This isn't for children."

The two workers who had spoken with us turned away; our communication really didn't seem to interest them. Why Bernhard wanted to tell them that was beyond me. I knew it was all a lie; he hadn't heard the police say anything like that. Bernhard gave me a satisfied grin. Then one of the men turned to us and repeated that we should disappear. We moved on, but slowly, very slowly: nobody should think they could send us away like that.

"What was all that about?" I asked him. "Why did you tell them that the police are headed for the bridge?" Then I corrected myself and said: "The bulls."

That's what the worker had called the policemen. I didn't know the expression, but I liked it, even if I had no idea where it came from. I liked the way you could say it. I had respect for real bulls—huge beasts that they are—everybody did, but the way the worker had said it, it sounded like they were the last thing anyone had to fear.

"Think about it. If they go back and find our little surprise, who are they going to blame?"

"You don't think they'll . . ."

"Anyway, they won't figure it was us."

For the next half hour nothing happened on the market square. A few of the workers went off and came back with an ax and a crowbar. They began tearing apart the white box with the peace dove, where the flags had been flying earlier. The slats splintered at the first blow, and within a few minutes the entire wooden structure was lying on the pavement. Little remained of the peace dove. You could make out one of the painted eyes and the red beak in the pile of broken wood. For the first time I saw the gray, rectangular monument that had been concealed under the big box, so I went closer. It was a memorial for soldiers who died in the world war—the first one, as was clear from the dates of death below the names. You could see bullet holes on all four sides of the monument, and on the top was what appeared to be the remains of an iron cross, but it was too damaged to say for sure. The men who had destroyed the box seemed pleased with their work; they laughed and pointed to the memorial and the broken wooden pieces lying beside it. Then the square quieted down again, as everyone looked at the monument that had been hidden since the end of the war. Suddenly I felt a hand on my shoulder; I turned around and there was Herr Frieder, who worked with my father and sometimes stopped by to take Father to work or to play skittles in the evening.

"Come on, boy, let's go now," he said.

I shook my head and freed myself from his grip.

"Come on," he said again. "The party's over. From here on out it'll be unpleasant."

He said it so quietly and so forcefully that I started feeling uneasy and looked over at Bernhard.

"It's always best to know when it's over. Come on."

I told Bernhard I had to leave. He just nodded. On our way home, Herr Frieder told me I shouldn't kid myself that they'd just stand by and let all this happen. They would deal with anybody who had taken any part in the goings-on at the market, one after the other, and if that didn't satisfy them they would turn to the spectators, including the ones who hadn't done anything, I could bank on that, and I should be grateful that he took me away, and my buddy had better leave as well. I just nodded. I was eager to know who he meant by "they"—the police or the people in the town hall or some people from outside. When I asked him he said he was sure I could guess who he meant.

Father and Mother were already home when I arrived and both were listening to the radio. They asked where I'd been and forbade me from going to the market square for the next several days. I was to come straight home after school, and they would check to make sure I did. Then they both went back to listening and tried to understand the agitated voice of the broadcaster that was barely audible through the crackles and scratches of the jamming station. I went to my room, took the blowtorch and the tools out of the wardrobe, and tested each one. When I heard steps in the hall I shoved them all under my bed and acted as if I were reading a book.

It was dumb to break into the truck and take the tools, since I really had no use for them. Even worse was the fact that I couldn't allow them to be discovered or there would be a huge row. I would have gladly given them all to my father, but I didn't know how to manage that. I couldn't simply take them into our small toolshed and hide them among his tools. Father would discover them soon enough and know that I had put them there. Nor could I give them to him. The tools were far too expensive—I couldn't tell him I'd bought them; and besides, they were all used. Nor could I think of any story believable enough to tell Father without arousing his suspicions; I was sure he'd grill me for as long as it took until I came out with the truth. And then who knows what might happen; even if Father decided to keep the tools, I would be in for a juicy thrashing. I told myself that probably the best thing to do would be to get rid of them at the first opportunity, to dump them in a ditch somewhere. Maybe the bridge workers would pass by, discover the tools, and take them back into their shed. That would be best, and no one would be any the wiser.

The next morning during recess I asked Bernhard if he had gone to retrieve his hoist and winch. He nodded. "And what are you going to do with it?"

He grinned and shrugged his shoulders.

"That stuff can get you in hot water, my friend."

"No, things will calm down. Let's just wait and see."

"What will we see? The truth is, I really don't need those things. That was a dumb idea you had."

"People always need tools. Tools are like gold."

"Well, as far as I'm concerned you can have my gold. I don't need it."

"Really?"

"There's no place for me to stash it."

"I could use those tools if you don't want them."

"And if somebody asks you where you got them? What are you going to do if your father asks?"

"Oh, I'll think of something. So you'll give them to me if you don't need them, agreed?"

"I'll think about it."

I left him and joined my classmates, who were talking about the strike and the Russian tank that had arrived during the night and was positioned on the square. After school we all wanted to go see it.

Three days later the whole incident had blown over. The tank drove off and people went back to work as before. Our teacher set aside an hour for current events, where we were supposed to discuss what had happened, but none of us had anything to say. We listened in silence to the teacher as he repeated what was in the newspaper. When he asked if any of us wanted to comment or had any problems, no one raised his hand, and the teacher seemed satisfied. Then he talked about the report cards we were getting in two weeks, and that worried us more, since they were our final grades for graduation, and in order to start our apprenticeships we had to finish school with passing marks. A little while later I heard that a few people in our town had been arrested—a woman and five workers—I didn't know any of them.

Two months later the paper reported on a trial in the district seat. Three of the workers building the new bridge were sentenced to two years in prison, and a fourth received three years for disparaging the police. He had insisted at his trial that policemen had stolen tools from his worksite while the workers were at the market square. He claimed he'd been tipped off by an eyewitness, but he couldn't name this witness, and so the accusation went nowhere, or rather was turned against him. By leaving the site he had enabled the theft, and the fact that he would direct such groundless accusations against the very forces who in those days were risking their lives and well-being to protect the socialist order was a sign of his outright depravity and hostile attitude. All four workers were ordered not only to pay the cost of the trial but also to cover the cost of the stolen tools.

The following September, when I happened to run into Bernhard on the street, I mentioned the article to him. He grinned and said, "What an idiot. How could he tell that kind of garbage to the court?"

"We were lucky. Imagine if he'd been able to give our names during the trial."

"What do you mean? Did you see any policeman stealing anything? Did you tell anyone that you did? I didn't. I would have denied everything—and I would have been telling the truth, too."

"Still, that poor bastard—if he ever gets his hands on us we'll be in for it."

"I don't know anything. And if the fool wants to come after me, he'll wind up with another trial. Calm down."

"I'm plenty calm." I was mad that Bernhard, who was still in school, was talking to me as if I were an imbecile or a small child.

"All right," said Bernhard, "so . . . what about the tools? Did you think it over?"

I shook my head, turned around, and went off without saying a word. I didn't want to have anything to do with him, and since I was already doing my apprenticeship I seldom saw him and finally lost sight of him altogether. I was working in Herr Merkel's metal shop, and once a week I rode into the district seat for vocational school. I didn't have any time to sit around and chat or hatch childish schemes.

The shop was tough; Merkel really worked his apprentices hard. At seven on the dot we had to be at work, dressed and ready to go, and then it was nonstop until four-thirty in the afternoon. There were two breaks but you couldn't extend them or Merkel would start yelling right away that we would ruin him and he'd have to teach us not to twiddle our thumbs. We did everything by hand. Only the journeymen were allowed to use the electric machines, so we had to drill and grind and deburr with Stone Age tools at least a hundred years old. We also had to haul a lot of heavy equipment. We had to lift cast-metal pieces that weighed a good hundred pounds and clamp them down. The shop had two cable hoists with electric motors, but Merkel didn't like our fiddling with them. He begrudged us the time it took to set up the hoist and carefully secure the piece and then steer it to a workbench or else store it along the wall. Merkel made all the apprentices carry the heavy objects themselves. This isn't summer vacation, he would say, we were training with him to develop our minds—and our muscles. Anyone who felt they were too good for the work or didn't want to get dirty should feel free to tell him and he'd give them a hand. The journeymen, who always used a hoist whenever they had to transport something substantial, would burst out laughing when they heard this, while we stood in the shop hall, our heads bowed, dragging pieces so heavy they brought sweat to our foreheads and tears to our eyes. The one good thing about Merkel was the fact that he treated everyone the same and didn't play favorites: he was equally surly and rude to everybody, but you could learn something, and that's what I was there for, so I never complained. And who could I have complained to? You can't get anywhere unless you put in your time, my father told me, and I should bear that in mind. In any case, after the apprenticeship I didn't plan on staying at Merkel's. I wanted to try to find work as an auto mechanic, since that seemed to have good prospects and I knew my way around cars.

The next I heard of Bernhard was this business with the collective that the whole town was talking about. I didn't learn about it firsthand, since I was out of town at the time on a large job: we were working on a steel scaffold at a gas plant and living onsite in a shed like the one the bridge builders used back then.

What they told me about Bernhard's role surprised me. I knew he had left school and started work as an apprentice somewhere. I assumed that sooner or later he intended to take over the shop from his father—a one-armed carpenter. The man must have been very skilled—I couldn't have even hammered a nail properly with one hand. I had no idea how Bernhard might have suddenly changed so much; it sounded as if he were a true believer—a party functionary or something like that. We had hardly talked about politics at school, at least not in the schoolyard, and certainly not during our free time. What was said in class didn't count; we simply repeated what was expected, and if someone wanted to show off for the teacher, all it took was an ironic remark after class and that was that. I assumed that the teachers told us what they had to, and that we should give them the desired answers so that nobody would be bothered. Of course in every class there were a couple students who saw the whole thing differently, who believed the official opinion and the teachers' explanations, and could go on for hours. Somehow I never had anything to do with them, and none of them were in my group. Naturally there were also a few who didn't agree with everything and refused to keep their mouths shut and insisted on contradicting the teachers. To this day I don't know why they did that; anybody could have seen it would bring nothing but trouble, but they kept on picking arguments with the teachers. For everybody else that meant thirty minutes or even a whole hour with no instruction during which we all had to pretend to be listening. Sooner or later it inevitably reached a point where the debater had to give in, or at least quit his line of reasoning lest he be exposed as a hostile element. The pupil in question would sit on his bench, flushed from exertion, while the teacher wrote something in the register, and then the lesson would continue. Then everybody was satisfied; the teacher had asserted himself and had the last word, and he could persuade himself that he had convinced the pupil, we had received an unexpected free period, so to speak, and the pupil who had argued with the teacher was visibly proud. Presumably he thought we would admire his courage; I found it idiotic. Swallowing his opinion wouldn't have made him choke, and he would have had one less bad mark on his record that he was bound to regret sooner or later. In any case, the teachers could tell me the stupidest nonsense, I never contradicted them, and I don't think I did that out of cowardice. All that political garbage simply didn't interest me, and none of the teachers, especially not the ones intent on teaching us political values, was so important to me that I would go to the trouble of contradicting him. In one ear and out the other was my approach back then, and that's how it is today, and I think it's served me well. Even if my final transcript wasn't exactly stellar, at least it wasn't marred by the sort of political comments that would make an employer hesitate to take me on as an apprentice.

I know that Bernhard never stuck out politically in school, either. As far as my friends and I were concerned—and I'm sure this applied to Bernhard's pals as well—you did what you had to do to make it through. At least I never heard that he thought otherwise—not from him or anyone else. The news that Bernhard had suddenly turned political and was putting on such a show, as if he really was somebody, surprised me. Presumably some people wanted to get ahead and so they joined the party—but I just couldn't see what Bernhard stood to gain. After all, he wanted to be a carpenter. You didn't have to talk like a newspaper for that; but maybe he had an entirely different career in mind and wanted to call attention to himself. In any case, he certainly distinguished himself when they were recruiting the farmers for the collective. Occasionally the farmers would latch their gates and not let the agitators onto their property: then the recruiters would stand for hours in front of their house and call the farmer's name over and over. They even showed up in the villages in vans equipped with loudspeakers, which they parked in front of the farmsteads, and would play very loud music for hours on end, interrupting it occasionally to demand that the farmer open the gate, that he not stand in the way of progress, and that he join the collective. In our town they didn't use any loudspeakers. The agitators would gather outside the door or the gate and knock vigorously from time to time. Some farmers opened up after a short while because they were embarrassed by the crowd in front of their home. Others stubbornly refused to open; but they, too, had to give up eventually when they needed to take care of the animals that were out to pasture, or had to drive the tractor out of the yard to tend their fields. The agitators would then stop them and tangle them up in a conversation, or pester them until they scarcely had any other choice but to sign the application to join. Nonetheless a few farmers still refused; they planned to go on working on their own, without giving up their property, but the state made it difficult for them: they received less seed and fertilizer, and often had to wait very long for equipment. Sooner or later they all gave up. A few joined the collective;

others dropped everything and fled to the West, to start over from scratch.

There were a few people in town who claimed the farmers were being terrorized, but no one said that out loud or in public. Most of the townspeople disapproved of what was happening, but they kept their mouth shut so as not to stick out and get into trouble themselves. They generally stayed away from the agitators, whom they held in low regard at best, although this, too, was never stated openly, only hinted at—such things could be communicated with few words.

Of course in Bernhard's case people were particularly indignant, and so they were more outspoken, since they had nothing to fear from him. They told him what they thought right to his face: that he was a refugee child, from whom people expected gratitude and not impertinence. And the fact that he picketed the very farmer who had first sheltered him and his family was particularly outrageous. During this period I only saw him a single time; he said hello, and I just nodded and went my way.

After my apprenticeship I left home and moved to Naumburg. I had been hired on there in a shop that mostly repaired farm equipment, but also some passenger cars as well. I liked the work and got along well with the boss and the other workers, so I made arrangements to stay in the town. With a little luck I even managed to wangle my own apartment. One of our clients worked for the housing office. On one of my many visits there to inquire about an apartment, I was walking down a corridor when a door suddenly opened. I glanced inside and saw our client sitting at a desk. The nameplate listed him as the head of the residential bureau. I waited for his guest to leave, then quickly stepped inside, held out my hand, and asked how his car was doing. He didn't recognize me right away, but then he was very pleased to see me, asked me to sit down, and even offered me coffee. I told him what I was doing at the housing office; he nodded and jotted something down. Then I told him my name, and he promised to call, which he did just one week later. When I went in to see him again he gave me an inspection form for a two-room apartment. It was nicely constructed, and I liked the location, so I immediately accepted and moved in the next week. Everything was going well for me, and I might have stayed in Naumburg my whole life and never seen Bernhard again. But then there was this whole mess with Gitti, and in the end I had no choice but to give up my job and the apartment and move out of town.

I met Gitti my very first week. It was a Saturday afternoon; I was on my own, taking a walk to look around. Outside the Golden Lion, I heard dance music coming from the banquet hall—a large wooden room, really, that you reached by crossing the dining area. I went inside; three old men were sitting at a table, playing skat. A hallway next to the bar led past the toilets to the banquet room. A little old man with a crippled hand was sitting behind the door of the men's room, selling tickets for the banquet room. I stood next to him and tried to get a glimpse inside. A three-man band was playing old hits; the guitarist was standing at a microphone, singing. As far as I could tell, the guests were mostly older; I couldn't see any young people on the dance floor. I asked the man how much a ticket cost and how long they would be playing. He said it cost three marks and that they'd play until six. I looked at the clock and said that that was very expensive for just an hour's worth of music. He simply repeated that it cost three marks, and I went to the bathroom. When I came back there were three girls standing there haggling with the man over the price, but he wouldn't budge. Finally they told him off and left. I followed them. One of the girls had caught my eye; she had very short hair and a strong nose and had been the spokeswoman for the group. The girls stood outside the Golden Lion. I lit a cigarette, waiting to see what would happen next. When they parted company I went up to the girl with the short hair and spoke to her. She said pertly that she was in a hurry, but then she let me walk her home, and in the end she agreed to meet with me the next day—a Sunday.

At two I was standing outside Gitti's house, waiting for her to come down. When she opened the door she told me I should come up for a moment. On the stairs I asked if her parents had gone out and if she was by herself; she shook her head and told me I should say hello to her mother.

"But why, for heaven's sake?" I asked.

"Oh, come on. It'll just take a second and then we can go."

Her parents were sitting in the living room, listening to the radio and reading the paper. When we entered and Gitti introduced me, both her parents looked up and nodded. They didn't offer to shake hands or pay any special attention to me. I didn't have the impression that her parents had asked to meet me.

"So what was that about?" I asked Gitti, once we were finally outside.

"They wanted to see you."

"It didn't seem that way to me."

"Don't worry about it. They're just funny like that."

"I had the feeling you wanted to show me off."

"Don't be so conceited. You're not so handsome that I'd be showing you off. So, what are we doing? I hope you have something in mind. I don't want to waste such a pretty Sunday."

"Maybe we could get out of town. Go to the woods."

"The woods? Great—now I feel like my own grandmother. And what do you want to do there? Hunt mushrooms?"

"Maybe. Maybe I'll look for something, and maybe I'll find something."

"You can forget about that. I don't think I want to go to the woods with you. I thought you were going to treat me to something. Like a glass of champagne."

"Champagne? My God—champagne in the middle of the afternoon? I don't even know if I have that much money on me. I'm sure I have enough for an ice cream, though."

"Anybody who wants to go out with me better not plan on saving money at the same time."

"I just started a new job and the little they pay me has to last the whole month."

"Well, I can tell I better not count on much in the way of extravagance from you."

"Just wait. Pretty soon I'll be earning tons of money. And a year from now I'll have a car. I'm already fixing up an old-timer, a gigantic limousine my boss let me have for next to nothing. I'm going to restore it. Then I'll have a car that really turns heads."

"From the junkyard?"

"You won't be able to tell where it came from. When it's finished it'll look like new. Everything under the hood will be spick and span. No other car will come close, believe me."

"Believing and seeing are two different things. So, are you going to buy me that ice cream?"

"Sure. Shall we go down to the market?"

"I'd rather go to Blumenreich's. Theirs tastes better."

Everything happened very quickly between Gitti and me. She didn't get along with her mother and stepfather and wanted to move out of the house as soon as she could. But she was just an apprentice seamstress, so she couldn't afford that on her own, and her mother wouldn't hear of it and refused to support her. When I got my apartment and showed it to Gitti she was very excited and immediately started thinking of ways to fix it up. She helped me get some old furniture for free or next to nothing from her friends and acquaintances. I told her she could move in with me, but she just laughed at my offer; nevertheless, ten days later she brought up the idea on her own and said she would. The next day during her lunch break I helped her move her clothes and the few pieces of furniture that belonged to her. Gitti wanted to move while her mother and stepfather were at work. She wanted to present them with a done deed so as to avoid discussion—namely, her mother breaking out in tears and her stepfather losing his temper—but she didn't succeed entirely. A week later both of them showed up at our apartment and told her off while treating me no better than a piece of dirt. When I butted in and said something, they went silent for a moment, and then went on yelling at Gitti without even looking at me.

Gitti spoke her mind as well. I had to cover my ears when I heard the way she treated them. She was a tough one all right. When the old man tried to hit her I stepped in between them and pressed his arm down, which was easy to do since he wasn't very strong. Then he acted as if I had broken his arm, and later he went around town saying things to that effect, but all I had done was stop him from hitting Gitti. Finally her mother ran out howling, while her stepfather started yelling something about the police and work camps for delinquent youth—but I knew they couldn't do anything to us. I had obtained the apartment according to regulations, and we were both registered at the address.

After her parents left, Gitti's face was covered in red blotches, though she wasn't crying.

"Well, that's that, I guess," she said and then began laughing hysterically.

I told her she'd really let them have it and they wouldn't be showing up here again anytime soon.

"Right," she said, "and I might as well forget about any inheritance, too. I'm sure my name won't be appearing in their will. But, then again, I have no idea what those two would have to pass on."

We had been living together for half a year when all of a sudden my mother showed up one weekend. She didn't know anything about Gitti, at least not from me, but she suspected something because I hadn't been home in months. When she rang the bell we were in bed, and since I was expecting a friend I didn't bother to get dressed when I opened the door. We were both stark naked, and Mother needed a while to recover from the shock. At least I didn't have to do much explaining, since she could see for herself how I was doing and how things stood with Gitti and me. She was obviously uncomfortable with the situation, but once I told her we were engaged to be married she made an effort to treat Gitti cordially. After I took Mother to the station, Gitti asked me what I had meant with that business about getting engaged and married, and if I didn't plan to consult with her about that. I told her I thought it was all decided.

"That's what you thought?"

"Yes."

"So you thought for me as well? Is that what you're saying?"

"Don't get worked up. What's wrong with you? Other girls would be throwing their arms around me for something like that."

"So tell it to those other girls. I never said a thing about getting married. And I didn't know I was engaged to anybody, either. Shouldn't I know something like that? Or did you go and get engaged when I happened to be out of the room?"

"My God, we've been living together for half a year. It's not as if getting married is something I just pulled out of the blue."

"I don't care where you pulled it from. But just don't go telling people that I intend to marry you or anyone else. Because when it comes to what I think, my dear, you don't have the faintest idea."

"What's eating you? Do you want to leave? Have you had enough of me? Is there somebody else?"

"Did I say that? Did I say anything like that? I just don't like it when people want to decide things for me. I might as well have stayed with my mother and her dimwitted bedmate."

"Okay. Calm down. I just said that about getting married on account of my mother."

"I don't have to calm down, I'm completely calm. But I'm not getting married just because of your mother, and don't you forget it, either!"

I told her I had to drop by a friend's and took off. I had no clue why she'd gotten so worked up, but I didn't have any desire to continue a senseless conversation. Truth be told, I hadn't given a thought to getting married; I'd never really considered the possibility. We got along fine living together, and that suited me. Whether I wanted to stay with Gitti for the rest of my life I couldn't say, but I couldn't understand why she'd blown up like that. All the other girls I knew were crazy about getting married. But Gitti was different.

Almost every day I stayed an hour or two after work to work on my old Adler—a large six-windowed limo that was already over twenty years old, a real classic, built in 1936. There were only a few thousand built, and probably no more than a dozen still on the road, if that. Gitti grumbled about my coming home so late. I told her that once the car was finished she would be the first to go for a drive in it, that everybody would be amazed, and that our car would be the envy of the whole town. In any event, I didn't let her moods keep me from working on my car. My boss, who occasionally took a peek at the car, once told me that if I kept at it the limousine would be in better shape than when it left the factory.

I heard a few things about Gitti through the grapevine. One or two people I knew had seen her with other men. Once I asked her about it; she denied it, and then made such a scene that she didn't speak with me for three days and I had to apologize. The next time I heard something about her I almost beat up the man who told me. In the end that helped. I didn't hear any more stories about Gitti.

We had been living together for exactly a year when she got pregnant. That didn't suit me at all; I had no use for a child, since I wanted to hurry and finish my journeyman's exam and then get my master's certificate as soon as I was allowed. After that I wanted to open my own shop. I was relieved that Gitti didn't want the child either, and we kept our ears open as to who in town performed abortions. I had heard of some old women, but I didn't know any details, and the only person Gitti knew was a friend of her mother's, and she didn't want to go to her. Finally an acquaintance gave us a recipe that involved drinking red wine infused with pepper and some herbs and scalding-hot sitz baths. One weekend we performed the procedure twice; Gitti moaned and cursed, but she endured it, and ten days later she had her period again. We were both relieved, or at least I was, because a few days after that Gitti said she was going to regret it and had a bad conscience. She should have had the child; we would have managed somehow. Since it was all over, I didn't contradict her, just nodded and said some soothing words. Six weeks later she told me she thought she was still pregnant, since she'd skipped a period again, and she had this funny feeling. I was stunned; I had long since considered her pregnancy finished and forgotten and had been more careful since then. I asked her if we should try the sitz baths and the peppered wine again, but she wouldn't hear of it. Without telling me, she went to a doctor, and he confirmed that she was in her fourth month and told her what she had to do. Now Gitti was looking forward to the child and really wanted it. She even began sewing children's clothes. I had some difficulty adjusting to the new situation; after all, I had just turned twenty and had other plans than pushing a baby carriage through the park. With every passing day I submitted to the inevitable, and at one point—I believe it was the day my boss saw me with a visibly pregnant Gitti and congratulated me—I began to enjoy the idea. I even neglected my car and built a crib in the basement.

I asked Gitti if we shouldn't get married. The child would need parents, and since we were going to have it, we might as well put everything in order right away. She still didn't want to marry me. She said she didn't want to stand before the altar with a fat belly, although I hadn't for a moment been thinking about a church wedding. I was surprised and asked if she was religious, since we'd never talked about that. Like me, she never went to church, and so I assumed that she didn't have much interest in it. She told me she was baptized and confirmed and hadn't been to church since, but she wanted to get married by a pastor, and the baby had to be baptized as well. I urged her that we should at least have a civil marriage before the birth: that would be better for the baby, he would have the right name, but she wouldn't hear of it. Naturally I was surprised, but I didn't think anything more about it. I was such an idiot back then; I didn't realize or sense a thing. I told myself that Gitti was always different from everyone else, and that she would get married after the birth, holding our child on her arm. At one point I went home and told my parents. They were both excited and concerned: I had the impression they were looking forward to their grandchild. They asked about the wedding. I told them we were planning to get married after the birth and would invite them in plenty of time, and my mother said that made sense because weddings were always stressful and too much to ask of a pregnant woman. Of course they disapproved of our child being born out of wedlock, but that was more on account of the neighbors and gossip. Otherwise my parents were very open-minded. They were hurt, however, that I had come by myself, and they couldn't for the life of them understand why my bride, as they called Gitti, hadn't come with me.

In October I finished the Adler. I had painted it silver, and it was magnificent—the people of Naumburg had never seen anything like it except in the movies. Gitti was in her eighth month, but that didn't stop her from riding in our car through town and joining me on smaller outings in the country. I didn't drive very fast, since half the motor was new and the parts still had to wear in. We had a good time with the Adler. Every day after work we took it for a spin through town, stopping here and there to talk with friends—just rolling down the windows without getting out. At Gitti's urging I occasionally let one of her girlfriends get in the back and come along. But I liked it best when it was just the two of us driving through the city or cruising down the tree-lined avenues. Once a week I crawled under the car to check everything and tighten bolts. Actually there wasn't that much that required attention; the car kept going and going, and my boss, the master mechanic, praised me. He was the only one I let behind the steering wheel, since I was sure he knew how to handle it.

On the second of November Gitti started going into labor. I drove her in the Adler to the district hospital. I had to stop twice on the way, because her contractions were strong and she wanted to get out and walk a few steps. I was afraid the child might be born in the car with no one but me to help Gitti, so I drove much faster than usual. At the hospital they kept us waiting for nearly an hour at the admissions desk; we were told there was a lot of paperwork to fill out and the doctors were busy. Besides, it was much too early, Gitti should take advantage of the chance to walk around a bit; once she was in the delivery room she wouldn't be able to leave her bed, and the more she moved around now the better for the birth. Finally I brought her into the women's wing; a nurse took my bag and sent me home. She told me to call in the evening; then they would let me know.

I drove straight to work from the hospital. My coworkers had guessed that Gitti's time had come and were making jokes. Just before closing time I called the hospital and was told that Gitti had been taken out of the delivery room and placed in the ward because her contractions had let up and it would certainly be another day. The next morning I called again from work and learned that it had happened at four a.m. and that mother and child were both well. They didn't want to tell me more, not even whether it was a boy or a girl: as a rule they didn't give out this kind of information over the phone. I asked when I could see Gitti, and they told me that visiting hours didn't begin until five p.m. I told my boss and left two hours early. At home I washed up carefully and then bought a huge bouquet of dahlias, which were the only cut flowers in the shop.

Gitti was lying in a room with five beds; she was excited and very happy. She had spent the whole day talking with the woman in the bed next to hers who came from some village or another. They had brought our baby for her to nurse four times already; it had barely drunk and kept falling asleep on her breast. It was a boy. I was happy, but I would have been just as happy if it had been a girl. Gitti got up carefully and then shuffled over to the neonatal ward together with me. We stopped outside a large window; Gitti rang, and a nurse came to the door. Gitti said that she wanted to see her child; the nurse nodded and disappeared. Then the curtain behind the large window was pulled back and we could see inside the room, where there were eight babies. The nurse picked one up and came to the window so we could see it better.

"That's our baby, our Wilhelm," said Gitti proudly.

I stared at it in silence while she went on and on about how beautiful he was. To me he looked strange somehow. His ears were crumpled, his nose was flat, his forehead had a large red spot, and one eye seemed swollen. I quickly glanced at the other babies; they didn't look any better; they were all reddish, and two of them were actually quite red. Our baby, on the other hand, had a brownish complexion I liked better. Since Gitti didn't stop asking me if I liked the baby and whether he wasn't simply the most beautiful thing, I said he was and that I'd like to have a chance to hold him in my arms.

"You'll have to wait a bit," she said. "They only give him to me for nursing. In three or four days we'll be back home, then you can hold him in your arm from dawn to dusk."

She kept waving at the baby, although he kept his eyes closed; only the swollen eye was a little open, but he couldn't have seen us.

"Real cabbage ears," I said.

"That will work itself out. That's from the birth. Imagine how hard the little thing had to squeeze to get out; he's all pretty squashed." Then she turned back to the windowpane and said to the infant, "Don't you want to say hello to your father? That's the polite thing to do."

At work I told them it was a boy and his name was Wilhelm, and then I had to buy a round of drinks. Every day after work I drove to the hospital, brought Gitti the things she needed, and saw the baby. Now he was feeding quite well, and had even gained a few ounces. His ears no longer looked so squashed and his nose assumed its proper shape; only his skin was still dark. On the fourth day after the birth I came to pick them both up in the Adler. When I got there, Gitti was in the hallway, all packed and dressed and ready to go; we had to wait for the doctor to sign the discharge papers. A nurse called us into a room where a doctor was examining the baby. The doctor had undressed the baby and was listening to his vital signs. Then he nodded, satisfied.

"A sturdy lad," he told Gitti. "You can dress him now."

He gave us some advice and urged us to make regular visits to the counseling center for new mothers. Then he asked whether we had any questions. Gitti shook her head, put a diaper on the baby, and swaddled him up.

When the doctor looked at me I said, "His head is more or less in shape, but what about his skin? How long does it take for that to get normal again? Right now my boy looks like a little Negro."

The doctor was surprised, looked at the baby, then smiled and said, "You should talk to the child's mother about that. I believe she can explain everything."

He nodded to us, then turned around and hurried out of the room without saying good-bye. On the way home Gitti went on talking about the baby and everything we had to buy. She talked nonstop, and I couldn't even get a word in. There was lots to do at home, and I had to wait until that evening, when she was nursing Wilhelm, to ask her.

"So what are you supposed to explain to me?"

"What do you mean?"

"The doctor said you could explain everything to me, how long the skin color lasts and all that."

"Oh," she said, and then talked to the baby. Only when I repeated my question did she say, "Yes, it's a pigmentation alteration. It's not that uncommon. It lasts a few days or a few weeks, then the baby gets his normal color, that's all."

"A pigmentation alteration?"

"Yes."

"Never heard of it."

"I hadn't either. It's not dangerous. A few weeks or months, then it's all over."

"Months? You just said days."

"Yes, well it might go a lot quicker. The doctor couldn't say exactly. If we feed him carrot juice it can last longer, even a lot longer."

"So we won't feed our baby any carrots."

"Are you crazy? Carrot juice is very important. And I could care less about your stupid skin color. He's a beautiful baby, not so pale as all the others."

"I wish he were a little paler. He looks like a baby Negro."

"Don't talk nonsense," she said, and then went on talking to the baby but not me.

I had never heard of a pigmentation alteration, and I don't know where Gitti came up with that, but then again she'd had enough time to think of something. Four days after she and the baby were back in the apartment, one of the guys at work came up to me. He'd heard something about the pigmentation alteration and wanted to know more details. Since Gitti had yet to take the stroller out into town, I was curious to know who had told him about it. He grinned and said he couldn't remember. I told him what I knew about it and added that it was very rare but not dangerous.

"That's right," he said. "It's not dangerous, and it's not that rare, either. It's estimated that there are millions of cases every year."

"Really?"

"Sure," he said. "About a million Chinese, and a million Negroes. Oh, and the Indians, too. All pigmentation alterations—but they manage somehow."

"You're an idiot," I said, then turned around and walked away.

But his remark had set me to brooding. Until then everything had seemed plausible to me, even if it did cause me to gripe a little. All I knew about small children was that they can have all sorts of diseases. That evening I cornered Gitti and kept asking about this ostensible pigmentation alteration. I even told her I'd drive to the hospital and would speak to the doctor, and she answered pertly that I should go right ahead if I insisted on making myself look ridiculous. In any event, she had an answer for everything, and I was at a loss. During those days I stood for hours next to Wilhelm's crib. I had dug up some old photos of me as a child and compared them with him, but that didn't help. The baby could have been mine or some other man's. When Gitti caught me holding one of my old pictures next to the baby's face, she burst out laughing. But it didn't get really bad until we started taking the carriage into town. All sorts of people wanted to see the baby, and as soon as they did they all made a strange face. Then I always said something about a pigmentation alteration, and they listened to me, but I could tell that a few had trouble suppressing their laughter. I spoke with my boss about it, since we got along so well, seeing as I was the best man he had in the shop. He told me that he had heard something about that and I shouldn't work myself into a state over it. Maybe it really was a pigmentation alteration and would go away someday.

"There's a simpler explanation, a more natural one, and that's something your Gitti can explain to you," he finally said. "But whatever the case, you now have a nice baby, and he's your child no matter what people say."

After that conversation I couldn't bear it any longer and drove straight from work to the hospital. I asked for the doctor who had delivered Wilhelm. I had to wait two hours for him to spare a minute for me. I asked him what was wrong with the baby and this pigmentation alteration. He weighed his thoughts for a very long time and then said that the skin color would not undergo any essential change, and that I had to accept that we had a colored baby.

"But how is that possible?" I asked him.

He shrugged his shoulders, hesitated a long time, and then said, "Perhaps you ought to consider the possibility that you are not the biological father."

I gulped, although by then I had already understood everything long before.

"And there's no other explanation?"

He shook his head and said, "You could have a test, if you absolutely wanted to. A blood test. But you might as well spare yourself the trouble."

"And what about the pigmentation alteration?"

He just smiled, shook his head, and said that he had to go back to the delivery room.

On the way home I kept driving faster and faster, until finally I had to stop just to calm down. It was already getting dark, and because of the fog hovering in the streets you couldn't see a hundred feet in front of you. I turned on the headlights and sat down in the ditch by the road. When the moisture started to soak through my clothes I pulled an old blanket out of the trunk. Clouds of fog were drifting slowly this way and that, as if they couldn't make up their mind. They covered the trunks of the trees along the avenue, so all you could see were the bare crowns, floating over the murky gray and looking like leafless shrubs on a mountain cliff. I cursed and laughed at myself. Everybody knew, everybody except me, because I didn't want to see it. I wondered whether the pigmentation alteration was Gitti's idea or a tip from someone at the hospital. I kept shaking my head at myself. You're running around with a magnificent pair of horns, I told myself, a real set of antlers. And Gitti and the baby have made sure everybody can see it, too. No one will fail to notice; they've probably all seen it already, and I've become the talk of the town, and the only one who didn't know. You are truly an idiot, I said out loud.

A car approached and braked. Without stopping, it slowly drove past the Adler. I stood up, climbed into my car and drove home. Gitti was busy with the infant—her infant, not mine. I liked the little baby; I'd started to take to it, but now everything had changed for me. I couldn't look at the little brat without my blood boiling over. I had no desire to raise some total stranger's child; I didn't want to be responsible for a kid I had nothing, and I mean absolutely nothing, to do with, and who every time I looked at him would remind me that somebody was his father but certainly not me. Surely the little creature had a father he would never lay eyes on, and I could not replace him, nor did I want to. He'd have to sort that out with his mother, who was the only one who knew anything and who had to accept responsibility. I felt sorry for the little guy, and I would have gladly helped him, but I knew I wouldn't be able to stand it. I couldn't take him by the hand around town, to kindergarten and school. Whenever and wherever I would show up with him people would whisper and make stupid grins. And what should I say if they asked: Are you his father? Obviously I wasn't. So I didn't want to attempt the impossible.

Gitti asked why I was so late and whether I had been working on our car.

"Wash your hands before you touch little Wilhelm."

"I was at the hospital," I said calmly.

She looked at me, surprised: "Did you have an accident?"

"No. I was at the district hospital. In the women's wing."

She didn't answer.

"In the maternity ward," I added, unnecessarily.

Gitti bent over the infant without saying anything. Now she knew that I knew. I stayed in the room and waited for her to say something, anything; she kept silent, or else talked to her baby. Then she laid him in the crib I had built and sang for him. When she left the room she asked if I wanted to stay another moment with the baby. Her voice was shaking a little; maybe she was afraid of what was coming. Maybe she was afraid of leaving me alone with the baby. I got up and followed her into the kitchen. She set the plates on the table, finished preparing dinner, and sliced the bread.

"Pigmentation alteration," I said. "Brillant. And how did you imagine things would turn out later? Or did you think I'd get used to it?"

She didn't answer me. When she had placed everything on the table, she sat across from me, looked me in the eye, and asked, "So what happens now?"

Her tone was mocking and shameless, and I would have liked to give her a good whack or two.

"So who really is the father of your pigment baby? There aren't any Negroes here in town. Where'd you get hold of him?"

She shrugged her shoulders and gave a disdainful huff.

"Very well," I said finally. "We aren't married, thank God. And presumably you're not going to claim I'm the father."

She grinned at me. I stood up and went out to the hall.

Then I packed my jacket and went to my usual pub. I hadn't been there much in the past weeks on account of the baby and the Adler. One of the guys from the shop was there and a few people I knew as customers. I sat down with them and ordered a beer. They were talking about motorcycles and stripping them down for performance. Then they asked me about my masterpiece, the limousine, and how expensive it was.

"It's priceless," I said. "I'll be driving that beauty until the day I die."

"If it doesn't fall apart on you someday, given how old it is."

"It won't fall apart, I'd bet anything on that. Now and then I'll have to change out something, but nothing I can't afford."

"Sooner or later it's over. Even today you can't get spare parts for it anymore."

"I'm not all thumbs, you know. If I have to I'll file an engine block myself."

"You do everything yourself, don't you?"

"You bet."

"Of course—a real man does everything himself."

"Makes his own children, too."

"I at least don't need strangers to help with that."

"Some do things themselves, others have them done. If a man's lying under a car day and night, maybe he doesn't get around to it."

"Or else he wants something really special. Something not everybody has."

"Like curly hair, a fat nose, and everything nice and brown."

"They say women really go for that. Get a lot of pleasure."

"What are you talking about?"

"Come on, Koller. Just a little talk among friends. You don't have to take it personally."

"I heard they've just started selling Negro dolls in the stores. Just came in."

"People who need that should be glad. Of course I wouldn't have something like that in my house."

"Of course not. You've got enough to do as it is."

"You bet I do. Nonstop. Every day."

"Or every night."

"Better watch out at night. Otherwise there might be a pigmentation alteration."

"That's the stupidest thing I've ever heard."

"Stupid yourself."

"Pigment alteration! My old lady should try something like that on me. I'd give her an alteration all right."

"Happens all the time."

"Really? Never heard about it."

"There's a lot you haven't heard of."

"So how does it work, pray tell."

"Simplest thing in the world, actually. When a nigger shoves his cock into your old lady, then there's a pigmentation alteration, get it?"

"That's what I thought. But leave my old lady out of it, otherwise I'll have to kick your ass. She's no floozy that plays around. Especially not with niggers."

"Very funny," I said. "Very, very funny."

I got up, went to the bar, paid for my beer, and went home. To my apartment. Because it still was my apartment. Gitti had moved in as my guest; she and her brat were lodgers and I could kick them out anytime.

Gitti was washing diapers in the kitchen. She kept poking down the cotton cloths as they came floating up in the seething water. I grabbed a beer from the cellar, sat down in the living room, and put on a record I had received from a customer—American rock and roll. Gitti came in and asked me to keep it down so the baby could sleep. I turned the dial a little, but you can't listen to that kind of music quietly. She stood there in the room and looked at me; I started leafing through a magazine.

"So what happens now?" she asked finally. "I take it there's no more getting married, right?"

I lit a cigarette, although I knew she couldn't stand that, and I hadn't smoked at all inside the apartment since the baby was there.

"I think you should gradually start looking for an apartment," I said, casually, without taking my eyes off the magazine. "Or better yet, right away."

"I understand. But it will take a little while. I don't have your good connections in the housing office. And I don't guess I can count on your putting a word in for me with your friend."

"You can move in with your parents. Or with the father of your child. You'll love that. He'll probably be overjoyed to see his baby. Or is he already miles away? Did he jilt you? Did he take off when he learned you were in the family way?"

"Think it over, Koller. If I go, it's for good. You won't ever see me again. Is that what you really want?"

"As God's my witness."

"And the baby? You like little Wilhelm too."

"Get lost, Gitti. Take your little nigger and get lost. I'd like you both to be gone by tomorrow evening."

"It can't happen that soon."

She went out and slammed the door, although the baby was asleep. I finished my beer and lay down to sleep on the sofa in the living room. I could barely shut my eyes. The laughing faces in the pub, the surprised expressions of my friends when they looked inside the carriage, Gitti's brazen smile, and the little curly-haired black brat were all dancing before my eyes and in my head. Once I had calmed down, I told myself that I, too, would make fun of somebody else if it had happened to him. The boys were all right; they weren't my problem. My problem was right here in my apartment, in the next room, and it would never go away; on the contrary, it would gradually get bigger and bigger and I would have to spend my whole life making explanations, responding to astonished questions and insinuating remarks. And Gitti's dumb attempt to deceive me, this stupid pigmentation alteration that I fell for and parroted to everybody, they'd never forget it, not in this town. I had no other choice, so that night I made up my mind.

As I was packing my breakfast, Gitti came into the kitchen with the little one on her arm and watched me. I packed my sandwich in the lunchbox, poured the boiling tea into the thermos, and stuck them both inside my bag. After I opened the door I turned around to her and said: "I've given the matter some thought—you don't have to look for another apartment. As far as I'm concerned you can stay here."

Gitti beamed and took a step toward me, and I quickly went outside because I didn't want to speak with her. After our breakfast break the boss usually went inside his office to write out the orders and the invoices. I followed him, knocked once on the door, and then stepped inside. I sat in the visitor's chair in front of his desk and waited until he raised his head and looked at me inquiringly.

"What's up, Koller?"

"I'm giving notice, boss."

"Don't do that to me, boy. You're my best man. With everyone else I have to explain everything step by step. But you—you don't just have two good hands, you have a good head on your shoulders as well."

"I'm leaving."

"Hang on a minute, boy! What's eating you? Am I paying you too little? Do you want to talk to me about a raise?"

"No, that's not it."

"We get along well with each other, Koller. No, I won't accept your notice. I'm declining. Understood?"

I shook my head.

"Koller, you can't leave me in the lurch. I need you, you know that."

"I can't, boss. I can't go on like this."

"What are you talking about? Get it off your chest and I'll settle things for you."

"It's on account of Gitti. She's made me the laughingstock of the whole city."

"Oh, so that's all? Just forget it. Talk to her. Maybe you'll work it out together. Or else you'll each go your separate ways. That doesn't mean you have to pack up and leave town."

"It's decided, boss. I can't stand it here any longer. Everybody knows, everybody's laughing at me. It's decided, I'm going."

"A pity, my boy. But you're probably right. That dumb goose messed up everything. Ruined her life, made you upset, and now she's taking my best man away. When do you want to leave, Koller? This month? Stay until the end of the quarter, so I'll have time to find a replacement."

"I want to leave right away. Today. I'm leaving this evening."

"What? What? You can't do that."

"I'm packing my trunk and taking off. I'm leaving all my junk for her."

"That's big of you, my man. My hat's off to you! After what she did to you."

"She'll have a hard enough time as it is. You can fill out my papers. Or if you don't want to I'll report in sick and disappear."

"Fine. Come by again this afternoon. Or an hour before closing time. I'll take care of the papers. I don't want to make things difficult for you."

"Thanks, boss."

As I was leaving the office, he called me back.

"Koller! In case you have second thoughts or change your mind later on, you can always find work with me. Just so you know."

"Thanks. But I don't think . . ."

He smiled at me encouragingly and I went back to the car I had on the blocks. I wanted to finish before we closed.

When I came home the table in the living room was set as if for someone's birthday. There was even a candle lit on the table. Gitti had completely misunderstood; she thought I was going to stay there with her. I went to the attic, took out our trunk, went in our bedroom, and packed my things. Gitti came into the room with the little one; now she finally understood. She asked if I wanted anything else. I shook my head.

"So then that's it?"

I simply went on packing. When I was finished I went through the apartment and looked in the cellar. Then I took the trunk and two bags to the car. I went back for my records and the record player. When I was about to leave the apartment once and for all, Gitti blocked my way. She hoisted up the baby and said, "Don't you at least want to say good-bye to Wilhelm?"

I set the record player on the stool in the hall.

"That's for Wilhelm," was all I said.

Then I walked past her, went down the stairs and out to my car. I drove out of Naumburg slowly, taking a thorough look around. I would never again come back to this town. Of course they'd talk about me at work and in town now and then, but after a few months all they would remember about me would be the little Negro boy and Gitti's idiotic pigmentation alteration. My blood boiled whenever it crossed my mind—it would be months before I stopped turning red every time I thought about Naumburg and Gitti and her little Wilhelm. When I drove the silver Adler past the city-limits sign, I honked my three-toned horn several times, as if for a wedding or a parade. I was certain I was leaving behind the stupidest and most humiliating event of my life, and resolved from then on to keep my eyes open and not let myself be taken in by anyone.

What I didn't know was that by running away—because that's what I was doing—I was running, or rather driving, straight into a misfortune that would cost me six years of my life and my beloved Adler, which made me madder than anything. A car like that was a miracle and impossible to find anywhere, certainly not with my pocketbook. Today it would be priceless, assuming the person who got it after me kept it in even halfway as good shape. Every single screw, every inch of the motor and the chassis had gone through my fingers. I had filed and polished parts, retooled the bolts, hammered out or replaced most of the sheet-metal; I fabricated and tempered pieces that were no longer manufactured, obtained material that could easily be mistaken for the original upholstery and sewed it myself on a sewing machine, and pulled it all into shape with an awl. I had never seen an Adler like mine brand new; all I had was the pile of scrap I had bought from my boss and a few pictures and descriptions in old magazines. The rest I filled in according to the way I imagined a limousine like that should look.

I don't know what roads my car is driving on today, what garage it's in, or who is at the wheel: I only know that it really still belongs to me. I still keep my eyes open and hope that one day I'll see my Adler. I'd be sure to speak to the driver, tell him about my work on the car, and how I lost it. If he's been good to the car—and I'd know in a glance if he had—then I might shake his hand and wish him well. Otherwise I'll steal my Adler from him, even if it means risking prison again. I'm determined to steal back my car if it isn't in immaculate condition. After all, I replaced the locks and ignition myself; so I won't have to fiddle with any bent wire. I would open the car with its very own key and drive off, because back then I didn't give them my extra key, and the idiotic official didn't think to ask for it. I don't imagine I'll get very far. My Adler is simply too conspicuous, and it won't help to repaint it. They don't make those kind of limousines anymore; it's as long as a presidential car, like you sometimes see pictured in a magazine, a one-of-a-kind custom model—certainly not mass produced. The cars they make today are just boxes for anybody and everybody. Sure, they're faster and more economical than my Adler, but they're two full yards short of being a real car. Nobody had to sit scrunched in his seat in my Adler, where even a man well over six feet could stretch out his legs.

Sometimes I think my car may have been lucky and wound up in some museum. I imagine grown-ups and children jostling to get a look and listening to somebody who doesn't have a clue tell them "Here is an original Adler like they built decades ago," and the people staring in awe and praising my work without knowing it, and everyone thinking the car had rolled just like that out of the Adler factory.

I do own a car again, but just one of the regular ready-made models. Your heart doesn't leap into your throat when you open the door or turn the ignition. I only use it to drive from point A to point B. Never in a million years would I take a mediocre car like that on a drive through the country, simply to listen to the motor and the shifting of the gears.

I still think of the Adler now and then—more often, to be sure, than I do about Gitti and her offspring, who must be a man by now, a man who never knew his father. He can't have had it easy. Growing up without a father, and having a mother like Gitti, that's drawing the shit end of the stick all right, especially combined with having to deal with a pigmentation alteration your whole life—now I can laugh about it. Anyway, that's one hand worth turning in for new cards, which certainly couldn't be worse than the ones he was dealt. But if I feel sorry for anybody, it is for myself first and foremost, because everything that happened to me later was all thanks to Gitti. For Wilhelm and me this girl was a catastrophe.

When I left Naumburg there were twelve days till the end of the year, during which time I planned to look around for work and visit a few old friends. Naturally I wanted to show them my car, and I wanted to see them and talk to them, to be with friends who didn't know anything about Gitti and Wilhelm, with people I didn't have to suspect were laughing at me and the Negro baby every time they made a comment or grinned.

I spent the first week in Berlin. I'd only been in the capital once before in my life, after an uncle died and our whole family drove up for a long weekend. We were staying in a family guest house across from the natural science museum. The funeral was on a Friday; we went to the cemetery and then to a restaurant, where we stayed late into the night. I didn't know my dead uncle, and that was the first time I had seen my aunt, his widow. I didn't like the way the sobbing woman kept hugging and kissing me, and when I had the chance I told my mother I needed to stretch my legs and I left for two hours to look at the neighborhood and the display windows.

The next two days my father took my siblings and me on the U-Bahn to West Berlin; Mother had to spend the whole Saturday with my aunt and the relatives and couldn't go sightseeing with us until Sunday.

On Saturday morning we visited several stores; Father bought a few small things for the kitchen and his shop, but he didn't have enough money to buy anything for us. He warned us several times not to touch anything so that he wouldn't have to pay for something if it broke. Although Father kept his eye on us, I did manage to steal a ballpoint pen. It was a thick pen in a plastic housing that showed a woman in a full-length black evening dress; when you twisted the pen, the dark color flowed to the bottom and the woman was suddenly wearing a skimpy bikini. That afternoon we looked at the newly erected high-rise district in the middle of the city, which they talked about at length on the radio. Nobody was living in the buildings yet; you could go in and ride the elevator, look at the apartments, and get a good view of the city. Then we went to a cinema and saw a very funny film, but I've forgotten what it was called or what it was about. We only went to the movies because that was something Father could afford: he would show his ID card and we could pay with our East German money, which the other stores in West Berlin didn't accept, unless it was at an exchange rate that made everything prohibitively expensive for us. After that we tried to talk Father into going to another cinema, and offered to pay with our allowance. Father told us our aunt was expecting us and we had to go back. I only remember that we ate a lot at our aunt's because all we'd had to eat had been the sandwiches we had taken on our trip.

On Sunday, Mother joined us to look at the window displays and visit the radio museum, which I liked a lot better than the natural history museum. Then we went to the cinema again, since Mother wanted to see one of her favorite actresses in an American film. Those two days were exciting for me, and I resolved then to move to Berlin for good someday—and now I had an opportunity. I didn't want to look up my aunt; I hadn't had any contact with her, and the thought of the funeral, when she kept kissing me, drove all thought of staying with her out of my mind.

I had several addresses in Berlin of friends I'd met on my vacations on the Baltic. Practically all of them had told me I should be sure and look them up if I ever came to the city and had offered me a place to stay. So when I arrived, I stopped at a post office, went inside one of the phone booths, and called the numbers in my address book. Three times a woman's voice answered saying their son no longer lived with them and they could only give me an address without a phone number. On my fourth call I reached one of my acquaintances; he didn't remember me, and when I asked if I could stay with him he explained awkwardly that it wasn't really possible at the moment because the apartment was being remodeled. No one answered at the other numbers; probably they were at work. I looked for a small hotel that wasn't too expensive, but wherever I inquired, all the rooms were taken. Then I drove to the address of one of the friends who had moved out of his parents' home.

It was a sorry-looking dump on the ground floor off the rear of a courtyard. The garbage bins were overflowing with junk that had evidently been there for years and completely covered the small bit of grass. You could see traces of the original plaster on the walls of the building, and the main entrance door was out of alignment and scraped the tiles on the floor. There were no real nameplates; the tenants' names were simply painted right on the doors. Sebastian, my friend from Rügen, opened after I had rung several times; the music in his apartment was so loud he could barely hear the bell. He recognized me right away, pulled me inside and introduced me to his new girlfriend, who was sitting on the couch in her underwear. She glanced up at me and went right back to her music. When I asked Sebastian if I could stay with him, he nodded as if it were a matter of course. Since he had a one-room apartment, he told me I could either stay with them in the main room or else have a mattress in the kitchen. I told him I didn't want to impose, but that I'd like to spend a week in Berlin since I wanted to look around for a job. If that was okay with him, I would happily sleep on the floor of his kitchen, since I hadn't been able to find a room in a hotel. He just nodded to everything I said and casually kept repeating "no problem" in English. He pointed to a corner in the hall where I could stash my things. He couldn't give me a key because he only had one.

"No problem," he said. "Whoever is the last to leave should lock up and leave the key with Kurt who runs the pub across the street. He's always open. At least when I get up he's already open, and after midnight you just have to knock on the shutters and he'll let you in. I've been doing that for years, it's fine, I don't need any other keys. And I'll tell Kurt that he should give you the key. I don't even have a key for the main door; it's usually open, and if it isn't you just have to give it a little push, no problem."

He pressed the key in my hand so I could go and get my things, then sat down on the couch with his girlfriend and started fondling her. I took one of my bags out of the car, and the suitcase that I had packed with some bedding and a pillow. When Sebastian saw me he groaned and asked whether I was really planning just to stay a week and why in the world was I hauling all of that stuff when a toothbrush and some underwear is enough for a week. I briefly told him that I had just moved out of my girlfriend's and that everything I owned was in the car. Then I said good-bye because I wanted to go into town. He already had his hand back in his girlfriend's panties and nodded his head to signal his agreement.

That week I went to the movies every night. In the morning I would go out shopping, because although Sebastian had a refrigerator, all it contained was a few bottles of beer next to an opened package of spaghetti. I bought fresh rolls for everybody and filled up their refrigerator, which they didn't bother to acknowledge. I had no idea what they lived on—neither of them worked, and when I asked him once, Sebastian gave an evasive, ambiguous answer, and I didn't ask again. After breakfast, around ten a.m., I set off to look for work. Three repair shops seemed interested in me, but since I didn't have an apartment in Berlin and didn't have permission to move, they told me I'd first have to take care of the necessary papers and find a room. When I asked how to go about it and whether they could help, they merely shrugged their shoulders.

One master mechanic in the south of Berlin agreed to see me. When I asked him for help, he laughed in my face.

"Good friends can be helpful," he said. "You can't have too many of those. If you have a good friend in the housing office, then you can obtain permission to relocate in three days, and maybe get a room or even a whole apartment."

"I know," I said. "That's exactly how I got my last apartment. From a customer who was always pleased with my work. I don't have any customers in Berlin though. But you do, and I'm sure some are from departments where they could help me."

"Maybe I do, maybe I don't. You know, my boy, I've helped people from the provinces twice now. They got their apartments—good ones, too, really nice places—and in less than a month they slapped their notices on my desk. Now they work in West Berlin. All they wanted from me was the apartment. So I'm more careful. Can you understand that?"

"Of course. But I want to work here, not in West Berlin."

"That's exactly what the two of them said. Their exact words. Come back when you have the relocation papers, my boy."

Finally I tried in West Berlin; they didn't need any mechanics there, and certainly none from the East. They had enough of those, they told me, and besides winter wasn't a good time to look; I should check back in the spring.

After four days I gave up looking for a job and drove all across the city, checking out the warehouses and spending hours in the tool stores and the shops for do-it-yourselfers. One day before I left, Sebastian mentioned a luxury sedan he'd seen parked in the street for several days.

"You mean the Adler?" I asked.

"Yes, I think it's an Adler. It's enormous."

"That's my car."

"Come on."

"Seriously."

"Really? I thought it belonged to a millionaire."

"I restored it myself. From a pile of scrap."

"No kidding. You mean you're a car mechanic?"

"Exactly."

"Now you tell me! Have you seen that old Opel P4? It's mine, but it doesn't drive. Something wrong with the alternator and the carburetor. The shop could fix it for me, but they want six hundred marks. Would you look at it, Koller? Maybe you can do it."

"Sure, I can take a look."

I spent a whole day working on his car. It was in terrible shape, hadn't been serviced or cared for in the least, but fortunately nothing serious was broken. The car looked exactly like the building he was living in, not to mention his apartment itself. Just as it was getting dark I finished; the engine sounded pretty good, and Sebastian drove it around the block. I told him he should remember to take it in for regular servicing, that that would cost him less in the long run. He nodded and said it was a good idea, but I knew he'd go on treating his car like an old sock. Because he asked, I drove him and his girlfriend, whose name was Barbara—he called her Babs—out to the Dämeritz See in Köpenick, to a friend of Sebastian's who was throwing a party. He urged me to come inside with them and join the party—bringing along an extra guest was no problem.

Sebastian's friend Klaus lived with his parents in a villa with its own access to the lake and a boat shed in the backyard. Klaus had his own apartment in the attic: two rooms, a tiny kitchen, and a small bathroom. His father was the superintendent of a medical clinic and he and his wife were away for a week at a congress, and so Klaus had the whole house to himself. Just as Sebastian said, he didn't mind my being there in the least; he merely nodded when Sebastian introduced me and asked if we'd brought anything to drink. I had bought two bottles of wine and one of brandy and gave them to him. He took them without saying a word, then left us to our own devices.

I liked the house. It was furnished with antiques that had to be worth a fortune. The living room had a huge table and leather armchairs covered with drop cloths so they wouldn't get dirty. A buffet five yards long was lined up against one wall; I wondered how they had brought the monster inside. The doctor's study was locked: that was the only room we weren't allowed to enter. Sebastian made the rounds through the living room, saying hello to all his friends. In the kitchen two girls were standing at the stove, trying to cook some soup, evidently for the first time. I went up to them and offered some advice. One of the girls asked me if I was a cook, then without waiting for my answer shoved a knife in my hand and told me that I should make the soup if I was so smart. She took the other girl and left the kitchen. I tasted the broth on the stove and looked to see what ingredients were available and what was in the refrigerator and then set about making a real soup. Now and then one of the guests came to the kitchen to cut a slice of bread and some cheese and then left. Half an hour later I found Klaus and told him the soup for his guests was ready. He couldn't have cared less; he was fiddling with the tape player, which he had turned up so loud that the bass was rattling. I went through the rooms, looking for Sebastian. Two rooms had mattresses on the floor and a few couples were making out in the dimmed light. Since I couldn't find Sebastian I fetched a bowl of soup and sat down at the big table in the living room. After a while other guests joined me. When one of the girls mentioned that I had cooked the soup, two of the boys praised me and asked what I did and where I was from. I told them what I'd been doing and that I was looking for a job but hadn't found anything in Berlin.

"You're from Guldenberg?" asked a young red-haired man sitting across from me. He was wearing a thick gold chain around his neck that struck me as peculiar: I'd never seen a man wear anything like that.

"Yes. You know the dump?"

He shook his head and thought a moment.

"Now I've got it," he said. "Guldenberg. That's where a buddy of mine is from. Maybe you know him. I mean, in a village like that everybody knows everybody."

"Guldenberg's not a village, it's a town. But what's your friend's name?"

"Actually, I forget his real name. We call him Woodworm. Does that mean anything to you?"

"Bernhard Haber," I said.

"Maybe. Yes! I think you're right. That's Woodworm's name. You know him?"

"We went to school together. He was a grade below me. His father was a carpenter, and he learned carpentry, too, as far as I know."

"Exactly. That's him all right. That's why he's called Woodworm. Well, well, fancy meeting someone else from that hole."

"I've lost touch with him. Does he still live there?"

"Uh-huh. But he's not a carpenter anymore. Now's he's working for my firm."

"You have your own firm? What do you do?"

"Oh, this and that."

"What does that mean?"

"It means it's a firm that does this and that." He laughed.

"I don't understand," I said. "Is that supposed to be a joke?"

"Of course not. It's just a firm that does this and that. Performing special services, if you know what I mean. People have a problem, we hear about it and help them out, that's all."

"And Woodworm's a carpenter there?"

"No. More like a driver. Gets around all right, your schoolmate. And he earns a whole lot more than a carpenter would. Everybody in my firm makes good money."

"I'm looking for work myself. I'm a mechanic, auto mechanic. Couldn't you use somebody like that? I'd like to work in Berlin."

"We don't need mechanics. Just drivers, really, and at the moment we have more than enough of those."

He smiled at me condescendingly and turned back to the girl sitting next to him. A while later I ran into him again outside the bathroom and asked about his firm and Bernhard, but he just gave the same vague responses as before. A little later I found Sebastian and told him I was going home because everyone there was drunk. He groaned, because he wanted to stay and if I left he and his girlfriend would have to take the S-Bahn. But he understood and gave me the key to the apartment.

The next morning I packed up quietly since I wanted to take off. Then I realized nobody had woken me up in the night, which meant that Sebastian and Barbara hadn't come back yet. I checked the living room; it was empty—they'd probably spent the night at Klaus's. Well, there certainly had been enough mattresses lying around. I ate a large breakfast, then stowed my trunk and bag in my car and got ready to go. I sat in the apartment for an hour waiting for them, hoping to be able to say good-bye and return the key. When they hadn't come back by noon, I wrote a letter to Sebastian that I planned to give to the pub keeper along with the key. Just when I was locking the door they showed up. I thanked them and reminded him to take his car in for regular servicing. I asked about the friend with the gold chain; all Sebastian knew was that his name was Frieder and he earned a lot of money.

"He has some kind of deal going," he said. "Something that beats working."

Barbara shook my hand. She could barely see straight and told me not to look at her, said she felt as if she'd puked her guts out and hadn't gotten a minute's sleep last night. I drove off and two and a half hours later was at my mother's in Guldenberg. I wanted to visit for a day or two to see some old friends and then drive to Leipzig to look for work. I had no desire to stay in Guldenberg; I was done with that town for good.

No sooner was I home than my mother asked about Wilhelm. In Berlin I hadn't given a thought to Gitti and Wilhelm; I'd managed to forget them, and now I had to tell Mother something. I told her we had split up, and when Mother asked if I wasn't going to see my son anymore, I said roughly that Wilhelm wasn't my son and that that's why I had split up with Gitti. When she kept on grilling me, I asked her to please stop, I didn't want to hear anything more about Gitti, didn't want to think about her, and didn't want to waste another word on her. Then I told my mother not to tell anyone in town about my flop with Gitti and left to see some old school friends.

I ran into Bernhard the next day early in the afternoon at the café by the parade grounds. I didn't want to talk with him, but there were only two other people in the café, so I couldn't exactly avoid a conversation.

"I heard you were back in town. You planning to stay?"

I shook my head.

"And how are you doing? That's a fine car you have. The whole town is talking about it."

"Yup, it's one of a kind. A real automobile. I built it up from scratch. All by myself."

"Nice work. I like it. Let me know if you want to sell it."

"I don't know if you can shell out that kind of money. It would be a pretty steep price."

"I guessed as much. Looks to me like it'd be worth it, too. What do you want for it, Koller?"

"Are you trying to tell me you have enough money to buy a limousine like that?"

"Speak up. Name your price. Just name a price. I won't bargain. I'll just say yes or no—isn't that the best way to deal?"

"I take it you're not a carpenter anymore, Woodworm. Carpenters don't earn that much."

"That's right. I found something better."

"I know. You're a chauffeur."

"Chauffeur? Who told you that?"

"I met your boss in Berlin. He told me."

"I don't have a boss. Someone must have been pulling your leg. Who the devil is supposed to be my boss?"

"A red-haired guy with a gold chain on his neck."

"I don't have a boss. I'm independent."

"His name's Frieder, I think. He told me a lot about you and your business."

"What an idiot. What did he tell you?"

"For instance that you're working as a driver for him and that you make a lot of money. He offered to hire me as a driver, too."

"What did he tell you?"

"Everything about the firm. How you make so much money."

"And how do we?"

"I certainly don't have to tell you."

"What an idiot."

Bernhard was mad, that was clear, and I hoped I could get him to talk without his realizing that I didn't know anything.

"Nobody will find out a thing from me," I said reassuringly. "And who knows, maybe I'll join you. Fixing cars for people you don't know isn't much fun in the long run."

Bernhard looked at me and said nothing. I knew he was wondering what Frieder might have told me. Finally he asked me to show him my car. He settled his café bill and we went outside. The Adler, needless to say, made a big impression on him, and he asked me if I could give him a ride. First we drove to the bridge. I hadn't been there since I'd moved and wanted to see what it looked like. I drove slowly across and stopped on the other side. We climbed out, walked back a few yards, and leaned against the railing to look at the river. The wind was bitingly cold; I didn't have a coat or a scarf and turned up my jacket collar. The murky water of the Mulde gurgled past the pilings. We looked at each other practically simultaneously and grinned, remembering the time we broke into the construction shed and stole the tools. But we didn't say anything, perhaps because we were ashamed or embarrassed—in any case, since Bernhard didn't mention our childish pranks, I saw no reason to, either.

When we walked back to the car, I asked if he'd like to go for a little spin, and suggested we drive to the Ox Head Inn, out on the heath. He agreed. The whole way he kept on talking about my car, and I tried to figure out how he was supposedly making so much money, without his noticing that I really didn't know anything about his firm. By the time we reached the inn, I didn't know much more than I had before—just that it was illegal, and if you weren't lucky you could wind up in prison. I'd already figured as much, given the sort of money Bernhard was ostensibly earning.

The inn was closed; it was only open during the season, so

we had no place to warm up and have a drink. We walked around the building, knocking on doors in the hope of finding someone who'd serve us some coffee, and all of a sudden the door to the kitchen sprang open. We knocked again and called out; not a soul could be seen or heard. For a moment we looked at each other, then back at the open door, each guessing what the other was thinking. Finally Bernhard shook his head and laughed.

"No," he said. "That's over. Too dangerous."

I nodded. Then I asked, "What ever happened to the hoist?"

He didn't understand me and looked at me questioningly.

"The hoist from back then! The winch!"

"Oh," he said, and laughed. "Father didn't want it. He didn't believe me when I told him I'd bought it from a friend. So six months later I sold it to someone who had placed a want-ad looking for a rope hoist."

He laughed again. We went to the car and started home. In the next town I stopped at an inn. When we asked for coffee, the proprietor said that he served beer and whiskey and for truck drivers he had a soft drink, but then he let us talk him into brewing some coffee for us. When at last he brought two cups and a pot of coffee, Bernhard ordered some brandy, which made him a bit more congenial.

I told Bernhard what I'd been doing, how I'd spent two years rebuilding my Adler, and where I'd been. I didn't say a word about Gitti and Wilhelm. When I asked him to talk about himself, he looked at me a long time and finally said, "What did Frieder tell you about us?"

"This and that. And how you can make a lot of money very quickly."

"And he really offered you a chance to join us?"

"He told me he didn't need any drivers at the moment. If something opened he said he'd let me know."

"It's not without its risks."

"I realize that."

"They managed to catch one of us. Five years."

"Death's always just around the corner. I guess he made a mistake."

"No. It wasn't his fault; we know that much. His client couldn't keep his mouth shut. That happens, too."

"If the money's right you have to roll with the punches."

"Don't talk like you know everything, Koller. It's bad for anyone they catch."

I refilled my coffee cup. I still didn't understand a thing. There were clients for whom you had to transport something with a car, and who paid well if it was dangerous, but I still had no idea what it could be that brought in so much dough.

"Your car is good. Very good. A small modification and it would be ideal."

"What kind of modification? It's true to the original. I'm not tinkering with anything."

"There's room to stash whatever you want; it's so big no one will notice."

"No alterations. It's an original; you have no idea how much that adds to its value."

"I know, I know. But the luggage has to disappear. If the guards make you open the trunk and it's completely empty, then you're clear. And now and then we get a client who can't be seen, because he might be on a list. That wouldn't be a problem with your car. Something like that would bring in a lot more money. They pay—man, they pay anything."

I nodded as knowingly as I could.

"Of course. I could think about it. A false bottom might be possible. Ten or twelve inches perhaps, but no more than that. Then it would stick out."

"A false bottom, exactly. Could you build that? I mean, could you do it all by yourself? You can't have it done in a shop or they'll nab you right away."

"No problem. I'd have to get hold of a few parts, some sheet metal, and once I have everything I can do it in a week. Three days, even."

Bernhard looked at me without saying anything. He was thinking, and that always took time with him, a long time. In school he'd always gotten on everybody's nerves the way he'd just stand there and think while everybody was waiting for him to answer. And I didn't want to push, especially because he was finally beginning to say something, and little by little I was getting an outline of how he and this Frieder were making their money. I lit a cigarette, took my time to enjoy it, and not until I had put it out did he open his mouth again.

"I could use someone," he said finally. "Someone with a car and a telephone—those are the requirements."

"Telephone? I don't even have an apartment at the moment."

"How can I get hold of you?"

"I'll let you know as soon as I have an apartment."

"That shouldn't be a problem. With a bit of money, with a large bit of money you can get an apartment with a telephone, can't you?"

"Sure. And then?"

"Then we'll talk again. Agreed?"

"So, what am I looking at? How much does a driver earn in your firm?"

"It's not a firm. We all work on our own, every man for himself. I don't know how many are involved. Nobody does. Or almost nobody. Frieder doesn't, either. It's better for everybody that way."

"How much would I make in a month?"

"Hard to say. One thousand, two thousand. Some months a little more, then you might go weeks without anything. You have to calculate it by the year, then it pays. And you need a permanent job, anything, otherwise you'll look suspicious. A permanent job where you can take off any time you want."

"That's not easy. What kind of job do you have?"

"Amusement operator."

"What's that?"

"Carnivals. Show up here, show up there. Always on the move."

"And what do you do?"

"Nothing at all. A friend of mine owns a carousel. I give him two hundred marks a month to keep me on the books as an employee. He needs the money for the taxes. I show up now and then when I feel like it. The two hundred marks are worth it to me. He doesn't know anything. He thinks I make my money betting on horses."

"A friend like that is worth his weight in gold. Do you think he might be able—"

"Forget it. That's out of the question. Carrying two men like that would be too dangerous."

"I understand. I'll have to see what I can do. I'll look around. And two thousand, that's guaranteed?"

"Nothing is guaranteed. Sometimes more, sometimes less is what I said. Once I made five thousand."

"In one month?"

"Um-hmm."

"A week from now I'll have a job, Bernhard. And an apartment, and a telephone, too. I'll take care of it right away. Maybe I'll go to Leipzig—I should have some possibilities there. How does that strike you?"

"Leipzig? That's good."

"And then? How does it work from there? When do I have my first job?"

"Everything else will work out. You'll find out soon enough. I'll give you a call, we meet, then we make the trip. That's how it goes."

My hands were sweating. The money was tempting, it clouded my thinking. The idea of making such a pile of money for a few drives kept me from taking the related dangers into consideration. I didn't pay any attention to the news about his colleague who got five years; I didn't even ask Bernhard what the man had been convicted of. The bills were dancing in my head—a new motorcycle, a small sailboat. I was dizzy, and on the way home I had difficulty concentrating on the road and listening to Bernhard. All I could think of was the money. When we parted I gave Bernhard a hug, which I had never done in my life and which turned out to be unpleasant as soon as I did it, especially because Bernhard bristled and looked at me annoyed.

"I'll call in a week," I said. "With my own phone from my own apartment. And just the right sort of job."

"First of all, fix up your car. A nice big secret compartment, that's what we need you for."

"It'll all be ready in a week, Bernhard. You have my word."

I said good-bye to Mother that same day and drove to Leipzig. A cousin of mine with whom I got along lived in an old house in Dölitz. I could stay there and work on my Adler in their garage when her husband was at work. I was easily able to put in a second bottom in a week. I fetched the necessary parts from the scrapyard and two garages near Leipzig. When I was finished you couldn't see the hidden compartment at all; even a mechanic wouldn't notice at first glance.

Finding an apartment with a telephone proved a harder assignment. I was in a hurry, and that made the heads of the housing offices suspicious: they suspected a trap. I told them I had a girlfriend who was pretty far pregnant, that I needed the apartment so bad on account of her, but that was a mistake. One of the men told me I should marry her and then come back; it would be easier for him to help a married couple with a child. In another district of the city I was very close to getting an apartment. The department head had his secretary bring a card file into the room and was already leafing through the cards when I said something that made him suspicious. I don't know what I said, what word it was that set him off, but suddenly he shoved the box away and was furious. He asked me if I thought he could be bribed and told me to get the hell out or else he'd report me to the authorities. When I finally did get an apartment it was a dilapidated hole in Connewitz where the only luxury was running water. Since I wanted to get into business with Bernhard as soon as possible I accepted it, though it meant forking over five hundred marks I had intended to put toward a respectable apartment. A telephone was out of the question, at least officially, but that wasn't a problem; for an additional five hundred I got one right away, and three days later it was hooked up. I thanked my cousin for putting me up and moved into the dark ground-floor apartment on the Nibelungring—two rooms with a kitchen and a tiny toilet. Then I called Bernhard and told him I'd taken care of everything and was waiting for news from him.

"Everything? You took care of everything?" he asked.

I told him I had, although I still hadn't found a job that would allow me to take off whenever I wanted without causing trouble. Bernhard wanted to see the car, and we agreed to meet the following Friday. He wanted to come to Leipzig since he had business there anyway. I had two days to find a job, but I was determined to make up something to tell him if I couldn't manage it in time. I wanted to start working for him, even if I still could only guess at what was to be transported. I wanted the money, and was getting more and more worked up in my head about bringing in that kind of dough every month. Even though I hadn't made a single drive for Bernhard and Frieder and didn't have a firm and binding offer, I was already living with the idea of having lots of money, and I was fantasizing and speculating about numbers so high that I wasn't worried about the considerable expenses I had already incurred; and yet, apart from those expenses, I had no connection with the firm at all. The longer it took for me to begin working for them as a driver, the more urgent was my desire to earn this money. I wanted it, I needed it, and I needed it urgently, because my savings were running out sooner than I had planned or expected.

By Friday I still hadn't found a job. All the factories had wooden display boards in front listing the skills and professions that were wanted, and mechanics were in demand. But I soon gave up applying after one of the foremen stared at me in amazement when I told him that for family reasons I wouldn't always be able to come to work. After that I tried a few pubs, where I expected a little more understanding, but they just laughed at me when I told them about some unexpected difficulties that might occasionally keep me from coming to work. Some of them pegged me for an alcoholic who had to sleep it off now and then. And just signing me on for appearance was out of the question; for that you had to know the boss, had to know him as a friend. I didn't dare suggest that kind of arrangement to any of the men I spoke to.

When Bernhard showed up on Friday he quickly looked around my apartment and had me show him the modified Adler. We drove out a ways toward Dösen. Behind the cemetery a road led off to a little forest; not a soul was in sight. We stopped, and Bernhard made a thorough inspection of my work. First I had to climb into the compartment, and then he crawled inside and told me to drive around a bit while he lay in the space below the false floor. When I opened the trap door and let him out he gave an approving nod.

"For that amount of money nobody could demand more comfort," he said, and grinned. He took a folding ruler out of his pocket and measured the hidden compartment between the floors, then noted the measurements in a calendar book.

On the way back he asked me about my job.

"It's all taken care of," I said. "I can take off whenever I want."

"So what kind of work is it?"

"Beekeeper," I said. It had occurred to me that morning. This ancient uncle of mine was a beekeeper; as a child I used to visit him now and then. He always had free time. In the spring and summer he had to rearrange his trailers every few weeks, inspect the combs, and extract the honey, and at the end of the season he was always pretty busy, but for that he had nothing to do all winter. He must have owned at least five hundred colonies, which he housed in three modified train cars. In addition to the proceeds from the honey, he got paid by farmers to set up his trailers on their fields, but the only ones who could afford that were those with large holdings or orchards, or else the collectives. They would haul his trailers into position with tractors or horses and then return them to his property in the fall. Throughout the summer he would drive out to his trailers every few days to look after the bees, but during the winter there really was nothing for him to do. In our family he was considered rich and everyone thought he'd hit the jackpot with that line of work. If I could work for him I'd have just the right job to be able to take off for a road trip at any time. I hoped I could persuade my uncle; he wouldn't have to pay me, just simply register me as an employee, and since he was already old enough to retire, that was bound to seem plausible to the authorities. In case he wasn't comfortable with the idea, and that was possible, since I really hadn't seen him in years—I didn't even know if he still had his bees—I still intended to make myself independent as a beekeeper. I would ask him to teach me and then I would submit my application for a license at the employment office. I didn't think it would be difficult to become a beekeeper, especially as I wouldn't be dependent on the income from the honey. I had yet to do any of this, but when Bernhard asked, I claimed that I was all set up. He seemed satisfied and told me I wouldn't have to wait long for my first fare; he would phone me. He warned me not to say anything over the phone; I should listen to him, remember everything he said, and not write any of it down. He would go with me on the first run, show me what I needed to know and introduce me to the contact. This also meant that I wouldn't receive anything for the first trip, other than my expenses and probably money for gas.

"That's your apprenticeship," he said, when I looked at him, surprised. "Don't worry, with your special car you'll get the best passengers. They'll have to pay extra for the hiding place, and that goes straight into your pocket. You see, we're very meticulous. Everybody gets what's coming to him, and nobody cheats anybody out of a single cent. That way no one gets any dumb ideas."

"I'll wait for your call. And where do we meet?"

"I'll tell you over the phone. Somewhere near the client, but never at his place. We're extremely careful about that. Don't forget that if something goes wrong it goes completely wrong. The district attorney will be overjoyed."

That same day I wrote my uncle and told him I wanted to visit. Three days later I called and asked if it was all right with him if I came by. He was surprised but said I was always welcome, even if he had a hard time getting around. Unfortunately he couldn't offer me a dinner, since his wife had died the year before and he was living on his own without any help. I readied myself for a difficult visit and was not proven wrong. The whole house stank of poverty and old age, and when I followed him through the kitchen into his living room, I thought my feet would stick to the floor; there was so much filth everywhere. I took a seat on the edge of a chair—the couch he offered me was just too awful—and listened to him for an hour as he talked about his wife, and about some neighbors who were annoying him. When he asked why I had come and I told him, he laughed and told me I was three years too late, he had given up his bees and sold everything to a man from the neighboring village. I had suspected he might be too frail to still be working as a beekeeper. He wanted to know why I had suddenly discovered a passion for bees, and I told him something about preferring nature to the dirty workshop, and that I'd been interested in bees as far back as school. I asked what I had to do and buy to work as a beekeeper, and he was able to give me some advice that seemed useful. He also knew how to obtain a license, and which districts were interested in having beehives set up. He lectured me for hours about beekeeping, till I was bored to tears: I mean, I wasn't interested in the fact that you couldn't put heather honey in the centrifuge but had to press it out of the combs. I had no intention of producing heather honey; I just needed a license and a few colonies that could buzz around wherever they wanted. As far as I was concerned they could eat their own honey; I didn't have any intention of taking their combs and risking getting stung. But I listened to the old man and even wrote a few things down. When he finally let me go he gave me the key to his shed. There were a few plunge-baskets, as well as some nets and a honey centrifuge, which he told me to take with me. I stowed the things in my car; I was glad to have something to show if someone came up to me and I had to present myself as a beekeeper. He also gave me a book about beekeeping, but I threw it out of the car once I was underway—it stank of my uncle.

Two weeks later I called Bernhard and asked when we would meet. I told him I'd been away a lot and might have missed his call. He was very curt and said only that he would call and I shouldn't call him again. I could tell by his reaction it was a mistake. But I'd already spent so much money; I needed to earn some for a change.

Bernhard called a week later and said he was expecting me at nine a.m. the next morning at the main post office in Altenburg. I told him I'd be there. He repeated the time and place and hung up.

I was a whole hour too early at the post office; I parked my car and walked through town, all the way to the Little Pond. Then I turned around, walked the other way up to the

Orangerie and the castle, and in the end I had to rush to get back to the post office on time. I didn't see Bernhard in the lobby, so I went outside and waited next to my car. Bernhard showed up half an hour late. He parked his car, walked over to me, and we sat down in my car. He said we had to take a couple with a small child to Berlin—the parents were teachers and lived on Brauhausstrasse.

"Where to in Berlin?"

"To the meeting place. Kiefholzstrasse in Treptow. I'll show you everything. Unless other arrangements have been made the handoff is always there."

"Handoff to whom?"

"You stop at the corner of Wildenbruchstrasse and just wait. If you get there at the right time you won't have to wait long—a man will come to your car, knock on the window, and ask if you can change a bill for him. That's your man. You have your clients get out, give them their luggage, and then leave as fast as you can. But first get the money, Koller, because there's no chance of collecting later. And you can't take anyone to court, that's for sure. If you're more than an hour late at the meeting point—and that's happened; after all, anything can happen—you might as well drive back with your clients, because no one will come to meet them. And if your man in Berlin keeps you waiting for longer than an hour, then you leave and take your freight with you. That means something went wrong. And then the people don't pay anything, you understand?

"Not even for gas?"

"No. Nothing. That's part of the agreement, and you have to stick to it if you want to stay in. Think about it, because if you try and get them to pay something, even though you drove them to Berlin and back, they might get annoyed. Then they might change their minds and say something about it somewhere. Then they have you by the balls. So, no handoff, no money. Is that clear?"

"Got it."

"You'll soon meet the men in Berlin—there are two, always the same. I don't know their names, I've never spoken with them, it's better for everybody that way. And that's what you should do, too. So . . . now drive past the church and then straight to the next big street and then turn left."

"Do you know Altenburg?"

"No. I've never been here."

"So how do you know where we have to go?"

"You have to take care of that beforehand. When you get the address, then get hold of a map of some kind. And memorize everything. Never ask anybody, not even in Berlin. Don't speak to anyone, don't stick out, nobody should remember you."

"My car sticks out everywhere."

"That's right. That's the dumb thing about your car. But that nice lower deck makes up for that. So, now turn left. And then left again at the second cross street."

He got out in front of the teachers' house and told me to stay in the car. It was bound to take a while; based on experience, the people almost always had much too much luggage. Then he had to explain to them that they shouldn't cross the border in a tourist bus but with the S-Bahn, and that they would be checked by the border guards. There were usually nerves and tears, and they usually ended up repacking everything. I should count on it taking about half an hour and stay near the car at all times. It was almost an hour before Bernhard came out with the people. I was about to stow the luggage in the special compartment, but Bernhard shook his head without saying anything and pointed to the trunk. I opened it and stowed two backpacks and a small suitcase. The couple climbed inside with the child; Bernhard sat next to me, and we set off toward the Autobahn. In the rearview mirror I could see the couple with their child, a girl three or four years old. The parents were in their early thirties; they were anxious and whispered between themselves. Bernhard answered their questions so curtly they soon gave up trying to converse with us. Once we passed Zeitz, Bernhard had me stop along a straight stretch of road that ran along a little forest. There, he and I hid the couple's luggage in the secret compartment. Bernhard told the woman that she should now give her daughter a sleeping tablet. While the couple tended to their child and ate the sandwiches they had brought along, we stretched our legs and smoked a cigarette.

We were stopped at the control point. At that time, before the wall, there were control points all around Berlin. Police patrols were stationed on the Autobahn and all the highways: you had to drive up slowly, and they either waved you on ahead or they noticed something about your car and made you stop. I had driven up very slowly, so as not to appear suspicious. One of the policemen saw my car and his eyes went wide. He waved us over; we had to show our IDs and tell him where we were headed. The policeman asked me to climb out and open the trunk. Since there was nothing there but a first-aid kit and a spare tire, he was satisfied. He glanced at the couple inside. Since the little girl was asleep on their laps, he signaled to me to drive on.

"Very good," Bernhard said to me quietly. "I've seldom passed through so smoothly. You know, your car sticks out all right, but if you can make the luggage disappear, it's all to the good. I ought to get an old classic like this for myself. Is it possible?"

"No. You have to rebuild it, piece by piece. It took me two years."

"Then I'll get an old truck instead. There's enough storage room, and it's less conspicuous."

"And probably won't cost as much, either."

"What kind of mileage do you get? Twenty miles to the gallon?"

"If I take it real slow and easy, maybe. But I've never managed that."

"Good lord. Looks like I'd better give you money for gas."

"That would be good. Because slowly but surely I'm getting pretty strapped. Lately I've had nothing but expenses, nonstop."

"Just wait. You'll be earning good money soon enough."

In Berlin he showed me where to go, and I tried to memorize the route. When we came to a main artery and I could go straight for a few miles, he turned to the husband and said, "Okay . . . we'll be at your destination in five minutes. Your first destination. A colleague will take you from there. You can give me the money now."

The teacher reached in his jacket pocket, took out an envelope, and handed it over. Bernhard opened it and counted the money; I could tell that it was several hundred marks. When Bernhard noticed that I was looking he winked at me, quite pleased.

We reached Kiefholzstrasse fifteen minutes after the agreed time. On our right was a railway embankment; to our left was a property in ruins and a green lot where a building had once stood. Not a soul was to be seen on the street. Scarcely had we stopped than a man appeared suddenly; he must have been waiting in some entranceway. The man eyed the car for a moment, then walked up to Bernhard and opened the door. We climbed out.

"That's our new man," said Bernhard, and pointed to me. The man looked at me attentively, without greeting me or changing his expression. Bernhard had the couple get out, then he climbed inside the car, opened the trap door, and fished out their luggage. The husband strapped one of the backpacks on his back, then picked up the other backpack and the suitcase while his wife carried the sleeping child. Bernhard jabbed me and we climbed inside, turned around, and drove back.

"So, now what happens?" I asked.

"As we arranged, I'll call you. And don't phone me. Ever. Understood?"

"I mean, what happens to the three of them?"

"No idea. I really don't know."

"Why don't these people go to Berlin on their own?"

"I didn't ask them."

"They just have to buy a train ticket and there they are. Why pay a pile of money for something they could do themselves?"

"I don't know, Koller. Maybe they're dumb, or incompetent, or too scared. Or maybe they need a guarantee for everything, and we give them that guarantee. You know, Koller, there are people who go to the end of whatever line they see; they can't help it, they're always lining up and waiting. And we show them a way to get ahead, that's what they pay us for. That's nice for everybody, isn't it?"

"You can make a lot of money off people's stupidity. I just hope they're not so dumb that they'll blab to somebody later. That could wind up hurting us."

"Yes, that's the real risk. That and their luggage. We tell them exactly what they can and cannot take, but you can bet that if one of the checkpoint guards looks at their luggage he can tell at a glance that they aren't just taking a vacation. No matter what we say, they insist on taking the family silver."

We drove to Altenburg, where Bernhard had left his car. When we said good-bye he handed me a hundred marks and then, when I looked at the bill and said nothing, added another fifty.

"I'll call," said Bernhard, when he climbed out of my car. "Don't worry. Just stay calm."

Over the next few days I read a book about beekeeping and applied for a license. The book was apparently for hobby gardeners, full of advice on how to fix up everything yourself, and it talked about the bees as if they were old aunts or little children that required loving care and putting up with their moods and pranks. But I learned what I had to and was able to make a list of all the things I needed to obtain in order to start. I underlined a few expressions and learned them by heart to be able to talk with beekeepers. I took out ads in three newspapers, in the hope of finding an older man ready to give up his bees who would sell me everything cheaply and all at once.

At the office they mostly made me wait. They had no time and no desire to deal with me and my request. It took three tries before I was able to speak to the official in charge, a fat man with a ruddy face. He acted as if he were very busy. Meanwhile, I had acquired enough experience with such people to realize right off that a little money would go a long way. I sat in front of his desk for some time, because his phone kept interrupting our conversation, and because he couldn't find a particular paper. As soon as his colleague left the room, I placed an envelope with some money on the table without saying a word. The fat man was on the phone and without so much as pausing his conversation he picked up the envelope, opened it, counted the money, and stuck it in his jacket. After he hung up he returned to the subject of my license. He made no mention of the money, nor did he thank me. Finally he told me when I should return to pick up the official document. I got up to leave and he went right back to his papers. I was impressed how matter-of-factly he had taken my money, without the slightest gesture of appreciation; he must be very experienced.

Whenever I went out I was worried I might miss a call from Bernhard. We had agreed on two times for phoning: eight in the morning and between seven and eight in the evening, but since I hadn't heard anything from him for days I was afraid he had tried to reach me in vain and had hired another driver. It took a while for me to realize I was one of two backup men to whom he passed along jobs he either couldn't do because he didn't have the time or had other passengers, or didn't want to do because they were a little too hot. I got the clients that Bernhard didn't want. But there was no point in complaining, and besides, who would I complain to?

For my first solo job I drove an elderly couple from Bad Muskau to Berlin. The day before I had had to visit Bernhard in Guldenberg, to get their names and address. He gave me a handwritten description of how to get to their house. The writing was extremely neat but used the old-style letters and I had a hard time deciphering them. The next day I was standing outside a four-story apartment building in Bad Muskau and rang the couple's bell. An old lady immediately opened; she must have been waiting for me. The couple had much too much luggage, and I told them so. They grumbled and moaned, then repacked, and an hour later we set off. I knew they still had more luggage than I could stow in my compartment during a stop along the way. I told myself that a single suitcase in the trunk wouldn't cause any trouble at the checkpoint, especially since the suitcase had nothing but clothes, as the couple assured me.

During the drive I tried to avoid conversing with the couple, as Bernhard had advised, but they were so talkative I couldn't manage. I asked why they wanted to move to the West, and the woman told me that her husband had been in the civil service for over forty-five years, and that he would get a decent retirement in the West, whereas he received a mere pittance in the East, precisely because he had always been a loyal servant of the German state. It was hardly enough to live on. After we passed the checkpoint I asked for the amount of money that had been agreed upon, though it embarrassed me to take so much from these two old people. On the other hand, it was their choice, and I'd had more than enough expenses for the past weeks and my bank account was empty.

I arrived punctually at the meeting place in Berlin and had to wait ten minutes before I could hand off the couple. The same man who had come when I was with Bernhard suddenly appeared beside my car. He didn't say anything to me and waited in silence until I had given the couple their luggage. When I drove off I looked in the rearview mirror and saw all three crossing the street; the two old people carrying everything, while the young man walked in front of them without carrying a single bag. I had seen him smirk when I shook hands with the couple and thanked them as I said good-bye. The boy is right, I said to myself: you're much too friendly to these clients. I determined to avoid any such conversations on subsequent trips.

Every month I would get four or five jobs, seldom more, and I earned a lot of money—easily twice as much as when I was working as a mechanic. If I smuggled a passenger to Berlin using the compartment, either because he was wanted by the authorities or because his ID didn't allow him to travel outside his district, then it meant a lot more money. But I didn't often have that kind of luck: once a month at best.

It took me some time and effort to build up my beekeeping operation, especially because I didn't have much incentive after obtaining the license. I managed to buy the necessary tools and a bee trailer with rubber tires that had been sitting in a dilapidated barn, but buying the bees themselves proved extremely difficult. I had no experience: I had almost reached an agreement with one farmer, but when he saw how little I knew he refused to sell me any of his swarms. By May I finally owned fifteen colonies and set up my trailer near Eythra, a village south of Leipzig, just half an hour away from my apartment. I had phoned a few of the collective farms, and Eythra was interested in my bees and prepared to reimburse all my expenses as well as pick up my trailer, take it to the fields, and move it to the next spot after a few weeks. When I showed up in the office of the collective, the two men from the administration were suspicious since I was so young, but I told them about the long tradition of beekeeping in my family, and that reassured them. Once the trailer was set up near a huge field of rape, I really did have little to do and could have traveled to Berlin twenty times a month, except that Bernhard wanted to earn money himself.

After a while the guards at the checkpoints knew me and my Adler, and I could predict exactly what would happen when I saw which of the uniformed men approach. One of them was keenly interested in my car and we always exchanged a few words; he himself owned a BMW motorcycle that was twenty years old, and we talked shop with each other. I thought it was a good idea, that being in the good graces of an official would spare me a more thorough inspection. After a few weeks I had to change my route so as to approach Berlin through a different checkpoint. The official had become so interested in my car that I was barely able to keep him from climbing inside, and then only with the promise that I'd show him everything on my next trip. He knew a thing or two about those older machines and could easily have found the false floor. I'm sure he would have noticed that modifications were made if he'd gone inside, and that was bound to make him suspicious. After that, I avoided telling the officials more than I needed to, especially when I noticed that my Adler had caught their eye and they wanted to talk about it.

I saw Bernhard regularly: I had to meet him before every trip, as he refused to pass any information by mail or phone. Now and then he came to Leipzig, if he was on his way somewhere or had business in the city, but mostly I had to drive to meet him at his home in Guldenberg. He owned a single-family house with a large garden on Moorbadstrasse, and lived there with a girl from Spora, a little gray mouse that flitted through the rooms, admiring her Bernhard. All he said about her was that she kept his garden in order and let him support her, and when she came to us in the room and asked if we wanted something to drink, he just rudely sent her away. She knew nothing about how he earned his money; as far as she was concerned he owned a carousel and had two employees who transported it from fair to fair, whom Bernhard had to check up on regularly. Bernhard added that I should keep my own mouth shut as well, even in bed, especially in bed, because you never knew how stupidly things could happen, and in his experience things happened as stupidly as possible.

After we had finished our business and gone to the Crown for a beer, I asked how he had started making these trips to Berlin.

"Complete coincidence," he said. "One summer I was at Rügen and I got to know a couple of people. We started talking, wondering how we might make some money, and somebody had this great idea. You don't need to know any more than that, it's better for everybody that way. And I really don't know anything about the others. I don't know a single name, and no one knows my name, either, except for you."

"I mean, how did it happen that you of all people started doing this? I would never have dreamed it. The last I heard about you was the business with the farmers."

"You mean the collectivization? That was a fun time back then," Bernhard said and laughed.

"You were even at Griesel's. At least that's what I heard."

"Of course. I wasn't about to let Griesel off the hook."

"I thought you actually wanted to be a party functionary."

"Me?" He laughed again.

"Absolutely. All the people pressuring the farmers to join the collective back then were party types through and through."

"Maybe. I don't know."

"So how did you wind up joining?"

"It just happened. I enjoyed it."

"But why you? And now we're smuggling people over the border."

"That's life, Koller."

"Why did you do it?"

"Revenge is sweet, Koller."

"Who ever did anything to you?"

"To this day I remember when we arrived. The way people looked at us. Whenever I went into a store, they watched my every move—everybody, not just the shopkeeper. And when I paid, I could see that they were talking about me behind my back. Where does this boy get the money for that, it's bound to be stolen. You know, Koller, I swore to myself I'd get my revenge. For them we were the starving paupers all those years, and that's how they treated us. And then suddenly the tables were turned. Let them see what it's like to lose everything. They didn't have to spend a long time persuading me: I joined right away. They had treated us like dirt."

"Even Griesel?"

"Griesel was the devil himself. He gave us the room with the storage closet, where the three foreign laborers had been housed earlier. And he treated us no better than them."

"So that's why you did it?"

"I only wish I could have gone after a few of my teachers. Voigt more than anybody. Or else Barthel, the policeman. Even today when I see him on the street, as old as he is, I'd still like to let him have it. It was a nice feeling back then. Suddenly they were all afraid of me. Everybody."

"It's true, people weren't too nice about taking in the refugees."

"'All these people who were expelled need to be expelled a little further, right into the Mulde.' Griesel said that right to my father's face. Another beer, Koller?"

"No. I have to drive back. Better not to have you as an enemy, right?"

"Let's just say I don't forget anything. Ever."

"And now? Are you doing this out of revenge as well?"

He looked at me closely and seemed surprised. Then he blew the smoke right in my face and said, "It's fun, Koller."

I called the waiter, paid, and got up.

"Have a good trip tomorrow, Koller."

"Piece of cake, right?"

That August they sealed the border and built a wall in Berlin. I heard about it on the radio one Sunday morning and immediately went to see Bernhard. He didn't know any more than I did, and just said we should wait and not use the telephone for the moment. It might be a temporary measure; and if not, then we could forget about our chauffeuring. He would go back to work as a carpenter, because the carousel only paid off if it belonged to you. On my way home I wondered whether I should give up the bees and go back to work as a mechanic, or else buy enough colonies that I could live off the honey. Although I was keeping the bees strictly as a camouflage, I had since learned to handle them, and had even extracted some honey.

Two weeks later Bernhard drove over to tell me that our enterprise would continue. He was coming from Berlin, where he had just taken his first customer since the wall went up, and he had an assignment for me: I was to take a family from Riesa to Berlin. Bernhard said that a few of the arrangements had changed. The clients were no longer to be dropped off during the day but at midnight, and at the Malmöer Strasse, in the middle of the city. Now they could take all the papers they wanted, but they were allowed only one backpack per person. The price went up, too—dramatically, because things had gotten really dangerous, at least for the people who had to smuggle the clients directly into West Berlin. Bernhard didn't want to tell me how that took place; as far as I could see, they were led through the sewers. Larger groups were smuggled all at once, so that on the appointed days all available cars were working to bring the clients together. Two operations would happen each month; at least that was the plan. For each drive there were fixed fees—five times the typical previous amount. For us it was easier, since there were fewer checkpoints around Berlin, but in general the business had become more risky, because the smugglers had no chance of talking their way out of it if they were caught, which was why the price for the entire operation went up, to, I believe, several thousand marks per person—Bernhard didn't know, nor did he want to know. All that mattered to us was that we were to receive one thousand for every passenger, regardless of whether it was an adult or a child.

"Are you still in?" asked Bernhard.

I nodded. I was just glad that things were finally starting up again and I could earn some money. I had gotten used to the danger, which added a sense of thrill that wasn't at all unpleasant.

"You realize that if they catch a group they'll squeeze them long enough until they have our names."

"They won't find out my name. And if you don't tell them, then nobody will know it. How would they?"

"Don't be so sure. If they pick up one of our clients, they'll probably be able to figure out the rest. If they really want to, they'll track us down."

"I wasn't born yesterday."

Just as Bernhard had said, we conducted two operations per month. The deliveries used to take place on different days of the week; now I drove mostly on Saturday nights—I don't know why. I had less to do, but since the fees had risen I still earned my money. The handoffs now had to happen very punctually, so that I always drove into Berlin an hour earlier and drove around the vicinity of the meeting place or parked until it was time to go to Malmöer Strasse. I was more careful than before not to talk with my passengers and to avoid anything that could help them remember me. On the other hand, almost everyone I took got a good look at my car, and there weren't many of these old coaches on the road, so it would be easy to catch me, based merely on the Adler. Since the hidden compartment was no longer needed, as there were no more checkpoints around Berlin, and I didn't have to hide passengers or luggage there, I considered obtaining a less conspicuous car, and put feelers out for a second vehicle. I had no intention of giving up the Adler: I wanted to keep it forever. I planned to remove the false floor, so that it would once again be in its original condition, but since this wasn't urgent, I kept putting it off, particularly since I was able to pick up an old Wartburg in February that required a lot of work just to get it streetworthy. At the end of March I drove this car to Berlin for the first time. It was a little faster, used less gas, and was less conspicuous. Above all, I no longer had to let strangers inside my masterpiece, people with no love whatsoever for old-time cars, who were careless and thought of nothing but the adventuresome flight out of the country that lay before them.

That May we temporarily halted our trips. A group of twelve people had been caught and arrested together with their guide in one of the sewers that led to West Berlin. Both Bernhard and I had driven some of these people, or so it seemed based on the information we read in the press and that Bernhard received from Berlin. The same night the group had been run in we had taken clients to Berlin, and Bernhard and I agreed to hold off making any more trips until we knew our names hadn't come up in the trial.

I had built up my beekeeping operation and now possessed fifty colonies. The old trailer was completely packed with beehives; it was a joy to hear the buzzing and droning and seething. Some days I drove out to the field, parked my car, and sat beside the old trailer to watch the bees and listen to their buzzing. If I kept very still I didn't need to fear them. They crawled around my head and on my hands without stinging me. I enjoyed being a beekeeper; I even caught myself talking to the bees, cajoling them to work hard for me. When I sat in my apartment and a spring storm came down, I thought about my bees and even wondered whether I shouldn't drive out and check on them. In the end I didn't go, but I enjoyed the fact that I could be so concerned about the little creatures. I enjoyed talking about the bees with the farmers. I tried to get on their good side; I was dependent on their help, and asked them to look in on the bees now and then when they were driving by, and contact me in the event of an emergency.

The thirteen people caught in the sewer went on trial at the end of June. Bernhard was very worried; up to the last minute he was afraid that the criminal police would show up at his door. I wasn't worried at all, and indeed we were spared. The people were given sentences ranging from eighteen to twenty-four months; the smuggler got four years.

So that's what we can expect, I told Bernhard, and he nodded darkly. Then he tried to cheer me up when I told him I was thinking of getting out. He tried to persuade me, saying that it was a unique opportunity to earn money, a lot of money. He succeeded in dispelling my reservations. And I didn't want to lose the income; I needed the money. On their own, the bees brought in too little. To live off them I'd have to have two or three hundred colonies, and that would have meant more work. The temptation of continuing to earn so much money so easily and quickly was greater than my fear.

Fourteen days later I had another delivery to Berlin; four people who squeezed into the Wartburg and didn't stop talking about all the things they were going to buy once they were over the border. Bernhard was driving as well, but we were no longer driving on the same day. There was also a new meeting place: now I was supposed to take the people to an ice-cream parlor on Karl-Marx-Allee. They were no longer being led through the sewers but by a different way I didn't know, and didn't want to know. Evidently the passengers had to pay more, but our earnings did not change.

For a year and a half everything went well. There were two fairly regular trips a month; very seldom, just once, there were three. I got the money as soon as I arrived at the parking lot behind the ice-cream parlor, then I handed them over to the next person, and left as quickly as possible. I convinced myself that I was out of danger because I really wasn't any more than a glorified taxi driver.

In December it was all over. Twelve days before Christmas I was arrested. I had taken two people to Berlin, a married couple from Dresden, who spent the whole time arguing about whether what they were doing was right. Evidently the man didn't want to go and kept trying to talk his wife out of it, right up to the end. There was no sign of my man at the meeting place, and I waited with the couple for ten minutes. Then I told them something had gone wrong and that I would take them back, because we weren't supposed to wait more than ten minutes. Just as we were about to leave a man came up to me and asked if I was waiting for Arthur. I shrugged my shoulders and wanted to keep going, since I didn't know the name of my contact, and we were never supposed to mention names. The man, however, would not be brushed off; he stopped me and took a bill out of his pocketbook, held it in front of my nose, and asked if I could change it. That was the agreed-upon signal for special situations, so I figured he was a replacement who in his excitement had made the mistake of mentioning a name. I pointed to the couple behind me and said he could take them at once and that next time he should be punctual, because another minute and we would have driven off.

"Wait a moment," he said to me, smiling. "You can come right along yourself."

At that moment five or six men jumped up and grabbed the couple and me. They took us to a small bus with the windows painted over and shoved us rudely inside. They sat us down, separated from one another, with two men on either side of each of us. The bus sped through the city; I had no idea where we were going. I sensed what was in store and tried to stay casual and amused. I told the men that there must be some mistake; I didn't know who they were or what they wanted, but in any case I hadn't done anything wrong. Then the bus stopped; we were told to get out and found ourselves in a courtyard surrounded by long new buildings. We were taken to one of the entrances and handed over to other men who were also in civilian dress. In the corridor we were separated; I never saw the couple again, not even at my trial. Then the interrogations began, lasting several days; I stuck with my story that I had agreed to bring the couple to Berlin as a favor; I hardly knew them and didn't know anything else. If the couple had done something crooked, I didn't know about it. I used the same tactic in court, and in fact they really couldn't prove anything against me; they had a few statements from the couple and from one of the men in Berlin. I denied everything and acted so outraged that the judge warned me about my demeanor. The two thousand marks in my pocket proved incriminating, however. I was unable to give any convincing explanation for that at the time of arrest—only later did I think up some good answers. In the end, the worst witness against me was my beautiful Adler; that was what got me convicted. They discovered the false floor, which I had meant to dismantle weeks before, but because I had to have the Wartburg ready and was building up my bees I had kept putting it off. During the trial it was this false floor, this secret compartment, that was considered an especially aggravating circumstance and irrefutable proof; it landed me a whole extra year.

They sentenced me to five and a half years. Both cars were confiscated as criminal instruments. I protested loudly and was given another warning.

Four men were accused along with me at the same trial; I had seen one of them at the deliveries. Without any arrangement we denied knowing each other during the questioning, and we withstood the cross-examination. Two of the accused were considered ringleaders and received two years more than I did. We had been betrayed by someone they'd caught shortly before they arrested us and who was ready to tell everything he knew. Bernhard wasn't caught; his name never came up, neither in court nor in the previous interrogations; he was lucky.

I had to serve my whole term. I was denied early parole because, as I was informed, I failed to show any understanding or regret. I spent the five and a half years in various prisons, and never had any visitors—except for one single time, when I was led into the visiting area because someone had registered and wanted to see me.

My mother wrote to me regularly. My father had forbidden her to visit me in prison. He wouldn't allow it—he didn't want either of them to have contact with a criminal. For a few months I expected Bernhard might visit me or write. I had hoped he would at least send a few things you need in a cell, things that can give a person strength, a little hope. Just a piece of chocolate or a magazine with the latest cars, or a book, any book—even a book of poems, although actually I've never been one for reading, least of all poetry.

I had expected that Bernhard would look after me now and then, because it was really on his account that I was in prison, at least that's what I told myself for two years. It was only because of him that I had started these drives, and later, when I had wanted to get out after the one group was arrested, it was Bernhard who convinced me to go on. I wanted to give it up; it was only because of him that I kept doing it. So I didn't exactly think highly of Bernhard, considering he didn't lift a finger to help me. I told myself that if I had mentioned his name during the interrogation or at the trial it would have been a plus for me: my cooperation would have gotten me a milder punishment, possibly much milder. In prison I heard that a few defendants in similar trials even got off with a suspended sentence, because they squealed so much. But I kept my mouth shut, since I didn't want to drag anybody else in, and I took it amiss that Bernhard simply left me there to rot. Later I accepted that it was entirely my own fault; after all, I hadn't gotten involved in smuggling people out of the republic because of Bernhard; and while it's true that I had wanted to get out after that group was arrested, the ultimate reason I went on was the money. And I would have gone on with or without Bernhard; I could forget about him and had to stop telling myself he was the guilty one. I alone was the idiot responsible for the mess I was in.

I had been in prison for over a year when I started borrowing books from the library. An older cellmate—he was over forty—told me about it; he was borrowing books to learn Spanish. At first I was annoyed because he kept pacing up and down our small cell, mumbling his Spanish words, always back and forth, and this constant mumbling, but then I realized that he knew how to put the time to better use than I did. I reported to the person who ran the library and asked for some English books for beginners. He gave me a thin paperback. I started with the numbers. Learning the pronunciation was difficult; the book kept referring to the corresponding records, but when I asked the librarian about the records he just laughed. When I wanted to know why they would have bought an audio course if there wasn't a single record player in the entire prison, he laughed and told me to think about it. When I asked again he said he was pretty sure the head warden owned a record player, and that he was in the habit of ordering books and records for himself through the prison library, a personal cost-cutting measure he was able to accomplish as all the orders were inspected by him. At first my older colleague helped me with the pronunciation, but we started quarreling at the slightest cause, and so I attempted to learn on my own. Because I wasn't making any headway I gave up the language study and borrowed other books—the only two books in the library about cars, and novels as well. I read all the things I should have read in school but never did; I learned three long poems by heart and said them out loud when I was feeling particularly bad. I can still recite one of them completely, Schiller's "Hostage." At the time, I wanted someone to send me something I could keep in the cell, a small personal possession such as a book, something that would belong just to me. Nobody, including Bernhard, thought about doing that for me. Perhaps he was afraid of being caught after the fact and wanted to avoid all contact with me and the others. Later I heard he was working as a carpenter in Guldenberg. Right after my arrest he must have given up the trips to Berlin and gone back to his old profession. I never saw him again, nor did I ever go back to Guldenberg. I was angry at my parents for writing me off when I was in prison. I didn't attend their funerals, not even my mother's.

I had one single visit while I was in prison. I learned about it the day before. The chief guard told me my fiancée was coming the next day, and since I never had any visitors, he looked at me with curiosity. I didn't show anything at all. I figured it had to be Gitti. She came in a short skirt; I could see her upper thighs, and that was all I thought about later when I recalled her visit. Her thighs and Wilhelm, because she had brought him along as well. Gitti lived by herself; she hadn't found a new boyfriend, which didn't surprise me—who wants a woman with a black child?

Wilhelm was already in first grade and had turned into a handsome, sturdy boy. Gitti had somehow arranged to bring him into the visiting room, though that ordinarily wasn't allowed. He sat on the chair the whole time and kept looking at me, without making a face or saying a word. When I spoke to him he kept on staring at me silently and seriously and didn't react at all. I liked little Wilhelm. I understood him. If I had stayed with him I would have had a completely different life and would never have wound up in prison. But that was impossible for me; I couldn't have pulled that off. If the stupid woman had betrayed me with just anybody I never would have noticed and the child would have been mine forever. And even if I might have found out one day, I think I would have stayed with the child and his dumb mother, because I would have liked the boy. To this day I don't know where Gitti scared up a black man, because back then there wasn't a single Negro anywhere in Naumburg or the surrounding area. I couldn't have managed it: every morning, every day, and every night, having a boy with a pigmentation alteration, and me supposed to be the father. So, prison it was.

After I was released—and I had to sit out my term to the day—I went to Leipzig and received an apartment within two days. The authorities also saw to it that I found work as a mechanic. The woman from the city district office didn't hide what she thought of me, but she performed her work correctly. The apartment I received was small, with a bathroom and a remodeled kitchen; and the auto shop was the largest one in Leipzig—there it made no difference that I'd been in the clink. Once during our morning break my coworkers asked me about it, and I told them my story. And when I added that anybody could easily wind up in jail for a few years, not even the foreman contradicted me, and several of the men nodded.

For a few years I kept searching for my car. Whenever there was a classic car meet anywhere in the country, or a race or an exhibition, I went. I would have recognized my Adler even if it had been repainted in the meantime. There were probably only two such big, six-window limos in the entire country, or so it seemed, because the same two always showed up at these meetings. Both of these Adlers belonged to idiots with lots of money but no real understanding of their cars; in any case, I would have been ashamed to show my car in such a pitiful condition. You don't do that to a car, not if you really love it.

My Adler had disappeared, and to this day it hasn't surfaced. Perhaps that's a good thing for me, because I don't know what I would do if I were to see it one afternoon on one of the display lawns closed off for the exhibition. Maybe I'd lunge at the new owner's throat, or just start fighting with him. I would move heaven and earth to get my Adler back. I'd offer the man all the money he wanted, or whatever he desired. And if he rejected all my offers, then I might just kill him. After all, it's my car, my baby.

Katharina Hollenbach

I moved to Guldenberg with my sister. When I was only eight years old, I remember declaring at home that I wasn't going to stay on the farm, that I wanted to see something of the world. When I said that, my mother just laughed at me and Father shook his head and sent me out to clean the chicken coop, or maybe it was the rabbit hutch. But I was determined, and every day I told myself that the minute I finished school I was getting out of Spora. I hated any kind of farm work, and marrying a farmer was out of the question—after all, I saw how things were for my mother. She'd thought she was marrying up since my father was due to inherit the farm. But all she wound up with was a chance to toil and grind for her in-laws, my grandparents, who owned the farm and treated her little better than a servant girl. They demanded a lot of work from their son and his wife. Moreover, they constantly wanted my parents to be grateful to them because they were going to leave them the farm. Grandfather and his wife stayed on the farm after he retired, and he never stopped ordering everyone around, and that included my mother. She never had any time off. There's no closing time on a farm.

As a young girl she had dreamed of marrying well, and the farm was one of the best in Spora: Grandfather was the largest landowner. And what did my mother get out of it? She thought she would be going to town now and then with her husband to buy clothes, or go to the pastry shop, or be invited out to dance in a fancy nightclub, but nothing of the kind ever happened! All of Mama's good clothes came from the time before she was married. After that the only new things she bought were work clothes, aprons, and slippers once a year, that was it. We didn't have lipstick or perfume in the house; I didn't know what those things were until my girlfriends from school invited me over. And my first lipstick came from a school friend as well: I stole it from her. As for dancing, my mother never went dancing in a club ever. The only dancing she got to do was at the two village festivals held every year, May Day and the Harvest Festival. People would dance for an hour in the village pub, by which time the men were so drunk they couldn't stand on their own two feet anymore. No, I had absolutely no desire to wind up on a farm. Whenever I met a boy I liked I immediately asked what kind of work he did, and if he or his parents had a farm, I just said thank you for the flowers but you'll have to milk the cows and clean up after the goats without me. The boy could look like Gérard Philipe or even Jean Gabin—I would have fainted if *he* had spoken to me—but if he had livestock and a farm, all his good looks were for nothing. He could be built like a bull but I didn't care.

When Grandfather died, the work didn't let up; Mother just wasn't ordered around so much. Now she could breathe more freely; she spoke openly even with us children about how the old man's death didn't trouble her, and she felt relieved because finally Father and she were the masters of the Hollenbach farm. In reality, however, nothing had changed. The day still began at five in the morning, because the animals had to be fed, and from then on it was constant work. At six in the evening we'd have supper, and sometimes, after eating, if mother didn't get up immediately to clear the table and wash the dishes with us girls, she'd fall asleep at the table.

We didn't have a TV. We asked Father several times to get one, because almost everyone at school had a television at home. All Father said was that there was plenty to see on the farm, no need to buy some dumb expensive box. Why should we watch horses, cows, and chickens on television when we have them all right here! There's plenty to see here! Look—a different program in every stall!

My parents never took a vacation; they didn't have time for that; the animals wouldn't let them. We children went to the same lake each year for summer camp. We spent two weeks in wooden cabins, going on hikes and sunning on the tiny beach near our camp. Every year there were swimming lessons for anyone who couldn't swim or who wanted to learn the backstroke or the crawl, and there was a night hike and a farewell party, but after the fourth summer I'd had enough of always going to the same place and begged my parents to take us to the Baltic or Lake Balaton like other families. Father shook his head and listed all the things I could do in the house or the barn. Of course there were the family parties, but that meant seeing the same faces year in year out and always having the same conversations. One Sunday I told my father he should do something nice with my mother, anything, like go for a drive in the country. Father just looked at Mother and said, "But, child, I do that every day. Every day I take Mother to the country—right here in our pasture." He laughed uproariously, and Mother smiled and looked at me as if I had lost a marble or two.

Things went on like that until they joined the collective two years after I left home. They had no choice, because they were too deep in debt. They hadn't fulfilled their quota and as a result received much less seed than they needed. My parents both signed the application to join the co-op, and that evening Father got drunk out of despair, as Mother explained to me. Father hadn't joined voluntarily; he felt he had been coerced. The truth was that they then had regular work hours, and except for harvest time they even got the whole day off Sunday. They'd never had that before, and the following year, for the first time in their lives, they went on vacation. For the rest of his days Father cursed the collective, although things were a lot better for him. Mother was assigned to fieldwork and Father managed to get the cattle sheds so he didn't need to drive a tractor all day, which he couldn't do with his bad back. Once when I visited them I told them they ought to be pleased, but Father didn't want to hear about it. The fields were no longer his property, and that made him mad. Even the TV they watched every evening until their eyes closed couldn't make up for that.

In eighth grade I got an apprenticeship and found an apartment in Guldenberg. The best I could wangle was a garden shop, since my grades weren't so good. I didn't really want to become a gardener: I was sick to death of digging in the dirt, and making bouquets was hardly my dream job, but to get out of Spora I would have even apprenticed as a salesgirl, which was offered to me but which I considered the absolute pits. I found a room with a war widow who lived with her son in a small house on Gartenstrasse. When I told my parents what I planned to do the coming September they were stunned and sent me out of the room to talk it over between themselves. Then Father explained that I was too young to live by myself in a strange city and said he would arrange for a proper apprenticeship so that I could go on living at home. I howled and the evening ended with Mother giving me a swipe and sending me off to bed. The apprenticeships Father proposed during the next weeks were no surprise—they all had to do with livestock and farming, or training to be a cook at the collective, where all I'd ever do is scour huge pans and dump shovelfuls of salt into enormous pots that were stirred with great wooden stirrers. I knew all of this from Rieke, who was employed there and had pains in the small of her back every evening from hauling around those heavy pots. Hardly what I was after.

Then heaven intervened, and it really must have been some divine power, because my sister fell in love with a carpenter who happened to come from Guldenberg and worked in Spora. Bernhard was a year older than Rieke. He was strongly built but no taller than me, and he was a quiet sort. I could tell right away that Rieke had a boyfriend. Whenever Mother complained that Rieke still hadn't found an admirer, even though she was already eighteen—and then Father would point out that the girl would be leaving the house soon enough, and Mother should be happy to have some help around the house—I would grin at my sister until she turned red.

Once I realized Rieke's boyfriend came from Guldenberg, I worked on her until she agreed to move there with me. It wasn't that hard to persuade her, because she idolized her Bernhard and would have spent the whole day kowtowing to him. The way she talked about him and sighed over him you'd think he shit gold. The hardest part was getting her to have the guts to tell Father and Mother, because just as I am Father's little girl she is her mother's daughter, always quiet and modest and careful not to stick out. Just like Mother, she was never loud and never demanded anything for herself, and if something good came her way, usually it was because I helped her. Rieke was simply the kind of girl a lot of men like, especially the ones who don't have much say in their lives and need a woman to feel complete as a man.

Rieke told our parents that the reason she was moving to Guldenberg was because she'd found a better job there in an inn called the Black Eagle. Father couldn't say anything against that, because Rieke was already of age, and she didn't earn much in the collective. After our parents swallowed that, I rushed right in, saying that it made sense to move in with Rieke, it would be cheaper and we could help each other out and keep an eye on each other. It only took me a week to convince my parents.

We planned to move into the widow's room that September: Rieke could then spend every evening with her Bernhard, and I would finally be free and out of that dump. I finished school by the skin of my teeth. Old Kossatz, the gardener, didn't care about my grades; after all, I wasn't going to keep his books or talk to the customers about atoms and molecules. All summer long Father worked me hard; I had to help him in the fields the whole time and could only get away for ten days to go camping, but that didn't bother me; I was counting the days until I could begin my apprenticeship in Guldenberg, and no matter what Father said or demanded, I was always in a good mood.

I had told Friederike not to tell our parents anything about Bernhard, especially not the fact that he lived in Guldenberg, and at home I covered for her when she wanted to visit her boyfriend, came home late, or claimed she was spending the weekend at her girlfriend's. The greatest danger was always Rieke herself, because she was incapable of lying and would have liked best to go running to Mother and tell her everything. I had to drum it into her twenty-four hours a day to keep her mouth shut in order not to jeopardize our move. When Bernhard showed up at our house and let slip the word Guldenberg, my plan nearly collapsed, but by then it was too late for Father to keep me from going.

It was his first visit to our house; he and Rieke had been going together for three months. I had met him a long time before that, but our parents had never seen him and wanted to know a thousand things about him, and Father actually took him to the cowshed on his first visit and showed him a trough that needed fixing, which Bernhard promised to do. When they asked Bernhard where he came from and he told them, my parents looked at each other knowingly and said nothing. As soon as Bernhard left the house, Father yelled at Rieke and me.

"And all of that behind my back!" he shouted. Then he turned to Mother and asked her in a threatening voice, "Did you know that?"

Mother assured him that she didn't know a thing about Bernhard or Guldenberg and that we had kept her equally in the dark. Then they sent both of us to the barn to chop beets and that evening Father told us that we hadn't heard the last word about Guldenberg, and that he intended to give everything a thorough thinking-over. Rieke immediately panicked like she always did and I had to calm her down. After all, I'd already signed my contract as a gardener's apprentice and ten horses couldn't keep me from moving to Guldenberg.

Father and Mother were mad because they felt we had pulled a fast one on them, and in that they weren't entirely wrong. But by then everything had been decided: the apprenticeships in Spora had long been taken; the contract was all wrapped up and Rieke and I had already paid the widow a month's security. Father threatened to have an acquaintance of his from Guldenberg check up on us, and Rieke cried and blamed everything on me when we were alone in our room.

"What do you mean?" I answered. "You're the one who had to see her Bernhard! And now you've got what you wanted. You should be grateful to me."

"Yes, but not like this. Not this way. We weren't honest."

"So? What if we weren't? The main thing is it worked out. Am I right?"

Rieke really was a sweet girl. If there was something she wanted, she always wanted it in a way that made everyone happy; problem is, that way you never get anything you really want, only what others can do without, and that's usually not very much. She could never understand that, and so she never got anything more than what people gave her. She should have been pleased I took things into my own hands. She would have stayed at home for another hundred years if Father had had his way—another pair of hands is always welcome on a farm.

On August 29th we moved to Guldenberg with a trunk, four cardboard boxes, and an old duffel bag dating from the First World War that Mother had inherited from her parents. It was stuffed to the brim. Bernhard had borrowed a car and drove us. Father was out in the fields when Bernhard arrived and we loaded the car with our luggage. Mother held back a few tears, and Rieke started sobbing loudly and the two hugged each other for several minutes as if we were going to the other side of the world. When I said good-bye I also said that I was very sad to be leaving, and Mother nearly whacked me because I was so obviously happy that even the buttons on my blouse were glowing. Then Rieke made Bernhard drive out to the field where father was turning over the soil with the horse and plow, so that we could say good-bye to him. I crossed myself three times when we finally left Spora.

Sharing a room with Rieke wasn't hard for me; at home we had slept in the same room, so I was used to it, and I got along well with my sister. She could never decide anything, she was always dithering about what to do, and when she finally brought herself to the verge of doing something, she immediately started having second thoughts. She was mostly relieved to have me make all the decisions, and consequently always did what I said. She liked having no responsibility, so that in an emergency if something went wrong she wasn't the guilty party but could just look at me, full of reproach. If I was too hard on her then she would fly off the handle and start shouting that she wasn't going to let me boss her around anymore, that she was four years older and could think for herself. That would usually blow over just as quickly as it came on; I just had to keep my mouth shut and not rile her any further. I had a way of nodding vigorously and saying that she was right, she should decide things the next time, and that I would listen to my big sister. Then she was satisfied, and the next time she had to decide something, she looked to me, as always, to tell her what to do. A real sweetheart, Rieke.

The widow's name was Schober, but between us we always called her the widow, because her living room was crammed with ancient photos of her bomber-pilot husband. She had a small attic room crammed with junk—probably including her war hero's uniform. She asked us if we wanted to rent this room as well; she wouldn't charge much because there was no way to heat the room. We thanked her and told her we'd think about it. Half a year later I rented it at my own expense, even though I wasn't making any more than the stipend from my apprenticeship—we got next to no money from home. I needed the room to be alone now and then, or at any rate to get away from Friederike.

My apprenticeship was easy enough. Frau Kossatz was a bitter old hag constantly in a foul mood who found fault with anybody and everybody. She would even bawl out the customers if something was eating her. But she didn't have anything to say in the nursery, since old Kossatz was in charge there. He and I got along well. Apart from me, there was one other apprentice, Helke, who was in her last year. Then there was Herr Förster, who took care of all the heavy work and all the building repairs, and Frau Gellag, who oversaw the greenhouse and had a talent for making bouquets; hers were much prettier than Frau Kossatz's or Helke's or mine.

Old Kossatz liked me, since I was never at a loss for words and was always in a good mood. He also liked me in other ways. He was always prowling around me, and whenever I had to work in the beds and had to bend over, he'd take the opportunity to look down my blouse. And there was something to see there, too.

Already at fourteen, I had beautiful breasts, and since I

refused to put on one of those horrible pink or white bras, they were free to move about. The men liked that, and so did old Kossatz. Naturally Friederike wore a bra. I told her that it would make her breasts sag because the tissue would grow slack. It's just like a muscle: if you don't exercise it, then it gets lazy and fat. Of course Rieke didn't dare run around without her old washed-out pink monstrosity, since no one did that and it was provocative and indecent. Well, to each his own. Old Kossatz certainly didn't complain that my little titties got to see something of the world. I liked it that way, and so did he, so we got along well. He was never fresh and never tried to force his attentions on me. Sometimes he brushed against my breasts, always as if by accident, and if I then grinned a sassy grin at him the old man turned red as a lobster. Frau Kossatz hated me for that, too; she thought I had something going on with her old man and made a scene about it to him and tried to pester me and give me bad marks, but old Kossatz always stopped her.

At the end of my apprenticeship I received highest marks for the practical work; I didn't give a damn about my bad grades from the vocational school, because I knew that if I ever wanted to work in a nursery again the employers would look at the practical grade and wouldn't give a hoot how I did in accounting or whether I could rattle off what family the alliums belong to. The boss would look at the practical grade, and at me, and I had something to show that was more outstanding than my school report—and which the men paid a lot more attention to than the assessments of my teachers at the vocational school. The teachers at school laughed when I told them I classified flowers according to their fragrance. They laughed and acted like I was crazy, but the clients buy flowers according to how they look and how they smell and no one ever bought a flower from me because of its Latin name, although I couldn't get that across to those fossilized teachers.

When Kossatz was ready to write up my final report, he called me into his office and told me that unfortunately he couldn't give me an A. He always enjoyed working with me, but he couldn't help notice that I let things slide as soon as his back was turned. For an A I would have had to work harder, much harder.

"I give my best," I told him. "I give my best, and anything beyond that I get someone to give to me."

He laughed at that and said, "That's right, my girl, that's absolutely right." Then he wrote down an A, and I gave him a kiss, a real one with fire and spirit. And he turned beet red once more. Even if his wife had been right there in the room it wouldn't have stopped me; even if she had screamed bloody murder and thrown a flowerpot at me. But there wasn't anything more than that between us; after all, he was at least thirty or forty years older than me, in other words, with one foot already in the grave, and could have been my father or grandfather.

After my apprenticeship I worked for four years in Guldenberg, but not as a gardener—that paid too little. A man from the city administration—I think he liked me a little—offered me a job running the youth center, and I earned almost five hundred marks there and got to work with young people, which was a little more exciting than dried flowers and cabbages day in day out. A few years later I moved to Leipzig; I had made an impression on a man from the district administration who visited our club and was enthusiastic about my work, and two years after that I managed to jump to Berlin, and then I was really able to earn some money. I had finally arrived where I wanted to be, while Friederike stayed in Guldenberg with her Bernhard. She didn't want any more out of life, and so each of us, in our own way, was content.

In Guldenberg, Friederike and Bernhard saw each other every day. When Rieke had the late shift and didn't come home until just before midnight, she ran over to Bernhard's the minute she got up to fix him breakfast. She did everything for him, or almost everything, because after two years I found out they'd never even slept together. I mean, really slept together. I was stunned. She'd spent the night at his place so many times it never would have occurred to me. What the devil did those two do with an apartment all to themselves and staying in the same room?

"I sleep with him," Rieke defended herself once I found out and called her to account. "We sleep together in the same bed. We caress each other and then we sleep. But just kissing and stroking."

"And Bernhard's fine with that?"

"He understands. He understands me better than you. After all, I'm not a sex maniac."

"My God, Rieke, you're twenty-one years old. What are you waiting for? A different man? A prince?"

"No. I don't want a different man. I love Bernhard. And I don't want him to love me just for that."

"For what? You mean your pussy?"

"The way you talk, Kathi! Like a floozy!"

"Oh, come on—floozy? The poor boy will wind up with a sperm overdose."

"Kathi! Please!"

"You mean you really lie there in bed next to each other . . . and you don't let him do it?"

"That's our business and nobody else's. And please don't go sticking your nose into it. I don't want to hear another word about it."

"So when will you give him the green light? On your silver anniversary?"

She ran out and slammed the door. She was furious, and I was sorry for that, but I was truly speechless. Maybe I did start a little early, and maybe I do really like boys—Mother was probably right about my being boy-crazy—but still, going with the same boyfriend for years and even spending nights with him and guarding your hymen like that struck me as wrong, and still does. I knew Rieke and knew that she was an odd duck, but I couldn't fathom why Bernhard would play along. He was good-looking, not very tall but sturdy. And he had something that I found attractive, and I'm sure I wasn't the only one. He was quiet, which would have suited me, because I always enjoyed talking, and Bernhard could sit in our room for a whole hour without saying a word. He would smile and say nothing, and when he looked at you, you could sense something. I'd say it was a kind of smell if that weren't so silly, because how can you sense a smell from someone's eyes? He was able to be silent and it wasn't because he had nothing to say. You had the sense he knew exactly what he wanted and that he would put into action whatever he decided to do. If he looked at me for several minutes and then touched my hand I immediately got goose bumps all up and down my arm. And the way he could look at you! It wasn't a dull staring; he looked straight into your eyes, friendly, and on the spot I could smell this smell, this scent of strength and determination. That's what a volcano must smell like before it erupts. He was a real man, and that's why I couldn't understand why he put up with my sister's dumb little games. I thought he'd had her right on their first date, because that's exactly the kind of smell he had.

After our quarrel Friederike didn't talk with me for a whole week and looked at me as if I'd said all sorts of things. When I ran into them two days later and smiled at Bernhard, Rieke stepped on my toes and glared at me, although I hadn't said a word.

Two weeks after that, Bernhard came to our room at the widow's—Friederike had called him from the Eagle and asked him to bring her fresh clothes because she had spilled some stinky oil on herself and had to change. When Bernhard came I was just getting ready to go out, and when he knocked on the door I quickly put on my robe. He asked me to help him find the right things for Rieke. I opened her side of the wardrobe and gave him a blouse and a skirt and then pointed to the drawer with the underwear and told him that he should pick something out himself.

"Take what you like," I said. "I'm sure you have your preferences, right?"

The poor boy couldn't decide and again asked me for help. I said I was in a hurry and couldn't. I let my robe drop and stood there half naked—all I had on were some tiny panties—right next to him and searched among my things for the one bra I owned. Bernhard gave me a frightened look, then started rummaging through Friederike's things, practically burying his head in the drawer. I waited beside him until he stood up and added the underwear to the other things.

"Can you help me, Bernhard?" I said. "Just help me fasten this bra. I always wrench my arm out of joint."

I held my white bra in front of my breasts, and when he stepped toward me I let it drop, as if by accident. We both bent over at once; he was faster, and I pulled my hand back.

"I thought you didn't wear a bra."

"You noticed that? Where have your eyes been! You shouldn't see things like that."

Now he smiled.

"Put it on me," I said, and raised my arms over my head. He looked at me, then at my chest, took a deep breath, and fitted the cups over my breasts.

"Here, hold it tight," he said, "so I can fasten it for you."

"How do you like them? Better than Rieke's?"

He mumbled something. I pushed my ass against him and then everything happened like lightning. He tore off my bra, sending the metal clasps flying through the room, grabbed my breasts, and carried me to the bed. In a flash he was undressed and lying on top of me.

"At least lock the door," was all I managed to say before he drove inside me like a wild man. He groaned and heaved, I tried to pull a pillow under my back, and then it was all over and he was writhing next to me and gasping, "Oh God, oh God."

"That must have been an emergency?" I asked. "I've never had it that quick before."

"Um-hmm," he said. "I guess it was."

I stood up, locked the door, and went back to him. Now he caressed me tenderly, and I grabbed his cock, and then we did it properly, and beautifully. The widow's eyes practically popped out of their sockets when she saw me leave the room half an hour later with Bernhard and I said hello. She hadn't expected me to be in the room. I accompanied Bernhard part of the way to the Eagle. When we said good-bye he said I mustn't let Rieke know anything.

"Did you like it?"

"Like isn't the word. Friederike would have my head if she ever found out."

"Don't worry about that, sweetheart. She's the least of your problems. With me there's also the public prosecutor. I'm only seventeen, did you forget?"

"Kathi! Please! I didn't rape you. You were the one. You seduced me."

"Calm down. I'm not going to the police. It was much too nice with you, love. And besides, I know how things are with you. Rieke's still a virgin. You'll have to marry her before you can do it with her."

"You know?"

"Of course I do, sweetheart. When you feel another emergency coming on, you know where to find me."

"You little devil."

"After all, you're my sister's boyfriend. It's all in the family, right?"

I tried to kiss him good-bye but he pushed me away.

"Stop it. Not here on the street, Kathi."

"Tell Rieke I said hello."

"No. That's exactly what I won't do," said Bernhard and shook his head as he added, "Such a sneaky little beast. I don't get it."

Over the next days and weeks he ignored me. Whenever I saw him, Friederike was always there. Bernhard avoided being alone with me, and he didn't come to visit me when Friederike had a late shift and I was alone at the widow's. Eight weeks later I got him to come see me—in a way he couldn't refuse. One Saturday night we had gone dancing and he managed to spend the whole evening dancing with Rieke and not once with me. I whispered that I wanted him to come see me Monday, right after he got off work. I didn't wait for Rieke to go to the bathroom, either—I just said it quietly while she was sitting right next to him watching the band. Bernhard shook his head coldly and gave me a black look, then put his arm around Rieke and paid no attention to me. When Rieke was talking to a friend who had come to our table, I took hold of Bernhard's nose and turned his head toward me.

"You really have to come. I'm pregnant."

Well, that gave the dear boy something to chew on. He swallowed hard and turned very pale. For a few minutes he sat at the table as if he'd gone numb and gazed into his beer glass. When the music started up he asked me to dance.

"Is that right? Is that the truth?"

"Just wait a few months and you'll be able to hold the truth in your arms."

"My God, what's Rieke going to say when she finds out!"

"Is that all you're worried about? Don't forget I'm underage."

He danced with me gloomily without saying a word. After three dances we went back to the table and he whispered, "See you Monday."

The weekend can't have been very pleasant for him, but why did he have to ignore me like that, even if there wasn't anything between us? Let him sweat a little. Monday he showed up right on time. He didn't want to go to bed with me, just wanted to know if I really was pregnant. I told him that if a bull like him, who's been led around by the nose for two years, is suddenly let loose, it's no wonder that the first girl he comes near gets pregnant. He insisted I have an abortion; he would pay for everything. I told him we could discuss that later. Now that the horse was out of the barn we didn't have to be careful anymore. He didn't want to and talked about Friederike, but all I had to do was touch him a little bit and stroke him to get him going. This time he was very careful; he didn't believe I was pregnant and didn't want to risk anything. After we were dressed he asked again, "So, are you pregnant or not?"

"Not entirely," I said and laughed.

He was furious, and before he hit me I told him that I couldn't stand the way he had been acting. He hadn't said a word to me for weeks and treated me as if I didn't exist.

"I'm your sister's boyfriend, not yours," he reproached me.

"Yes, and I'm helping you so that something doesn't blow up inside you one of these days. We have such a nice thing going—it would be a horrible pity, wouldn't it?"

He looked at me for a long time and finally smiled. When he left he even gave me a kiss. We never went to bed again. He didn't want to. I could have easily seduced him, but in the end I didn't want to have trouble with Rieke and my own boyfriend. I liked Bernhard, and since my sister wasn't opening up, and I mean in every way, I merely wanted to do them both a favor. That way Bernhard wouldn't go looking for some other girl and Rieke wouldn't lose a boyfriend she hadn't earned and then wind up with somebody who might suit her better but not me. Anyway my relationship with Bernhard was a lot friendlier after that, and I also got along better with my sister. Whenever she had one of her rare outbursts and played the older sister, all I had to do was think about Bernhard and his five-second eruption. Then Rieke could throw whatever she wanted at my head: I would nod and do exactly as I was told, and that rendered her completely helpless. Rieke always needed someone to call the shots, she was a born hausfrau, and any man who got her at least wouldn't have to worry about not wearing the pants at home.

During the last year of my apprenticeship, crazy Bettina, a.k.a. Babsy, showed up in Guldenberg. She was visiting her grandfather for four weeks to take care of him while her grandmother was in the hospital to get something cut out of her stomach. There couldn't have been very many people who witnessed Babsy's arrival in Guldenberg, but the next day the whole town was talking about it.

Babsy rode in on a motor scooter. They were the latest fashion, and both available models were frequently pictured in the magazines, but nobody in town had one. Judging from the photographs, these scooters were mostly designed for women, for whom motorcycles were either too heavy or too unwieldy, at least the magazines always showed beautiful women posed sidesaddle, so that it looked easy as pie. I wanted to save up for one as soon as I finished my apprenticeship and was making a decent wage.

Babsy appeared on the market square one Tuesday riding her white scooter and wearing a red dress. Several of my girlfriends told me that she circled twice around the square, until everybody had seen her, and then drove onto the sidewalk and parked the scooter right in front of the Rathaus steps. Her red dress was a rag held up by two thin straps, and so thin you could see everything. The best thing about it was the length. When she rode her scooter everybody could see right up her legs, and they probably all thought that her dress had slid up. When she got off, you could still see her legs, because her dress ended two hands above her knee. Years later that came into style and was known as a minidress, but those weren't around back then, and people called them schoolgirl frocks because only little girls wore skirts that short. Anyway, the whole market was staring at Babsy, and that's probably what she intended. The policeman who spent the day walking around the square, because that's where the mayor was, and the party headquarters, came running up to her right away and told her it was against regulations to park a motorcycle on the sidewalk, especially right in front of the Rathaus steps.

"Does that apply to scooters as well?" Babsy asked him. She beamed at him so that the policeman was fully embarrassed.

"Of course. No motorized vehicles have any business on the sidewalk."

"Oh God, I didn't know that."

"Do you have a driver's license? If you have a license you ought to know. Please show me your license."

She went to her scooter, where she had a small red suitcase fastened to the luggage rack, untied the straps, removed the suitcase, and set it down in the middle of the sidewalk.

"Just a moment, please, Mr. Policeman," she said. She opened her suitcase, evidently not in the least concerned that everybody could see what it contained. Then she bent over the wide-open suitcase and began rummaging through her things. She bent down so far that the whole square could see her white panties. The policeman, who was standing right next to her, and whose eyes were fixed on her panties, turned bright red and looked uneasily around so as not to be staring constantly at Babsy's rear end. It must have been three minutes, said one of the girls, before Babsy got back up and handed the policeman her driver's license.

"I knew I had a paper like that somewhere," she said, opening her eyes wide. "Is that the right certificate, Mr. Policeman?"

"Yes, that's your driver's license. If you have that, then you should know you're not allowed to park here. You could be fined."

"Oh God, I really am a naughty girl! What are you going to do with me now?"

"Roll your scooter off the sidewalk. And you can't park in front of the Rathaus: there's no parking."

"Not on the sidewalk and not on the street? Where should I take it? Can't you make an exception for me?"

"Impossible, miss. You can park at the pharmacy, over there by the cars."

"But the scooter is hard to roll. And I'm just a girl."

The policeman was at a loss and puffed out loud. He looked around uneasily, then walked over to the scooter without saying anything and actually pushed it to a spot in front of the pharmacy. Babsy stumbled after him in her high heels, carrying the half-open suitcase in both arms.

"You are the nicest policeman I have ever met," she said, once he had parked the scooter between the cars, then kissed her finger and touched it to the policeman's forehead.

"That's what we're here for," he said, flattered. Beads of sweat were breaking out precisely on the spot she had touched.

"You really ought to bend me over your knee and spank my bottom. I deserve it after all."

"Now, miss!" was all he said. He looked around helplessly, since everyone on the square was watching. When he discovered two young men standing next to their motorcycle and staring at them, he excused himself from Babsy, quickly touching his hand to his cap, then curtly ordered the two men to leave; their motorcycle was an obstruction to traffic he would not tolerate. The men protested and demanded an explanation since they were not aware of any fault. The policeman walked around their motorcycle, pointed to the dirty taillight, and said that a taillight like that posed a considerable danger to traffic that would have to be punished with a fine if they didn't disappear immediately. He opened his shoulder bag and made as though he were about to write a ticket, whereupon the men got on their motorcycle and drove angrily away.

Babsy ran to the policeman and asked him something out of earshot from everyone. The policeman turned bright red again and then pointed toward the parade grounds. Perhaps she'd asked him for directions to a café.

Within three days Babsy was friends with every Tom, Dick, and Harry in Guldenberg, and when she crossed the street she was always engaged in conversation. She must have enjoyed that; in any case, she was always cheerful and in a good mood. I met her in the garden shop. On the day she arrived she ordered roses from old Kossatz—and actually got them, although roses were in short supply and the old man normally saved them for his friends and regular customers. Babsy showed up and told him that she absolutely had to have a big bouquet of roses because it was her grandfather's birthday, and then she needed another one for her grandmother, who was in the hospital, and Kossatz nodded and took the order. When Babsy returned for the bouquets the next day, Kossatz went with her to the rose beds and let her pick out the flowers herself, something he had never done before. For half an hour she stood with the boss by the roses and showed him which he should cut for her. She'd never seen such a beautiful nursery in her life, she told the old man, and he didn't want to let her go. I was planting a peat pyramid while she was talking to the boss, and as I was sticking the plants inside the wire netting and covering them with layer after layer of peat, I could hear and see everything. Now and then Babsy gave me a conspiratorial glance. When Kossatz was called to the phone, she came up to me and asked where you could have fun in this town. I told her we had a cinema, a skittles alley (though you had to sign up for that), and that there was dancing once a month at the Eagle and every two weeks at the health resort, but that was about all the place had to offer.

"And then there's the museum up at the castle, but that's probably not the type of fun you had in mind, miss."

"You're right," she said, very informally. "Hey, would you like to go to the movies tonight? When do you get off?"

I was taken aback and looked at her so startled she burst

out laughing. I didn't think she was laughing at me, though; it was a warm and contagious kind of laugh. We agreed to meet that evening.

I was so excited I got to the cinema far too early. When she came she kissed me on both cheeks and asked what my name was and told me to call her Babsy, that's what everyone called her and that was her stage name as well. When I asked what kind of stage she meant she said she was a singer and toured all over the country. Mostly she performed in nightclubs, where she had to sing old hits, but really she was a jazz singer, except people didn't want to hear jazz, they always wanted the same old songs they knew as children.

"You know, 'Isle of Capri' and things like that."

I nodded.

"My passion is gospel. Do you know what that is?"

I started to nod again, but then shook my head.

"That's the music of the American Negroes. Dreamy. And I have the voice for it, too. In America I could be big, I think. When I cut loose the air starts to shake, Kathi. I have a black voice—that's what an American told me once—a genuine black voice, straight out of Harlem."

I didn't know what a black voice was, but I took her word for it, and then in front of the cinema she sang a song in English but all I could understand was that it had to do with Jesus. It sounded good, very good, and I told her that, too. I didn't tell her that I really just liked listening to hits and not much else.

"And don't you have to perform now? Are you on vacation?"

"No, the boys from my band are in Berlin. We want to make a record, and they're trying to make the right contacts."

"A phonograph record?"

"Of course. Without contacts that's hard. If you have connections, then you can have the voice of a mouse and it doesn't matter, they'll produce your records. But without connections, and then doing jazz or gospel on top of that, you could have a golden throat and it wouldn't matter. Oh well, maybe the boys will manage it. Then I'll go to Berlin for two months for the recording sessions."

I didn't know what to say, and I stood there in front of her like the dumbest twit in the world. I'd never seen anybody who was going to be on a record. The singers on the records were kings and queens as far as I was concerned, unreachable and from a different world. I never thought that they could be normal people you might meet on the street and talk to. And now I was about to watch a movie with one of these dream princesses!

"Have you ever heard about us? We were on the radio two times—Babsy and the Ricks."

"I don't think so. I just listen to Hits of the Week. Otherwise I hardly listen to the radio at all."

"Hits of the Week," she said disdainfully and laughed.

"When can I hear you on the radio? I'd love to hear you sometime."

"I don't know. Maybe next year sometime. Or if we take part in a contest, then they'll broadcast that. Next month we're in Gera, and then in Leipzig for six weeks, but that's all bar music. 'Red Roses,' 'Isle of Capri,' 'Dark Eyes'—that's what the people there want to hear."

In the four weeks that Babsy took care of her grandfather we became best friends. Almost every day we spent a few hours together; I'd visit her on Schützenstrasse, where her grandfather owned a tiny house, or we would walk through town and talk. Whenever she suggested we do something together I immediately said yes, even if I had a date with Manfred, my boyfriend at the time. And sometimes I even forgot to tell him, so that the poor boy would be standing somewhere for an hour waiting for me. The only time we didn't see each other was when she was visiting her grandmother in the hospital, and later, when she was with Bernhard and hardly had any time left for me.

All of Babsy's clothes were very short. She had had two suitcases sent by train because there wasn't room on her scooter and she didn't want to travel like a packhorse. Her clothes caused quite a stir: sometimes they had a dramatically plunging neckline, or else the back had a deep cut, and even if a dress was closed up tight it somehow had panache; and besides, she could move in it as if it had been custom tailored for her. And almost every day she wore something different. But no matter how shamelessly short her skirts were or how much she turned the men's heads, no one got mad at her, not even the older married women whose husbands would stare at Babsy for minutes at a time and practically devour her with their eyes. She had a way of winning people over that silenced even the most malicious tongues. I think that any other girl in town who had the idea of running around revealing as much as Babsy did would have been called a slut and a whore, but Babsy always repaid the most outrageous comments with something nice, and that was enough to break the ice. I was with her when the pharmacist's wife stopped her on the street and told her that her dress was awfully short.

Babsy looked down at herself, put her hand over her mouth as if shocked, opened her eyes wide, and said, "You're right! I outgrew that dress a long time ago. I better sew a hem on quick—and a real broad hem, too."

Then she laughed that laugh of hers, so that the pharmacist's wife had to smile and the mean look in her eyes went away.

There was something about Babsy that fascinated everyone—men and women, and the old pious types, too. Once old Dr. Wilkert was in the Eagle and said in front of everybody that if this girl, meaning my friend Babsy, stood too long in front of a mirror, he feared she'd be blinded, because wherever she goes the sun seems to go, too. And that was the truth, even if Rieke, who told me that, would later be venting her spleen whenever Babsy showed up. Rieke was the only person in Guldenberg who talked badly about Babsy—Rieke and old Frau

Kossatz, but she'd never met Babsy in person, only heard about her, and besides, she ran everybody down, even the old Catholic priest, whom most of the townspeople regarded as a saint. Once I told my boss, Herr Kossatz, that his wife was the rarest flower in the whole nursery. He laughed and grinned at me.

Babsy and I talked about men a lot. She didn't think much of Manfred, the electrician I was going out with at the time, and who had fallen terribly in love with me.

"Watch out, Kathi. Something's wrong with that boy. I don't know what it is but I'd bet my right arm. Does he bite you?"

"Like a madman! I've already let him have it once."

"Drop him, Kathi. He needs a different kind of woman, he needs a strict mama."

"What's that?"

"Some men are strange. They're sweet, and a little twisted, and they're looking for a strict mama. That's what they need. Your Manfred is one of those; at least I think he is—no, I'm sure of it. And if he doesn't find one he'll snap. Better cut him loose."

As it turned out I didn't have to drop him. After I kept canceling on him on account of Babsy and then stood him up three times he called it quits. Two months earlier he had threatened to kill himself because I was interested in someone else. For him I was the one, he said through his tears; but then he dropped me just because I didn't show up at the market square to meet him or I was late. Eternal love—and all of a sudden it's over just because I kept him waiting for an hour. Twelve years later, long after I moved to Berlin, a friend from Guldenberg wrote to say that Manfred got caught fiddling with his girlfriend's six-year-old daughter and was sent to prison for five years. I don't know if Babsy really sensed something back then, but she did know her way around men.

She also talked to me about Bernhard. She liked him, which surprised me. After all, she was a singer; she performed in public and might have her own record out soon, and Bernhard was just a simple guy who earned his money doing something at fairgrounds and who didn't have much to say; he had yet to bowl anyone over with his charm and wit. Babsy was of the opinion that there was something of a real man about him, at least he smelled like a man, and I answered that he had once smelled like a woodworm, since he was a carpenter by profession. She wanted to know if I had slept with him and I asked where she got that idea. Her question caught me by surprise and I'm sure I turned red, because I'd never told anyone about my little fling with Bernhard.

"What do you mean? He's my sister's boyfriend."

"Exactly. So you already have a relationship with him. And if your sister likes him, you might like him, too. It's in the blood, there's nothing you can do about it. It's just nature, Kathi."

For a moment I considered telling her about Bernhard and me. She laughed so rowdily I was unsure if she was serious or just making fun of me, so I decided to keep my mouth shut.

"Sweetie," she went on, "I don't think you know much about men. Let Aunt Babsy explain some things to you. They're all sweet, even the ones with bellies and bald spots—that doesn't matter. The only thing that should matter to you as a woman is whether he's a real man or not. And that's where experience comes in. First and foremost is how he smells. If he smells like a man, then you've hit gold."

"If he smells like a man? You mean, if he stinks?"

"No. That's something else. Though he can stink and still smell like a man. No, I'm talking about a very specific scent that can't be described. Something that smells like strength and determination. In other words, like a man. And quiet men are better than loud ones, because all the loud ones ever do is bluster and roar. They talk big and act bossy and have to be the center of attention. Whenever they open their mouth the whole room has to listen to all the important things they have to say. They're no good in bed. They crave recognition, they can't love you, they just love themselves and are so insecure that they need to be acknowledged everywhere, and that's why they're so loud. If you run into a loudmouth like that, whether he's seventeen or fifty, just keep walking. But the quiet types are worth a closer look. If they can't look you in the eye because they're simply too embarrassed or uncommunicative or don't have anything to say because there's nothing upstairs, well, those are bound to be duds and you can forget about them. But if you get a look from one of the silent types, someone who doesn't say one word too many and doesn't take his eyes off you, someone who makes you tingle, then you'd be smart to get a whiff of his scent, because you might have something there. Quiet strength and smelling like a man, that's what I'm talking about, girl."

"And Bernhard? Is he a man like that?"

"At least all the pieces fit."

"He's with Rieke. My sister will scratch your eyes out if you take him away."

"Who said anything about taking him away? I just want to get a whiff, that's all."

"And he's younger than you. Three years younger."

"I know. That's what makes it so appealing."

And then she laughed again, and again I wasn't exactly sure where I stood with her. With Babsy I was never sure.

Two days later she had him wrapped around her little finger. I got it all firsthand and up close because I was friends with Babsy and sharing a room with Rieke. And, just as I thought, Rieke wanted to scratch somebody's eyes out, but it wasn't Babsy, since she had too much respect for her, and it wasn't her Bernhard, either, which I would have understood. It was me, which I really couldn't understand, because she didn't know about me and Bernhard, and I couldn't do anything about the fact that he let Babsy lure him away. And that's exactly what I told her, too, but she was angrier with me than she was with

Bernhard and Babsy put together. At one point I told her she could suck her thumb as far as I was concerned, and I moved up to the tiny attic room for the next few days so I wouldn't have to listen to her yammering in the middle of the night.

I don't know how Babsy managed to win Bernhard for herself; on the other hand, she had bewitched the whole town, and Bernhard was the icing on the cake for her. Nobody was amazed to see her start something with a boy from our town; they were only surprised that it was Bernhard. I'm sure most of them assumed she would take one of the tall handsome types—we had a few of those and they were always lining up in front of her. They were probably all too loud for Babsy, or didn't have the smell she told me about and that I didn't really understand until a few years later. Of course everybody knew she had taken him away from my sister, but I never heard a bad word about that, except from Rieke, of course. Apparently the people in our town felt that whatever Babsy did was all right. My sister demanded that I never see her again, or at least that I give her a good piece of my mind, but I refused. On the contrary, I was proud to be Babsy's friend, and that she went around town with me when she had time. Twice I even went out dancing with them. My sister was particularly outraged at that, but I loved it, because in a way Bernhard belonged to all three of us, even if he and I were the only ones that knew that.

When I went to the resort hall with them and Bernhard asked me to dance, I said to him, "All in the family, right, Bernhard?"

"What do you mean?"

"You know—you and me and Babsy and Rieke."

He smiled. "As far as Rieke goes, I like her very much. I think I love her. And Babsy—that just came over me."

"And what about me?"

"You tricked me, Kathi. You seduced me, you little beast."

"Seduced! You saw my ass and went after me like a wild animal. That's how it was."

"You must be joking. You had set your mind on it and then it happened. It doesn't mean anything, not a thing."

"Maybe not for you. I almost got pregnant, did you forget? First you bed your girlfriend's little sister, and now Babsy—it's like you can't get enough."

"Shut up, you stupid brat."

"You'd like me to shut up, wouldn't you? Things could get unpleasant for you, huh? I'm still underage, you know."

"Kathi, please."

"Then be a little nice to me."

"Take your hand away from there, Kathi."

"Ow! Don't be so rough, you're hurting me."

"Behave yourself, Kathi. Please."

When we went back to the table, Babsy asked if we had quarreled. I said yes and Bernhard said no, at the same time.

"She's a devil in disguise, this Kathi," she said to Bernhard. "A real Beelzebub, you better watch out for her. That sweet little girl's a sly one all right."

"Don't you worry about me," said Bernhard. "I eat little girls for breakfast."

Babsy asked about his work at the fairgrounds, and Bernhard explained that he was responsible for a carousel—setting the dates, renting the space, and maintaining the equipment. He had one employee for the day-to-day operation, and apart from that he employed one or two people by the hour so that he didn't always have to be there and had ample free time.

"Does a carousel make that much money?"

"If you go about it the right way, anything can make a lot of money," Bernhard said and grinned. He didn't want to talk about it and ordered a bottle of champagne.

Four days later Babsy asked me if I knew Manolow, the old farmer from the outlying farm, and when I nodded, she told me she'd had a conversation with him.

"That must have been a pretty one-sided conversation. He barely opens his jaw."

Babsy looked at me surprised, shook her head, and said that he had told her about his youth, the first war and his years in France.

"Did you know he was a balloonist?"

"A what?"

"A balloonist. You know, those big balloons with the gondola hanging below?"

"He told you that? And you believe him?"

"He showed me the balloon. He has it mothballed up in the hayloft. The gondola is tiny, it only holds a single person, but he's flown in it."

"Old man Manolow? I never heard that."

"I'm going to his place tomorrow to look at the balloon fabric. The silk is gray and matted, but maybe the thing can be fixed. If I can manage it, the farmer promised he'd take me up with him for a flight."

"In a balloon? What if you crash?"

"It's not dangerous at all. It's a lot safer than an airplane, he said, because if there's an accident a balloon goes down slowly."

"You've got nerve all right! Are you really going to fly in that?"

Babsy laughed, took my arm, and we walked from the market square to the parade grounds and then up Gärtnerstrasse to the resort, while I asked her about her band and her performances. I told her that Rieke was pissed off at her and would scratch her eyes out if she got her hands on her.

"I guess so," said Babsy. "In her shoes I would have given my ass a good tanning long ago."

We didn't discuss Manolow and his balloon again until a week later, when she told me the balloon was cleared for takeoff. The farmer had bought several propane gas canisters and on Sunday they would fly over the town. She had inspected the fabric piece by piece and mended all the rips and tears; Manolow had inspected her work and was very satisfied. As a reward he was going up with her and Bernhard. I looked at her in disbelief until she told me to close my mouth.

"This Sunday?"

"Yes."

"And you're climbing into that balloon?"

"No, I'm not climbing in. You can't climb into a hot air balloon, Kathi. There's just the gondola, and it's so small that old Manolow can barely squeeze into it, what with his gut and all. Bernhard and I are riding on the trapezes."

"What on earth are you talking about?"

"That's what they used to do in the old days. Two trapezes, one on each side, where people sat who couldn't fit in the gondola."

"You mean you're flying underneath the gondola? On just a trapeze? And what if you can't hold on?"

"What's that supposed to mean? Then I'll drop right on you, my dear. And I hope you'll catch me, so I won't land on my pretty little ass."

"You're crazy, Babsy. The police will never allow that."

"We're getting permission right now. Are you coming on Sunday? Tomorrow we're having a dress rehearsal at Manolow's farm. We're puffing up the balloon to see if everything's airtight. And the day after tomorrow we'll take the whole mess by horse cart up to the old mill. And then it's up in the air. Sunday at ten a.m. sharp you can admire your Babsy from below."

"You're completely crazy. And Bernhard's flying, too? Also on the trapeze?"

"He doesn't know how lucky he is yet. I haven't told him anything."

"He's not as crazy as you."

"He doesn't have any choice. There always have to be two people on the trapezes. Two or none, otherwise the gondola won't be balanced. So he has to go. Or else you do, Kathi."

"That'll be the day. I'm planning on living a few more years."

On Sunday I didn't get to the meadow by the old mill until

eleven because I had caused a flood in the widow's laundry room and had to wipe up the hot suds under her nasty scolding. The balloon was already pretty fat when I arrived: I could even see it from the gas station and hurried to be on time. Apart from Manolow, Babsy, and Bernhard, there was just Manolow's neighbor, Becker, and a few children on the meadow watching the goings-on. Manolow was holding a kind of Bunsen burner up to the opening of the balloon in order to heat the air inside, while Becker was regulating the propane. The balloon was tethered with cords fixed to tent stakes that Babsy and Bernhard, who were constantly running around the balloon, had to keep pounding into the ground, since the balloon was tugging at them harder and harder the more it wanted to rise. The gondola sat next to the balloon. It was an old worm-eaten wicker basket that looked so rotted out I wouldn't even use it to transport flowerpots. Nothing in the world could have forced me to get into a basket like that and go flying through the air. Next to the basket were two wooden rods, probably the trapezes; they looked like the farmer had fashioned them himself with his ax. I couldn't for the life of me see why Babsy trusted this crazy old farmer and wanted to go floating into the air with him. She called out to me to help, so I ran around the balloon, checking the tent pegs. One of them came tearing out of the ground just as I was about to grab it and flew a hairsbreadth away from my face. I was just able to grab the rope, and Manolow shouted that I should hold on to it with all my might, which I did. I swore to myself that if the balloon lifted me up so much as a half an inch off the ground I would let go because I had no desire to be part of some aerial show.

Half an hour later Manolow climbed into the basket and told us in what order we should release the tethers. Then he rose up with the balloon. When Becker let go of the last rope, the balloon jerked up so suddenly that Manolow lost his balance and nearly fell out of the basket. The balloon was held by a single long rope that Becker and Bernhard slowly let slip through their hands, to allow the balloon to ascend smoothly. When Manolow was two or three yards over the meadow, the balloon started drifting toward the lake, and Becker and Bernhard had to work to keep it in place. After a few minutes Manolow waved that he wanted to be brought down; he didn't want to let out any air but just wanted them to pull him down. The two men reeled him in so carefully that the balloon settled leisurely on the meadow and the old man climbed out unharmed. He was satisfied with the test flight. Now everybody had to hold the balloon; even the older children were handed a rope, and Manolow and Becker heated the air in the balloon for another minute through the opening at the bottom. Then Manolow asked Babsy and Bernhard if they were ready and told them they could take off. Babsy nodded enthusiastically; Bernhard was very pale. He was breathing heavily. I told him he was crazy to get in there, or rather hang there, like that.

"What are you going to do if you conk out up there?"

He didn't answer, just gave me a dull look, like an ox being led to slaughter, and blew air out of his open mouth.

"Come on," said Babsy and she picked up one of the wooden rods that were fastened with thick ropes to the side of the basket. She positioned it under her bottom so that she would be sitting on it as soon as the balloon began to climb. Manolow clambered heavily into the basket, now wearing a cracked leather pilot's cap strapped beneath his chin. He looked like an enormous old hoot-owl.

"Get going!" he said to Bernhard, who walked over very slowly to the other rod, lifted it up, and stood there, helpless, as he held it in his hands.

"Hold it under your bottom," Manolow bellowed from the gondola, "just like the girl. She's not making a fuss like you. She has spunk, my boy, you could learn a thing or two from her."

Bernhard squatted down and tightly gripped both ropes

that were tied to the dowel. He looked so funny that Babsy and I had to laugh.

"Hold on tight, my little doves, we're taking off," said Manolow. He ordered the children to let go of their ropes and nodded to Becker, who alone was holding the lead line. Then Manolow loosened that from the basket, and the balloon rose heavily, much more slowly than before. Once the basket was floating five feet over the meadow, Babsy could dangle her legs, while Bernhard could still touch the meadow with the tips of his shoes. Then Manolow lit his Bunsen burner and directed the flame into the opening. After a few minutes the balloon began ascending. This time it headed leisurely toward town, and we could all follow it comfortably on foot. I could see Babsy, who was constantly waving her feet around, looking down at us and shouting something I couldn't make out. Bernhard, on the other hand, sat very stiffly on his trapeze, without moving a muscle; he kept his eyes fixed on the balloon and didn't dare look down. I couldn't see Manolow at all, just the flame from the Bunsen burner, glowing conspicuously against the dirty gray of the balloon. After they were thirty or forty feet in the air, I couldn't really tell—to me they were high as a tower—Manolow turned off the burner and the balloon drifted on in the direction of town. At first it looked like they were moving steadily along at one height, and then all of a sudden the balloon started to pick up speed. I ran with Becker and the children down the paths of the resort gardens so as not to lose sight of it, and wondered whether the old farmer could steer the thing, because they were headed right for the church steeple, and if he ran into that, then Babsy and Bernhard wouldn't be able to hold on to their trapezes and would fall. Or else the peak of the roof or one of its metal coverings would tear the balloon open and they would all come crashing down. I called up to them to fly back but they didn't hear me. Manolow waved to us from the gondola and Babsy let one hand go so that she could wave, too. The balloon again changed course, and we had to run around the resort in order to follow. I could tell from the glow that Manolow had once again lit the burner. Now they were headed for the playing field, where a soccer match was going on, a play-off between our town and the leading team from Plünnen. I ran panting after them and could soon hear the voices of the spectators and the players. Suddenly the whole place went quiet: they had spotted the balloon. When I reached the field the game had stopped and everybody was looking up at Manolow, Babsy, and Bernhard. The balloon was approaching the field, then it slowly rocked a few yards over toward the graveyard, only to head back to the playing field minutes later. Now I could see Manolow's hands working away at the bottom of the balloon. The balloon came down very slowly. It was rocking sharply, and Babsy and Bernhard clearly had to work to hold on to their ropes and not fall off their trapezes. Manolow again lit the burner and held it up for a few moments; he was trying to slow the balloon's descent. Now the balloon seemed about to land right in the middle of the field; Manolow must have had some way of steering it, although I couldn't imagine how he could maneuver that huge bulky globe. The players had all moved behind the wooden barriers where the spectators were standing. Everyone was looking up; a few shouted to Manolow, but most were talking about Babsy's bright red panties showing underneath her white dress; at least the people I ran past were talking about that and laughing. The referee was cursing the interruption and saying something about filing a report; he was from out of town. When the basket was eight or ten feet above the playing field, the balloon suddenly started drifting back toward the resort. Manolow pulled excitedly on the ropes to change direction and shouted to Bernhard to release the mooring cable and throw it down so that the balloon could be held from below. Bernhard kept both hands tightly clenched around the trapeze ropes, too frightened to dare let go with one hand and free the cable from the cleat over his head. Manolow cursed and hastily let out air. The balloon plummeted more quickly. When Babsy's and Bernhard's feet were a few feet from the ground, Manolow ordered them to jump, which they did immediately. At the same time the balloon jerked up. Manolow let out more air, pulling quickly on the vent line, in order to land on the playing field. The balloon sank and the basket landed right in front of one of the soccer goals, but then the ropes got tangled on the goal, uprooting it and dragging it off toward the trees, in the process destroying part of the wooden barrier that separated the spectators from the playing field. Everyone ran toward Manolow, who had been thrown out of the basket and was lying on the cinder track. I went over to Babsy, who was jumping up and down and gave me a passionate hug when I reached her.

"It was wonderful!" she said. "What I'd like most is to go right back up into the air. Oh, Kathi, you have no idea what you missed. I saw the whole town, I recognized every village. I saw your house! It was fantastic."

She kissed me and then ran to Bernhard to give him a hug. His face was completely white.

"Wasn't that fantastic?" Babsy asked him.

"Yes. I feel like I'm going to vomit. One more minute and I would have done it, too."

Babsy laughed and asked where Manolow was. I pointed to the people gathered around him. It looked like something had happened, and we went to the group and pushed our way up to the old farmer. He was lying on the ground, rubbing his leg. A man with a small medic's bag was kneeling beside him, feeling his leg. Manolow cried out and told the man to leave him alone or else he'd box his ears. When he saw Babsy he beamed.

"Well, my girl, did I promise too much?"

"No," called Babsy, bent down to him and kissed the old man on the mouth.

"What's wrong?" she then asked. "Did you hurt yourself?"

"It's nothing. This man here's playing doctor and he's nothing but a lousy medic. Get your fingers off me, Karl."

"We'll need to put that leg in a splint," the medic insisted. "I'm fairly sure you've broken a bone."

"And what if I did. I have enough broken bones, one more won't make any difference. There's not a balloonist around without a broken bone. Well, and you, girl? Everything all right?"

"Everything's wonderful! I could go right back up with you, Herr Manolow."

"Well, that's not very likely. Not so soon. First I have to let this leg heal. But then, girl. Come and look me up again. Promise?"

"Promise."

"I haven't been up in twenty years. The last time was when the war was just starting up. Without you, my pretty, I would never have gone up again. And don't forget that when these old bones are back together the two of us will fly again. In the meantime find yourself another boyfriend, one with a little spunk. Because this boy was too dumb to toss a line down, I have a broken bone. He's no use, girl."

Some of the men standing around Manolow nodded in agreement.

"That's right, he's not from here."

"They should have taken every one of those refugees and drowned them in the Mulde the minute they got here."

"They're all completely worthless."

"That one they should have made into a pound of soap. At least then he'd be of some use."

"But Herr Manolow! What are you saying! Bernhard's a nice boy."

"He's not one for flying, girl. You can't tell a man until he's in the air or on a mountain, or in a war. I'll go up again with you, girl, and by then I hope you find yourself a real man. But now you have to take care of the balloon. Have Becker bring his carriage around and haul everything back to my place. He can unload me there, too, while he's at it, because I'm not setting foot in a hospital. Not on account of a simple fracture. And tell my old woman she'll have to feed the animals this evening. I won't be doing much feeding in the next few days."

The medic demanded they call an ambulance, because the leg had to be X-rayed. Manolow simply replied that he wasn't getting into any ambulance, that he was driving home in the same carriage together with his balloon, and if the doctor wouldn't come to him, he'd wrap the splints himself.

"I've long been able to do for myself what little the doctor knows. I don't go to the dentist, either: I've already pulled two teeth at home. A piece of string, girl, tied tight to the doorknob—one swing and the tooth is out. And broken bones I've always fixed myself. You just have to be careful that the pieces fit back together the right way, and nature takes care of the rest."

Before the medic could get to a telephone to call an ambulance, Becker showed up on the playing field with the carriage. We carefully pulled the balloon shell out of the trees, where it had gotten caught, and loaded it onto the carriage. Then three of the soccer players took a wooden board from the damaged barrier and used it to lift Manolow onto the balloon silk. Babsy asked Bernhard whether he was coming along; she wanted to see the old man home and help him out. Bernhard shook his head and said, full of hate, "No." His face was still completely pale.

I asked Babsy whether I should come. She stroked Bernhard on the head and said to me, "Yes, come on. We'll help the old man."

The next week I heard that Manolow had been cited for endangering public safety and vandalism and wanton destruction of a sports field that had been erected as part of the National Reconstruction Program. I never learned who reported him; maybe it was the referee. It didn't come to a trial; the old man just had to pay for repairing the goal and the barrier. The police confiscated the balloon, because it had been instrumental in the commission of a criminal offense. Everyone in town agreed that they only took the balloon away from him because he could have used it to sail over the border, which had been sealed off two years earlier with a wall and barbed wire. Manolow just laughed at all that. He spent eight weeks at home, and later he limped because the break never healed right and his right leg was a little shorter than his left. Whenever I ran into him he always asked about Babsy, even years later: that's how strong an impression she made on him.

One Thursday at the beginning of October, Babsy left. That morning she had told me good-bye, but so casually I thought she was going away for a few days to check in with her band or visit her parents.

"And when are you coming back?" I asked.

"I don't know. The season is starting, Kathi. We need to make some money, but most of all I need to perform again. I live for the stage."

"Will you give me your address? Maybe I'll visit you. Or at least we can write to each other."

"I'm here today, there tomorrow. Visiting me is impossible. Maybe you'll come to a city sometime where I'm performing."

"Absolutely. Write me when you're going to be near Guldenberg again."

She shook her head. "No, Kathi, I don't write. I never write letters. Maybe I'll come back to see my grandparents, maybe we'll see run into each other somewhere. That's better than writing. And much more exciting."

She hugged and kissed me good-bye, and that was that. She never came back to Guldenberg, not even when her grandparents died; I took off from work especially for her grandfather's funeral, and went to the cemetery, but she wasn't there. I never found any record by her, and her picture never appeared in the papers, although I looked through all the ones we ordered in the youth center. Maybe she left the country and was in West Germany or somewhere else abroad. She was the best friend I ever had, even if she only spent a month in Guldenberg, and despite the fact she was six years older. I would have liked to have her as a friend for my whole life. Or as a big sister, because although Rieke was older than me, she wasn't really ever a big sister, rather a silly girl I had to take care of.

After Babsy left, Bernhard came by to see Rieke. He showed up on a Friday evening, one day after Babsy had gone; he went straight from work to the widow's and knocked on the door to our room. When he stuck his head inside Rieke screamed hysterically that she didn't want to see him and he should get lost. He stood in the open door for fifteen minutes, not daring to enter and confront her. He told her that Babsy had seduced him, and that he didn't know what had come over him, and she should forgive him this huge stupidity, he was cured of it for good. Rieke sat in the chair by the window with her face bright red and acted as if she was looking outside, and every minute just repeated that he should leave. I sat on the bed, sewing sequins onto my red blouse and acting as if I wasn't there. When I walked past Bernhard to get the scissors I winked at him and stroked the tip of his nose. He swatted angrily at my hand and I blew him a kiss. When he left and the front door locked behind him, I told Rieke that if she let him go now he would never come back, because Bernhard was as pigheaded as they come. She wanted to say something but no sooner had she opened her mouth than she sensed I might be right. In any case, she jerked open the window and called him back. One second later Bernhard was in our room and Rieke asked me to leave them alone. An hour later Rieke came up to the attic, where I was lying in bed, and asked if I could stay up there for the night.

"Of course. Anything for the sake of love."

"We had a talk and made up. And I want him to stay with me tonight."

"You don't waste time, Rieke. And now give your heart a little nudge. The first time isn't really all that bad."

"Do you mean that you've . . . ?"

"Of course."

"With Manfred?"

"Yeah, him, too."

The poor girl couldn't close her mouth. When she left I called after her: "And say hello to your Bernhard for me. Let him know who he has to thank for picking that cherry."

Since that day the two were back together, and Rieke evidently acquired a taste. In any case, they spent the night together more often than before, and whenever Bernhard was at our place for the night, I had to sleep upstairs.

After my apprenticeship I said farewell to old man Kossatz. I didn't want to spend my life thinning and transplanting and haggling with old ladies over funeral wreaths. Herr Leberecht had asked me to take over the youth club on Altmarktstrasse. It was called the Youth House, even though it was really just a few rooms above a shoe store. I received a better salary from the city and got to work with young people, with none of the overpowering smell of age and poverty from the people who came to the nursery to spend an hour looking for something green for a grave. Kossatz was sad to see me go; he desperately wanted to keep me. I was far from his best apprentice, but I had other qualities the old man considered more important.

I had met Herr Leberecht at the resort, at the party marking the halfway point in our apprenticeship. He kept coming to our table to ask me to dance. The other apprentices joked about it, because he was already old and halfway bald, but I danced with him four times, and he was well-mannered and didn't start pawing at me like the younger ones. Besides, he was a terrific dancer—he could waltz right and left and even tango, and didn't just hop across the floor like most men, with whom you were never sure if they were going to tramp on your toes because all they could think about was holding you as close as possible while they moved across the floor. Herr Leberecht danced properly, with his arm bent and a straight back, just as we had learned in dance class, and he also made conversation, while the boys just sweated in silence when they danced, or at most hummed along with the melody or parroted the text of some hit. Herr Leberecht told me that he worked for the city council and was responsible for health, family, youth, and sports, which is a huge and important area of responsibility. He asked where I worked and then said that being a gardener was the nicest profession for a woman and that he'd always wished his wife had had such a nice profession, but she was completely untalented in that regard, and anyway they barely lived together because she was always driving out to look after her sick mother, who lived in Halle. When I told him I was hoping to find something more interesting after I finished my apprenticeship, he promised to help me. I should pay a call on him up in the Rathaus; he thought he might have something for me.

The very next week I went to visit him and he offered me coffee and cookies as if I were an important guest. We spoke for about an hour, and he gave me a thorough interview, asking about the strangest things, because he had to determine whether I was suited for him and the position he had in mind for me. He had me come back several times to talk with him, but he never asked me over to his house at night or any other awkward place, and he was never pushy and always called me Fräulein Hollenbach. When we said good-bye he kissed me on both cheeks, and back then there was nothing more between us.

Four months after I took my final examination he offered me the job of running the Youth House, and I accepted immediately. I had to oversee four groups and supervise on the evenings when the rooms were open for the young people. Then there was the Wall Newspaper, which I had to renew every two or three weeks, and the gatherings I had to invite people to and make sure that no one said any political nonsense. Because I had to work longer in the evening, my days didn't begin until ten, which I really liked, because I loved sleeping in.

Once a month I had to go see Herr Leberecht, to give him a report; there were never any difficulties and he was quite pleased with me. And every year I had to attend an additional training seminar that lasted a week and took place at a holiday resort that belonged to the district administration. Once I went there with Herr Leberecht and slept with him; it was my own decision. He never pushed me to do anything, although he'd liked me ever since we'd danced at the apprenticeship party, and the next morning at breakfast he was as polite as before and went on calling me Fräulein Hollenbach.

The best thing about working at the youth center was the kids. I soon won them over, and they came to me to talk about every little thing and told me everything they couldn't discuss with their parents or teachers. For them I was the aunt they could talk to about their romantic woes, and I listened carefully when they told me their stories and their unsolvable problems. They were only a few years younger than me, but they were absolute children, and the things they told me were so hilarious that I could have split my sides laughing, but I listened to them without batting an eye and then told them very seriously what they should do. Aunt Kathi's advice column. I also helped them when they had real problems. Two sixteen-year-olds got pregnant during my time at the youth club, and I was able to give them addresses. And when one of my boys landed in juvenile court for breaking into the cellar of some building, I drove out to the district seat and testified as a character witness on his behalf so that he got off very lightly and didn't wind up in one of the feared youth work reform yards.

Two years after Babsy's visit to Guldenberg, Rieke and Bernhard got married. Bernhard had given up his carousel business and bought a workshop. He must have made tons of money off that carousel. When I once asked he laughed and told me he'd tell me about it someday.

"Someday," he said. And then, after a moment he added, "Or maybe never. Because the most important thing about running a business is keeping your mouth shut, Kathi."

In any case, Bernhard had the most modern carpentry shop in Guldenberg. All the equipment was new or almost new, and he even had a gigantic vacuum for the sawdust, which none of the other carpenters owned. Since Bernhard had yet to obtain his master's certificate and therefore could not get a license from the city council and the Guild Chamber to run his own shop, he brought in a colleague who was already a master carpenter, and ran the workshop under the name of that man for the first four years. By the time he became a master himself—I was long gone from Guldenberg and living in Leipzig—he employed five journeymen and owned the largest carpentry shop around, since Beuchler's had burned down in the meantime.

Rieke was in seventh heaven when they married. Bernhard was her one and only, and no matter what he said or did she immediately nodded and did what he asked. I don't think Rieke needed a TV: it was enough for her to spend the whole evening staring at her Bernhard—for her that was the most beautiful thing in the world.

They got married in our parents' house in Spora. Mother was very proud of her son-in-law, because he was a self-made man who owned his own business. She had always wanted her daughters to find a husband exactly like that, someone who could stand on his own two feet and didn't make his money working the land; she wanted to protect her children from that. It was a big wedding, just like the Hollenbachs used to put on a hundred years ago when they were large landholders. Father cleared out the barn and set up tables. Mother and four neighbors cooked for three days to make sure they could properly feed the eighty guests, and Bertels, the collective's one-legged accountant, played the accordion all evening long. I had gone to Spora alone, since I couldn't let my parents see the boyfriend I had back then. I had met him in my youth center and he was only seventeen—in other words, a good deal younger than me, and that would have upset my parents. Mother sat me next to a cousin named Frieder, and he and I walked together into the church behind the bride and groom, because everyone got married in church in our village, and I sat next to him the entire evening and had to dance with him. Frieder and I got along well, but that evening did serve to remind me how extremely glad I was to have gotten out of Spora. I also danced with the groom. I had to ask him, because Bernhard avoided touching me or being alone with me. The sweet thing was afraid of me, so afraid that I was never again able to spend such a nice time with him like back then.

When I was living in Guldenberg, I seldom saw Rieke and Bernhard—really only on birthdays or when our parents visited. Rieke did keep inviting me, especially after they had moved into the large villa, which was the ultimate for Rieke, the perfect happiness of her life with Bernhard, but I avoided visiting them. It was too boring. Everything there was cleaned and polished; the tables had lace mats, and I'm sure Rieke washed the net curtains once a week. At Rieke's I had the feeling I had to ask permission to sit in one of her armchairs. And evidently that's exactly what Bernhard was looking for. Back then I told him I wouldn't be surprised if he had a fat paunch and a bald head in ten years. I think Babsy would be amazed if she saw him. She really did have a nose for men, but in Bernhard's case she didn't realize that this kind of buttoned-up, middle-class happiness was exactly what he dreamed of. After a few years the guy she went out with, the wild animal I had seduced, no longer existed. His shop prospered more and more, and he and Rieke became downright rich, at least by Guldenberg standards.

As Rieke proudly related, her Bernhard was an important person in town, and nothing was decided in the Rathaus without consulting him.

They had two children: first a girl named Sybille, and eight years later a boy named Paul, and both children were uncommunicative and mean. On the very day Rieke turned sixty Sybille gave birth to a grandchild and that was Rieke's best birthday present. All babies are supposed to be beautiful, but I remember looking at this child as a baby and thinking that it, too, looked uncommunicative and mean.

On that occasion I took Rieke aside and asked her if she had ever been unfaithful to her Bernhard. She was completely outraged. That never even occurred to her, she said, indignantly, and I believed her. In her own way she really had hit the jackpot with him, even if for me he proved to be a complete dud.

Sigurd Kitzerow

I first met Bernhard Haber when he opened his carpentry shop. We must have run into each other before that, but I never noticed him. He was two years younger and three or four grades below me in school, so we didn't have anything in common. I'm sure his classmates called him Woodworm the same as they did me, because that's what everybody was called if their father was a carpenter or a sawmill owner like my father. I never spoke to him in those years: as a rule we had nothing to do with the younger kids, particularly somebody who had been held back and had to repeat a grade. In addition to that, his family were refugees who'd been expelled from the East, and we stayed away from those people. They owned nothing and let the city give them everything; they lived at our expense. If one of them ordered wood from our mill, Father demanded they pay in advance because these people barely had pants to cover their ass and all they knew how to do was whimper and whine and not pay their bills. The way they talked, every one of them had owned and lost an estate in Pomerania or Silesia. Father said there wasn't room in all of Germany for the number of estates they claimed and wanted compensation for. In any case, he always wanted to see cash before he delivered anything to the refugees. That way he didn't have to go chasing his money afterward.

Bernhard's father frequently came to our mill, and Father did business with him, because old man Haber ordered wood from us every now and then. Father constantly made jokes about his having one arm, and we all laughed, because who ever expected to see a one-armed carpenter? Old Haber might have been able to hold a piece of lath, but he certainly couldn't lift one of the squared timbers we delivered to his place. Still, he must have been very skilled with that one arm, because he squeaked by somehow, even if he did have his share of bad luck. His first workshop burned down, and nothing seemed to go well for him. He had blurted out some terrible suspicions about the fire, which didn't win him many friends in town, if he had any to begin with. Wood burns and that's that, was what Father said back then; one match is all it takes, but the refugees are too dumb to understand that—not one of them can add two plus two. The people who came from Pomerania and Silesia were all nitwits and loafers and didn't deserve better than they got. The fact that they wound up in Guldenberg of all places was a punishment from God that this poor town didn't deserve.

After the fire, old Haber set up a new shop that he couldn't possibly have paid for on his own; presumably he got help from the city authorities or the Church—at least the pastor gave him some work. From what I heard, the insurance didn't have to pay him a penny, since you're not allowed to set up diesel machines in a wooden barn. Haber never had many customers: the other refugees may have hired him, and a few of the farmers from the outlying villages sometimes gave him business, because he accepted any project and was cheap, but the Guldenbergers didn't go to him. They didn't like dealing with the refugees, and Haber had accused the entire town of arson, so they weren't about to send a penny his way.

By the end of the 1950s he seemed to have made it. He had a few commissions and was even able to employ a journeyman now and then, which as a cripple he very much needed. But then he had an accident that nearly killed him and he spent four weeks in the hospital. A timber must have fallen on his head one evening in the shop, which can easily happen to somebody with one arm. He was lucky, because an inch-long nail was embedded in the wood and missed the back of his head by a hair, so that he got off with just a fracture. Once again he started throwing around accusations that someone was trying to kill him, but he had no evidence.

Then one week after the old man got out of the hospital he hanged himself. No one could figure out why he did it. People thought he might have been in debt, or maybe it was that missing arm that tied the noose.

The police conducted an investigation; detectives even came from the district seat, but that was mandatory with suicides and didn't necessarily mean anything. Two of them spent a whole week in Guldenberg. They must have found something that aroused their suspicions, and a few people were called in for questioning. As always on such occasions the rumor mill was running fast and furious. In the pubs people talked about murder and some kind of evidence. I even heard some names whispered—one of old Haber's competitors and two of his neighbors. No one said the names out loud, though, at least not to the detectives. You don't wash your dirty laundry in front of strangers. Old Haber wasn't liked in town; he was a refugee, but that someone should hate him enough to murder him was something I refused to believe back then. There was enough work for everyone, and the one-armed man certainly wasn't taking customers away from anyone, especially since he hardly had any of his own in town. No one had ever exchanged more than two words with him; people merely nodded and went their way. He simply didn't belong.

The old case of the workshop burning down was reinvestigated, as was the accident Haber claimed was an attempted murder. After five days the officials released the body and left without having established anything. Haber was buried in the suicide corner of the cemetery, and that was final proof for everyone that he hadn't been murdered. The suicide corner was located behind the pump and the compost heap; that's where all the suicides used to be buried, even though after the war that practice was prohibited, and suicides were no longer supposed to be buried in a place strictly reserved for them. So the name suicide corner no longer existed officially, but no one in town would let himself be buried behind the pump, and the suicides were laid to rest there just as before.

Two years after that Bernhard's mother died. She was buried next to her husband and so became the first person who did not die by her own hand to find her final resting place there. But things like that didn't matter to the refugees.

Bernhard wasn't living in Guldenberg when his parents died. I heard he was running some fairground business, a shooting gallery or a carousel, so he was always moving around; in any case, he never appeared in town. He probably wanted to let the dust settle a bit, and that was sorely needed, too, because after he finished school he had gotten mixed up with some political agitators and made a lot of enemies among the farmers, whom he and the party comrades bullied into joining the collective. In doing so he not only harmed himself but all the other refugees, since he made everyone even more hostile toward them than before, if that was possible. That was the source of the quarrel between him and his old man, the way I heard it, and when Bernhard started working at the fairground instead of in his father's shop it came to an open break between them. But those are all stories I didn't hear until much later, because at that time I hardly knew him.

At the beginning of the 1960s I received a tip from town hall that Bernhard Haber was planning to open a carpentry shop. He had taken over a farmstead that had belonged to Herr Morak, who had fled to the West with his family, and hired masons to begin remodeling it. His friend Hermsdorf applied for a license to open the shop, since young Haber still did not have his master's certificate. Hermsdorf was a master and lived off a disability pension, because he had sawed the fingers off his right hand two years earlier. Everyone realized that Hermsdorf was merely the front man for Bernhard Haber, but since everything was legal no one could say anything against it. And I was pleased because a new carpenter in town meant one more customer.

At first people didn't take young Haber seriously, and they particularly laughed at the idea of his setting up shop with a cripple, what with his father having been a one-armed carpenter. They predicted he'd be bankrupt or burned down in two years and that he'd end up just like his old man. I never took part in this gossip. Like I said, for me a new woodshop meant a new client. I heard about his plan in October, and in December I sent him the new wall calendar I had printed for my regular customers.

Back then a calendar like that was something special. It was difficult enough to get a new calendar each year, since things were in such short supply, but one that had the name of my sawmill on every page, and which only fifty people received at Christmas—there was nothing else like it in the whole town. Whoever got it was proud to have it and hung it prominently, where his customers could see it. Two years later I had a hundred copies printed, because all the relatives wanted one, as did a few friends who didn't order wood from me but were helpful in other ways. Naturally I just gave the calendar away, even though the printing wasn't cheap; there's a reason printers call their trade the black art. My idea with the calendar paid off. Now and then people would ask me in the summer if there'd be another one next year, and once our local paper even wrote an article about it with a picture of me and the calendar.

Between Christmas and New Year's, Haber visited the mill. He phoned first, and I told him the business was closed until after New Year's but that he should stop by if he had time. The workers had the week off and the equipment was shut down; my wife and I were finishing the year's accounting and would be in the office every day. Haber stayed for over an hour. I showed him the mill, my equipment, and the various stocks of wood, and his questions demonstrated he had learned a lot. He asked me for the prices and I gave him the list, adding that I gave discounts to regular customers and that beyond that there were other ways of keeping the costs down.

"You understand?" I asked.

He nodded and said, "That's exactly what I meant. Self-employed people like us have to stick together, otherwise the state will flay us alive."

He didn't smile when he said that and I knew right away that everyone else was wrong. Bernhard Haber wasn't going to take a bath with his new shop. The man had strength and the ability to assert himself, and I realized that his colleagues and a few loudmouths were in for a shock. No one was going to get away with treating him the way they had his father.

When we said good-bye I wished him success and asked him when he planned to open.

"And your first cubic yard of lumber is on the house, for the opening."

He simply nodded, as if a gift like that was routine.

I asked if he had received my calendar, since he hadn't mentioned it.

"Yes," was all he said. "Thanks."

Once again he acted as if he hadn't expected otherwise and was entitled to it.

"That boy is ice cold and tough as nails," I told my wife, after Haber had left and I went back to the pile of receipts. "He'll make it all right, they won't scare him off."

"Isn't he a refugee? Not a single one of them has managed to make a success of anything."

"He will; you'll see. He knows what he's after and he gets what he wants. I'll bet you."

That May he opened shop. Hermsdorf's name came first on the sign, but everyone knew who the real boss was. There was no celebration. Haber took out three announcements in our paper and otherwise put his trust in his new machines. And they were indeed amazing. The day before he opened I took him the wood I had promised—not the very best boards, but they were well dried and aged the way carpenters prefer. I drove the truck myself, because I was curious. Haber led me around his shop, which struck me as well thought out, and showed me the machines. There was none of his father's junk: all the equipment was either bought new or had been well-maintained. He gave me a demonstration, since I didn't know what all the machines were for. When he turned on the giant vacuum for the sawdust I was really impressed.

"That puppy must have cost twenty thousand."

"On the nose," he answered, without offering anything more.

"You have a fine shop. Can't say a thing against it. The jobs are just going to start flying your way. Beuchler and the other carpenters will be dragging their tails between their legs."

"Let's hope so," he said, reservedly. "It cost enough."

"I believe you. Is everything paid for or do you have a lot of debt?"

"Yes," was all he answered, leaving me to choose for myself what he meant. I think most of all he was trying to signal that he didn't want to discuss it. And that was as it should be. Never talk about money and debts; the only people who do are those who don't understand a thing about either. Haber wasn't a fool; they wouldn't be finished with him so easily. The boy won my respect.

Together we unloaded the wood and sat down in his office, where he poured us each a beer and a chaser.

"Every second Friday of the month the skittles alley at the Eagle is reserved for our club," I told him. "If you'd like, I can ask whether you can join in."

"Who is we?"

"A few friends, all from here. There are twelve of us. Twelve upstanding citizens. All businessmen."

"That sounds good."

"I'll ask. I'll put in a good word for you."

"Is Beuchler there?"

"Of course."

"He might have something against it. After all, we're competitors."

"That's not a problem, Haber. That's why we have the club, to clear up problems before they happen."

"Great. Then count me in."

"Not so fast. The others have to agree. And you'd be the first . . ."

Haber looked up, waiting for me to finish the sentence. Then he said, slowly, "The first refugee?"

"Yes," I said. "You realize not everyone has good things to say about you. It's a small town, you know? People are afraid of strangers. And back then there were too many who wanted to settle here all at once."

He took in what I was saying, as if he were simply registering the news. He didn't agree or disagree with me; it was impossible to tell what he was thinking.

"A skittles club," he said at last. "I'd like that."

"The skittles isn't the main thing. We sit and discuss the things in town worth discussing."

"I figured as much."

"We have to, Haber, if we small businessmen want to survive. And whenever we've been united, we've managed to get things done. Even with the mayor. He doesn't ignore us anymore; he listens to what we have to say."

"With unity comes strength," he proclaimed. The way he said it, the words sounded pompous and full of sarcasm.

"That's it," I answered, and laughed.

"And the party doesn't have a problem with your club? It sounds like a secret society."

"You don't have to worry about that. Four of us are in the party. Or, rather, in each of the official parties. We keep politics out of the club, and what we say inside doesn't leave the room. None of us wants any trouble. Besides, who could have anything against our meeting? Strictly speaking, we're out for the common good."

"I think I'd like skittles. Ask your twelve upstanding citizens if they'll accept me."

We finished our beer. Haber offered another dram, but since I'd come in the truck and had to drive it back, I placed my hand over the shot glass to decline the offer.

As it turned out, the other members did have doubts and objections to letting Haber join. Beuchler said that Haber had to wait his turn, there were other businessmen from Guldenberg who wanted to get in; and Pichler, who owned the Eagle and the skittles alley, recalled Haber's performance during the collectivization. Haber had been at Pichler's stepfather's, had stood for hours in front of the farmstead and tyrannized the old man. He'd even shown up at Griesel's, who'd taken the Habers in after the war.

"Sins of youth," I said. "Now he has to get along with us, and we with him."

"And how do you know he won't go on the political bandwagon again?"

"How do I know? The boy wants to build up his business,

and a license from the authorities isn't enough for that. He'll have to get along with us; otherwise things will be rough for him. If we accept him into the club we can train him."

There was a formal vote; eight were for letting him in, two opposed, and two abstained.

"But I'll never forget what he did to my stepfather," said Pichler.

"What do you want? The old man's better off than he was before. He works an eight-hour day and has a paid vacation. And when he's sick he stays in bed. He never used to live like that. You said as much yourself."

"That's one thing. But it's something else that he was forced. That's a different pot of fish."

"Kettle."

"What?"

"A different kettle of fish."

"Don't get on my nerves, Sigurd. I say pot. I don't have any kettles."

Haber knew how to build up his business. He left the talking to Hermsdorf and his wife, since he wasn't very sociable. Unlike his father he succeeded in winning clients among the Guldenbergers. He worked well and his prices were good, so I heard, and with his machines he was able to land large contracts the other carpenters couldn't think of taking on. He became one of my regular customers, and within four years, once he had his master's certificate and the business was running under his name, he was using more of my lumber than any other carpenter in the region. When he bought the house at Neumarkt and fixed it up we even became neighbors. We started inviting each other to family parties and spent New Year's together at the Eagle—which we do to this day. Haber has a very peculiar sense of humor; when he makes a joke you really have to pay attention to get the point, and I've told him more than once that he should make it clear that his jokes are jokes, because otherwise people might get scared.

He made a good start in the Skittles Club. For half a year he listened, played decently, drank his beer, and seldom said anything. Pichler and he avoided each other. He didn't spout any political nonsense like back then when he was running around pestering people with the agitators, and I couldn't imagine how he'd ever been part of that in the first place. He was a reasonable man who knew his trade, and was as good as his word. He was one of us, even if he was a refugee. No one who didn't know that would have ever been able to tell.

One Friday evening about two years after he opened his business, Haber surprised us with the announcement that his shop had been the target of an arson attack. We were sitting at the long table that was set up at the upper end of the skittles alley, drinking our beer, and had just started to sort out who owed whom, because we always played for money, when Haber said, "Someone in town doesn't like my shop. Do you have any idea who that could be?"

He looked at Beuchler, and Beuchler glared at him, and I had the feeling the two men were going to stand up and start hitting each other. Haber had said the sentence very quietly, emphasizing every single word, so that everyone immediately paid attention. No one said a thing; everyone looked at him and waited. Beuchler squinted and stared at him blackly.

At one point someone asked what was going on, but no one answered. Finally Beuchler said, "I like your shop."

"It's better than yours, I agree. That's no reason to burn it down."

Beuchler stood up and shouted something; the man next to him pulled him back onto his seat, and everyone told Haber to say what he meant, because when all was said and done there hadn't been any fire, not at his place or anywhere else in town. Haber nodded and said that, yes, there hadn't been a fire, but someone had tried to set one, and he explained how that morning he had found a broken beer bottle in his shop that had obviously contained gasoline and some burnt bits of rag.

Someone, and Haber again looked at Beuchler, had thrown it in through one of the windows; the bottle had landed on a stack of lumber, then rolled onto one of the veneer presses, where it exploded. There were burn marks on the metal; and the veneer in the press was charred but fortunately hadn't caught fire. If the bottle had landed a few feet farther on, or rolled off the press, his whole shop would have burned down. He had of course treated the wood in the shop, but that probably wouldn't have helped if it had been doused with gasoline. Beuchler was furious and asked Haber if he suspected him, and Haber replied that he had no proof, nor had the police found anything they could use; consequently no one was above suspicion.

At that point the others protested and said that he should watch his tongue. If there had been an attempt at arson, that was bad, and the police should inspect everything as thoroughly as possible. But accusing honest people was just as bad as arson, and he should watch his words. Pichler grabbed him by his lapel, and the skittles evening nearly ended in a fight. I separated them, then took Bernhard by both arms and pushed him back into his chair. Not until I had banged on the table and raised my voice did things quiet down.

"Like children!" I shouted. And when everyone was back in his chair I said, "And now to you, Bernhard: Do you know who threw the bottle in the shop?"

"No."

"Then think twice before you open your mouth. No one in this room goes around tossing bottles filled with gasoline."

"Somebody did."

"Not one of us."

"I'm not going to end up like my father. I swear that to you all."

"Is that supposed to be a threat, Bernhard?"

"I'm just saying how things are. I have two hands, and I'll catch whoever it is."

"Fine. And then you'll hand him over to the police. Everything according to the law. But until you catch the perpetrator you should keep your mouth shut and not cast aspersions on honest people. Understood?"

No one felt like playing any more that evening. Most finished their beers and left. When Bernhard stood up to leave I asked him to wait a moment, so we could walk home together.

We had almost reached my house when Bernhard finally opened his mouth. "Thank you," he said, without looking at me.

"It's all right."

"But I'm still convinced that Beuchler is behind it. My shop is simply too successful."

"That might bother some people. But it's still no reason to burn it down."

"Don't forget I've lived through it before. I know what a fire is like."

"It could have been some dumb kids. You should invest in some security. Wire-glass and iron bars."

"I'm not going to end up like my father. Whoever did it has to pay."

"Yes. If you can prove it. But don't set yourself against the town, Bernhard. You've made it. Your business is doing well. You're more successful than your father ever was. Don't destroy all that."

A bitter silence, then he nodded and shook my hand good-bye.

"Best to keep an eye on things," I said. "With us woodworms, fire is always a danger. I've made a habit of checking on my wood stores in the middle of the night. If it's late or I'm awake at night I just drive out there and have a look around. And whenever there's a dance at the Eagle I don't go to bed before midnight, and not without first checking. And New Year's Eve—that goes without saying. Better to be on the safe side."

"And? Have you ever caught anyone?"

I smiled at him and thought for a long while. Then I nodded.

"Well?"

"Well. I took care of things with a wooden slat. And when he was lying in the sawdust with two broken legs, I told him he better leave town. He said he planned on doing that anyway."

"That's exactly what I mean, Sigurd."

"I thought so. But you can't go around raising a ruckus beforehand. And you have to make sure you have the right person. It certainly wasn't Beuchler. He does his work and lets others do theirs, he's no arsonist. So don't go sinking your teeth into Beuchler. He's not your man, Bernhard."

"Then who is?"

"No clue. If I hear anything I'll let you know. We woodworms stick together, right? And whoever it was is bound to mention it somewhere, brag about it. He'll present himself to you on a silver platter. And then you'll have your man. Now go check on your shop. Since he didn't succeed this time, he'll probably try again soon. It's all just part of business, Bernhard, so don't go chasing ghosts. I don't want you to end up like your father, either. After all, you're one of my best customers. But I promise you this: when you're sure you have the right man, when you're really sure, then I'll help you out with a wooden slat."

A year and a half later there was another fire, and this time there was no lucky accident to prevent it; the whole shop burned to the ground. Firemen pumped water day and night onto the glowing pile of wood, which spewed dirty plumes of smoke when the water hit it, and shot up in flames as soon as the firemen turned away and their water had evaporated. All that was left were the foundation walls and a few remnants of machines that weren't worth a thing, even as scrap. But this time it wasn't Haber's shop—it was Beuchler's, on Kupferstrasse. Once again there were many rumors and lengthy investigations. I, too, was questioned by the criminal police, but there was nothing I could tell them. In town people suspected

Haber, and there were even some who pinned the blame on Beuchler, claiming he had set the fire to cash in on the insurance. I took no part in these speculations; I had a business to run, and you can't help that by spreading wild and dubious rumors.

I looked over the site of the fire and then went to Beuchler to offer my help, but he said he was giving up. He was almost sixty and had neither the strength nor the time to build up a new shop. Besides, Haber was set up to handle every conceivable job, and he'd win over all Beuchler's customers before Beuchler could get back on his feet.

"What are you going to do? Go into retirement?"

"I don't have enough for that. I don't know what the insurance is going to pay, but I'm sure it won't be enough to live on. I'll probably go on working as a carpenter. Work is what I know how to do."

"You're going to hire yourself out? To whom?"

"Certainly not Haber. I'll see."

"Maybe you're right. So, we'll see each other Friday?"

"Of course, if Haber's no longer in."

"Haber is in. You know we don't throw anyone out of the club."

"It's Haber or me. You'll have to choose."

"Be reasonable."

"Haber or me. We should never have taken him in. They aren't our people, those refugees. They're not like us."

"He's lived here his whole life."

"That doesn't mean a thing, Sigurd. It's in the blood. They just don't belong here."

"You think that Haber is responsible for . . ."

"What I think is one thing. What I know is another. And that's what counts."

"And what do you know?"

"That a year from now I'll be sixty, and then I'm officially an old man. And I understand something I never understood before, something I never took seriously—namely, that we all have a place on this earth. Each of us is allotted one place that belongs to us, and we to it. If you give up this place, then you don't belong anywhere, that's just the way the world is. It has something to do with where you're born, with the only place you can really be at home. And if you leave this place, then you give up your homeland. You might get a lot done in life, maybe even more than if you hadn't gone away. But you've still lost your homeland. That's something you don't realize until you're as old as I am. Before I used to laugh at this kind of talk. I didn't understand why our parents set themselves against the refugees. Now I know why, and I know that they were right."

"Where were they supposed to go, these people?"

"That's a different matter, Sigurd. I don't know where they should have gone. But I believe that they didn't then and still don't have the right to take other people's homeland just because they lost theirs. Ever since the war, Guldenberg hasn't been the Guldenberg where I was born, it's no longer our town. We never had so many fires before the refugees came. Not even during the war! Back then we all belonged together. But that's over now. There are too many strangers. Too many people who weren't born here and don't belong here."

"Maybe you're right, Reinhard. But the fact is, we're living in a different time, and we have to face that fact. And Haber isn't a bad guy. He's not exactly sociable, and he's a crazy stubborn mule who always has to assert himself everywhere, but he's reliable. In short he's no worse than any local. He fits in, he's a Guldenberger."

Beuchler shook his head. "Either you can't understand me or you don't want to. Whatever the case, at least fires were something we didn't have."

"Was it arson?"

"Yes. That much is certain, according to the police."

"Then wait to see what they find out."

"What are they going to find out? The same as always. Nothing."

"How are you so sure it was one of the refugees? The Habers had their share of fires, too—first the old man, and just last year at his son's."

"That's what they say. But who can say for sure who it was back then. Maybe they did it themselves, who knows. There's no way old Haber could run a carpentry shop. With one arm? Sigurd! He had every reason to want the insurance settlement. And as for young Haber, my God, who knows why there was a fire. Or why there wasn't one. Isn't it odd that a burning bottle of gasoline wouldn't do any damage? In a carpentry shop? With wood and sawdust everywhere? Strange, don't you think? That's what I would investigate if I were with the police. Why didn't the place burn down? Something's not right there. No, it's all different than what you think. A fire means nothing to these people. It's not their town they're putting in danger. They don't care what might get destroyed. They just don't have a heart for the place; they landed here by chance and can go on their way at any time. Like the Gypsies. The town, the church, the castle, our resort, the old streets, everything we hold dear doesn't mean a thing to them. Believe me, they're strangers, and that's what they'll remain. You can't build on that, Sigurd, you can't count on these people."

"Bernhard Haber is my neighbor, Reinhard."

"Yes. You didn't exactly have a choice."

"I get along with him."

"Right. So, as I said: it's me or Haber. Let me know when you've kicked him out of the club. You know I like skittles."

I had no intention of bringing this up with the others; I had no desire to throw Haber out of the club. There was no reason to do that, and he and I got along well, but apparently Beuchler had approached the other upstanding citizens. In any case the atmosphere that next Friday evening was bad; everyone was talking about the absent Beuchler and his shop that had burned down. You could feel that everyone was afraid. The fact that not a single one of the fires in recent years had been solved made everyone afraid that they might be next in line. Everyone believed all the fires were the work of one person, an arsonist, who seemed to take a perverted pleasure in his actions.

After Beuchler's shop burned down I started worrying as well and acquired an Alsatian from our local sheepherder, who had a good eye for dogs. The dog was a male, just under a year old, and did what he was told. He spent the day in a cage and at night I let him run around the mill yard on a long chain. In a few weeks, after he had gotten used to me, I intended to give him free run of the place. I had hired two young men for the season in addition to old Hubert, who had been there since my father's time. I had the three of them extend the fence from the two sides that bordered the street to include the whole yard. During Father's and Grandfather's day access to the pond and to the small woods had always been open; they'd never needed a watchdog. People didn't worry about security in the Kaiser's time or under Hitler. Back then there were some things that were definitely not right, not right at all—we learned all about it in school, and the papers printed a lot about the past and how everything was better today. But there was more order than there is today, at least for us businessmen, who don't want to get involved in politics. Your life was safe, and your property was better protected.

I told people about my dog and about my habit of checking up on things in the evening or the middle of the night, and someone suggested that we should organize a kind of citizens' watch, that every night one of us should run by our shops and businesses and look after things, but the proposal failed to gain a majority. The shopkeepers preferred to install new rolling shutters, and Pichler said that he didn't get off work until after midnight, and the only place he wanted to go was bed.

Haber didn't comment on any of this. He stood next to the

skittles alley, apparently interested only in the falling pins, and since no one else wanted to play, he rolled one ball after another, eagerly watching for the results. Then Grebe, who owned the clothing boutique on the market square, whispered that Beuchler had been to see him and demanded that Haber be kicked out of the club. Unless that happened Beuchler wasn't going to show up anymore. A few of them nodded and mentioned that they had spoken with Beuchler as well. Haber was bowling away, undeterred, as if in preparation for a tournament, when we all looked over, undoubtedly with the same thought: Could Bernhard Haber be the arsonist? Was it possible that one of us, a successful and well-off businessman, would roam through town at night setting fire to his rival's shop? Of course no one likes his competitors, and we always wish they'd go to hell—a second sawmill in Guldenberg and I might as well pack up, or else tighten my belt, and I mean really tighten it. Still, you might bad-mouth a competitor, but that doesn't mean you destroy his shop.

In a way I had to admit Beuchler was right: some things had changed. Maybe because of the war, which had taken its toll, or the postwar period, which lasted longer and caused even more suffering in town: the actual fighting in Guldenberg had lasted no more than an hour. One hour of bombs, then as far as Guldenberg was concerned the war was almost over, and the fire brigade and the inhabitants were able to put out the fires. Apart from that, Guldenberg had seven fallen soldiers; their families had paid more than all the other inhabitants, and for them the war was surely more horrible than all time before and after. But after the war came the refugees, first those who had been bombed out of the neighboring villages and nearby cities, and then the ones who had been expelled, and they didn't stop coming until the middle of the 1950s. They demanded a place to live, and work, and ration cards, although Guldenberg itself had nothing to give. At one point the people who had been bombed out of their homes left; only a few stayed more than a few months before going back to their hometowns. The expellees, on the other hand, simply stayed, and everyone knew they would never leave, at least not willingly, because they no longer had a homeland. And with the expellees, life in our town changed. They *were* strangers. You didn't know exactly where they came from, or how they used to live, or what they considered acceptable and unacceptable. Maybe people in Pomerania and Silesia did make money off insurance for arson and natural catastrophes like some of our locals said—who knew for sure?

When Haber noticed we were all looking at him, he smiled awkwardly, racked up the pins, and joined us at the table. He picked up his beer, took a swallow, put the glass back on the table, and said, "Strike that idea out of your heads. It wasn't me. And if someone has something to add to that, then he should say it here. To my face."

No one said anything, and Haber looked each man in the eye until he turned away.

"Fine," he said at last. "Then we're agreed."

"None of us assume that you—" I began, but Haber cut me off.

"There are worse things," he said. "My father didn't just have his place burned down. He was murdered."

"No he wasn't," Parlitzke answered sharply. "Your father hanged himself."

"Do you know that for a fact? And the attempted murder? Just one month before?"

"The police determined that it was an accident. A timber fell on his head. Things like that can happen when you have just one arm. It's understandable that your father thought someone had hit him on the head. I'd think the same thing. But it was an accident."

"So why did the police investigation go on so long for this ostensible suicide?"

"I don't know. I heard that it's required with suicides. Maybe it wouldn't have happened if you had stayed here."

"Maybe. Whatever. But there's not just an arsonist living in this town; there's also a murderer."

"Stop talking nonsense, Bernhard. Your father couldn't manage any longer and so he reached for a rope. It wasn't murder."

"It wasn't a rope. It was a wire snare, Erhard. A wire snare, just like back then. It was a long time ago; I was still in school; someone killed my dog. With a wire snare. And you can say what you want, but I'm convinced it was the same bastard who murdered my father."

"Do you know who works with wire snares? The Gypsies. Have you ever thought about that?"

"He's right, Bernhard. And Gypsies eat dog meat, too. Everybody knows that."

"My dog wasn't eaten. They killed him. They strangled him and left him lying around so I would find him. Besides, it happened before the Gypsies started coming to our town."

"But maybe with your father . . ."

"No, my friend, you're on the wrong track. The police investigated thoroughly in that direction—they would have preferred to arrest a Gypsy. But my father had nothing to do with Gypsies, nothing at all. What should they have against him? He was a refugee, right, and that was almost the same. Gypsies or refugees: people in town didn't really differentiate."

"Haber, don't jump to conclusions."

"We have to get used to the idea that there's an arsonist and a murderer living in our wonderful town, among all the upright citizens and kind neighbors."

"That's completely absurd."

"Are you suggesting one of us? Do you think that one of us had something to do with that?"

"No. I don't."

"Well, thank you very much," said Parlitzke sarcastically. "If you have proof for your accusations, then show it. If you are simply imagining such a monstrous idea, next time think before you say anything. Let's call it quits for today. For me the fun is over."

We didn't kick Haber out of the club, and true to his word, Beuchler never came back. We felt sorry about it, but then again, Beuchler no longer owned a shop: after the fire he worked as a simple carpenter in the state-owned furniture factory in Eilenburg, and since our club was only for independent businessmen, his staying on would have become a problem sooner or later. For all intents and purposes, our group was the secret businessmen's association of Guldenberg; someone who wasn't running his own outfit would neither help us nor benefit from our efforts. Beuchler understood that and maybe that's why he never returned. After all, we weren't meeting just to knock down a few skittles; we had things to discuss and decisions to make in order to keep the local government from riding roughshod over our interests. We exerted what pressure we could, and occasionally we succeeded. Naturally, we couldn't get the mayor to do anything about the outrageous taxes that forced each of us to work under the table now and then to keep ourselves from bankruptcy, because while the municipality did indeed live off our taxes, it had no say in what we had to pay or how much of it they got. Any time a building was planned, we made our voices heard, and because we consulted with each other in advance, our united front gained more and more influence. After years of debate on resurfacing the roads around the Polish settlement, the outlying areas, and the Schwarzer Berg, we were even able to assert ourselves against the collective farm, which otherwise always had its way. And although the mayor stressed indignantly that Guldenberg did not need a chamber of commerce and industry, by which he meant our Skittles Club, we were still often able to force a majority vote in the council assembly.

Our club was a thorn in the side of the party, as we found out from Wessenburg, who owned the Homeland Publishing Company and the print shop. He had joined the party six years after the war, when he took over the business from his father, and the occupying power made it difficult to renew his license. Wessenburg told us the party viewed us as a hostile element; he had to submit regular reports to the local party organization. Whenever he sensed it was time to file a report, he would sit down with Pichler and me and we would tell him what to say. Pichler had joined the Peasant's Party—one of the parties allied with the government—at some point, because he wanted to have his peace and quiet, as he put it, and that particular group would not tell him how to run his hotel and pub. Furthermore, they considered him an experienced accountant, which left him with no choice but to become treasurer. So Pichler was familiar with such reports and knew what was expected. If the report sounded too positive, he would protest, and then make up some criticisms of our club for Wessenburg to pass along. Pichler assured us that these complaints had no consequences and would only make the report more credible. When Wessenburg finally read his report out loud, and I felt uneasy at some of the formulations, Pichler smiled and said that now the report was just right and there was no reason Wessenburg couldn't submit it. And so he did. Wessenburg then received instructions from the party as to how he should act with us and influence the club, and the next report would contain a few success stories, although Pichler was careful that Wessenburg never declared more than a partial success, and that he always included a few self-critical remarks highlighting what he had yet to accomplish. In that way, the party had the impression of being fully informed, and we could skittle away and speak openly and undisturbed, and everybody benefited.

In the mid-1960s Haber married his girlfriend; they had been living together for a few years. He purchased some property next to my house at Neumarkt, including an old villa from the previous century. After the war, the place had served as a home for refugees, who managed to run it down completely, so that Haber acquired the building at very low cost. The windows and floorboards had been torn out and the roof had so many holes that the whole truss had to be rebuilt. Haber was determined to fix the place up. I told him it would be cheaper to tear it down and build something new, but he liked the old house—the two rooms with bay windows, the large entrance hall, the turned flight of steps leading down to the riverbank and the barrel vault in the cellar. Moreover, since he was a craftsman and able to do most of it himself, he wasn't scared by the amount of work, but rather enjoyed watching it progress, satisfied with his handiwork and looking forward to its completion. I delivered the wood for the truss and cut it to his specifications; when needed I also lent a hand like a good neighbor. Eighteen months later he was finished; the solidly rebuilt villa had acquired its old luster and was the best restoration in all of Guldenberg, more beautiful than the townhouses at the marketplace, and more impressive than the ostentatious new building the veterinarian had built behind the nursery.

Haber invited his friend and partner Hermsdorf as well as my wife and me to join his family for the housewarming. Since then our families have often gotten together; our wives have become friends, advising and helping each other with their gardens, and jointly decorating our homes for various holidays.

Friederike, Haber's wife, was a young and somewhat naïve woman who had worked as a cook in the Eagle before giving up her job to devote herself to home and husband. She came from the country, of strong build and plain-looking, but without a mean bone in her body. If you tried to joke with her she would listen in gullible amazement to whatever you were saying, and then you'd have to explain it was a joke or else she'd take it seriously. The most beautiful thing about her was her boundless admiration of her husband; she hung on his every word, and he, along with their glorious villa, was the fulfillment of all her dreams. I once slept with her, just once—it somehow happened even though neither of us was particularly looking for it. She came running over late one afternoon looking for Veronika, my wife. I told her Veronika wasn't due back from Leipzig until later that night, and invited her in, since she seemed distraught, completely beside herself. She went on at great length, constantly breaking into tears and saying how much she loved her husband, about how she had been taken in by a swindler, who had promised to procure an old Ford for her—a car that Bernhard had dreamed of. She had put down a sizable payment, convinced that Bernhard, who had often talked about that very same model, would happily pay the purchase price. But the seller failed to show up at the appointed time; the Leipzig address he had given turned out to be false—the street existed, but there was no such number. He had shown a work ID as well, but that, too, proved to be fake: the place existed, but the man did not work there. Some of the employees recognized his name, though, since a number of other victims he had swindled into paying for a car had gone there asking for him.

I tried to calm her, and told her that while Bernhard was hardly going to reward her with flowers, her home would soon return to its blissful order after a purifying storm. But she was determined not to let her husband find out about her stupidity and the swindle, and so I offered to lend the money she needed. And then it just happened. She thanked me and hugged me, I stroked her shoulders, she kissed me lightly on the cheek, and I returned her kiss a little more forcefully. Suddenly she was in my arms, I touched her breast, and seconds later we were on the carpet, tearing off our clothes and making love with a hasty urgency, and, at least as far as I was concerned, without passion. Afterward, Friederike started howling again, this time not because of the swindle, but because she had betrayed her Bernhard, and it took me an hour to quiet her down. I assured her that Bernhard would never find out, that we would take our moment of weak will and bury it in the bottommost depths of our hearts, and that it would have no effect on our friendship.

And that's exactly how things went. Now and then Friederike would blush when she saw me at a family get-together or if the conversation turned to affairs and marital fidelity, but our little secret didn't disturb our good relations; in fact it inclined her to be almost as forthcoming and obliging toward me as she was to her Bernhard—either out of gratitude for my discretion or because in her eyes our intimacy had underscored our bond.

This little episode meant nothing to me. I didn't find Friederike attractive; as far as I was concerned she was Bernhard's wife, more a neutral quantity than an object of desire. Besides I was and am the monogamous type; I can count all the women I've slept with on the fingers of both hands, and none of these extramarital incidents deserved the name of affair or even infidelity. They just happened without much interest on my part. Perhaps my limited experience was due to a lack of opportunity: after all, at a sawmill you only deal with men.

Pichler, on the other hand, who owned the Black Eagle, enjoyed talking at length about his conquests. In a hotel you meet women who are total strangers every day, women who have this or that requirement and maybe a few more requirements at night, so there it's natural, so to speak, to have a flirt or a fling or something even more involved—to some extent it's all part of the business. At a sawmill, though, the only surprises are when a tree trunk rolls onto your feet, or something like that. So I simply didn't have the opportunity, and I wasn't interested enough to actively seek them out. For me it's not so much about marital fidelity, just a tendency toward monogamy. I was married to Veronika and didn't have any sexual needs beyond that. And the laughably few incidents that did occur, such as with Bernhard's wife, had nearly nothing to do with eroticism—just a bit of biology, nature having its own way; I was barely a participant. My promise to keep it all under wraps was entirely genuine, since Friederike didn't mean anything to me and I would have forgotten all about our ridiculous coupling if she hadn't kept reminding me with a blush or a frightened glance.

After Beuchler's shop burned down, Haber enlarged his own place with an annex and a heating shed, hired on two more employees, and within two years he had become the most important carpentry shop around. Then some political changes went into effect that had an impact on our Skittles Club, which the mayor disparagingly referred to as "our local chamber of commerce." A campaign against independent businessmen was launched throughout the republic. The private capitalistic enterprises, as they called us, needed to be brought into the new era, and that meant expropriation, plain and simple. The state assigned its own managers or controllers, and half of each targeted business henceforth belonged to the state. To add insult to injury, all the independents had to sign that they had voluntarily requested to have their business half-nationalized.

At that time I still had only one permanent employee, Hubert. The others I hired were just temporary, with contracts that ran for a matter of weeks. The official allotment of wood that the state delivered did not allow me to expand. Also, when clients came with their own wood, they would usually help out with the cutting. That saved me from having to pay for a journeyman, and it also meant there would be no complaints after the fact, in case the lumber wasn't sized exactly, since the client himself had been present to supervise the cutting. As a result my firm was too small to make it desirable to the state and so I escaped the new campaign. Of course as an independent business owner, I still had to pay the ridiculously high tax imposed on all private enterprise and had to put up with the usual discriminatory regulations at every level of government. I also had to accept the fact that neither of my daughters—Liane had already started school and Jenny was just four years old—would be allowed into the advanced high school or the university, since the offspring of all independent businessmen—the kulaks' brood, as the mayor called them late one evening at the Eagle—did not deserve to be sponsored and promoted by the state. Still, I was lucky to be spared the partial takeover, which was otherwise enforced for independents in the whole district and even beyond.

Haber, too, had to submit to the new arrangement. All he managed to work out was that he was hired as manager of his own business, which was now called Guldenberg Carpentry—Haber's name appeared only in small letters on the wooden sign, accompanied by the word "formerly." Three other members of our club—Pichler, Wessenburg, and Plehnert—also had to accept the state's intrusion.

Plehnert, whose family had owned the chair and upholstery factory for four generations, refused to work as hired manager in his own firm, especially since his son had no intention of taking over the factory, but had gone to Berlin where he traded in used cars—not exactly legally—and from what we heard was highly successful. Plehnert declined the post and instead came up with a new position that hadn't been planned: he became the senior consultant, received a small salary and went every two or three days for a few hours to his former factory, to check on things and advise the new management.

All four stayed on in the Skittles Club. What they lost in independence they gained in privilege. Once Pichler was no longer sole owner of the Eagle, he had hardly any problems with deliveries. His hotel and restaurant were given the same rank as the state hotels, and he received the same order lists as the large establishments, offering products he never could have dreamed of before. Plehnert's factory soon became part of a larger combine, which produced both for domestic use and export. Wessenburg's publishing house was dissolved, but his print shop went on receiving commissions from the entire district for several years, until it was liquidated at the beginning of the 1980s. By then the machines were worn down and not worth replacing, given the small capacity of his print shop. Haber's woodworks, on the other hand, received so many orders he had to expand his business practically every year. He needed more wood than I could deliver, and so he began ordering from other mills, and received some types of wood I had never seen before.

In our club we joked about the fact that it was precisely our party loyalists—all except Haber belonged to one of the official parties—that were hardest hit. At times, however, when we complained about the poor deliveries and they smiled and listened in meaningful silence, we sensed that we were the ones who had been outmaneuvered, and not them.

My relationship with Bernhard Haber continued unaffected by these changes; we kept up our friendship, and our families socialized as regularly as they had before. Bernhard never talked about money, but I had the impression that he managed to circumvent the state oversight and took in enough orders under the table so that he earned practically as much as before, despite his less-than-lavish manager's paycheck.

Bernhard and Friederike had one daughter and a son. Paul was one year younger than Jenny, my youngest daughter. They grew up together and were nearly inseparable. If something stupid was going on in town I could bet that the two were involved or even the instigators. None of our children cared much for school; they always passed by the skin of their teeth, and I had a hard time finding an apprenticeship for them. Since I didn't have a son who could take over the business, and women were not suited for work that was so physically demanding, I hoped that one of my girls would bring me a hard-working son-in-law, to whom I could pass on the mill.

Paul, Bernhard's son, was a real rascal, who liked nothing better than spending the whole day running around pulling pranks. But I liked him anyway; he was witty, never at a loss for words, and both my daughters were fond of him. After he finished school he learned carpentry in his father's shop, not by his own choice; he had wanted to do something with cars, but Bernhard convinced him or somehow forced him to apprentice in his shop, and he turned out to be a solid, reliable worker who knew his trade. He and Jenny stayed close, and that was fine with me. I thought that if they ever got married, I'd have the right man for the mill. Paul had next to no chances of taking over his father's former business, which now employed eight carpenters and would in time surely be entrusted to someone with the right party affiliation. Paul certainly wouldn't have been unhappy if I gave him my sawmill.

When Haber turned forty—it was a Saturday—I went over to congratulate him and raise a glass. The two of us sat on the benches at the round table in his summerhouse, a kind of gazebo that Bernhard had built the year before, based on an old engraving in an album about castles and princely residences, with a built-in stone grill. We were drinking beer and talking about old times when suddenly Friederike came in, very worked up, and told us that the Catholic priest wanted to speak to Bernhard. I was just about to make a joke, because I couldn't imagine that Bernhard was Catholic, since he never went to church, when Father Gessling came into the garden. We put down our beer bottles, somewhat embarrassed, and Father Gessling shook Bernhard's hand and wished him a happy birthday, then shook my hand as well.

"May I offer you something, Father?" asked Bernhard. "Some coffee or a beer?"

"I'll gladly take the beer, but I'll save it for this evening and drink to your health then. For the moment I'd prefer some tea."

Friederike nodded, still worked up, and rushed off to fetch some tea. We sat at the round table; Father Gessling looked around the garden, then praised Bernhard's gazebo, full of admiration for the execution and the quality of craftsmanship.

"I like it a lot. A little house behind the house—a refuge where you can retreat and collect your thoughts."

He paused for a moment, lost in thought.

"Do you think you might be able to build me a gazebo like this? Of course it would have to be smaller. Just for one person."

"Of course, Father. I have a few photos and some sketches I found when I designed this. You can take them along, and take all the time you need to decide what you want."

"The deciding factor is the price, Herr Haber. As you know, in our country the Church is far from wealthy."

"That's something we can talk about; price shouldn't be an obstacle."

"I could supply the wood. We still have two forests: they didn't take everything we had."

"That's fine. That would lower the price considerably. Of course that means my friend Sigurd won't have any business, but he'll survive."

"And how much might it cost?"

"I can't say until you've decided what it should look like, how big it should be, what kind of roof it should have. If you want rose-windows like these it will cost more."

"No. It should be very simple."

Friederike came back with the tray. She placed an unopened bottle of beer in front of the priest, who thanked her as he stowed it inside his leather bag, and then she served him tea.

"But I didn't come about the gazebo, Herr Haber. I have a rather delicate mission, very awkward for me."

"I'll be on my way," I said. "Veronika and I will see you this evening."

"You can stay, Herr Kitzerow. What I have to say is not a secret. Or rather, it is a secret that I am bringing out into the open. It concerns your father, Herr Haber."

"What about him?"

The priest stirred his tea without looking up.

"Did he leave something in your hands? A note to pass on to me?"

"No. It's about his death. As you know, he was buried as a suicide—"

"It wasn't suicide," Bernhard interrupted. "It was murder."

"How do you know that?"

"I just know it. Even if the police were unable to prove it, it was murder."

"You are right, Herr Haber. Someone killed him."

The priest now looked at Bernhard, who stared at him in amazement. The pronouncement hung for a few seconds in the small gazebo, and when its echoes faded we all felt paralyzed. Finally Bernhard reached for Father Gessling's hand.

"Father," he said, and his voice sounded hoarse, "what are you trying to tell me?"

"What you suspected, Herr Haber, was correct. Your poor father was murdered. I heard it half a year ago in private confession. The man who told me died within the hour. He was an unhappy man, deeply in conflict with himself."

"Who was it?"

"I am bound by the seal of confession, Herr Haber, and I have told you what I could, keeping my obligation to myself and to my duties. I wanted to and had to tell you this, in order to free you from the burden of an otherwise unholy paternal sin. Your father did not die in sin; he died as a righteous man and he will receive his heavenly reward."

"Who was it?"

"A very unhappy man, who could find no rest after his evil deed. I cannot and will not tell you more."

"And why? Why did he hang my father?"

"He said it was on account of a wager. A drunken wager, that all of them had been drinking."

"All? Who are they?"

"I don't know. And even if I did know, I couldn't tell you. You shouldn't dwell on it. I came to tell you that you may remember your father without pain, because he did not forfeit his state of blessedness."

"What you are telling me I already knew, Father. What I don't know is the name of the murderer."

The priest shook his head. "Whoever it was, he is dead now."

"And the others?"

The priest shrugged his shoulders and shook his head once more.

"Did he murder my dog as well?"

"I don't understand."

"And the fire? Who set my father's shop on fire?"

"Herr Haber, please. I don't know anything about all that. I came to you with a heavy heart, in order to give you comfort. I have told you what I know and what I can say. I have done so in order to sort things out in my own mind. I believe I have done my duty in taking a burden from your soul without breaking the seal of confession. If you think of your father, or if by chance you pray for him, you should know he died without guilt and free of sin."

"Thank you, Father. But I have known that for some time."

Bernhard and Friederike accompanied the old priest to the garden gate. When Bernhard came back, he smiled at me.

"I'm sorry," I said.

"What do you mean? I always knew that my father had been murdered. And besides, it was fifteen years ago."

"And who—"

"Forget it. Another beer?"

"No, I promised Veronika I'd help her transplant some bushes. We'll see you tonight."

"OK. See you then."

At the party he said nothing about the conversation with

the priest. When Friederike mentioned that Father Gessling had dropped by to wish Bernhard happy birthday, he gave her a look that silenced her.

In the following weeks he never mentioned Gessling's visit, and I assumed he didn't want to know anything more about the whole business, but at the end of October, when we were working together in our gardens, raking leaves for burning, he said, all of a sudden: "I'm certain it was Lachmann, Ernst Lachmann. Did you know him?"

"Lachmann the old boozehead? What about him?"

"He was the one. He put the noose around my father's neck."

"Lachmann? He couldn't even walk straight."

"That may be. But he was perfectly capable of hanging someone."

"How did you figure that out?"

"Gessling said that the murderer had confessed during last unction, half a year before my birthday. I inquired at the town hall and in the church registry. The only one it could be is Lachmann. What was he like?"

"Lachmann? An alcoholic. He sat all day in the pub and drank away what little brain he had."

"And his friends?"

"Lachmann didn't have any friends. Nobody wanted anything to do with him."

"He obviously had some friends."

"He didn't have any friends, Bernhard. In all of Guldenberg he didn't have a single friend. Who would want to go around with a drunk like that?"

"There had to be someone he could bet with." Bernhard smiled grimly. "I did a little research. The city had to pay for the funeral, since he didn't have a penny, and there were no relatives to bear the costs. But his rent had been paid for years. The dump he lived in only cost a few marks, but the money was always transferred right on time. There was a standing order."

"From a bank? I can't even picture Lachmann having a bank account. He couldn't write his own name."

"He didn't, Sigurd. It was Beuchler who paid his rent . . . Don't know what to say to that, do you? So why? Why did Beuchler pay his rent? They weren't related."

"Who knows. Maybe Lachmann worked for him now and then, and Beuchler was sensible enough not to pay him directly. That's possible."

"No, Sigurd. And you know it. What's possible is something entirely different."

"What do you mean?"

I felt a shudder as something dawned on me.

"Back then neither of us was in the club. But Beuchler was. Maybe they used to have a little bet now and then. And a few people in the club used to hire Lachmann."

"Should we go to see Beuchler together and ask him to explain?"

"No. I already know what I want to know. I don't want to wake any sleeping dogs. I don't want to have to go through the whole circus all over again. Once in a lifetime is enough for me. I can't help my father anymore, so what's the point?"

He took his potato rake and scratched some leaves together and then heaved them onto the wheelbarrow.

"I'm through with them, Sigurd. The only thing that's still unsettled is Tinz, a mutt I used to have and someone killed. But I'm not going to start a war on account of a dog. Not today, anyway."

I nodded and didn't say any more. I had a suspicion that Bernhard wasn't entirely off the mark; in fact, it made a lot of sense.

Lachmann had occasionally visited our mill, and Father sometimes gave him work. He wasn't allowed near the machines, because he always reeked of alcohol, but he was strong and could carry logs that normally took two men. After Father died he showed up two or three times asking for work:

I sent him away. His hands were always shaking and he stank; I didn't want to see a wreck like him around, and I didn't believe his talk about Father owing him something. Those boozers always had some claim or another, and when they didn't get what they wanted by begging they would turn aggressive. At one point I took him by the collar, hauled him to the front gate, and gave him a kick. After that he never came back, and whenever I saw him in town he would quickly cross the street.

I couldn't stop thinking about Bernhard's comments. I wanted to know whether my father had had a hand in this horrible business, and if Bernhard didn't want to go on with it, I did. First, I dropped in on Beuchler, spoke about this and that and the old times, then mentioned the name Lachmann and indicated that I knew what Lachmann had said shortly before his death. Beuchler contested everything: finally he came out with a few details and a name. The fact that he paid the rent for Lachmann had no connection; he had had an affair with Lachmann's sister for years and managed to keep it a secret: it was for her sake that he took over the rent, since she was worried about her alcoholic brother. Then I went to see Wiesner, who had owned the smithy back then; he had to give it up when the co-op succeeded in running its own shop. From what the two of them told me and what I could piece together, the whole thing happened after a night of skittles in the club. People had already said good-bye, and most of them, including my father, had already left. Four men were standing at the bar and having a last drink. Beuchler was there along with Wiesner, Schmöckel and Pichler. They were going on about the town and all the refugees, who would soon be straining the city budget to the limit. They made some dumb jokes about the one-armed carpenter, and one of them—neither Beuchler nor Wiesner would say who—stated that he would shell out one hundred marks for every dead refugee, as a personal contribution to municipal hygiene. Everybody laughed, and someone else said he would add a hundred of his own, because he, too, would rather live in a town that was clean. At that point Lachmann, who had been sitting alone at one of the tables, stood up, went over and joined the conversation. As always he was drunk and asked whether the gentlemen were as good as their word, and they joked back that their word was solid enough to build a house on. They bought Lachmann a beer and left. Two days later old Haber hanged himself. Or was hanged, because they never spoke about it with Lachmann, and they certainly didn't give him any money, at least not that Beuchler or Wiesner knew of. Wiesner assured me the whole conversation had been in jest, and that Lachmann had definitely realized that. Besides, old Haber seemed to magically attract misfortune, and this was just more of the same.

I was relieved to learn that my father hadn't been part of it; he wasn't there when the conversation took place, he hadn't offered any money, there was no blood clinging to his fingers.

I thought long and hard whether and how much to tell Bernhard. Because he was my neighbor and friend, I at least wanted to let him know that my father hadn't had anything to do with it, so I went to see him one Sunday morning. Friederike answered and told me Bernhard was in the garage, but would be right in to have some coffee, and invited me to wait in the living room.

"I'll go check on him," I said, and went around the house. Bernhard was building a rack to hang his snow tires from the ceiling; he was standing on a ladder, gave me a brief nod and asked me to lend a hand. I passed him screws and tools and told him what I had discovered, although the only name I mentioned was Beuchler's. Bernhard went on working the whole time, without reacting. He wasn't surprised, and he wasn't upset. He didn't even seem to be angry; at any rate he didn't say anything and didn't interrupt me. When I had finished he kept on twisting away at the screws, calm as could be, as if I had been speaking about the weather.

Then he asked: "And who were the other three?"

"Do you really want to know?"

"Yes. I think so."

I hesitated a moment, but before I could tell him, he cut me off.

"Wait," he said. He climbed down from the ladder, walked to a corner of the garage where the cases of beer were standing, took out two bottles, opened them and handed one to me. He sat down on a stool in the open garage door, looked out at his garden then up at the sky and drank his beer. He didn't say a word and neither did I. At one point his wife called, but he didn't answer. After he had finished his beer, he held the bottle upside down to pour out the last drops, then turned around and smiled.

"I don't know, Sigurd. I want to know and I don't want to. I want to know because I spent years chasing after that truth. And I don't want to know because I'm afraid it won't help me. I'm afraid that I'll be right back where I started, that everything will begin all over again. Do you understand?"

"I think I do."

"Everybody was against us; we never belonged. And now I finally feel that I do. Should I give that up? If I bring those guys to trial, I'll have the whole town against me just like before. Then I might as well give up and move away. And what would I gain? I can't bring my father back to life. Sigurd, I don't know. I don't know if I want to hear it."

I nodded.

"The murderer is dead. And the others involved could only be sentenced for being accomplices or inciting murder or reckless endangerment. Besides, it's been fifteen years; they won't get so much as a probational sentence. Because of the statute of limitations my father's murder will never come to trial. How can there be a limit for murder, Sigurd? I understand completely why most crimes aren't subject to prosecution after a certain number of years have passed. If someone stole something or betrayed someone: sooner or later you forget it. Angry as he may be, the victim will ultimately get over it. But a murder! The dead person will never again be alive, and his friends and relatives won't forget his death for as long as they live. Nor will the murderer ever forget it either. Because a crime like that never disappears. At least for my father's murderer it didn't: he had to talk about it, fifteen years after the fact. There can be no statute of limitations for a murder—that's just nonsense cooked up by judges and legislators."

Once again I simply nodded in silence.

"But what should I do? What would happen if I bring accusations against three Guldenberg businessmen and make a huge fuss? I'm in the right and I might even be vindicated, but I would only be told that the offense is no longer punishable. Then I'd have to start all over. Somewhere. Because after that it wouldn't just be these three businessmen sending me into exile."

I knew he was right and took care not to contradict him.

"In the middle ages," said Bernhard, "at least the way I heard it, cathedrals and churches and other large buildings were always built with blood. The blood of an innocent—best, that of a child—had to be mixed with the mortar if the building was to hold. That may be superstition, but maybe it's still like that. Maybe what was needed was the blood of my father, my innocent father, for me to be accepted here, for this to be my home."

I laughed out loud, chucked him on the shoulder and shook my head. I found what he was saying odd, disturbing, but something in his thoughts fascinated me, at least I never forgot it, and found myself thinking about it years later.

"So what are you going to do?" I asked.

Before he could say anything, I decided to step in.

"I think it would be better for you, Bernhard, if you could forget it. Knowing the names won't help you. Apart from Beuchler none of the others are still around. Two are dead and one is in an old folk's home somewhere down south."

He looked at me and I held his gaze. It's ok to lie for the

sake of a friend, and Bernhard had become something like a friend for me. Friederike called him again.

"Thanks, Sigurd," he said shortly, and together we went inside.

Friederike, who was busy in the kitchen, asked if we wanted a beer, and brought some into the living room.

"What were you doing so long in the garage?" she asked.

"Just talking," said Bernhard. "Swapping memories."

"Talking about old times?" she said, mockingly, then suddenly turned red and looked at me, alarmed.

"That's right," said Bernhard. "The good old days."

Over the next five years everything went on as usual. There were a few small improvements for us businessmen; our complaints were taken seriously, and three members of our club actually became part of the municipal administration and were able to ward off the most idiotic things. The demonstrations in Berlin and Leipzig came as a complete surprise for me. Party members and the police crept into hiding; people ran into the street and let loose, as if roasted piglets were flying through the air.

In Guldenberg there were a few spontaneous meetings, so-called citizens' forums, where a handful of excited teachers, a few members of the local church council, and some young hotheads shouted their demands. Our Skittles Club held back. We hadn't discussed what we would do, but as it happened none of us chose to step into the limelight. We had seen too much come and go than to lose our heads at a few wild speeches made by a bunch of screaming kids who had no experience with political promises and even less with the reality that always follows. We didn't let ourselves be carried away by the enthusiasm that had taken hold of the city and the entire country, instead choosing to remain quiet observers. The word from town hall was that everything would be over in a week at the latest, and that the police and the army would soon get things back to normal. Then the wall opened up in Berlin; the mayor appeared at the citizens' forums and spoke just like the people he had earlier derided as petit bourgeois, and the manifestos and slogans that appeared on the pillars and in the shop windows were no longer taken down.

At our club's next meeting, we sat in the special guest room beside the skittles alley to talk about what the changes might mean for us and the town. We agreed that Wessenburg should become the new mayor as soon as the situation had cleared up a little. We would nominate him and give him our unanimous backing, and we had no doubt he would prevail. Schmöckel advised us to rummage through all our old papers; he believed that property expropriated by the Russians and the Communists would be returned sooner or later, so we should be ready with deeds and titles.

That same night I took my files out of the attic and looked through the papers. My father had carefully sorted everything: the excerpts from the ancient land register, the paid receipts for the property tax, the confiscation papers, the articles in the regional paper calling him a kulak, which also gave a detailed listing of our family's former holdings and could thus serve to corroborate my claims. When I had finished I raised a glass to my old man; unlike me, he always believed that some day we would get everything back, so he kept a very careful account and didn't throw anything away. I knew that the two townhouses near the parade grounds had once belonged to us, as well as the three gravel pits, but I also found documents for some tracts of forest and the deed to the alum pond, which I hadn't known about.

Three months later the gravel pits were returned to me. I negotiated with the new government trust, signed a waiver, and they compensated me for the decades of lost profits by letting me keep the two bucket dredgers and the crane shovel purchased by the former combine and installed at the pits. I kept three of the employees, hired another four workers I knew personally, and made the operation more efficient. In the spring it looked like our region was going to see some major road construction, so I ordered another dredger for the summer. I left Hubert in charge of the sawmill, and only checked in on the fly. Hiring was done with a handshake; there was no need for contracts, and since I paid well, no one complained, at least not to me.

In April Uncle Gustav came to visit. He owned a construction firm in Reutlingen in West Germany. The year before, when he turned seventy, he had handed his company over to his son and began traveling around the world with his wife. He had just returned from Canada and decided to visit me, his only brother's son, before flying off to the Maldives for two months. He inspected the gravel pits and the sawmill and pored over my files for a whole day until deep into the night. The next morning he said we had to talk. We sat down in the living room and asked Veronika to make coffee and make sure we weren't disturbed.

Gustav looked at me for a long time without saying anything and then said, "Sigurd, you are a Kitzerow. So you're bound to succeed, like all Kitzerows do."

"I think so too."

"You have it all, boy. Everything you need."

"The gravel pits are a real gold mine."

"Exactly. So why are you giving the gold away?"

"I'm not, Gustav. Right now the price is good, and it keeps on rising. Road construction will be a thriving business for years. Even decades. And there's no end to the gravel."

"So why are you giving everything away?"

"I'm not. Brönner and Karlitz, the two construction firms, complain about my prices, but they're dependent on me if they don't want to drive a hundred kilometers to get their gravel."

"Mistake number one. Why isn't the gravel transport in your hands?"

"I don't have the trucks. A rig costs two hundred thousand, and I'd need at least four. How am I supposed to pay for that?"

"Mistake number two. Why are you selling the gravel in the first place? Why aren't you in charge of construction yourself?"

"I don't own a road construction company. I don't know the first thing about it. I know about wood, and I don't want to get kicked in the pants."

"So that's why you're giving away money, Sigurd?"

Then he put my files on the table, took a notebook out of his jacket pocket and outlined his plans, ignoring my doubts and objections. When I asked where I was supposed to find the money for the projects he was describing, and whether I could count on him to put up the capital, he just laughed.

"No, that's not how it's done. Of course I could loan you the money, but that would be too expensive for both of us."

He telephoned and made an appointment for the next day with the director of the bank. Then he called his wife in Reutlingen and told her to cancel the trip to the Maldives, because he would be busy here for a few weeks getting me on my feet.

We took all the documents to the bank. I knew Sandler, the director; he gave us a friendly greeting and asked what we needed. When Gustav laid out his calculations and started talking about a loan of one and a half million, Sandler laughed: he thought it was a joke. Gustav then showed him the papers, totaled up my possessions and became increasingly determined with every objection raised by Sandler. In fact he seemed to know more about credit and lending than the banker, and repeatedly referred to regulations the other man had to look up. Two hours later we said good-bye. Sandler had told us he needed one or two weeks to have a loan of that size approved, but Gustav got him to agree to change that to three days. Gustav didn't give me any money, but he acted as my immediate guarantor for an amount in the millions, in order to speed up the process, and he spoke with the bankers and their lawyers as if he owned a bank himself and knew every law.

Gustav stayed at our house for two months. By the time he left I owned a construction firm with more than fourteen months' worth of advance orders, but I was also in debt to the bank for over three million. When I told Gustav that the debts made me nervous and that I was sleeping poorly, he laughed and said: "It's when you don't have any debts that you should worry. You've now acquired a very good friend, one who will trouble himself on your behalf and will do everything in his power to make sure you don't suffer any damage—your bank. Because if you go bankrupt they stand to lose a few pennies, and that's not something banks like to do. Believe me, Sigurd: your bank will do enough worrying about you and the loan. So leave those worries and sleepless nights to them. And now don't just sit there, go deeper into debt. Money isn't cheap at the moment, but you can't pass up an opportunity like this. In ten years it will all be a done deal—the gold rush will be over. Now's the time for pioneers; you have to set down your stakes. So keep at it, Sigurd. When I come back a year from now I want to see some real growth, understood?"

I had more than enough sleepless nights, but I expanded my businesses like Gustav told me to. Because I used the gravel for my own construction, and stopped selling to outside firms, Brönner and Karlitz had to drive far away to get gravel, and their transport costs went up considerably, allowing me to undercut them in all bids. Brönner, who had come from Hesse, was quick to catch on and went back home. Karlitz struggled on for a year before declaring insolvency. That left me as the only road construction firm in the region, and nobody could get around me.

Wessenburg became the new mayor, as we had agreed, and the new town counsel consisted mostly of members of our skittles club, so that local businesses received favorable consideration in all city contracts. Eight years after the collapse of the wall I owned ten separate firms in Guldenberg, and had a sizable interest in twelve other companies. I even owned a stake in the port at Rostock, which was advantageous for overseas transport, because in the meantime I had started importing and exporting gravel as the market required.

Today my only worries are my two daughters. They're both of marriageable age, but they have yet to come to their senses. Liane can't keep a job for more than a few months, and gets her mother to support her, which Veronika does despite my orders not to give the girl a penny. Every time she changes jobs she switches boyfriends as well, so that two or three times a year I see a new face at our breakfast table and have to put up with my daughter's cooing and petting. Unfortunately Jenny is no longer with Paul; she moved to Leipzig, where she lives off welfare or theft or something—in any case not off her work. I once visited her to straighten her out. She laughed at me and told me to my face that she was either going to marry money or inherit it, so that in any case she was taken care of, and I shouldn't worry about her.

I still hope that at least one of the girls will settle down so I can hand over my small empire to her and a reasonable son-in-law. Most of all I'd like it if Jenny and Paul would marry, because then I wouldn't have to worry about the businesses: Paul works with his father, is almost shrewder than his old man, and is always on the go from morning to night. Bernhard lets Paul handle all his contracts, and even I have to watch out whenever Paul shows up in my office with that innocent look of his and suggests some lucrative business. Although I was a kind of uncle to him and he ate at our table almost every day of his childhood, that devil has tried to take me for a ride. I would gladly leave Paul my firms, and who knows, if my daughters keep acting as dumb as they have been, I might disinherit them one day, so that all they get would be the legal minimum, and give the rest to Paul.

Bernhard Haber hasn't let opportunity pass him by either, and I've advised and supported him as best I could. The carpentry shop was returned to him along with the buildings and the heating shed, and all investments that had been made were given as compensation. Consequently he started his new life as an entrepreneur with little capital but considerable property. I talked him into building up a heating oil delivery firm alongside the shop, accompanied him to the bank, and shared Uncle Gustav's advice.

When we celebrated the fifth year of our new businesses, Haber and I were the biggest employers in Guldenberg. No one could get around us, and certainly not city hall. There was a small difference between us of just a few million marks, but that didn't affect our friendship. After all, we both knew that I'd been able to build on what my grandfather and father had left me, while as a refugee, Bernhard had had to do it all on his own.

Our Skittles Club did not survive the changes. We kept meeting every other Friday at the Eagle, but no one had time for skittles. Instead we spoke about what was going on in town; since the mayor was also a member, we were a kind of kitchen cabinet that set municipal policy. We had a couple of new members—a few Guldenbergers who had become independent businessmen, and a few former residents whose property had been returned or else newcomers who had come to set up business. Apart from that there was a notary, two tax advisers, and a lawyer from the former West Germany. Since we no longer had to keep our proceedings secret, we gave up on skittles and met in the club room at the Eagle instead.

At one point a proposal came up to form an official club, and we considered the most interesting propositions. Pichler suggested that we call ourselves the Chamber of Commerce—just as the former mayor had called us disparagingly, but the lawyer objected. Wiesner suggested we start a carnival club, pointing out that such an organization had existed in Guldenberg up until 1927. A few of us had reservations, since anyone and everyone had the right to join a carnival association, which none of us wanted. Wiesner said that we could avoid that by demanding yearly dues. He suggested setting annual dues at five thousand marks, which would keep unwanted citizens away. We took a vote and the proposal passed, so we contracted with the lawyer to draft bylaws that would allow our club to be considered not-for-profit and exempt from taxes.

That November the establishment of the Green-Gold-Guldenberg Carnival Association was announced in the press, and we held our first official session, where we elected Haber president. The following February, exactly seventy years after the first carnival association had been disbanded, the city partied for three fantastic days. We rented the school gymnasium and Guldenberg's two large restaurants for our celebration, and the townspeople took part in a parade to which we donated a considerable portion of the club's budget. The day before Shrove Tuesday we held a big meeting in the gym. As president, Bernhard opened the proceedings and then handed power to the carnival prince and princess. The town's young girls strutted across the stage, and the brass players from the church orchestra squawked out some carnival tunes, which would have sounded just as good if not better at a funeral.

The next day was the parade. The prince and princess stood on the steps in front of the town hall, to review the parade along with the members of the association, and to cheer on all the carnival fools. The prince held a golden papier-mâché key that symbolized the municipal power that had been handed over to the fools. I stood next to Bernhard, waving to the crowd, and told him through the din of the brass players that we had no need for keys like that, since we had the real ones right in our pocket, that he and I were the kings of Guldenberg. Bernhard went on waving with his right hand but turned his head to me and said casually: "Of course, Sigurd. But never forget there are some people down there who would gladly see our heads roll. And today even more than a few years ago."

Then he laughed, applauded the carnival oxcart that was passing below, and greeted a few business friends who were coming up the stairs. Two hours later we were frozen through and went to the town hall to warm up with some glühwein. That evening our club spent three hours at the Eagle before moving to the Crown, where we traded places with the prince and princess, who then transferred their court to the Eagle. Paul came up to us with a girl who was a little drunk and told us he had found his carnival princess. He asked his father for some money. Since Bernhard just eyed the girl suspiciously, I took out my wallet and handed Paul a hundred marks. Bernhard shook his head at me, but Paul gave me a satisfied grin and a patronizing pat on the shoulder.

"I'll make it good some other time, Sigurd."

"You can do that right now, Paul. Just promise you won't turn me down next year. Next year you'll be our prince, all right? It has to be a Guldenberger, one of us, and someone who represents something."

Paul laughed out loud and shook his head: "No, I wouldn't be a good choice. Besides, your prince only gets one single princess for three days of carnival, that's not enough for me." He grinned at his father and kissed the girl.

"What was going on in the square earlier?" I asked him.

"Earlier? What do you mean?"

"I saw something, Paul. Some kind of free-for-all."

"Oh, that. That wasn't anything. We just pulled a couple of slant-eyes out of the parade."

"Leave them alone. If they have a costume they're fine."

"This is a German tradition. What are they doing here?"

"What happened? Get in a fight?" Bernhard joined the conversation.

"Come on. We just pulled them out and sent them home. Why should they be marching in our carnival?"

"Leave the people in peace, Paul. They're just poor refugees, they have it bad enough as it is. They aren't doing anything to us or taking anything away from us."

"Who asked them to come here? Not me."

"Your grandfather was a refugee."

"That's different. Grandfather was a German. He had a right to live here."

"What do you know about it, Paul? I'll say it one more time, leave those people alone."

"Okay, okay. Come on, kitten, let's go."

The three-man-band in the Crown struck up a carnival hit. Paul grabbed the girl around her hips and took her to the dance floor. Bernhard watched him and smiled proudly.

"He's a good boy, your Paul."

"Um-hmm."

"Maybe my girls will come to their senses some day."

"Never give up hope. If Jenny and Paul end up together, that'd be fine by me."

"Let's drink to that, Bernhard. My treat."

The band played a waltz and the drunken couples stumbled across the dance floor. A woman shrieked, and an old man fell flat on the ground. Bernhard slowly pushed his way toward the bar, and I followed. The three-cornered hat on his thick skull had slid down; I fixed it so it wouldn't fall off.

Procession

Two costumed girls on two stocky dappled grays bringing up the rear of the parade were the last to leave the square. Children were running around both horses, petting them and holding out colored candies. A few seconds later the plaza was almost completely empty. The grandfather with the two small children went to Thomas Nicolas, the man who had taken the crying child to the microphone and who was now standing next to the parked cars in back of the Rathaus.

"Thank you for taking care of my little Nadja," the grandfather said.

"Of course. I hope she calmed down."

"I let go of her for a second and she disappeared just like that. I'm sure I'll hear from her mother about it."

"Hello, Nadja. You have a beautiful name. A very beautiful name."

The child looked at him without changing her expression.

"It's a big day for your town."

"Yes, it's carnival. The little ones have been raring to go since early in the morning. That's why Nadja got away from me. But I think we've seen enough for now, so we can go back home. Right, Nadja? Shall we go back to Mama?"

Both children nodded but said nothing.

"You have a nice little town here."

"Have you had a good look?"

"Yes. All morning. I was down by the Mulde and up in the castle."

"Yes, it's a nice town, though I'm sure it's not as exciting as your Berlin. I saw from your license plate where you come from. Here everything is more peaceful. And friendlier. You have neighbors you can talk to, who help you out. In a big city it's completely different. I don't think I could live in a place like Berlin."

"I can understand that. I grew up in a small town myself."

"Well. So have a good trip. And thanks again."

The old man cut across the square with his grandchildren and disappeared in the direction of the green. Thomas Nicolas climbed in his car, started the motor, and then turned it back off. He climbed back out, locked the car, and went to the pharmacy. For a few seconds he stared at the large display window, then climbed the three steps and opened the door to the shop. No one was in the store, but the buzzer called a woman from the back room. She asked what he might need, and he requested a package of licorice lozenges. She placed three different boxes on the counter, the man pointed to one and handed her some money. While she went to ring up the purchases the man carefully looked over the old pharmacy.

"Anything else?" asked the pharmacist. The man thanked her, took the lozenges and the change, and stuck it all in his coat pocket. He said good-bye in such a friendly way that the woman stared at him in surprise.

He got in his car and drove off. He steered once around the parade grounds, then drove down to the Mulde. He stopped in the middle of the bridge and got out of his car to look at the water. A few minutes later he started up again and drove through town, following the signs to the Autobahn. On Sandstrasse he was stopped by a policeman, who was halting traffic for the parade. Since the driver could already see the girls on the horses bringing up the rear of the parade, he didn't bother to turn off his motor. After they had passed, the policeman waved him on. He drove past the resort and past the settlement. When he reached the ramp that led to the Autobahn, he accelerated very quickly, as if trying to win back some lost time.

About the Author

Christoph Hein, a novelist, poet, playwright, and essayist, is considered one of Europe's most respected literary and political voices. He is the author of the widely translated and internationally acclaimed novels *Willenbrock, The Distant Lover,* and *The Tango Player,* among others. A former president of PEN Germany and the winner of several literary prizes, he lives in Berlin.

About the Translator

Philip Boehm has won numerous awards for his translations from Polish and German, by authors such as Franz Kafka, Ingeborg Bachmann, and Ida Fink. Based in St. Louis, he also works as a playwright and theater director.